TECHWITCH BOOK FIVE

WICKED WAYS

M.J. SCOTT

"This is a marvelous book. The world building is unique and complex. The characters are well developed and likable and there is intrigue for days. If you've read the first book in the series it only gets better in this one."
—*Lissa - Goodreads reviewer*

"'Forbidden Heir' is a great rarity: a sequel that I liked better than the original book."
—*Margaret - Amazon reviewer*

Fire Kin

"Entertaining…Scott's dramatic story will satisfy both fans and new readers."
—*Publishers Weekly*

"This is one urban fantasy series that I will continue to come back to…Fans of authors Christina Henry of the Madeline Black series and Keri Arthur of the Dark Angels series will love the Half-Light City series."
—*Seeing Night Book Reviews*

Iron Kin

"Strong and complex world building, emotionally layered relationships, and enough action to keep me up long past my bedtime. I want to know what's going to happen next to the DuCaines and their chosen partners, and I want to know now."
—*Vampire Book Club*

"Iron Kin was jam-packed with action, juicy politics, and a lot of loose ends left over for the next book to resolve that it's still a good read for series fans."
—*All Things Urban Fantasy*

"Scott's writing is rather superb."

Blood Kin

"Not only was this book just as entertaining and immensely readable as Shadow Kin—it sang in harmony with it and spun its own story all the while continuing the grander symphony that is slowly becoming the Half-Light City story. . . . Smart, funny, dangerous, addictive, and seductive in its languorous sexuality, I can think of no better book to recommend to anyone to read this summer. I loved every single page except the last one, and that's only because it meant the story was done. For now, at least."
—*seattlepi.com*

"Blood Kin was one of those books that I really didn't want to put down, as it hit all of my buttons for an entertaining story. It had the intrigue and danger of a spy novel, intense action scenes, and a romance that evolved organically over the course of the story. . . . Whether this is your first visit to Half-Light City or you're already a fan, Blood Kin expertly weaves the events from Shadow Kin throughout this sequel in a way that entices new readers without boring old ones. I am really looking forward to continuing this enthralling ride."
—*All Things Urban Fantasy*

"Blood Kin had everything I love about urban fantasies: kick-butt action, fantastic characters, romance that makes the heart beat fast, and a plot that was fast-paced all the way through. Even more so the villains are meaner, stronger, and downright fantastic—I never knew what they were going to do next. You don't want to miss out on this series."
—*Seeing Night Book Reviews*

"An exciting thriller . . . fast-paced and well written."
—*Genre Go Round Reviews*

Shadow Kin

"M. J. Scott's Shadow Kin is a steampunky romantic fantasy with vampires that doesn't miss its mark."
—*#1 New York Times bestselling author Patricia Briggs*

"Shadow Kin is an entertaining novel. Lily and Simon are sympathetic characters who feel the weight of past actions and secrets as they respond to their attraction for each other."
—*New York Times bestselling author Anne Bishop*

"M. J. Scott weaves a fantastic tale of love, betrayal, hope, and sacrifice against a world broken by darkness and light, where the only chance for survival rests within the strength of a woman made of shadow and the faith of a man made of light."
—*National bestselling author Devon Monk*

"Had me hooked from the very first page."
—*New York Times bestselling author Keri Arthur*

"Exciting and rife with political intrigue and magic, Shadow Kin is hard to put down right from the start. Magic, faeries, vampires, werewolves, and Templar knights all come together to create an intriguing story with a unique take on all these fantasy tropes. . . . The lore and history of Scott's world is well fleshed out and the action scenes are exhilarating and fast."
—*Romantic Times*

About Wicked Ways

If there's one thing I've learned about the magical world, it's that you never know what's coming next. Monsters lurk in the dark, and even in the light, danger is never far away…

I've rolled with everything the magical world has thrown at me. Training with a Fae warrior, honing my witchy powers, and navigating life as the girlfriend of tech god billionaire Damon Riley. Until a witch from England arrives to meet with the local Fae and new trouble begins to stir, revealing that some Fae view me as a threat to be eliminated rather than an ally in the fight against demons.

Which means the last place I should go is into the Fae realm. But to try to stop a witch bent on bending technology to his own dark purposes, I'll have to do just that. Worse, I'll have to take Damon—who doesn't have any magic to protect him—with me.

It's a race against the clock through a land where the ancient magic is more complex than any code and there are no new lives or save points. To find my way safely home, I'll have to embrace every scrap of magic I've learned and hope that it's enough….

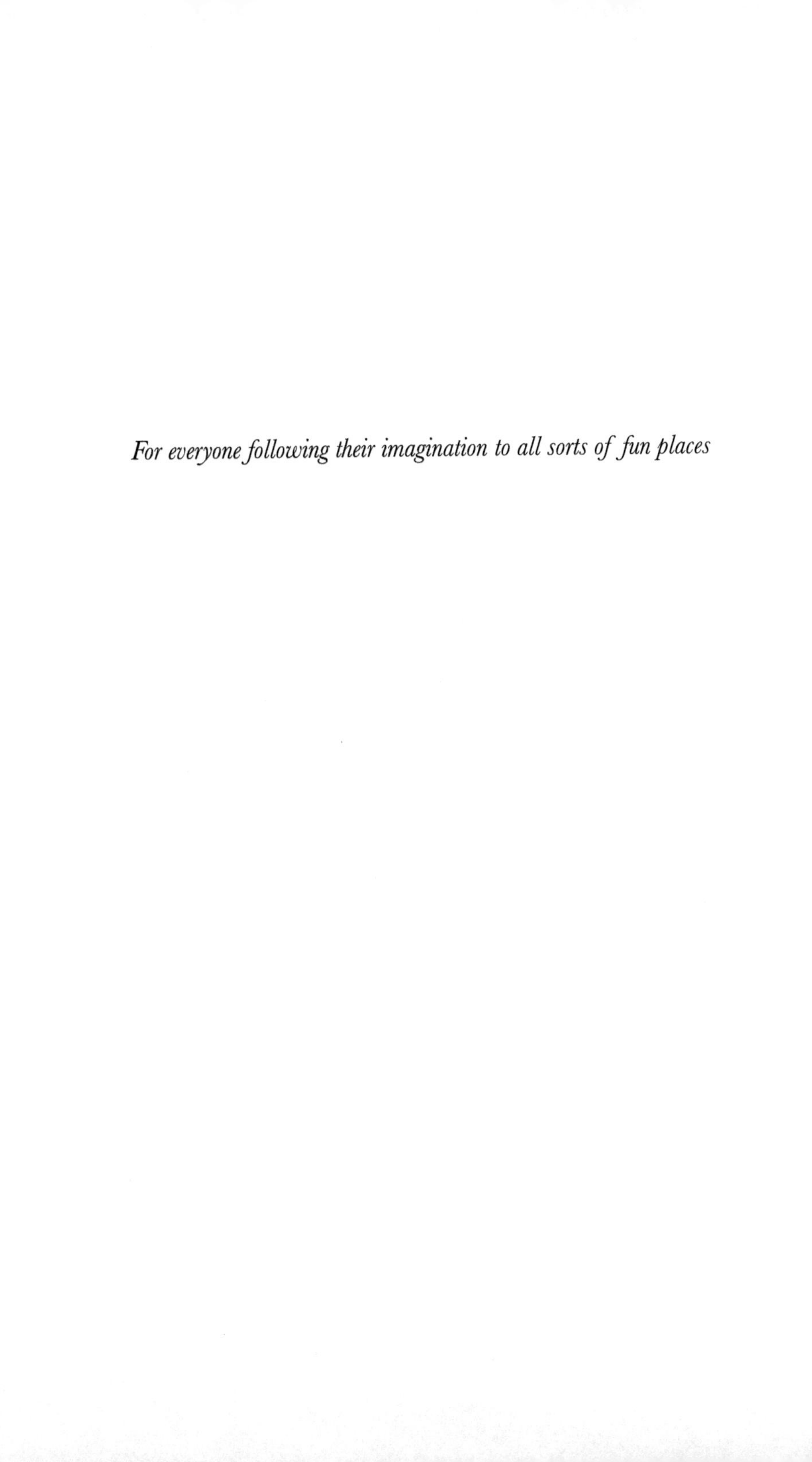

For everyone following their imagination to all sorts of fun places

Chapter One

WHEN I WAS EIGHT, I wanted a dog. *Badly.* But I never told anyone. Because I knew there was no chance in hell that my mom would agree. Sara Lachlan had no time for things that cost her money or time and served no purpose. I mean, I was her kid and she barely tolerated me.

Of course, at eight I didn't know that she had a plan for me. To sell my magic to a demon and, well, I never knew her ultimate goal because she died a few months after she did exactly that the night I turned thirteen. I had no memory of the demon part, and I went to live with my grandparents in Berkeley after Sara died.

They had a cat, though, a big fluffy black guy who sort of liked me. I'm sure they would have tried to make a dog work for me—they were determined to give me some sort of normal life to make up for not having known that I existed—but after seeing my grandpa get hives from petting a neighbor's chihuahua, I never asked them about a puppy.

I never asked for magic, either. But, apparently, even though the universe hadn't delivered me a puppy back then, it had delivered magic. And ever since my magic had broken free of the demon and I'd discovered that I was a witch, it had a way of messing up my life. Nine months or so ago, the Fae had restored the door to their realm in Berkeley. The one they'd closed after the earthquake we called the Big One had leveled half of San Francisco.

Reopening the gate shouldn't have impacted my life. After all, I wasn't one of the *tanai fol*, the humans with Fae blood. But, because of my link to a demon, the Fae wanted to keep an eye on me. Which meant I'd started lessons with Cerridwen, one of the Fae elders charged with defending their realm against demons. Working with her had shown me some of the weird things that lurked in their world. And those that guarded the realm could be weird themselves.

Like the giant black wolf dog currently pacing beside me through a Dockside back alley. Not exactly the dog I'd always yearned for. His name was Callum. Most of the time he was a man. A *s'ealg oiche*. One of Cerridwen's best demon hunters, along with being a shapeshifter.

Also a pain in my ass. He was cocky and, of course, being Fae, also far too handsome. And very good at what he did. Luckily for me, I already had my very own version of cocky—far too handsome, and very good at what he did—in my boyfriend, Damon Riley. Tech genius, billionaire, and, well, swoonworthy. Which meant there was no risk of falling for Callum's charms in the romantic sense of the word. Particularly not after he had managed to extract an unnamed future favor from Damon as payment for helping me several months ago. I'd mostly gotten over my immediate fury with Callum, particularly after he'd told Cerridwen he wouldn't call the favor in. But I was still aware that, deep down, he would act for himself if forced to choose.

But he was the one that Cerridwen had assigned to teach me the kind of fighting and weapon skills a demon hunter needed. So I also had to trust him. Which made for some interesting moments. Cerridwen occasionally set foot outside the Fae realm—she'd even been stuck in Berkeley for a few weeks when the door to the Fae realm had…glitched for a few days—but mostly she preferred to send others to the human world when something needed doing here.

I still went into the realm for lessons with her, but after Callum and I had battled a *bruadhsiu*—a dark walker—that escaped from the realm, she'd decided that it would be a good idea if we continued to practice here, too.

Which, so far, meant I was spending too many late nights with Callum dragging me around the city so we could hunt down imaginary magical critters. Hardly the girl and dog bonding time I'd once imagined.

But, like magic, it was my life now.

Tonight it was cold, foggy, and threatening to rain. My left boot kept rubbing my pinky toe and, frankly, what I really wanted was to be home in bed with Damon. Preferably fast asleep after some smoking-hot sex.

"How much longer?" I asked, failing to stifle the yawn that half-garbled the words.

Callum's ears flicked back, and he made an annoyed little doggie rumble I took to mean "patience, human".

"Rude." I retorted.

"It's not even midnight," Callum's voice said in my head.

"Some of us like to sleep. And have to work in the morning."

"You're working now."

"I'm training *now. And last time I checked, this didn't pay the bills."*

He rumbled again, this time sounding amused. *"I could organize some Fae gold for you."*

"Pass." I wasn't dumb enough to want any part of that.

"Well, then, concentrate and we can get this done."

We were supposed to be tracking a group of afrits. The lowest form of demonkind, but still capable of wreaking mayhem. They came in quite a few varieties, all of which could injure or kill a human if they attacked in groups. Or worse, lead the cleverer, stronger varieties of demonkind to a human, so that they could take that human over. Fortunately, tonight we were hunting illusory afrits created by Cerridwen, rather than the real thing. But I had learned from our previous sessions that not-real didn't equal not-booby-trapped-to-keep-us-on-our-toes. Also, that Cerridwen liked to plant her tests in parts of the city where they were least likely to be accidentally stumbled over by well-meaning humans. Which meant those parts hardest hit by the Big One. The ones no one had cared enough about to rebuild in the twelve or so years since.

Which also meant that tonight I was once again in Dockside, wondering what weird magical shit might be about to go down. It didn't improve my mood.

The very first time I'd used magic—accidentally—I'd been in a Dockside alley being hunted by an imp. I'd had time since then to get used to the idea that I was a witch, and to get a handle on my magic. I wasn't sure I'd ever get used to the fact that demons and their kind sometimes walked the same streets as me.

Maybe that was healthy. After all, letting myself get complacent about the existence of demons and imps and whatever other nasty critters like the walker might be lurking in the Fae realm might be a good way to end up dead.

I shivered.

Callum's head twisted back toward me, one ear cocked in inquiry. *"Do you sense something?"*

"My impending doom. Does that count?"

"If your doom is fake afrits, then that's just embarrassing. If you have a doom, make it one worthy of being remembered in songs."

"Humans just do obituaries."

"Yes, but you're not the average human, are you?"

"I'm feeling average right now." I stifled another yawn.

"Then let us catch the afrits and you can retire gloriously from the field of battle."

Most of the time, Callum talked in a mostly modern fashion. Sometimes he slipped back into the kind of language I associated with fantasy books and Shakespeare, reminding me just how old he was. He'd learned things in all that time, no doubt, things that might just keep me alive one day, so I mostly didn't tease him about it when he slipped into orating at me. Instead, I just nodded, to show I was done complaining.

He glanced briefly up the street where we stood. *"Which way do you think we should go?"*

He didn't need me to tell him. He could sense whatever magic Cerridwen had left for us. But he wasn't the one in training, I was. If I ever wanted this particular lesson to end, I needed to make a decision. I stood still and concentrated, trying not to breathe the ever-stinky Dockside air too deeply. My first few months of training with Cerridwen had mostly been learning various forms of combat and how not to be overwhelmed by the sheer weight of magic in the realm. Once Cerridwen had decided I had some chance of staying alive in a fight, we'd moved on. I was still training with various weapons, but now I was learning Fae magic, too. Or the forms of it that I was actually able to wield.

Sensing Fae magic in use was one of the things I was working on. Or not magic, exactly, but the traces it left in the energy fields. Fae didn't think about magic in the same way as witches, but that was the analogy that worked for me. I sent my own magic out, seeking for things that felt…wrong.

With witches, I saw magic as light and color. But, for some reason, with Fae magic, the sensation was often more akin to touch. Like reaching an invisible hand forward through the air, one that was sensitive to every faint change in the air currents, the shimmer of even the slightest vibration of energy.

Dockside wasn't exactly a bastion of magic. No respectable witch would set up shop down here. Of course, that left the less respectable ones—those who, like my mother, used their magic to cheat and prey on human weaknesses. But, here in San Francisco, the less respectable ones were either small fry who kept their heads down, or the occasional actual criminal witch with a hazy grip on reality. After all, this city was home to the Cestis, the ruling council of witches in the US. With four of the most powerful witches in the country in residence, witches who wanted to skirt around the law tended to take their criminal enterprises elsewhere. My mother certainly had.

So any magic I could sense should be Cerridwen's. There were more Fae in the city now that the gate to the Fae realm had been reopened, and more tanai, but the Fae who left the realm were watched by those within the realm and the treaties the Fae had with the witches were literally ironclad. Fae misbehavior was not tolerated.

Humans knew about witches, but the fact that the Fae were real was a closely guarded secret, along with other knowledge about the darker parts of the magical world. The Fae weren't keen on that changing. And the tanai fol weren't either. So I doubted any of them would be in the most dangerous part of the city for nefarious magical purposes.

I assumed that was part of the reason Cerridwen liked to set her challenges in the seedier parts of the city. Less chance of any magical interference, along with way less chance of the human police getting the wrong idea. Add in a greater chance of actually getting into the kinds of trouble that would mean I needed to use my newly gained fighting skills, and for Cerridwen's purposes, Dockside was perfect.

Though, with a huge black wolf dog at my side, the physical violence part had so far been avoided. And, as I had told both Callum and Cerridwen, if some Sandman-addled idiot jumped me in a Dockside back alley, I was likely to shoot first and ask questions later. And whether I would attack with magic or the gun that I always carried during training runs was anybody's guess.

"Anything?" Callum asked.

I pulled my attention back to the task at hand, pushing my senses further ahead. My head started to throb slightly from the exertion, and I was about to pull back when I finally felt something, like the brush of a sticky cobweb on the edge of my awareness. Ahead of us and off to the south. "This way." I followed the sticky sensation, ignoring the slow roil in my gut as my instincts protested. *Not real,* I told them firmly. *Just a test.*

My stomach was not convinced. My spine crawled in tandem with each churn of my stomach.

But I ignored the fear and focused on the sensation, trying to home in on it. Because scared or not and real or not, with Callum by my side, it was unlikely we would run away if we encountered an actual threat. The Fae have no tolerance for demonkind. Demons feed off magic. If one ever broke into the Fae realm, it might grow powerful enough to kill the whole damned planet.

I didn't blame the Fae for wanting to wipe out whatever traces of demons they found. I shared those sentiments. I was just a lot less practically immortal than a Fae. I'd survived one encounter with a demon. Not everyone who'd been with me had been so lucky. There was no guarantee I'd survive a second encounter. Imps and afrits I could likely deal with, but anything more powerful and I needed all the help I could get.

The sticky sensation intensified with every step, pulling me down a couple of blocks and then to the left when the feeling moved at a cross street. If you could call it a cross street. If we'd kept going straight ahead, the sidewalks were mostly intact and the road itself only had normal-sized potholes. But in the direction the magic wanted me to go, the road was crumbling, the footing uncertain. The lighting was no better. Dockside wasn't the kind of place the city bothered spending much money maintaining the street lighting. Around the fringes, where there were still apartments and things officially connected to the power and water supplies, there was some lighting, though not as much as in the rebuilt parts of the city.

The deeper you went into the broken parts of Dockside, the darker it became.

Callum had excellent night vision, so he paced happily at my side, but I eyed the darkened street with apprehension. There were some old apartment blocks on the right-hand side, and a couple of the barred and shuttered windows showed cracks of light around the edges. But on the other side, the buildings were crumbling, the windows that weren't broken revealed nothing but darkness. I sighed. *"You'd better take the lead,"* I said to Callum. *"You'll hear trouble before I do."*

He tilted his head at me, a doggy smirk revealing his too-large teeth. *"The point of this is that you take the lead."*

"The point of this is that I follow the magic and complete the test. If I fail because I trip on a chunk of cement and break my ankle because I can't look down, then that's going to put a stop to all my training." I knew the usual arguments. Demons wouldn't choose places where it would be easy for me to find them or fight them. And usually I was happy to try my best to learn the lessons that Cerridwen and the others were trying to teach me. But I was cold, tired, and unwilling to cripple myself for a stupid test.

I made a shooing motion at Callum. *"The faster you move, the faster we'll be done."*

"That feels like it should be my line. But very well. I agree the night grows late and both of us could find more entertaining ways to spend the rest of it. But you still need to tell me which way to go. If I find the target for you, then there's little point to the exercise."

The sticky sensation was still tugging at me, so that was an easy enough thing to do.

"Down the block to that third building. Then left again, I think. Unless it's inside the building itself."

Callum thumped his tail once in acknowledgment and then stalked off ahead. Even with his Fae sure-footedness, he chose his path on the crumbling concrete carefully. I did the same. I managed to make it to the building, which was mostly intact, though the number of broken windows and the lack of any form of lighting suggested it was unoccupied. Officially, at least. Not that the city officials paid much attention to what happened down here. Anyone or anything could have taken up residence inside.

My hand curled around the grip of my gun, holstered on my hip, hidden by my jacket and a charm or two to make sure humans didn't notice it. It was licensed, but I didn't see any point in drawing trouble to myself by carrying a weapon openly. I disguised the sword I carried, too, because that was even harder to explain.

"Do we turn or go in?" Callum's ears angled forward toward the front door.

A heavy chain had been wrapped around the handles, reinforcing my earlier assessment. And making it harder for us to find a way in. But my magic was telling me that in was where we needed to go.

I doubted anyone would pay much attention if we broke the chain, but there might be an easier way. If anyone was using the building illegally, then they must have a way to get inside that was less obvious. *"Let's see if there's another entrance."*

Callum set off again. There was a narrow gap between the building and its right-hand neighbor, and he headed down it. I followed, angling my shoulders to avoid brushing against the grimy walls. It was hard to distinguish between the gluey sense of the lure surrounding me, and what was actually real. My hands flexed briefly, the urge to rub my arms and legs, to brush off whatever was sticking to them, growing stronger. *Ugh.* Next time I'd tell Cerridwen to choose something more pleasant.

I'd never been that bothered by spiderwebs, but after defeating a bruadhsiu, which while not exactly a spider, was definitely heading in that direction—way too many eyes and legs—I had less fondness for small skittering creatures. So feeling as though I was walking toward the lair of one that might be as big as the sort of giant spiders you saw in movies wasn't my idea of fun.

Afrits were small. They didn't all look the same, though insect like was a good way to describe many of them. Like imps, they could vary in size, but none of them ever got much bigger than cat sized. Hopefully Cerridwen had stuck to the smaller end of the range.

The gap finished at the rear of the building. Which would have been great if it wasn't blocked by a chain-link fence, about eight feet tall and topped by razor wire. Though both the fence and the wire had rusty patches. Which probably meant that no one was checking them regularly. Still, it was enough of a barrier to deter anyone sane. If anyone was getting past it, they weren't going up and over. I bent and tugged at the wire closest to me. It was still attached, but a rattle a few feet away suggested that wasn't true for the entire length of the fence. Sure enough, another minute of searching and I discovered a flap where the fence had been neatly cut. The gap was big enough for me to get through, but I wasn't so sure about wolf-Callum.

Neither was he. He shimmered back to his human form about ten seconds after I started tugging the wire back. Annoyingly, even standing in a Dockside ruin, surrounded by rotting garbage and all kinds of other things I was trying not to think about, he was inhumanly gorgeous. His green-gold eyes gleamed at me as he straightened, pushing his dark hair back off his face. He wore black leather pants, and a decidedly human nano leather jacket that somehow looked tailored to within an inch of its life. His whole face looked tailored, to be honest. Or, rather, drawn by an artist who'd had a particularly inspired vision that day. He was all sculpted bone structure, golden skin, and long lean muscle.

"Let me," he murmured. He reached past and bent the flap back with ease. There was only a faint noise of protest from the fence and if there was anyone around to notice, they didn't show any sign of wanting to investigate. The building and its neighbors stayed dark.

Callum gestured me forward. "After you."

I wriggled through, trying not to catch my jacket on the jagged ends of the wire, and then moved away to give Callum room to follow, moving cautiously. It was still dark and, judging by the smell, the ground was covered by a wide variety of nasty things. The sticky sensation of the lure was worse than ever.

I needed to get Cerridwen to teach me a spell for magic gloves. Or magical hand sanitizer. Either would be welcome.

Callum bent the fence back into position, presumably to hide the entry point from anyone dumb enough to pass by. Personally, I thought that anyone deliberately heading down the alley to the back of this building already knew about the gap or knew how to break into places like this.

But Callum had many more years of hunting things in the dark than I could ever manage, even if I wanted to. Fae lived very long lives. So I turned my attention to the building. Where there was another door. But it wasn't chained and padlocked. So that was progress.

"Let's see if it's open," I suggested softly.

Callum nodded. I moved cautiously, checking for traps. The sensation of the lure made it difficult to feel if there were any wards, as though it was an actual web lying between me and any other magic.

Gross. I needed the world's longest, hottest shower when I got back to Damon's. One of the benefits of having a tech-god billionaire boyfriend was that his shower was amazing. Multiple heads and more settings than a girl could ever need.

"Can you feel any wards?" I asked.

"Can you?" Callum countered.

I grimaced. "The lure is making it hard. If Cerridwen was trying to be subtle, she missed the mark."

"Afrits are seldom subtle." He tipped his chin at the door.

"But no, I can't feel anything." He reached out and tugged at the handle.

To my surprise, it actually turned, and the door opened easily. That wasn't necessarily a good thing. It kind of suggested regular use. Regular use meaning that we could well have company once we got inside.

Guess it was our lucky night.

I had to assume Cerridwen wasn't actively trying to get me killed. Sure, she'd only been training me for what was a mere blink of the eye to an ancient Fae, but surely she wouldn't want her investment to go to waste?

Unless this had all been an elaborate plot to kill me in the first place. The Fae didn't like demons, and I had a demon who was interested in me. Currently it was gone from the world, after I'd hit it with a bolt of lightning, but there were no guarantees it was actually dead, according to Cassandra, the head of the Cestis. If it wasn't, it might decide to have another go at taking my magic for its own purposes. It had had sixteen years to use it while I'd been unaware of the fact that my mother had sold my magic out from under me, binding me to the demon when I turned thirteen. She'd died not long after and, for whatever reason, the demon had never taken enough from me to do me any permanent harm. What its long-term plans for me might have been was something I avoided thinking too hard about.

Inside the building, it was darker than ever. If people were living here, they either had excellent night vision or they carried torches.

I had a small torch tucked in one of the inside pockets of my jacket. But the light, as I had learned from previous late-night training sessions with Callum, was bright enough that it made you effectively blind if you had to drop it suddenly. So instead I turned to another trick I'd been learning: how to summon a magical light. Inside the Fae realm, I'd been able to make a small ball that could hover over my hand. Cerridwen and Callum could make fleets of them. Even Pinky had managed to make more than me, and there weren't many areas of Fae magic where she outdid me. But apparently the light thing was a skill that Cerridwen's descendants all had to a degree, and Pinky was no exception.

Out in the real world, the light took more effort and didn't glow as brightly, but it was enough to let me see where we were headed. Callum nodded approvingly once I had it stabilized and set it to float near my shoulder. He could probably light the whole room with a snap of his fingers, but we were trying to be stealthy.

The lure felt stronger above me, so I assumed we were supposed to go up, not down. There was an elevator at the far end of the lobby, but even if it had power and was in working order, I wouldn't have wanted to chance it. Buildings that looked like this didn't have regular maintenance and I had no interest in plummeting to my death.

Instead I scanned the room, looking for the entrance to the fire stairs. Which wasn't hard to find, because the peeling red paint on it stood out against the peeling what-had-once-been-white paint of the walls. It was propped open, but the space beyond was dark. Just what I wanted: a dark staircase to explore when all my senses were telling me giant spiders were lurking around every corner.

I tried to ignore the mental image. Between the gap in the fence and the doors being open, I was fairly certain people were squatting in this building. That would be unlikely if there were giant spiders. Or, at least, the Cestis would have heard about them. Some of the residents of Dockside might be a bit too fond of illegal substances, but rumors of huge arachnids would either be enough to have them fleeing the area or for word to get around. The Cestis had an information network that rivaled those of the human government, though it relied a lot more on a system of cooperation. No one was funding them to the tune of billions of dollars, after all.

In fact, I wasn't entirely sure how the Cestis were funded, but they did employ witches to work for them, so there was at least some money. And, of course, given that only a small percentage of the population had magic, there was less trouble to police. But that didn't mean it was easy, given the nature of the trouble when it did happen.

But Cassandra and Lizzie hadn't mentioned giant spiders to me, so I needed to get my mind off imaginary arachnids and onto the issue of finding and disabling Cerridwen's lure.

I pointed at the door. Callum nodded. We checked for wards again, found nothing, and moved on cautiously. Fortunately for my thighs and calves, we only climbed two flights before the spiderweb sensation became so strong we'd either found the right place or there actually was a big-ass spider waiting to eat us. I pushed through the door from the stairwell into the hall beyond. It smelled of mold and damp, but also other more human smells. Stale cooking scents and a touch of smoke in the air that I hoped was from a cooking fire rather than drugs. I wasn't wearing any nose filters and some of the substances sold on the streets in Dockside were dangerous even in small amounts.

But despite the scents, there was no sound, so I continued down the hall, wading through the sensation until I reached the very last apartment.

Callum stood behind me while I scanned for wards again and undid the one that was clearly recognizable as Cerridwen's magic. I had hoped that would be the end of it, but, sadly for me, the spiderweb feeling remained.

"I guess we're going in, then," I said, without looking back at Callum.

He grunted agreement.

The first few times I'd done this kind of test with him,

merely finding the correct destination and untangling the first level of magic had been enough. But Cerridwen had been layering additional complications into the last few challenges she'd set me.

I dissolved the illusion that had been hiding my sword, resting my hand on the hilt while I studied the door, trying to make sure there wasn't another ward I'd missed. When I was satisfied, I pressed a hand against the door before twisting the handle.

It turned and I pushed the door open. Not entirely unexpectedly, the room suddenly exploded into light, the contrast blinding. My eyes watered and I blinked back tears as the walls started to crawl with small creatures that looked like something you might get if you crossed a cockroach, a hedgehog and a crab and made them shades of black and dark purple and green that were entirely wrong. They varied in size from teacup to dinner plate, but they moved fast, the movement skittery as they ran down the walls, heading for the floor and…me.

I drew my sword, and started trying to analyze the illusion so I could undo it as I chanted *not real, not real, not real* in my head. Fake afrits started leaping for me and the room fairly sang with magic as I stabbed at them. The sound of their shells splitting, and squeals of rage were disturbingly realistic. Ugh.

I really hoped Cerridwen had made up whatever these were, because they were disgusting. But at least they didn't stink like imps, and they vanished in little zaps of sparkling light when my sword made contact with them rather than splattering me with bodily fluids. Callum fought beside me, his movements easy but focused. I started to sweat as the creatures kept coming, new rows of them appearing at the top of the walls and crawling down as we killed the ones that reached us.

It was a bit too reminiscent of old VR games I'd played.

"Have you been showing Cerridwen games again?" I panted at Callum, as I flicked two more of the horrible critters into magical oblivion.

"No," he said. "She thinks of these things on her own."

She'd missed her calling. Instead of ancient Fae demon hunter and whatever else it was she did, she could work for Damon designing monsters for his games.

I made a mental note never to suggest that. I was trying to keep Damon's contact with the Fae to a minimum. Though he and Callum seemed to have gotten past their initial dislike and were far more friendly these days.

Which would have been fine, if Callum wasn't Fae. He would always put himself—or at least the interests of the Fae—ahead of any mere human. He'd already wangled one promise of a favor out of Damon in a moment of duress. I didn't trust him not to try again. And Damon, unlike me, was just human. Not even a shred of magic to help him defend himself if the Fae ever decided to toy with him.

Part of my agreement with Cerridwen was that Damon was to be left alone. She seemed to honor that, but her word couldn't bind all Fae. Callum had already shown that the Fae definition of "letting someone alone" was somewhat flexible.

I slashed at another not-afrit and another and another. At first it seemed like there was an endless swarm of them, but eventually we gained the upper hand. I swiped at one of the last ones I could see and felt my sword connect with something far more solid.

"Wha—?" I started to say, the word dying on my tongue as hot liquid splashed over my hand and something thumped to the ground in front of me.

Callum made a startled noise and waved a hand. Almost instantly the remaining illusions vanished. Except for one nearly dead critter waving its legs feebly a few feet from me.

I stared at it, trying to understand what had just

happened. Callum, more sensibly, struck it again with his sword, chopping it in half.

A familiar acid-rot scent filled my nose as black blood pooled on the floor.

"Okay," I said slowly. "Where did Cerridwen get a real afrit?"

Chapter Two

"WHAT THE *FUCK* IS THAT?"

I whirled to see who the hell was yelling at me. Not Callum. Callum was standing right beside me.

Standing in the doorway, looked understandably freaked out and undeniably bedraggled, was a guy wrapped in an old, torn, gray wool jacket, jeans that might have started off blue but were now also gray, and a black beanie pulled over straggly blond hair. His shoes were incongruously white. He stared at both of us, mouth hanging open, pointing at the now deceased afrit.

"Who are you?" I snapped back, before he could yell again.

He sputtered silently at me before he recovered his powers of speech. "What the fuck? I live here. Never seen you before. Never seen anything like that either. What the fuck is that?" He leaned forward, neck craning, looking like he was deciding between coming closer or bolting, his face twisted between anger and fear.

Beside me, Callum took a step forward, one hand raised, the other hastily sheathing his sword.

"Hang on," I said, grabbing for his arm, though I wasn't

sure exactly what I was trying to prevent him from doing. Callum wasn't likely to strike down a civilian—mostly because he was well aware how much shit he'd get from the Cestis— but the truth was we now had a problem beyond just the all-too-real, all-too-dead afrit.

The guy in the doorway took a step back. "This is nothing I want anything to do with. Bad trouble." The expression on his face changed from frightened to something less fearful and more calculating. "Bad for you two," he added, reaching into his pocket.

I cursed under my breath as Callum broke free of me and closed the distance to the door just a fraction faster than a human would've been able to. Luckily, our wide-eyed friend was too busy rummaging in his pocket to notice.

Callum grabbed his wrist. "You don't want to do that, friend," he suggested in a soothing sort of voice.

The guy froze and then raised his free hand. "Hey, man, I was just reaching for my datapad. I don't have a gun."

Crap, I hadn't even thought about a gun.

I was a terrible demon hunter.

Callum, though, apparently *had* thought about a gun. He didn't let go.

"I hope that's true," he said, his voice dripping with skepticism, "But, for both our sakes, just let go of whatever you have in your pocket and pull that hand out easy." He used a tone that was both reassuring and commanding. How many troublesome creatures had he practiced that on in his long life? No doubt he'd had to talk his way out of dangerous situations caused by his insatiable curiosity and penchant for pushing boundaries many many times.

Beanie Dude seemed to consider Callum's words, weighing his options. Fortunately, he didn't make the dumb choice. Slowly, he pulled his hand free of his pocket, showing that it was, indeed, empty. Callum's grip remained firm around his wrist, not taking any chances.

"See, no gun," Beanie Dude protested, tugging at his arm. "Let go of me."

Good luck shifting a Fae warrior's grip. "How about we all calm down?" I suggested.

Callum's back stiffened, but his gaze never wavered from Beanie Dude.

Beanie Dude stared at me, his eyes darting between the two of us. His mouth made an "oh" when he finally clocked that I was carrying a sword. His eyes bugged out when he realized Callum had one, too. And then he tugged harder, looking like he was regretting all the life choices that had led him to this point.

"Relax," I said, aiming for soothing rather than annoyed.

He shot me a panicky look. "You've got a sword." He jerked his arm again. "So does he. This is *messed up*."

"I don't suppose you'd like to believe that we're the exterminators?" I asked brightly. If soothing hadn't worked, maybe funny would.

"Lady, there's not enough Levitator in the world to make me think that."

Well, crap. If he was on Levitator—which was what you got when bored chem nerds messed around with cocaine and some of the newer synth drugs for kicks—then he'd be paranoid and wide wide awake. The up-for-days kind of awake. Why couldn't he have taken something that made you sleepy and less coherent, like Sandman? Which would have also helpfully turned him into an unreliable witness, given it tended to give most people pleasantly mild hallucinations.

"What now?" I asked Callum, who was still holding Beanie Dude's arm, unbothered by his struggles.

"Well, I can take care of him, but your friends may not approve of my methods. Or you can call Cassandra and get some help."

Gah. Rock. Hard place. We meet again. I didn't see an easy way out, unless Callum was going to knock the guy out and put a whammy on his memory. And he was right. The Cestis wouldn't love it if he did that. Phoning home it was.

I transferred my sword to my left hand, resisting the urge to curse out loud, and reached into my back pocket for my datapad. "Hang on, I'm going to call someone who can explain everything," I said, eyeing Beanie Dude as I took a few steps back, avoiding the dead afrit.

He didn't seem to like that idea. He jerked back against Callum's grasp, but Callum was Fae; it would take someone stronger than this guy to break his hold. "No cops."

"Don't worry, it's not the cops," Callum said.

Not entirely true. The Cestis were the magical equivalent of the police in the United States. In fact, they had more powers than the police, given that they could also judge a witch guilty without the need for human courts if they decided to. But I didn't think explaining that to Beanie Guy was going to improve his mood, so I just dialed Cassandra.

She didn't take long to answer, despite the late hour, once again leaving me wondering when exactly she managed to sleep.

"Maggie? Is something wrong?"

I could almost hear the sigh in her voice. Fair. The only conversations we'd ever had this late at night had all been dealing with various kinds of trouble. And I guessed that, as head of the Cestis, people didn't call her in the wee small hours of the morning to talk about rainbows and sunshine.

"Callum and I are in Dockside," I said. "I think there's something you're going to want to see."

"What kind of something?" she asked .

I heard a rustling noise as though she was throwing back the covers and climbing out of bed and hid a wince of guilt. Yup, I'd definitely woken her.

"Just something," I said. "Something that's best not discussed over the phone. Oh, and we have a civilian here."

This time she sighed out loud. "I see," she said crisply.

"Alright, let me call Lizzie. Give me the address." Lizzie Reagan was both my roommate, my bestie and the youngest member of the Cestis. Which meant Cassandra thought she needed backup. Great.

I pinged her the address and ended the call, turning my attention back to Callum and our friend. The guy was clearly determined to try to get away from us, randomly jerking his arm against Callum's grip. Slow learner, it seemed.

I kept my eye on him as I did the math in my head.

Cassandra had been home in Berkeley. It would take her at least an hour to get to us, which meant we needed to keep what's-his-name contained until they arrived. If I was actually part of the Cestis, I'd have a better idea of how to do that, but for the moment I would have to wing it.

I slid the datapad back into my pocket and walked a bit closer to Callum, though I made sure I stayed out of Beanie Dude's reach.

"Who were you talking to?" Beanie Dude demanded.

"Just a friend who can help."

That made him pull harder. Callum grunted softly, but otherwise stood still, his grip unbreakable.

"I don't need any help," Beanie Guy whined. "I just want to bug."

"And that will be fine," I soothed, "Once you've spoken to our friends."

That was the wrong thing to say, because his struggles redoubled.

Seriously. Hadn't he figured out it wasn't going to work? He'd hurt himself if he kept fighting. *What now?* I asked Callum. *It'll be an hour before the others get here.*

Callum, apparently two steps ahead of me, abruptly took three quick steps backward, dragging Beanie Guy into the room. I darted forward and slammed the door closed, then slid the rickety bolt home. It wouldn't stop anyone really intent on getting in, but it was something. At least we'd hear it rattling if someone tried it.

Beanie Guy started to say, "You two are going to kill—" when Callum slapped a hand over his mouth, his expression finally annoyed.

"It's going to take a while for our friends to get here. You need to relax or you're not going to enjoy the wait," he growled.

"Tactful," I said. *"Perhaps it might be easier if we talk this way. He seems to think we're a pair of serial killers and he's already freaking out. If he's on Levitator, he's not going to see sense. And that stuff takes forever to come down from."*

Callum muttered a curse then winced. *"He* bit *me."*

He sounded outraged.

"Haven't you been bitten before?"

"Not by a human. At least not in this kind of situation." He raised an eyebrow at me. *"Do you really want to spend the next hour wrestling with this guy?"*

No. No, I did not. But I wasn't sure what the alternative was.

Callum winced again and a low rumble escaped him. Beanie Guy had the sense to freeze. *"I'm not supposed to magic him. So you need to do something."*

"Like what?" I asked. *"I don't know how to put a magical secret whammy on him."*

One of Callum's eyebrows arched. *"Secret whammy?"*

"You know, that Fae glamour stuff like putting someone to sleep."

"Ah," he said, looking enlightened. *"We'll have to get Cerridwen to add that to your curriculum."*

"How about I ask you to do it. That way we can tell Cassandra it's my fault and she won't be mad."

"You think she'll buy that?"

I shrugged. *"Got a better option? We can try to ward the doors, of course, but that might not work over Cerridwen's magic, right?"* The whole point of Cerridwen's lure was that it was magically detectable. Which I suspected meant designed not to be silenced by a simple ward. *"And if he really starts to kick up a fuss, other people are going to hear."*

"Do you think the people that live in this building are the kind who are going to investigate if they hear screaming?"

Good point. *"Probably not, but I don't think we need anyone else joining this party."*

"Very well," Callum agreed. He stared at Beanie Dude and said, "If I let go of your mouth, will you be quiet?"

Beanie Dude nodded, and Callum continued, "Good, because we can do this the hard way or the easy way, and you won't like the hard way."

Beanie Dude nodded once again, and Callum withdrew his hand. Almost instantly, he slapped it back against Beanie Guy's forehead. "Sleep," he commanded in a tone so authoritative that I felt my own knees begin to buckle. Magic shimmered through the room, and Beanie Dude slumped forward. Callum was ready for the reaction and caught him, lowering him gently to the floor. Luckily, the pool of blood from the afrit hadn't spread too far.

Probably just as well to be magically knocked out if you had to lie in whatever was coating the nearly destroyed carpet. "How long will he stay that way?"

"Until I wake him up again." Callum straightened, clearly not finding that statement as alarming as I did. But what was done was done.

Which meant we now had to go back to dealing with our initial problem.

I pointed my sword back at the dead afrit—what was left of it. "Where did Cerridwen find that?"

Callum stared at the small black critter, his mouth twisting. "I don't think she did. Summoning one of the dark goes against everything she stands for."

My gaze snapped to him. "What do you mean?" I asked.

"This was supposed to be a test. I mean, the whole place was teeming with afrits a few minutes ago."

Callum shrugged. "Those were illusions, not the real thing." He prodded the dead afrit with the tip of his sword. "This one definitely feels real."

"If it's not Cerridwen's, then how did it get here?"

He shrugged again. "Your guess is as good as mine. Perhaps the illusion drew it, the scent of its own kind. I mean, it's not entirely unheard of that such things exist in this city. You have, after all, had demons and lesserkind here before, and where there are those…" His mouth curled with distaste. "Their…companions follow."

Or even led the way.

Demons rarely managed to cross over into our realm, and I only knew of one instance of a lesserkind in San Francisco in recent years. Well, one instance that I'd been involved in at least. But, given that Cassandra and the rest of the Cestis seemed to think that I was the thing most likely to interest any demon paying attention to San Francisco recently, if there'd been others it was doubtful they would have left me alone. So far, I'd only had to deal with one demon; hopefully that meant there weren't others.

Just their creepy-crawly pets. I tried to remember everything I'd learned about afrits. Basically the hierarchy of demonkind went: demons, lesserkind—far less powerful than their masters, but still intelligent and more easily able to get into our world than demons—then the imps, which were the attack dogs of the demon world, and then "afrit", which was a term that covered a wide range of various small demonic creatures that the lesserkind and even imps used for various purposes. The afrit in front of us didn't look like any of the varieties that Damon had built for me in our VR training system.

Afrits were hard to get rid of entirely, apparently. Like the rats of demonkind, though, perhaps fortunately for humanity, they didn't seem to breed like rats. Cockroaches were the better analogy. Hard to kill. Quick to scurry away to dark places and hide away.

But regardless of how the afrit came to be, I knew what had to happen next. I shoved my sword back in the scabbard, hoping that afrit blood wasn't going to do anything too nasty to it before I could clean it, and then hunkered down against the far wall to wait for Cassandra.

Fortunately, no one else interrupted us while we waited. Which didn't make the waiting any more enjoyable. The room was freezing, despite the fact it was early June, Cerridwen's spiderweb sensation was back, and the acid smell of the afrit blood had done nothing to improve the pre-existing stench. But at least we didn't have to deal with any more unfortunate encounters with innocent bystanders. Callum split his time between establishing some additional wards—presumably to prevent anyone else from stumbling across us—and watching over Beanie Dude.

I mostly just stared at the afrit, trying to ignore the way its scent brought back a lot of bad memories, and worried about what Cassandra was going to say when she arrived.

She'd agreed to my training with Cerridwen, but sometimes I got the feeling that occasionally she regretted her decision. The return of the Fae to San Francisco had dumped new complications and responsibilities into the Cestis's lap. Technically the original agreements that the Fae had had with the Cestis before they'd removed their door the first time were still in place. But, in reality, the return of the door and the inhabitants of the Fae realm—not to mention the fact that there'd already been one instance of something escaping that realm that really shouldn't have—meant that things were still being…negotiated.

Mostly by Cassandra. I hated feeling like I'd caused more problems for her.

I knew both sides of the argument for me learning Fae

magic. Having Callum and Cerridwen on our side had helped with the nightwalker. And if they could teach me ways to better fight demons, that was a definite plus. And then I could share what I'd learned with other witches. But the other side was that not all the Fae were on board with Cerridwen teaching me. And if she hadn't taken me on, it was possible whoever was behind the nightwalker getting free wouldn't have decided to push things quite so far. I only hoped the afrit wasn't the next gambit.

But the history of the Fae was long. And bloody. Their power struggles were the stuff of legend—literally—and that was only based on the few glimpses humans had gleaned of the process.

Humans could be remarkably stupid about taking risks to gain power. I had no reason to think that there wouldn't be those among the Fae who weren't equally deluded.

And if I was wary of the Fae, given how little I knew about them, then the Cestis had even more reason to be.

I scowled at the afrit.

"It's dead," Callum said eventually. "You don't have to watch it every second."

"That may be true," I said. "But it makes me feel better."

"It would be wiser to keep an eye out for any friends it may have."

I stiffened. "You think there are others?"

"I do not know. This room smells too much of Cerridwen's lure for me to get a sense of the building and the afrit died too fast for me to learn much of its magic."

"You're the one who chopped it in half," I said.

"You'd already dealt it a fatal wound. It would have died soon enough without me."

"Sorry," I said, not sorry in the slightest. When it came to demonkind, dead was always better than alive.

"My wards will be keeping anything that might be looking for it out," he said.

Meaning if the afrit was traveling with others, they'd be roaming around the building trying to find a way in? My hands flexed involuntarily. "We should warn Cassandra."

"Your Cestis will be fine," Callum said. "They are well schooled in dealing with such things."

I rose from my crouch and circled the afrit once more. "If I had my way, we'd do a cleansing ritual and be done with it."

"That is one approach. The other would be to wait for Cassandra and see what she wants to do."

Given Cassandra generally had the same 'kill it with fire' attitude to demonkind as me, I doubted she'd disagree. But it was a moot point. The cleansing rituals I'd been taught for dealing with imps usually required hot water and various herbs and oils. And a bucket. None of which I had readily available.

"Perhaps you could explain the cleansing ritual to me while we wait," Callum said, after watching me pace for another minute.

I stopped, surprised. "You don't know how to do one?"

"I'd imagine our approach is somewhat different to yours," he said with a liquid shrug. "Explain it to me. Then our time waiting won't be wasted."

I couldn't tell if he was genuinely curious or merely offering me a distraction. Either way, knowing him, he wouldn't drop the subject, so I began to outline the steps Cassandra had taught me for erasing the trace of demonkind from the earth after they'd been killed.

Callum listened patiently, asking me questions every so often. Annoyingly, explaining it helped me understand it better. I could see how it would shift the energy fields, soothe them back to what they should be without the presence of the afrit pulling at them.

I'd just finished explaining the final steps when someone knocked on the door with three no-nonsense raps.

Callum lifted an eyebrow. "That is likely the Cestis."

I nodded. I recognized Cassandra's knock. "If your wards are doing their job."

"My wards always do their job."

"Careful or your head won't fit back through the door."

He snorted at me, the sound close to some of the disapproving huffs he made in his furry form, and I laughed. He beckoned me over and after he'd unwound his wards, I took down mine.

"Here goes nothing." I cracked the door open a cautious inch.

Cassandra stood in the grimy hall, along with Lizzie and Zee Anderson, none of them looking particularly happy to be there. The fact that she'd brought both Lizzie and Zee, who worked for the Cestis sometimes and was Lizzie's undefined something, didn't bode well.

I opened the door wider, stomach twisting, and Lizzie pulled a face as the smell wafted outward.

"It doesn't improve," I said to her.

"Not chill," she muttered, and then pulled a surprisingly subdued rust-brown cotton scarf over her mouth and nose, leaving only two disgruntled brown eyes between the scarf and the dark purple beanie hiding her hair. Rust and dark purple and covering her neon-orange hair were her concession to wearing colors that blended in. Zee wore black, his dark hair and skin well suited to nighttime activities requiring stealthiness. Cassandra wore a navy sweater and dark gray pants, with a large black purse slung across her body. Unlike Lizzie, she wasn't hiding her silver hair with anything.

"You always find the best places for us to hang out," Liz grumbled as she followed Cassandra into the room.

"Don't blame me, blame Cerridwen," I said. "I wasn't planning on an afrit party."

"No one should plan on an afrit party," Zee said as he trooped through the door as well. "That would be very, very wrong."

"Apparently Cerridwen thinks differently. You would have liked it," I said, smiling lopsidedly at him.

"Liked what?" He was breathing shallowly, his expression suggesting there was nothing about the situation he was prepared to enjoy.

"Cerridwen's illusion. It was impressive. I didn't even realize there was a real afrit until my sword hit something solid."

Cassandra turned to me, frowned, then turned the frown on Callum. "Your Lady needs to be more careful."

He nodded once. Acknowledging the point but unlikely to tell Cerridwen that. Cassandra shifted her attention to Beanie Dude. She squatted beside him, briefly laying her fingers against the pulse point on his neck before she rose again and came over to the afrit.

Lizzie came to stand beside me. "Are you okay?" she asked in a low voice.

"Yeah." I bumped her shoulder gently, "Not a scratch. Everything was going smoothly until we encountered that." I tipped my head toward the afrit.

"And what about him?" Zee asked, glancing at Beanie Dude.

"He is a case of wrong place, wrong time. He must have heard us. He just kind of popped up out of nowhere."

"You didn't ward the room when you entered?" Cassandra asked, looking as though she thought I should have known better.

"I was busy fighting imaginary afrits," I protested.

"The lure should have discouraged him," Callum added. He'd circled back to the door, his hands moving rapidly to reweave some of the wards. "Maggie says he's taken something called…" He glanced at me.

"Levitator," I said helpfully. "Well, that's what he said it was. And he was acting pretty smoked up."

"A drug might have suppressed his reactions enough to

make him ignore the usual sort of go-away wards we use for these exercises," Callum said.

Cassandra huffed out a breath. "Perhaps."

"He is just sleeping," Callum said, his tone turning soothing. "I can wake him easily enough. It seemed the easiest way to limit his exposure and stop him doing something stupid. He was quite upset."

"I know how he feels," I said. I didn't do drugs, but wouldn't have turned down a shot or two of scotch if someone had offered it. Something to take the edge off my nerves.

Cassandra peered at the afrit again. "I thought this was a training exercise. How does a live afrit come into the equation?" she asked Callum.

Callum shrugged and offered her much the same explanation as he had offered me about the lure possibly attracting a real afrit. Cassandra didn't look any happier than I had when he'd finished.

"Alright," she said after a moment, "We can clean this up. Zee, Lizzie, why don't you check the building quickly, see if you can find any trace of more of these." She flapped a hand at the afrit. "Callum, you make sure our visitor stays asleep, and we'll deal with him last."

The three of them made various noises of agreement. Lizzie and Zee slipped back out the door.

"What do you want me to do?" I asked.

"For now," Cassandra said, "I think you should probably just go home."

Not what I'd expected. And unlike her not to turn this into a teaching opportunity. Maybe she was pissed at me. "You don't want me to help clean up?"

She shook her head. "Maggie, I can deal with one afrit, if it's one afrit. If it wasn't, there'd probably already be more of them. Even if they couldn't get into this room, they'd be lurking outside. I didn't sense anything when we came in; I doubt the others will find anything either. There's been plenty of time for the creatures to gather if they wanted."

She turned back to Callum. "Though I think I need to have a word with the Lady about how she did this. I don't agree with her methods, but if the afrit was actually lured by her illusion, perhaps we could put that to use."

"I will convey your interest," Callum said.

"Good," Cassandra said. "Maggie, we'll talk more about what happened tomorrow. You should get going. No need for you to miss any more sleep.

I nodded, but then paused, thinking about where we'd left the car. "I'm not sure that walking back through Dockside by myself is the best idea. I can stay. I'll keep out of the way. Besides, I drove Callum. Can't leave him stranded."

"I see," Cassandra said. She glanced at Callum. "Will he stay asleep if you take Maggie back to the car?" she asked, pointing at Beanie Dude.

Callum nodded. "He'll stay asleep until I wake him again."

"And if you don't?" Cassandra asked.

Callum made one of his oddly fluid shrugs, the casual gesture a reminder that he wasn't human. "In my realm, he'd just stay asleep forever."

A shiver ran down my spine. Fae magic was too strong. Terrifyingly strong. "But out here?" I asked.

"I'm not entirely sure. I expect he would die, eventually. The way your kind do when they have injuries that they don't wake from. Like a coma."

A coma like the one that the dark walker had put Boyd into. Another bad memory.

"Well," I said, "that's not going to happen. A few blocks won't take you long." Without me slowing him down, he'd be able to move at a speed no human could manage on his way back.

"No," Cassandra agreed. "It won't, will it?" She arched an

eyebrow at Callum and at first I was confused why she'd asked.

Until Callum said, "No, Lady Cestis, I give you my word I will return as fast as I can." In other words, he wasn't going to decide he was done with the whole situation and leave.

Cassandra looked satisfied at that. The Fae don't lie. And Callum, as much as he could be annoying and flirtatious and distracted when he wasn't focused on a task, was a demon hunter. He wouldn't vanish into the night and leave only witches to deal with his prey. "Good. Maggie, I'll see you tomorrow."

I felt a little like a naughty child being sent from the room. Or to bed while the adults talked of adult things. But, on the other hand, I was tired and cold, and I wasn't exactly sure that my nasal passages weren't just going to give up the ghost permanently if I had to stay in this room much longer. So I decided not to argue and just leave the Cestis to do what they needed to do.

Chapter Three

By the time I reached Damon's house in St. Francis Wood, I'd mostly warmed up thanks to the excellent heating in the Jeep. But I still smelled of Dockside and dead afrit. Or maybe the lingering stink of Cerridwen's illusions. I'd been studying illusions with Zee for months now and we hadn't covered how to add smells yet. Maybe witches didn't do that. Or couldn't do it.

But if anyone could do it, it would be the Fae.

And, in the end, it didn't really matter whether the stink on my clothes was from the actual afrit or Cerridwen's fakes. The fact was the smell was real and disgusting and if I didn't clean everything I was wearing I'd risk smelling this way forever. I'd wiped off my sword as best I could when I returned to the car, Dockside not being the kind of place where you wanted to hang around longer than you had to while casually cleaning a weapon. I must have missed some of the blood. Or some of it could be inside the scabbard from when I'd sheathed the blade earlier. I added it and the sword to my "to-be-cleaned" list.

At this rate, I wouldn't be getting to bed before dawn. It was nearly two a.m. already.

Of course, just letting myself fall asleep in the car was an option. A very appealing option.

My eyelids were heavy, my thoughts a weird combination of sleepy and still on edge from what had happened. The Jeep was comfy. I could just lower the seat back and I'd be fine. The temptation was strong. In the end, only the eau de afrit and derelict buildings forced me to open the door, wincing as I stepped down onto the pebbled drive. Apparently the journey home had been just long enough for me to start to stiffen up. These days I was fitter than I'd ever been, but that didn't mean I just waltzed through training sessions and exercises with no effort. Or aftereffects.

I hauled my bag and the sword out of the trunk and padded up the front steps, toeing off my boots and carrying them and everything else through to the laundry. I cleaned my sword, decided to leave the scabbard until I could ask Callum exactly how I could clean it, and put everything that was soakable in to soak.

Which was all my clothes except my nanohide jacket and my boots. The nanohide required specific cleaners and the boots…well, I'd figure that part out when I had the brainpower. In the meantime, they and the jacket could air out and hopefully that would take care of the worst of the stink.

I hung the jacket on one of the drying racks and put the boots near the sink, making a mental note to buy Amy, Damon's housekeeper, some of her favorite candy, if she got to them in the morning before I did. Damon paid her very well, but technically she worked for him, not me. And before I'd come along, I doubted she ever had to clean anything that smelled like afrit blood out of Damon's clothes, so she deserved extra.

Luckily there was a pile of clean towels stacked on the counter next to the sink. Perfect. Wrapped in fresh-smelling fluffy cotton, I tiptoed back through the house, heading for one of the guest bathrooms so I wouldn't wake Damon.

But I should have known better. I reached the bathroom, set the lights to low, asked the house comp to turn on the shower, ditched the towel and washed my hair once. I was standing under the water, telling myself I had to finish the rest of me, when the bathroom door opened and Damon walked in, wearing black boxer briefs and an old white T-shirt.

Hot, my tired brain registered, but then stuttered to a halt, unable to think anything more profound.

He gave me the once-over, his eyes scanning for signs of injuries. I just smiled at him, half asleep, wavering between happy to see him and my increasing desire to curl up on the tile and sleep.

"Did everything go okay?" he asked when he'd completed his inspection.

I nodded and reached for the shampoo. "Everybody's all in one piece."

His mouth twisted. "That's not exactly the same as everything being okay."

"It's complicated. Do you mind if we talk about it in the morning? No one got hurt." I waved a hand vaguely down my body. "All as it should be."

"So I see." He grinned, his expression turning from concerned to…interested. "And technically, it *is* the morning."

"Yeah, but I just want to shower and sleep. I'm not sure I could be coherent if I tried." I stared at the shampoo bottle, trying to remember why I'd picked it up, then held it out to him. "You could scrub my back. That might make things go faster."

His grin widened and a wave of heat that had nothing to do with the shower suddenly bubbled through me, chasing away some of the fatigue. Parts of me I thought would be too tired for anything but flopping face down on the mattress came to life.

"It's late," he pointed out.

"Between your schedule and mine, when isn't it late?" I

countered. "Get in here or get ready to carry me to bed when I pass out in approximately three minutes."

That made him laugh. "Well, if you put it that way. Let me see what I can do to keep you awake long enough to reach the bed, at least. I don't have any meetings in the morning." He gave the shampoo back to me. His eyes were very blue in the half-lit bathroom, the kind of blue that would usually wake me all the way up.

"Work fast. I can't guarantee I'll stay awake once I'm anywhere near a soft horizontal surface."

Damon chuckled, hooked his thumbs into the waistband of his briefs, jerked them down, and stepped out of them. "In that case I guess I might just have to keep you in the shower for a while."

He stalked into the stall, which, like all his bathroom facilities, was more than large enough for the two of us. One hand reached toward the control panel, and he flicked several buttons without even looking. The strength of the shower decreased but the width of the water tripled so that we'd both be caught under the stream.

Another day I'd have more appreciation for the benefits his high-tech shower offered, but I had little time to think more than *Hot-wet-pretty-naked* before he pulled me close and kissed me.

I wound my arms around his neck, the shampoo falling from my hand, and kissed him back enthusiastically, letting the solid reality of him chase away all the weirdness of the night.

After a minute or so, he broke the kiss. "Hold that thought." He bent and retrieved the shampoo. "Let's take care of this before we try anything too ambitious."

I groaned as he started washing my hair, his fingers massaging my head and neck with just enough pressure to turn my knees wobbly with a whole different kind of satisfaction. If he ever wanted to change careers, he'd do well in a hair salon with those hands.

I let him take care of me, the hot water and the soft sound of his voice lulling me into a kind of trance. It took me a few seconds to catch up when he rinsed the last of the conditioner from my hair and swept it over one shoulder so he could start nibbling on my neck. His arm around my waist was just about the only thing holding me upright. I made pleased noises and lifted one hand, turning my face into his to catch his mouth again.

His lips chased away the languor of the massage, turning the relaxation humming through me to something hotter as we kissed. I twisted in his arms, running my hands over his body, appreciating the feel of slick hard muscle. Of him. I could touch this man a million times, more, and I would never get used to it. Never lose my fascination with the way we sparked together, a sensation both heady and familiar. I slid my hand lower, pausing at his hip, flexing my fingers slightly. He groaned and his hips arched forward as he tugged me closer. "Don't tease me," he said.

"But it's fun." I smiled at him, moving my hand down over his ass. His hips arched again, his cock pushing against me, hitting me just right. I sucked in a breath.

"Two can play at that game," he reminded me.

My very favorite game, the one we played together. Wicked and wild. But he was right. At some point, as much as I wanted him, the fatigue was going to catch up with me. Falling asleep would be a waste of his talents.

"Fine," I said with a grin. I slid my hand between us, wrapping my fingers around the head of his cock. "Let's not waste time." My fingers were wet and slick, and he sucked in a breath as I moved them over him.

He made a growling noise and my back thumped against the tile as his hands gripped my butt and lifted me. I gasped as he held me, his cock rubbing over my clit, and he grinned at me. "Like this?"

"Exactly," I purred, and he thrust into me with one steady

movement that stole my power of speech. All I could do was hang on as he drove himself into me, mouth hard on mine, the sound of the water rushing over us mixed with our gasps. The tiles were slick at my back, but he held me in place like I was weightless. I was no help. Heat and need drove rational thoughts from my head. I just wanted the sensation, the feel of him thick and hard sliding into me, filling me, sending sparks burning through me.

I growled against his mouth, nipping at his lip and he moved harder, somehow managing to hold me with one hand, sliding the other one between us, to pinch and tease my clit until I thumped my head back against the tile, blind with pleasure, as I came.

I woke with a start, convinced I'd slept through my alarm. Then the vague memory of Damon murmuring something about canceling it to the house comp as he'd carried me to the bedroom post-shower shenanigans, floated through my brain.

He rarely slept late, but he'd apparently been telling the truth about not having a meeting. His arm was curled around my waist, the warmth of him against my back comforting. He made a sleepy noise as I shifted, soothing me back to sleep. My body definitely wasn't keen to wake up just yet, the haze of sleep tugging at me. But as much as I wanted to, I couldn't stay in bed all day.

I cracked one eye open. The room was still dark, but the few cracks of light showing at the edges of the curtains were bright. So, not that early. And regardless of my body's opinion on the matter, I had work to do. Cerridwen was somewhat accommodating of my mundane human schedule, but the fact was that for training exercises like last night's, late at night on a weekday was the safest time to do them. On the weekends, the streets were busier, regardless of the hour, and Dockside, for reasons I would never entirely understand, attracted steady streams of tourists and pleasure-seekers eager to try the seedier side of San Francisco entertainment. Even with the best illusions and wards to turn attention away, there were just too many people around for it to be safe for us.

The Cestis had agreed to my training, but both they and the Fae were determined to keep the non-magical world living in blissful ignorance with regard to the fact that the Fae were real.

Just like I wanted to live in blissful ignorance about the fact that I really should get out of bed. I closed my eye again, snuggling back into Damon.

He made a muffled noise of contentment. "What time is it?"

"Morning. But not early."

He pressed a kiss into my neck and, for a few seconds, I thought that he shared my desire to go back to sleep. But no, apparently now that he was awake, his brain was kicking into gear. He let go of me, rolled over toward his side of the bed, and asked Madge, his house comp/AI, the time.

"It's 9.28 a.m., Damon."

He made a resigned kind of noise as the system asked whether he wanted anything else. "No. Thank you."

"Don't tell me," I sighed. "You have to get up now."

"Yeah, but you should go back to sleep."

I rolled my head side to side on the pillow reluctantly. "No, I have work to do. Besides, I need to check in with Cassandra."

"About last night?"

"Yes." I pushed myself upright, wriggling back to lean against the headboard. I yawned and my jaw cracked.

Damon pushed back the covers. "Are you going to tell me what happened last night?"

"I will, but let's do that over breakfast. If I'm going to make it through today, I need coffee." I wasn't sure even coffee was going to help. My whole body felt heavy. Moving was going to involve a certain degree of "ow".

"Deal." He sounded far more awake than me.

He seemed to survive on less sleep than most people. It was a handy trait when you controlled a massive global corporate empire. But sometimes it was hard to appreciate when he hit the ground running the instant his eyes opened and I needed caffeine and time to get my brain working.

Damon headed for the bathroom and, after another minute of arguing with myself, I climbed off the bed. As expected, my thighs and calves and back complained when I took a step. Maybe the first order of business for the day needed to be stretching. I took another step. Make that definitely.

I moved gingerly over to open the curtains and then rummaged in the drawers for some underwear and a sports bra and started to move through some stretches. I was feeling slightly looser by the time Damon came out of the bathroom and began rummaging in his closet. He grabbed me and kissed me as I walked carefully past him, but then let me go again and turned his attention back to clothes.

Another hot shower helped more and by the time I joined Damon in the kitchen, I was feeling a little more alive. Just. Somewhere slightly above zombie. The kitchen smelled of toasting bread and coffee. I was more interested in the latter, making a beeline for the mug that sat steaming slightly at my usual place at the table, next to a plate of fruit and berries. I headed for the coffee and gulped a few mouthfuls before I turned back to Damon, who had peanut butter, butter, and plates in front of him.

Peanut butter sounded perfect. "Can I have some of that?"

"Breakfast of champions," he said with a smile. Then he nodded at the toaster, which was, like everything in the kitchen, state-of-the-art and large. There were already four slices of bread in it.

"Have I told you lately that I love you?" I asked gratefully. I stirred sugar into my coffee and took another swig, trying not to gulp it down. I could have eaten a horse, but the peanut butter would be a good start. Fat, salt, carbs. All the good stuff. Using magic tended to leave me hungry, and Fae magic even more so. I should have eaten something when I'd gotten home, but I'd been distracted. And then asleep.

I started munching melon slices while Damon did the honors with the toast. When it was ready, we ate in silence, me too hungry to manage breakfast chat. Damon just checked his messages on his datapad, which was his usual morning ritual if I wasn't feeling chatty. The Riley empire didn't sleep and there were always multiple things needing his attention. But whatever was in this morning's quota of fires to fight, there was nothing urgent enough to send him to his study to jump on a call or summon Boyd, his driver, to take him into the office. He put the datapad down and reached for some of the grapes on the fruit platter.

"Nothing important?" I asked.

He pulled a grape from the bunch. "Nothing urgent."

Which wasn't exactly the same thing. But meant that he could take his time with breakfast. And with asking me what had happened the previous night.

As though reading my mind, Damon said. "So we have some time to talk." He nodded at my coffee mug. "Refill?"

"Yes, please. Or you could just start an IV."

"I don't think Meredith would approve." He grinned while he grabbed our mugs and went back over to the coffee machine.

I couldn't argue. Meredith Dempsey was a witch and a healer. She didn't approve of my coffee habit any more than Cassandra did.

Future Maggie would pay for the extra caffeine, but, for

the moment, I needed the boost. I had client work to do, and then I would have to talk to Cassandra to debrief what had happened.

I'd recently finished up a gig and had to finish my final report, but didn't need to go to their office again. But I wanted to get it done and finish the billing, so I could plan out the next few weeks. I'd settled into a routine of taking on my own clients when they had issues that wouldn't take me out of California, and taking projects for various divisions of Riley Arts when they needed me.

I'd resisted taking too much work from Damon at first, but the fact was, it was easier when I was working for someone who understood the other unique demands on my time. And Riley was, after all, a tech company, so even though he hired the best and brightest, having someone like me around who had a knack for solving unsolvable tech problems helped them work through issues faster. Especially now I had a chip.

Which made the situation win-win.

I wouldn't have agreed if he'd been throwing me make-work.

Damon came back to the table with coffee, breaking my chain of thought. He nodded at the fruit plate, which still had a decent pile of strawberries, raspberries, melon and pineapple. "Eat," he said. "You need fuel."

I pulled the plate closer and started eating again. My stomach rumbled. Second helpings required. Or I could rummage through the fridge and see what goodies Amy had left for us. But that would have to wait.

"So," Damon said, settling back into his chair. "What happened last night?"

Straight to the point, then. I stalled, sipping coffee, wondering how to explain it so he wouldn't freak out. "Callum and I were doing a training exercise," I started.

He rolled his eyes. "Get to the part you don't want to tell me about."

"We were meant to be hunting a nest of afrits."

He stiffened, brows drawing down.

"Don't panic. They were illusions. Mostly. Cerridwen set them up."

His frown didn't ease. "What does that mean?"

"Well, I managed to find the nest, but the test was to deal with the threat we found. We were fighting the illusions when a real afrit turned up."

He put his mug down with a thump.

"I said, 'don't panic'," I repeated. "I'd already mostly killed it before I realized that it was solid." Which had been more luck than skill, but telling him that wasn't going to help.

"Still, a real afrit? That can't be good news."

I speared a raspberry, trying to act unconcerned. "I don't know. They're not entirely uncommon." He'd been studying what he could from the Archives as he worked on the project to create a digital version of them. And he grilled me about what I learned. He claimed it was to help him build the VR versions to train me, but I figured he was also equipping himself to face whatever demonkind threw at us next.

"They're not like a lesserkind, or even an imp. Sometimes they get left behind." Or get through from the demon realm on their own. Or were sent. They were small enough that they didn't need the power a demon did to cross the barriers between the realms.

At least, that was what Cassandra and Lizzie had taught me. It had to be more complicated than that, but I had enough nightmares still about demons crossing over to risk making it worse by learning how the mechanics of it worked. I was happy just to accept that afrits passed over from the demon realm more easily than lesserkind or imps. The good news was that, unlike the bugs they sometimes resembled, they didn't breed over here, which was why humankind hadn't been overrun by afrits centuries ago. "I'll find out more when I talk to Cassandra."

"So it was just a coincidence that it appeared where you were?"

"The number of people who knew where we would be is pretty small and, unless you've turned to the dark side, doesn't include anyone who'd be summoning demons. Callum said it's possible the illusion that Cerridwen set caught its attention. Maybe it wanted to hang out with some buddies."

"Is that likely?" Damon's frown deepened. "I thought the different kinds of afrit didn't always get along."

Because they were being controlled by, or created by, different demons or lesserkind. From what I had learned, demons didn't exactly cooperate, acting more like feudal lords, working to their own agendas and desires and plotting against their rivals. Which was another reason that humanity had survived so long.

"There are lots of different kinds of afrits. These were kind of…cockroachy." I shuddered. I'd be dreaming about gross giant roaches for weeks. "I hadn't seen anything like them before. Maybe they're a type that works in groups? I mean, there were plenty in the illusion and presumably Cerridwen based them off something she knows about." A point I'd have to clarify when I saw her next. See if she knew more about these particular afrit. Or Callum did. That thought stopped me. I tried to remember how much I'd asked him last night.

"The fake ones are not what I'm concerned about."

Me neither, but I didn't want him to overreact. He was pretty good at accepting the risks my life entailed, but that didn't mean he didn't also do his best to keep me safe and worry like hell when he knew he couldn't. If he thought there was an actual real imminent threat, then my security detail would triple before I could blink. "Cassandra and Zee and Lizzie didn't seem that concerned. And we were in Dockside."

"Zee and Lizzie came, too?" he asked. "Doesn't that suggest Cassandra was at least slightly concerned?"

"I think she probably just wanted some help checking the building out. It was ten floors." I tried to downplay the situation, but my thoughts were racing. Damon was right, Cassandra had brought backup. She could deal with imps on her own, why bring three for an afrit? Unless she was just covering her bases, given it was me. Which I wasn't going to mention to Damon.

"I would have thought that if demon activity was happening, the Cestis would know."

"I think they're mostly worried about imps, not afrits. And they haven't told me about anything lately. Until I talk to Cassandra, your guess is as good as mine."

Damon still didn't look happy, but he shrugged and nodded, which I took to mean he was dropping the subject. For now.

"What are your plans today?" he asked.

"I have to finish some reports for Triton and then I guess I'll be going to Cassandra's."

He nodded. "Then we'll meet there."

I blinked. "You want to talk to Cassandra, too?"

His expression turned amused. "You really do need coffee. Have you forgotten what today is?"

I blinked at him, mind blank. "I barely remember what your name is this morning. Remind me."

"Today's the day that the representative from the UK Cestis is coming to look at the Archives. See the digital stuff we've been working on."

My stomach fell. Damn and crap and…yikes. I had a hundred percent forgotten. Apparently last night's adrenaline rush had fried my brain. "Yes. Right."

"You really didn't remember?" He sounded concerned. "You didn't hit your head on anything last night, did you?"

"Nope. I'm barely awake," I said. "I would have remembered." Or, at least, I would have checked my calendar and seen the meeting reminder. In my defense, it had been a busy week between finishing the job for my client and Cerridwen throwing in the training exercise among my normal lessons. And the Brits—or Brit—were coming to see the Archives, not me. I'd only been invited because I had been spending a lot of time helping Damon with the project.

"Okay." He studied me a moment, as though reassuring himself that I really was okay, then picked up his datapad when it chimed. "Boyd's here. I need to get my things." He came around the table and kissed me quickly. "See you later. Stay out of trouble."

"Worry about your own trouble," I retorted.

"Mine is the boring kind of trouble. No swords involved. Well, other than virtual ones."

I ignored that comment and went to the counter to make more toast. While the toaster was doing its thing, I pulled up the holoscreen and checked my calendar. Yep. There it was, plain as day. A meeting at the Archives at 3.30 p.m.

I stared at the holoscreen, wondering if it was too late to cancel and leave Damon to do his thing and dazzle everyone on his own. But no. Sleep deprivation might have made me temporarily forget the meeting, but it was a big deal for an actual member of a foreign Cestis to visit. Not only did it leave their own country short a member, but there were protocols and rules to be followed, or so I'd gathered in the last few weeks since the request from England.

Damon had done a good enough job with the virtual cataloging of the Cestis's Archives that Cassandra had mentioned it to some of the foreign Cestis and now they were curious to see the results. But the Brits had been the first to actually ask for a demonstration.

I was curious about the other Cestis and how they did things in their jurisdictions, but wasn't sure how I actually felt about meeting one of their members. Zee had dealt with them when he'd been undercover in the UK for a time, but he'd never talked about the members of the Cestis. But there were five of them, like here. Well, like there *should* be here. The Cestis still hadn't replaced Antony. Apparently finding the right witch took time.

The toaster popped and I slathered the slices with peanut butter. I munched on the first as I carried my plate to the small study that had become my de facto office. I was spending more and more time at Damon's house, and it was getting to a crunch point where Lizzie and I were gonna have to discuss the apartment and what we wanted to do with it. She and Zee were still spending a lot of time together, too, though she'd never told me the exact nature of their relationship. They hung out a lot, but I'd never seen them get touchy-feely, though there was a definite something in the air between them. If they were sleeping together, they apparently weren't ready to talk about it. Or they were both very good at not giving in to that first flush of sex-addled inability to do much more than grin at each other and find excuses to make contact.

If they weren't already sleeping together, I would put money that they were headed in that direction. Which meant that, at some point, Lizzie and I were going to go our separate ways. Damon had suggested I move in, but I'd resisted so far, not quite ready to give up another piece of my independence. But the fact was that, since we'd gone public with our relationship, me living separately from him cost him extra money and extra headaches.

I still had my suspicions that he'd actually bought my apartment building—though I'd never quite worked out how to ask—and was paying for my security. And not just Maia and Jake, who were usually my bodyguards. I knew there were others that I never saw. I still felt weird having a security team, but Damon was who he was and that meant I was a target for more than demons.

Another reason Damon didn't love my late-night training sessions with Callum, and I suspected that someone would have been watching us in Dockside last night. I hadn't spotted them, but that only meant that they were very well-trained.

But today wasn't the day to worry about whether I was ready to move in. Today I had to stay awake, finish my work for my client, find out what the story was with the afrit, and then meet one of the most powerful witches in England. No big deal.

Chapter Four

When Maia parked in front of Cassandra's house, I realized that, at some point, I'd crossed the line from needing more caffeine to having had too much. My stomach felt jittery, and my fingers were drumming a matching pattern on my thigh.

On the plus side, I'd gotten my reports finished and sent off, but that meant I'd had time to kill before Maia had arrived to take me to Berkeley. Which left me with plenty of time to wonder where exactly the afrit had come from, and what it would be like meeting a member of a foreign Cestis, and stew myself into a mess of nerves. I'd done another round of stretching, followed by a session on the treadmill, but it hadn't really taken the edge off.

The drive over hadn't helped either, the traffic over the bridge slow, leaving us sitting in the middle of the bridge for a few minutes, which I always hated, part of me braced for another quake to hit and collapse the bridge.

None of Damon's vehicles were parked on the street, but that didn't mean he wasn't already here. If he wasn't planning on returning to Riley, he would have sent Boyd home, knowing he could ride back with me.

Maia had been quiet during the drive, though I'd told her

what had happened in Dockside. As my bodyguard, she needed to know what she might be coming up against. And she was a witch into the bargain. She seemed to take the news of the afrit in her stride, only asking a few quick questions before dropping the subject. Perhaps Damon—or Cassandra, even—had already briefed Mitch Angelico, Damon's Head of Security, and he'd briefed his team in turn.

"I'm going to check the perimeter," Maia said to me, once she'd killed the engine. "Then I'll be out here if you need me."

Cassandra's house was probably the best-warded house in the entire country, but there was no point telling Maia not to do her job. I pushed the door open, exiting cautiously as I'd been trained to do.

Maia held up her hand for me to wait, her expression turning focused in the way it did when she was listening to something coming through her earpiece. I braced myself, but then she said. "Boss man is already inside. Boyd dropped him off a little while ago."

My grin was instinctive. "Thanks. See you soon." Maybe the fact that just knowing Damon was inside made me happy meant that I was a sap, but I'd take happy and sappy over stressed out and alone these days. It had taken me a long time to find someone who could get through the walls I'd built in childhood, thanks to my mother. At first I'd resisted, but now I liked the fact that being around him made things better.

It took me the usual amount of time to navigate the security measures guarding the Archives below Cassandra's house, but nothing new had been added to them. Hopefully that meant her guest had arrived safely and there'd been no more fallout from last night.

I passed through the last door and walked into the long, brightly lit room. As always, the size of the Archives was a little startling. They were bigger than the house above them, with rows and rows of dark wooden bookshelves that filled about three-quarters of the room, stretching on in an impressive—or alarming—display of accrued witchy knowledge. I scanned what I could see of the shelves, then focused on the long table that dominated the open space at the front of the room. Cassandra and Lizzie sat to the right with a tall blonde I didn't recognize. Radha Morgan and Ian Carmichael, the other two members of the US Cestis sat opposite them. Damon was standing at the far end, setting up a portable holoscreen. He saw me first, a smile breaking over his face. "Hey, Maggie."

Everyone at the table turned in unison. The blonde woman had a narrow but beautiful face, with eyes an intensely icy shade of blue-gray. Her hair was pulled back in a slick ponytail and the pearl studs in her ears matched the creamy shade of her silk shirt. Another pearl on a slim gold chain adorned her throat. For someone who'd recently flown halfway around the world, she looked far too awake and put together.

She kind of matched Ian. He wore a pearl-gray button-down shirt, open at the throat as some concession to informality. It fit him so beautifully, it was obviously made for him. I couldn't see the rest of his outfit due to the table but, if I had to guess, I'd say he was wearing equally elegant charcoal trousers and Italian leather shoes to go with them. His silver-streaked dark hair was tamed as always, brushed back from his face. At least Radha looked a little more relaxed, in a rust-colored linen tunic that made her blue eyes pop against her brown skin and matched the tones in her beaded earrings.

Cassandra, dressed in a sunshiny yellow shirt that brought out the gold in her eyes, stood and beckoned me forward. "Come and join us."

When I reached the table, she gestured toward the blonde. "Maggie, this is Aubrey. Aubrey Carter. From England."

I nodded politely. "It's very nice to meet you, Ms. Carter." I took a seat beside Lizzie, who flashed me a quick smile. Her hair was electric blue, which she'd paired with a vivid green shirt covered in a design of silver skulls and daggers. The kind of thing one might wear to unsettle a stuffy Brit, perhaps. I couldn't decide if that was funny or whether I should be worried that Lizzie was wary of Aubrey.

Aubrey smiled, though it wasn't particularly warm. "Please, just call me Aubrey." She tipped her head to one side, studying me as though I was an interesting specimen in a museum, the gaze coolly assessing. "So you're the famous Maggie Lachlan."

Her tone was as cool as the gaze. Not the best start. I shook my head, telling myself not to be paranoid. "I don't think I'm so famous."

"Believe me, Ms. Lachlan, anyone who's survived being bound to a demon, let alone managed to kill one, has a certain amount of notoriety in the magical community beyond the borders of the United States," she said briskly.

That was something I didn't really want to think about. "These days I just try my best to be boring." I glanced around the room, then caught Cassandra's eye. "Is anyone else joining us?" I meant Callum or Cerridwen. Or even Zee. Trick, the witch who was one of the agents employed by the Cestis full time, was off on assignment again, so that ruled him out.

"Not yet," Cassandra said. "I thought we'd let Damon do his demonstration and then we can move on to other matters." Meaning I just had to wait to find out if there was anything more to our visit from the afrit the night before. Hopefully not. Ugh. Coffee overload and patience didn't mix. But I wasn't in charge, so I had to suck it up. I sat quietly next to Lizzie and turned my attention to Damon.

***

Damon ran through his demonstration with ease, reeling off technical information in a way that made it easy to grasp as he went through the features. He didn't mention the virtual monster simulator that he'd built me for training, sticking solely to the database that contained the information that had been uploaded so far. Perhaps Cassandra thought that the Brits wouldn't approve of virtual imps. She didn't particularly approve of them herself, but she and Damon had come to some sort of accord where he made monsters for me to fight and she didn't interfere, as long as I stuck to fighting them with weapons, not pretend magic.

Aubrey watched the demonstration with those icy eyes and only interrupted twice, asking intelligent questions that made it obvious she had a reasonable grasp of the tech.

When Damon finally wound down, leaving the last image of the login menu hanging in the air behind him on the holo-screen, I had a few questions of my own to ask. He'd added a few tweaks I hadn't seen before, but I decided to wait until we were alone before I asked about them. No one else would want to geek out with us about algorithms and metadata taxonomy.

"Any questions? Ms. Carter?" he asked, reaching for his datapad.

Aubrey shook her head. "No. Or, rather, yes. But I think I need to digest all of this before I ask them. Otherwise I would just be wasting your time. Thank you for this though, I know you're a busy man."

Damon looked pleased. His eyes found mine briefly, a quick smile curling his mouth before he focused back on Aubrey. "If you have questions at any time when I'm not available, I'm sure Maggie could explain. She's done a lot of work on the project as well."

Aubrey's gaze shifted to me. "Oh, yes, you have a technology business yourself, don't you?"

Apparently she'd been doing her research. I wasn't sure how I felt about it, though in her position, I would have done the same. I smiled politely back. "Yes. I work freelance. A troubleshooter is the easiest way to describe it."

"A tech witch," she said softly.

"The tech part is more lots of study and hard work, rather than magic." She didn't need to know that we'd decided it was likely my magic did, in some way, power my knack for finding ways to sort out systems issues that no one else could. After all, it wasn't like we could explain to her how it did.

Aubrey twisted a ring on her right hand. A gold signet set with a dark-green stone. Not an emerald. Something more opaque. Enamel or something like jade, perhaps. Protection and wisdom and harmony. Suitable for a witch with her role.

As she turned the band, I glimpsed some sort of carving or engraving, but couldn't make out what it might be.

"It's good marketing. Clever." She twisted the ring again, her expression skeptical. "You really had no idea that you had magic?"

I exchanged a quick glance with Lizzie, wondering how much Aubrey already knew about me. "No. My mother was a witch, but she told me I didn't have any power."

"And yet, from what we hear, you have quite a bit."

Because my mother had lied to me and sold my magic to a demon, an act that could have killed me in the end. But that wasn't something I wanted to discuss with a stranger, no matter who she was.

"I'm merely learning," I countered, wondering why exactly she was so interested in me. "But I can help. As Damon said, I understand the project well."

"Isn't it unusual for an inexperienced witch to spend time in the Archives?" Aubrey asked. "You're not employed by the Cestis, are you?"

"Maggie's not employed by us, no," Cassandra cut in. "But we are training her, since she has come to her magic late, and she has been kind enough to lend us her skills in undertaking this project. In fact, without her, we wouldn't have met Damon. He came up with the idea. One that is proving useful." Her tone was tight, her expression a little annoyed. My interpretation was she was probably telling Aubrey to back off.

Apparently Aubrey respected Cassandra enough to take the hint. "Of course," she said with a small smile. "You must run things here as you see fit. I'm just interested in the differences to how we do it back home."

Cassandra inclined her head slightly. "I understand. It's some time since I've been to England, but I've always found my visits there to be…instructive."

"Yes. The last time you were there I hadn't even joined the Cestis."

"No. Verity was still alive. I was saddened to hear that she had passed away."

Aubrey looked down briefly, twisting the ring again. "Yes, it was a great loss to the community. But she had a life to be celebrated. She left quite the legacy." She straightened and turned her attention back to Damon. "Thank you for the demonstration, Mr. Riley. I can see how such a thing might be very beneficial. Definitely plenty of food for thought. I hope you don't mind if I ask for your contact details, so I can ask some of these follow-up questions?"

"Of course not." Damon smiled politely. "Cassandra has my assistant's number; that's the quickest way to get to me. And please call me Damon."

Annoyance flitted across Aubrey's face. Had she hoped for his personal number? That seemed…optimistic at best, and rude at worst, given she seemed to know plenty about me and that had to include the fact that Damon and I were together. Hopefully the former. Which, as I said, was optimistic. He was one of the richest men on the planet. He didn't hand out his personal details easily.

He'd told Aubrey the truth: Cat was the one who acted as the traffic controller to his schedule and who got access to him. Perhaps Aubrey thought that, because she was one of the Cestis, she would automatically earn his trust, but he hadn't gotten to where he was by being fooled easily. He was cautious. Even more so since Jack had pulled his stunt. If he hadn't offered Aubrey his number, that meant he hadn't yet decided how he felt about her. Neither had I.

"Of course, thank you. And I'm Aubrey." Aubrey turned back to Cassandra. "Will you remind me to get that from you later? I fear the jet lag is catching up with me. Perhaps we should move on to the next topic?"

There was another topic? Had I forgotten that, too? Or had Aubrey sprung it on Cassandra? I shifted in my chair, suddenly uneasy.

Cassandra nodded. No one else moved, which made me feel like somehow I'd not been given an agenda and everyone else had. "Of course. And yes, why don't you go ahead and explain your proposal."

"While I am here, I hope to pay my respects to the Elders. Now that they've reestablished a door here, it is only polite," Aubrey said, as though talking to the Elders, aka the oldest and most powerful Fae, was no big deal.

Lizzie stiffened beside me. I resisted the urge to look at her. If I looked, I'd blurt out some dumb question and break some rule I didn't know existed. I knew nothing about the protocol for a meeting of Cestis and a Fae council. I'd barely scratched the surface of the protocol just for dealing with Cerridwen. And she was friendly. Was this usual? Certainly the Cestis here had reacted with caution when the Fae had returned, not eager for the Fae to interact with anyone they didn't have to. Of course, it could be different in England.

Cassandra held her hands out, palms up. "As I've already told you, I can make a request, but I can't offer any guarantees. They are still settling back in here and keep mostly to themselves."

Which none of us were sad about.

Cassandra glanced around the table. "But I will make the request." Either she'd already discussed it with the others—though I wasn't sure why Lizzie would be surprised if she had—or she was telling them there was nothing to talk about. Radha and Ian were paying attention, but they didn't look alarmed.

Aubrey smiled. "Yes, I imagine they are. You needn't fear I'm going to do anything to upset them. Dealing with the Elders falls under my responsibilities back home."

She said it so casually, I couldn't help a little squeak of surprise. I found the realm an uncomfortable place and so did Pinky and Lizzie. Cassandra hadn't expressed an opinion, but she preferred to remain on our side of the door whenever possible. "You work with the Fae regularly?" I asked, unable to help myself, even though this conversation wasn't really any of my business.

Aubrey looked startled at the question. "I deal with the Elders, yes." She frowned at me. "You speak freely of them here?"

"We have had some dealings with them since the door was restored," Cassandra said. "They do not mind the use of Fae, if it is spoken with respect. And their secrets are maintained, of course."

"I see," Aubrey said.

Apparently things were more formal in England. When I'd first learned about the Fae, Cassandra had called them the Elders, too, and cautioned me about using other words for them. But since working with Cerridwen and Callum so closely, we'd all become a little more relaxed about saying the word "Fae" among ourselves. "Fairy" was still taboo, though. They didn't like that one.

"What does 'dealing with them' involve?" I asked.

"I'm our liaison with the realm," Aubrey said calmly. "So whatever comes up, really."

How often did things come up? Dammit. Why hadn't I

asked Zee more about his time in the United Kingdom? He'd dealt with the Fae on occasion and spent time with the tanai fol over there. Had he met the Cestis as well? But if that was the case, why wouldn't Cassandra have asked him to be here? Was he still mopping up after last night? Or did he just have a more mundane reason like practice with his gaming team. I tried to remember what was the next big competition that Trueno Diablo were competing in, and drew a blank. Which made me guiltily aware that I hadn't spent as much social time with Lizzie—and Zee—recently as I should.

"I will be talking to the Lady Cerridwen soon," Cassandra said. "I'll ask then. It may take a little while to arrange, if they agree."

Aubrey nodded. "I expected as much. I can wait. I'm not in any particular hurry."

Cassandra raised an eyebrow. "You're not eager to return home?"

Was she keen for Aubrey's visit to be a brief one?

"We have planned for me to be out of the country for several weeks, at least," Aubrey said, with a smile. "Given that it's rare for any of us to travel to this part of the world these days, I took the opportunity to have some time to play tourist, alongside my official duties.

"That makes sense," Cassandra said. "So. I will talk to the Lady, and we will see what she and the others have to say." She rubbed her hands together and rose from her chair. Apparently the formal part of the meeting was over. "Well, perhaps we should all just get on with it. Aubrey, please feel free to explore the collection, and we can discuss anything you're interested in later on. I'll show you the basic layout."

Did the Cestis share resources? The collection in the Archive was full of mostly old books and scrolls and ledgers. Some were even handwritten. One of a kind. Irreplaceable. Or, they would have been until Damon had suggested digitizing the records. Most were simply too valuable to risk transporting between countries by any method other than being taken individually by a witch and, even then, I doubted some of them would stand up to the travel. We'd come across several that were becoming very fragile and had consulted with a few museum conservators on how we might best approach scanning them. Luckily, there were museum conservators with magic, who understood the precise nature of the problem. Cassandra limited access to the Archives, but she was in touch with the other Cestis. So maybe, if there was a need for more information than could be summarized in an email or vidcall, coming in person was the only way.

Aubrey and Cassandra headed toward the long rows of bookshelves, speaking softly.

I rose and went round to Damon, kissing him hello quickly. He dismissed the holoscreen and was packing his datapad into his backpack.

"Hey, you," he said. "Good day?"

"I finished my reports. So that was good. The rest of it remains to be seen." I tilted my head back toward Cassandra. "Has she said anything?"

He shook his head. "Ms. Carter was already here when I arrived. Cassandra introduced us but that was about it."

That made sense. Cassandra didn't know how much I'd told him and she probably didn't want Aubrey to find out about the afrit. And if she hadn't brought it up, then damned if I would be the one to let the cat out of the bag.

Before I could say anything else, Lizzie, still sitting next to Ian, burst into laughter, pulling my attention back. Ian was pulling a mock annoyed face at Lizzie, but then he waved her away with an affectionate grin and focused back on his datapad as though he had work to do. Lizzie left him to it and came over to us.

"Hey," she said. "How are you feeling today?" She studied me a moment, and I wondered what she was seeing in my energy field.

"Tired," I admitted, "And, right now, over-caffeinated." I lowered my voice in case Cassandra heard. "But don't tell Cassandra. She'll make me drink something terrible to counteract the effects."

Lizzie made a little zipping motion across her lips. "Your secret's safe with me. Today is so one of those days."

"What time did you get home?"

"A little after three. Luckily, I wasn't working today, so I slept in."

I glanced cautiously over at Cassandra and Aubrey. "And everything was okay?"

Lizzie followed the direction of my gaze and nodded. "Yes, everything is icy. We'll tell you more about it later."

I'd half expected that, but it was still frustrating. But at least it confirmed my instinct that the Cestis were reluctant to discuss everything in front of Aubrey. "Sure. But even the… complication?" I asked delicately, miming the shape of a hat over my head.

Lizzie's expression lightened. "Yeah, even him. He woke up fine, and Callum managed to convince him that he'd just been having a bad trip."

Had that involved some Fae persuasion? Not one that the Cestis objected to, if it had. "Well, that's a relief."

"Yes. But also, can I just say, Callum's kind of intimidating? That much power. It's so effortless for him."

Good to know it wasn't only me who found Fae magic scary. Beanie Dude had been out for the count. If Callum had been called away or killed, anything could have happened to him.

But that was one of those things we weren't going to discuss in front of Aubrey. I for one, wouldn't be spilling any secrets until I decided if I trusted her. "I thought Zee might be here."

"He had to do some team stuff." Lizzie dropped her voice. "At least, that's what he said."

"Does he know Aubrey? From when he worked in England?" Damon asked.

Lizzie grimaced. "I think so. He didn't seem that happy about her coming here. But he doesn't talk much about what happened over there."

Zee had been working undercover for the US Cestis. Things had gotten…complicated. I wasn't in on the details, but some of it must have been bad because he'd been called home and hadn't done another serious undercover job for the Cestis since.

Would he tell me anything more about it if I asked? If I pitched it as wanting to figure out how far we could trust Aubrey? It seemed ridiculous that I'd known the woman for a whole half an hour and felt so wary. But she seemed wary of me, so perhaps my instincts were merely repaying the favor.

Before I could ask Lizzie more, Cassandra headed in our direction, stopping to say something to Ian I didn't quite catch. Aubrey was still studying the contents of the shelves, seemingly engrossed.

"Maggie, now that we've dealt with the formalities, perhaps you and I should go back upstairs, and you can have a lesson. Ian can keep Aubrey company. Damon, do you mind if I steal Maggie for a while or do the two of you have to get back to the city?"

"No," he said. "I can wait, no problem. We have an update to the cataloging program I can run, anyway."

"Excellent. Thank you. I promise I won't keep her long. Come on, Maggie. You, too, Lizzie."

"Have fun," Damon said, raising an eyebrow at me. "Bring me back a cookie."

Cassandra snorted. "No cookies down here. But I'll pack some for you to take home."

Chapter Five

"I don't want this to take too long. Damon needs to get back. He already had a late start, thanks to me," I said as Lizzie, Cassandra, and I walked into the kitchen.

Cassandra's gold-brown eyes studied me critically. "You do look tired."

Ouch. "Well, I was up late. We all were." She looked somewhat tired herself, but bringing that up didn't seem helpful.

"You can't push yourself too hard. Perhaps I need to discuss your schedule with Cerridwen again."

As long as I wasn't there when she did it. Cerridwen was ancient and scary powerful and I, for one, preferred not to argue with her. But Cassandra was just as stubborn as she was. "Did you ask her about the afrit?"

"Not yet. Aubrey arrived first thing, and there have been other matters to attend to."

She didn't offer another explanation, so clearly, whatever those matters were, they were above my pay grade. "I guess you can ask her when you ask about Aubrey."

Cassandra didn't take the hint to tell me anything about how she felt about Aubrey's request, just nodded. She moved behind the counter and started setting out her tea things. "Most likely, yes. But right now, let's focus on you. Lizzie and I will talk you through what we did to cleanse the room from the afrit over some tea."

I hid a groan, aiming a pained look at Lizzie, who merely grinned.

"Tea sounds good," she said brightly.

Traitor. I wrinkled my nose at her. Cassandra was an expert herbalist, but she didn't waste time making her concoctions taste good, she was more interested in making sure they were good for you. Some of the teas she'd given me in the past had tasted like compost that dead things had rolled in. Or worse. Though, I had to admit, they usually did work, despite the taste. "Does tea mean cookies?" Unlike the teas, Cassandra's baking was always delicious.

Cassandra smiled and dumped more herbs into her teapot. "Of course. I wouldn't have promised Damon some otherwise. I made a fresh batch last night. Plenty for you and Lizzie." She pushed the cookie jar on the counter in my direction and I pulled off the lid, inhaled the aroma of sugar, fat, and chocolate appreciatively and then carried the whole thing over to the table.

By the time Cassandra had finished fussing with the tea, I'd eaten two chocolate-chip cookies and was feeling slightly happier. Having something in my stomach took the edge off the caffeine jitters, at least. Cassandra slid a mug in front of me and set the teapot on an iron trivet beside it, making it clear she intended for me to drink more than one cup. I piled up more cookies. One probably wouldn't be enough to counteract the taste.

She settled herself opposite me with her own mug. The steam rising from hers was faintly minty. Mine smelled… earthier. Like mushrooms and damp wood. It was a deep red-brown. I regarded it with a decided lack of enthusiasm before taking a tentative sip. Yep. Tasted like it smelled.

"So, last night," Cassandra said. "Tell me again what happened."

I'd expected the question and had spent some of my free time earlier running through my memories of the night. I focused on them again as I explained each step of the training run.

Cassandra stayed mostly quiet, just nodding until I mentioned the sticky cobweb feeling and she started to look more interested.

As did Lizzie, her blue eyes narrowing at me over her mug. "You didn't mention that last night."

"There were other more important things happening." I paused. "You didn't feel it?"

"Not the way you're describing," Lizzie said. "But it wasn't aimed at me." She looked at Cassandra, who shrugged. "I could feel the magic. And it felt kind of weird," Lizzie continued. "But it didn't feel like cobwebs." She pulled a face at the thought. She didn't like spiders any more than I did.

"No," Cassandra agreed. "I didn't get cobwebs, either. Just a sort of pull."

"Whatever Cerridwen used for that lure, it was strong." Lizzie still didn't look happy. "It had to be to bring that afrit out alone. They can be sneaky little bastards. That's how we never seem to get rid of them all."

If afrit found that sticky cobweb feeling pleasant, then that only cemented my opinion that they were weird and gross and stabbing them was the best action.

I shook off the memory of the lure and reached for another cookie, trying to focus on chocolate rather than magic. And taste something other than the tea. "I guess that's what you get when ancient Fae try to get creative in our world."

Cassandra sipped her tea, and then sighed as she put the mug down. "Apparently. Perhaps she needs a reminder on how to be more discreet."

"Nobody else noticed," I pointed out. "It needed to be strong so I could find it."

"There was your unfortunate bystander. It's not entirely impossible that he has a trace of magical ability and was drawn by the lure. I think we were fortunate that no one with more nefarious intentions noticed," Cassandra said, looking thoughtful.

"Or even a witch with good intentions. If I'd been walking by and noticed something that felt so weird, I would have checked it out." Lizzie added.

"You're Cestis. It's kind of your job. I expect most people roaming around Dockside at night would know better. Even if they were curious," I countered.

Lizzie screwed up her nose, as though she didn't like the thought of people just walking by without seeing if something was wrong. "Maybe. Still, imagine if somebody other than you or Callum had gone into that room. Even if they had magic, it's unlikely they would've dealt with an afrit before. Even one can do damage if you can't defend yourself. They would have been lucky to get away unharmed."

"Can one afrit kill someone?" I asked. Should I have been more freaked out than I was?

"Not often." Cassandra's tone was soothing. Which worked until she added. "A lone one startled, or hungry, and put on the defensive, well a normal person wouldn't necessarily have much time to get away. Nor would a witch who didn't know what they were dealing with."

And there were plenty of witches who were unaware about the true extent of the nastier side of magic. The Cestis made sure of that. Their job was to keep the black hats of the magical world under control and out of sight.

"This particular one had some nasty stingers on its front two legs," Lizzie said, grimacing. "And way too many teeth. Like a piranha. I wouldn't like to see what it could do to skin and bone."

A shiver crawled down my back. I hadn't really taken in that detail.

"Yes, I hadn't seen one like that before," Cassandra agreed. "So probably best if your training exercises don't draw more of them out of the woodwork. At least not unless we all know ahead of time that's what we're trying to do and can be there to deal with them."

I was fine with that. "So, when will you talk to Cerridwen?" I asked.

"When Aubrey goes back to her hotel. She's staying at the Edwin."

The Edwin was a pricey boutique hotel closer to the center of Berkeley. Not far away, but enough to give her some distance from Cassandra and the Archives. I felt weirdly relieved about that.

"I'd prefer not to share all the details of what happened last night and what you're doing with Cerridwen straight away. It might be better for her to get to know you a little first."

Yeah, I wasn't being paranoid if Cassandra had noticed Aubrey's frostiness toward me. "You mean, satisfy herself that I'm not possessed and have fooled you all into letting me close so my demon overlord can attack when it's ready?"

Cassandra chuckled. "That's not exactly how I would put it."

"But it's not too far off." Lizzie hitched a shoulder, eyeing me. "It's a long time since the UK had to deal with an actual demon."

Meanwhile, lucky San Francisco had had two in less than fifteen years. "It's not like I summoned the demon," I protested.

"No. But you must understand why they find the idea of you, an untrained witch with enough power to kill one, to be a matter of interest, if not concern," Cassandra said. "But don't worry, they'll relax once they realize we're telling the truth about you."

"So, was this trip an excuse to check me out, or are they really interested in what Damon's doing here?"

"I'd say a little of both," Cassandra replied. "Plus, as Aubrey said, it's not that often we have an excuse to travel abroad. The rules when you go outside your own territory are…complicated. Aubrey can probably operate fairly well across Europe where the ties are closer and her counterparts mostly cooperative, but the farther you go from home, the harder it is to exercise the kind of authority a Cestis usually can without falling foul of rules and regulations you don't know."

Hopefully that meant that Aubrey couldn't go all vigilante on my ass if she did come to the wrong conclusion.

Cassandra reached for the teapot and refilled my cup. Which was only half empty. I took the hint and started sipping again, wondering if the sensation of my tongue shriveling from the bitter under taste was just in my head. I had to concentrate on not pulling a face. Because even though the tea was terrible, Cassandra was helping me by making it. And everything else she did. So, no point being rude.

"Aubrey is young. She may be eager to make an impression. So tell me if she says anything to you that you think is out of line," Cassandra said after she'd watched me drink for a minute or so.

"Has she been with the Cestis long?" I put my mug down, needing a break. Four cookies would be pushing it, so there was nothing to soften the taste of the remaining tea. And any subsequent mugs Cassandra made me drink.

Cassandra's brow creased. "Five, no, six years I think. I'd have to double-check the exact date. But she's well qualified. She's strong and comes from a strong line of witches. Her grandmother was Cestis as well."

"Is that normal?" I asked.

"Not here," Cassandra said. "But you have to remember that the Cestis in England has a much longer history than we have. And there are magic families in the United Kingdom and Europe that are very old. That much time means politics and traditions."

"And hierarchies," Lizzie chimed in. "Zee told me there are a lot of rules."

"So, what, the Cestis there are like, what do they call them, aristocracy? Lords and ladies and that sort of thing?"

"One of the current members is," Cassandra said. "But no, on the whole, they have become more…egalitarian over the years. But in general, Zee is right. They have more rules. Or, if not rules, expectations of what is acceptable." She arched an eyebrow, peering at me like a teacher regarding a problem student. "So let's try to keep the drama to a minimum while she is here. Not give her anything to disapprove of."

Lizzie snorted. "Judging by earlier, she's already disapproving. She probably thinks we're all uncivilized Americans."

Yeah, that was definitely the vibe Aubrey had been giving out.

"I can't imagine where she'd get that impression." Cassandra said drily, looking Lizzie up and down. To go with the vivid blue hair and chartreuse-and-skulls shirt, Lizzie had gone with neon pink mascara and lipstick and her favorite light-up orange high-top ubersneaks over shiny white pants. Her ears were pierced in multiple places and adorned with a magpie's trove of various earrings. About as far from cream silk and pearls as one could get.

"I don't think it's so much my hair color as the demons and the demon killing," Lizzie said with a grin. "It's Maggie she's in a snit about, not me."

"I'll be a perfect angel," I said. "It's not like I go looking for trouble." It just had a way of finding me. "Do you think the Fae will agree to talk to Aubrey?"

Cassandra shrugged. "What the Fae will agree to is anyone's guess. It's true that the Cestis in the UK have more dealings with the Fae than we traditionally have. So it may be that they're perfectly happy to talk to her."

"Or it may be that some want to, and some don't, and then that will only add fuel to the fire," Lizzie grumbled.

The Fae had returned to San Francisco, but they were hardly in lockstep about the decision or how they should conduct themselves now that they were here. So far, the factions that wanted to maintain the status quo and the friendship of the Cestis and the humans were in control. But there was dissent. Callum and Cerridwen wouldn't talk about it in any detail, but someone had helped the bruadhsiu who'd terrorized the city a few months ago get through the door.

Hardly a sign of unanimous love for humans from those who lived inside the Fae realm.

"Does the fact that the English Cestis deal with the Fae over there mean that Aubrey could have met the Fae who live closest to our door?"

"I doubt if anyone knows all the Fae," Lizzie said.

I waved a hand. "You know what I mean. Does the Fae realm work like our realm? Different countries, for different clans, or is it all connected?" I hadn't thought about the geography of the realm before. For one thing, because it was infinitely fluid, at least to my human eyes. Fae magic let them change the world around them. But there were families and clans and such, of a kind. Not as simple as in the fairy tales with high and low courts or light and dark Fae but they weren't all one unified group.

"As I understand it," Cassandra said, "it's all connected. But of course, the territories belong to various families or clans, controlled by the Elders like Cerridwen. The Fae who use the doors in England are different to those who live here."

"Where did they go?" I asked.

Cassandra blinked. "Where did who go?"

"The Fae from San Francisco, when they closed the door here. Which door were they using to connect with the human world then? Where did the tanai that went with them live?"

Her brows lifted. "That's not something I've actually asked."

Neither had I. I knew precisely one tanai: Pinky Andretti. Cerridwen's many times great granddaughter. She and her mom had been among those who had stayed behind when the doors closed, so she might not know either. The splits in families and friends had been painful and I hadn't wanted to pry. Maybe I might have to ask her the basics at least. If Pinky knew, of course.

"San Francisco has always been the main door here in the US," Cassandra said. "There are other, smaller, well-hidden ones here and there. Mostly in the wilder areas still. Places where the Fae dealt with the indigenous peoples before we came here. The door here in San Francisco was opened when the English arrived. Some of their Fae were curious. They came, too. But that's as much as I know. If any Fae were still living in the United States while the door was closed, they made themselves scarce and kept out of trouble. Certainly I've never been contacted by one."

Her tone suggested that had been just how she liked it. The Cestis were busy enough policing human witches without having to deal with the fallout from Fae choosing to interfere with humanity. But now they were back. Because of my demon. But if they'd been concerned about demons, surely some of them should have been watching San Francisco anyway, given the demon that had caused the Big One was the last demon to break through before mine. Was that the role of the tanai fol? To keep an eye on things and alert the Fae to trouble.

"So you'll pass Aubrey's request on to Cerridwen, and then she'll talk to the other Fae?"

"Yes, to the other Elders connected to our door. Each door

has a kind of council…a group of the leaders of the closest territories. They'll be the ones who make the decision. Unless they disagree, then it gets escalated somehow to a wider vote. I don't understand much about how that works. Cerridwen is very good at avoiding my questions when I try to ask her about their politics."

"Would all the council members have to agree to meet Aubrey? Cerridwen could choose to meet with her personally if she wanted, couldn't she?"

"Of course," Lizzie said, "Cerridwen is powerful enough to do what she wants. She could meet Aubrey outside the realm. But that didn't sound like quite what Aubrey's after. She sounded like she wanted to pay her respects from the British Cestis to the Fae, rather than speak to an individual."

"And what if Cerridwen tells Aubrey she's training me? If Aubrey doesn't like the fact that I tangled with a demon, how's she going to feel about me working with the Fae."

"Well, if she has any sense, it should convince her that you don't have any demon taint," Lizzie said. "That is one thing the Fae wouldn't tolerate."

"True, but it's not my preferred method of proving that to her," Cassandra said.

"Better than demon stone," I muttered. I had zero desire to ever be tested with demon stone again. I'd done it twice. It was painful and terrifying. Thinking about it turned my stomach. So, nope to ever doing that again.

"Demon stone has the benefit of being traditional," Cassandra said. "Your arrangement with Cerridwen is unconventional at best."

"Meaning not done in the UK?"

"Not that I've ever heard of."

Lizzie shot her an assessing look. "Are you worried that they'd try to stop Cerridwen teaching Maggie?"

Cassandra snorted. "I'd like to see them try. For one thing, Maggie isn't under their jurisdiction. And for another, they can hardly tell Cerridwen what to do. And they can hardly argue it's not important that Maggie learn to control her powers."

"But they might not think I should be training with the Fae?" I asked.

Cassandra waved her hand back and forth. "Perhaps not. But then, perhaps they would. Perhaps they might even know if others have learned Fae magic."

"Wouldn't that be something that would be shared if there are skills that are transferable?"

We hadn't found anything buried in the Archives specifically about witches using Fae magic. But that didn't mean it never happened, particularly in other countries, where witches may have had different relationships with the Fae over a longer time.

"Zee might be able to help," Lizzie said. "There wasn't time to talk much last night."

"Yes, it would be good to get his input. We debriefed him after he returned, but we weren't specially focused on how the Cestis over there was dealing with the Fae."

"But if Cerridwen tells them, then maybe that's easier," I said. "After all, if she says she asked to train me then it's not your fault. More a sort of, well, a Fae accompli, pun completely intended."

Lizzie groaned.

Cassandra merely rolled her eyes. "Aubrey will be less able to argue if the Fae said they initiated it. I'm not sure many witches would turn down the opportunity if it was offered."

I wasn't so sure about that. Smart witches would stay wary of the Fae. As I fully intended to.

Lizzie also didn't look convinced. "This isn't getting us very far in terms of teaching Maggie how we dealt with the afrit."

"No." Cassandra nodded and then pointed at my mug of tea, which I'd been leaving neglected on the table, hoping she wouldn't notice. "Drink your tea while we tell you what we did."

Damon was still sitting at the table, a portable keyboard connected to his datapad, typing furiously when I arrived back in the Archives. Probably coding. He did a lot of his work just by talking to the house comp at home and the same at Riley. The programmers there were increasingly working in VR environments, constantly dreaming up new ways to interact with the code. But the system he'd built for the Archives wasn't yet at that level. For one thing, not a lot of witches had interface chips. Zee and I did, but we were the exception, not the rule.

The virtual version of the Archives was highly secure and, yes, you could use a game chair and hook up with a headset to stroll through the catalog, but you could also access it via a terminal. Provided you had all the right codes and passed the various scans. The system was as well warded as the building. Possibly better. Since Jack Miller had hijacked VR to trap Damon in it and try to kidnap him, Damon kept adding layers of security to the Archives as fast as he could invent them, much like he did at home and at the Riley campus.

He was smiling faintly, gorgeous blue eyes focused with laser precision on the screen. In his element. He hadn't said as much, but the Archives project was fun for him. He'd started out programming his games and these days he got to do a lot less of that than he liked.

He looked up, blinked, and then smiled more broadly. "Finished already? Everything…sorted?" He lifted an eyebrow, which made me think the actual question he'd be asking me once we were alone was whether everything was under control.

"All done," I agreed. "No drama." At least nothing immediate. "We can head back when you're ready."

He nodded at the screen. "Just let me finish…" his voice trailed off as he started typing again.

I watched him for a minute, then pulled out my datapad to send Maia a message that we'd be out sometime soon. She replied almost immediately, asking if we were going home or back to the Riley campus.

"Maia wants to know where we're headed," I said to Damon.

He held up a finger, typed another blur of characters then grinned in satisfaction as the datapad chimed. "I don't have to go back to the office, we can go home."

Where hopefully I could eat dinner and crawl into bed early.

Damon started to grab his things as I pinged another message in Maia's direction.

Aubrey, who stood by the end of one of the rows of bookshelves, a slim, blue, leather-bound volume open in her hands, raised her head at the movement. She slid the book back into place and joined us. "Are you leaving?"

"Yes," I said. "I'm done for the day. We have to get back to the city." Which was going to take longer than I liked given it was now after five and we'd be hitting the worst of the commuter traffic. At least we were heading into the city, not coming out.

"I am looking forward to exploring San Francisco," Aubrey said. "It seems so beautiful when I see it on the vids. And the recovery seems to have moved fast."

"Have you been here before? Before the Big One?" I asked. She was right. The recovery had been fast, but there were still parts of the city that were yet to be rebuilt. And some that never would be.

"No. My travels have mostly taken me around Europe. I've

been to Japan and China. And New York, twice, but never the West Coast. Have you traveled much, Maggie?"

She didn't bother asking Damon, I noticed. Apparently she just assumed the billionaire was a jet-setter. And while he tried to stay home when he could, she was right. Damon owned properties in cities we'd yet to get anywhere near. We'd snatched a few nights in some of his other properties in the States, enjoyed one glorious long weekend in Tuscany, and managed another in the Caribbean after my birthday, but I couldn't have named half the places his business empire took him.

"Around the States, for my work, yes. I've had a few global clients, but mostly worked on their facilities here or in Canada. I'd like to see more of the world."

"It must be difficult juggling both your schedules to find time alone, particularly if Maggie is still learning to control her magic."

Damon shrugged. "We make it work."

"I guess you must." Aubrey looked at him with a speculative expression that I didn't entirely like. "Perhaps we could have dinner one evening in the city? I would like to hear more about Riley Arts."

If she'd managed to find out something about my background, she should have had no problem finding out about Riley. It had to report a buttload of information every quarter and, being as huge and successful as it was, also had a buttload of media coverage. People wrote theses about it. "You're interested then?" I asked.

She nodded. "It was definitely impressive. It would be a lengthy task, I imagine, to convert our Archives. They are a little more…substantial than these." She gestured back at the shelves. "And I would have to convince my colleagues, of course." She smiled at Damon. "I may have to fly you into London to charm them."

I lifted an eyebrow, and she made an apologetic face.

"My fellow members can be somewhat resistant to change. The others are all quite a bit older than me."

"You're the baby, like Lizzie," I said, unable to resist poking back at her, just a little.

That earned me a cool look. "Not quite so young, but they have been a stable group for a while, and we tend to move more slowly in our part of the world. It would be better for them to hear from the source, so to speak. I'm sure someone with Damon's reputation would make them more open to the idea."

In other words, if she could get the billionaire to come along and perform for them, she'd look good, and they'd take her more seriously. I glanced at Damon. He was used to people wanting things from him, but I found it irritating. Cassandra and Lizzie and Ian and Radha were scrupulous about not asking him for any favors, so it was grating from Aubrey.

But, then again, her being willing to digitize the British Archives would help us as well. If Aubrey and I weren't ever going to be friends, I had to grin and bear it and be as civil as possible for the duration of her stay.

"Let's start with dinner, if we can," Damon said, deftly avoiding promises. "When do you leave?"

"At this stage, on the twentieth."

"Very well, I'll get my assistant to look at my schedule and see if there's a free evening. We have a launch in a few months, so it's beginning to get to the crazily hectic stage."

"Of course. I'd appreciate it if you can, but I understand if it's not possible. Will you be holding another tournament this year?"

"Yes," Damon said easily. "Though we haven't announced it yet, so please keep that to yourself. It worked well to launch *Serenity Falls* and, of course, I always want to support the gamers."

"Everyone was talking about it back home, last year," Aubrey said.

"Do you game?" I asked politely. The cuffs of her shirt hid her wrists, so I couldn't see if she had a chip.

"I used to when I was younger, but not much time these days. Occasionally I play something old-school, if I want to relax. Nothing that requires a chip, of course."

"You've never been curious what it would be like with a chip?" I asked.

"It's impressive enough without. I've seen enough odd things in real life not to need the whole experience in a game."

"I know what you mean," I said sympathetically. I'd avoided magic in games for a long time, because I hadn't wanted to be reminded of Sara.

Aubrey turned her attention back to Damon. "I assume you'll be upping your security measures this time?

He frowned, "What do you mean?"

"Well, Jack Miller is still on the run, isn't he?"

"What," Damon demanded coldly, "do you know about Jack Miller?"

Chapter Six

"I KNOW that you have been sending your security teams around the world searching for him," Aubrey said, matching his chilly tone.

Not intimidated by the billionaire. Points for that. Damon in master-of-the-universe mode was formidable.

His mouth flattened briefly. "We've been keeping that well under the radar."

"All the Cestis in Europe play a part in the legal system, just as they do here. Your security teams are good, but you can only send a team poking around the continent so many times in a relatively short period of time before law enforcement will notice. Even those not informed directly by your organization. We talk to each other when there seems to be an issue that crosses jurisdictional boundaries," Aubrey said.

"Knowing we're after something is one thing," Damon said. "Knowing who it is, is another."

"We have our own networks, and investigating crimes and other matters is part of our job. Jack Miller has had business interests beyond the borders of the United States. Though it seems he had kept his magical abilities to himself before now.

We haven't found anyone he's had dealings with who was aware he's a witch."

That was actually something of a relief to hear. Jack had fooled everyone. "He kept those abilities close to his chest," I said.

Aubrey nodded. "Criminals often do."

I winced, thinking of my mother. Did she know about Sara?

"It might have been easier to just tell us you were looking for him," Aubrey continued. "We could have helped. Cassandra should have known better."

I bristled, ready to defend Cassandra, but Damon spoke before I could. "As I said, we were trying to involve as few people as possible. Clearly Jack has networks of his own, keeping him informed."

He was doing a good job keeping his voice from revealing his level of frustration that Jack still evaded him, but I could see the signs. Every time one of his teams failed to catch Jack, Damon became a little more laser focused on finding him.

"So far, that strategy hasn't yielded the results you want, has it?"

I was reluctantly impressed. There were a lot of people who wouldn't be willing to be so blunt with Damon. People who wanted something from him often thought sucking up was the way to go. Until he bounced them. Hard. I'd been leaning toward thinking Aubrey might be one of them earlier. But perhaps not.

Damon, however, frowned, his eyes shading to the chillier side of blue, jaw tightening. "It's not always easy when we're working from the other side of the world. We have leads, but sometimes the trail gets cold before we can get there, even with suborbitals." He tilted his head. "After all, as an American company, it's difficult to leave security teams running around a continent for any length of time without violating a few dozen treaties. Which we try not to do."

Aubrey nodded at that. "Yes, I guess it would be. But again, for that reason, may I suggest that next time you think of asking for some assistance?"

"I'll keep it in mind." Damon looked at me and then made a show of pulling back his cuff to check the time. "Perhaps we can talk more about this another time. But I'm afraid Maggie and I need to get going."

Damon didn't say anything until we were safely back in the car, and several blocks away from Cassandra's.

Maia drove in silence, focusing on the traffic and doing her best to be unnoticeable, but we'd brought the Jeep, not one of the larger cars where the backseat could be cut off from the driver with a privacy screen.

So I waited for Damon to start talking, figuring he needed time to process what Aubrey had just said. He trusted Maia and she, as one of the witches on his security team, knew more about our lives than most, but it was up to him to decide how much to tell her about this. It took a while. He ignored both of us, initially, typing out a stream of messages on his datapad with more force than strictly necessary. Eventually he shoved the datapad away, shook his head irritably, and huffed out a breath before turning to me.

"What do you think of Ms. Carter?" he asked.

She was back to Ms. Carter, not Aubrey. Definitely still annoyed. "I'm not sure. I don't think she likes me much, unlike you."

He snorted, but his expression lightened a little. "Not sure she likes me much, either. Or she doesn't approve of my methods, clearly. But I get the feeling she thinks I could be useful to her. She wouldn't have offered to help otherwise."

"It's kind of her job to help," I pointed out. "That's what the Cestis do. And at least she wasn't sucking up to you."

"No. I'll give her that."

"Do you know much about the British Cestis?"

He shrugged. "Do you?"

"No. It hasn't exactly been a priority. I have enough dealing with our Cestis without worrying about other witches in places I'm unlikely to go."

"I'll take you plenty of places," he said. "At some point, things will calm down enough."

"Let's hope so." I smiled at him. "But when we travel, my plan is that we don't do anything that would require us to be talking to the local Cestis. I'd prefer dinners and cocktails and sightseeing and…other activities."

That earned me a smile. "Me, too."

"So can you tell me anything about the Brits?"

"Bits and pieces," he said. "Names, but not much more than that. I've never had to deal with them in person. Until you came along, Riley Arts managed to stay clear of magical mishaps."

"I know," I said, making an apologetic face. "I'm sorry."

"It's not your fault." He patted my thigh and then reached for my hand, winding his fingers through mine.

"I could ask Mitch to put together a briefing," Maia piped up. "Background information. Whatever you need."

Damon smiled. "Good idea. Tell him to focus on Aubrey Carter. She's the youngest member."

"She's the one who's visiting?" Maia asked.

"Yes," Damon said. "They're interested in digitizing their Archives, so we might be dealing with them for a while. Better to understand what we're walking into."

"All right," Maia said. "I'll tell Mitch once I drop you off. I doubt it will take long. I'm sure Mitch already has some of the information."

Damon laughed. "I'm sure he does, or he wouldn't have let me come to this meeting. But he needs to do a bit more of a deep dive. Aubrey didn't exactly greet Maggie with open arms. Which might just be due to her being English, or maybe she's just naturally cautious due to her job, but I'd like to find out more about her. And tell him he needs to be discreet. The Cestis apparently have their own feelers out."

Maia frowned, concern clear in the expression I could see in the rearview mirror. "Anything I need to know about, boss?"

"I've already briefed Mitch, he'll fill you in."

Her expression didn't ease, but she nodded and didn't ask any more questions.

"There's someone else we could talk to," I said.

"Who?"

"Zee. He worked in the UK for the Cestis. Our Cestis, I mean, but he was over there a while. So he has to understand the basics of how they operate. If we want the lowdown from someone who might have had direct contact, then he's our best bet."

"Do you think he'd be able to tell us much?" Damon asked. "After all, he was working undercover, and the Cestis tend to be close-lipped about things."

"Well, he probably won't be able to tell us about exactly what he was doing, but I'm sure there's no reason he can't tell us about personal opinions he's formed about individuals," I said with a grin.

"You think Lizzie would agree to him telling us?"

"I don't think Lizzie liked Aubrey any more than we did. If she hasn't already grilled Zee about her, I'm sure she will tonight."

He squeezed my hand. "You're probably right about that. So, perhaps we should see if we can be in on that conversation."

"I could invite them for dinner?"

"Good idea. I don't think I had anything urgent tonight, but let me check." He pulled out his datapad again, swiping through his calendar. "Nothing that can't be rescheduled. So yeah, if they can come tonight or tomorrow night, that will be helpful. When do you think Cassandra will ask Cerridwen about meeting with Aubrey?"

"I'm not sure. I don't think she'd wait terribly long, though," I said. "So if we want to get the skinny on the Brits before then, then we need to move fast."

"You think the meeting request will cause problems?"

"I don't think we can assume the Fae will have a united view on the matter. Which could cause problems. And if they say no, then I get the feeling Aubrey wouldn't take it well."

"No," he agreed. "All right. Talk to Lizzie, see what she has to say."

"Sure." I grabbed my own datapad out of my backpack and sent Lizzie a quick message.

Dinner?

It didn't take long before the reply came back."

Tonight?

Yeah. With Zee. At Damon's.

I see. Would I be wrong in guessing that there's a specific topic of dinner conversation you had in mind?

No. Unless you already had this particular conversation.

Some of it. :D But after today, I have more questions. And I think you should know some of it, too. Zee should be around. Let me check what time we can get there.

Sure, let me know.

Is Amy cooking?

"Is she in?" Damon asked.

I nodded. "Yes, she's checking if Zee's free."

"A double date." he said.

"The two of them would have to admit they're in a relationship for it to be a double date. And we wouldn't be talking shop."

"They still haven't said anything to you about—" Damon made a back-and-forth gesture that I assumed was his attempt to suggest that Lizzie and Zee were doing it.

"Nope. But they spend a lot of time together. They're either sleeping together or they're officially BFFs."

Lizzie would tell me when she was ready. I understood being wary about relationships. And she and Zee had messed things up once before.

"Sounds like talking shop might be easier." He grinned and then yawned. "But it kind of nixes your plan for an early night."

Yeah. By the time Lizzie got back to the city and then to Damon's place, it wasn't going to be an early night for any of us. "My new plan is more coffee. Lots of it."

It was after eight by the time Zee and Lizzie arrived. Any good that Cassandra's tea had done me had been undone by the coffee I'd drunk since getting to Damon's. I'd managed to grab about a thirty-minute nap when we first arrived home, but that just left me feeling groggier.

Damon had investigated the contents of the kitchen and announced that he was making some sort of quick curry thing, with a name I didn't recognize. He actually liked to cook, though he didn't often have time. I happily let him take charge and chopped, poured, fetched, and carried when requested. The task distracted me for a while, but I was flagging again when the doorbell rang.

Did coffee go with curry? Probably not.

Leaving Damon to his culinary duties, I padded to the front hall to let Lizzie and Zee in. To be fair, neither of them looked much more awake than I did, but Zee at least kissed me on the cheek, and then said, "Something smells good," appreciatively as they came inside.

Lizzie nodded agreement, taking off her sparkly jacket. The temperature had dropped after sunset and there was a chill in the air. At least I didn't have to run around Dockside in the cold tonight.

I smiled at Zee and held my hand out for his jacket. "Thanks for coming."

He shrugged out of the leather jacket he was wearing over a blue hoodie a few shades darker than his eyes. "Free food, what's not to like?" He handed me the jacket, sniffing the air. He was a year or so older than Lizzie, but still ate like a teenage boy rather than a man in his late twenties. Lizzie told me once that he said it was the magic burning calories. But more likely it was just good genes. Using a lot of magic made me hungry, but Zee would have to be walking around using his constantly to justify the amount of food he put away.

But he was a big guy, so there was a lot of him to fuel. And he worked out, like the rest of his gaming team did. Virtual reality gaming took stamina and good reflexes, despite what many people assumed about gamers and lifestyles consisting of stims and junk food. The top teams trained like athletes.

I rolled my eyes and flapped my free hand back toward the kitchen. "Damon's cooking. If you go join him, I'm pretty sure there's beer or whatever else you want."

"Sounds like a plan," Zee said. He glanced at Lizzie. She made a shooing motion much like mine, "Girl talk."

"Say no more." He held up his hands in surrender and then loped away down the hall.

"Did you ask him about Aubrey?" I asked Lizzie. We went into the small office-slash-study area off the entrance that Damon sometimes used for guests he was trying to keep away from the main part of the house. It was furnished in a lot of stark white and black, more formal than his office at Riley. "Yes, he's willing to tell us what he can."

"What about you?" I put the jackets over one of the architecturally severe sofas. "I imagine you know more than he does."

"I've never met any of them face to face, unlike him, but I can tell you the parts I'm allowed to."

The parts that didn't come under the heading of "secret Cestis business". As expected. "Did Cassandra talk to Cerridwen yet?"

"She hadn't by the time I left," Lizzie said. She wrinkled her nose. "Rather her than me."

"Hard agree." Telling Cerridwen what to do was not a job for the fainthearted. "Okay, so we worry about that when it happens."

"Are you worried about the afrit, or the fact that Aubrey wants to talk to the Fae?"

"I can worry about both," I smiled a little lopsidedly. "I was enjoying the fact that we'd had some peace and quiet for a few months."

"No rest for the wicked," Lizzie agreed. "Besides, some of us have still been dealing with the not-so-peace-and-quiet stuff."

"Which I am extremely grateful for. But I'll leave it to you. I don't need a third job."

"More like a fourth," Lizzie said.

"A fourth?"

"Being Damon's girlfriend takes a chunk of effort," she pointed out. "Even if it has its perks."

She was right about that. Damon and I had kept our relationship secret for some time, but now we were public, which meant that I had to accompany him to far too many weird rich-people events. It was fun to wear gorgeous clothes and jewels and eat nice food in interesting places, but the reality was that those nights were mostly work for Damon. Lots of networking and keeping up connections. Not exactly relaxing. Luckily the only perk I was really interested in—being with Damon—made up for it.

"True. So I don't need yours." I studied her. "Any news on a new fifth?"

"Not that I can share," Lizzie said. "But we're looking."

The house comp chimed, and Damon's voice said, "Enough girl talk, food is just about done."

"Coming," I called back.

"Better be quick," he answered. "Or Zee and I will eat it all."

Given he'd made enough curry to feed at least ten people, that was doubtful, but I was starving. And food might help me stay awake. "We'd better join them," I said. "Thanks again, for this. I'm sure whatever you can tell us will be helpful." I snapped my fingers to make sure the house comp wasn't still relaying our conversation. "Damon's got Mitch looking into the Brits as well."

Lizzie's eyebrows rose. "He's that worried?"

"He just likes to understand who he's dealing with," I said. Damon had always been cautious, but especially since Jack. "While you were still with Cassandra, Aubrey mentioned that she knows about Jack."

Lizzie's eyebrows shot upward, eyes widening. "She does?"

"She said that Damon couldn't have people poking around Europe on the regular without it coming to the attention of the various Cestis over there."

"Well, I guess that's right." Lizzie was frowning, not looking any more pleased by the news than Damon had been. "Interesting that they didn't contact us, though." She meant the Cestis, not her or me.

"Well, maybe they were willing to look the other way while it wasn't stirring up any trouble," I suggested. It was a nicer option than the Brits not wanting to play nice with the upstart colonials or something.

"If it isn't stirring up any trouble, it's interesting that Aubrey brought it up."

"Isn't it? It felt like a bit of a power play, letting Damon know that she knew."

"This is a conversation it will be easier to have with the guys," Lizzie said. "Otherwise we'll have to go over it twice."

As if agreeing with her, my stomach rumbled.

Lizzie giggled. "Hard agree with that. And Zee. It smells delicious."

"It's chicken curry. Well, it has a fancy name, but I can't pronounce it as well as Damon, so I'll let him tell you. But yes, I'm starving.

"Me, too. Curry sounds perfect. And one of those beers you offered Zee sounds pretty good too."

"Yeah. This will be easier with food and alcohol."

"Yep, that's my plan. Eat fast, talk fast, and see if we can all get to bed at a decent hour tonight." She stretched her arms above her head and yawned.

"I'm on board with that plan."

Seemed we were all equally hungry, because, for the first half an hour or so of the meal, the food was firmly the focus. Damon's chicken curry was delicious, and he'd made rice and naan and various sauces and sides that went along with it. Everyone kept the conversation away from magic while we ate. Damon mostly talked with Zee about how Trueno were doing and what their next few competitions were. Zee told him the latest and they both avoided talking about the upcoming Riley tournament. Zee was too professional to press Damon for details, even if he'd had any thought that Damon might give them to him. The tournament was going to be in November, the new game Riley was launching even more complicated than *Serenity Falls*.

Lizzie and I half participated in that conversation and half caught up on stuff we needed to coordinate about the apartment and schedules and grocery shopping and more boring life admin that was easier to do face to face than by the datapad messages and voicemail we had been resorting to for the last week or so.

Zee ate two serves of curry in the time I ate one.

"Oh, for that metabolism," I said to Lizzie, watching Zee making short work of the last of his second helping.

"He's always eaten like a horse. Him and Carlo both." Lizzie smiled but there was a hint of something sad in her tone.

Idiot. I'd never really thought about the fact that Zee never missed an opportunity to fuel up because there had been a few years in his teens where he and Lizzie and their other two friends, Carlo and Jaali, had lived on the streets, not always knowing where their next meal was coming from.

Zee pushed his plate away and reached for his beer, grinning at Damon. "That was great. You missed your calling."

Damon tipped his beer in acknowledgment of the compliment, "No. I don't mind cooking now and then, but it would be less fun if I had to do it every day."

Zee swigged beer and nodded. "I know what you mean. You should do a cooking game. Weren't those popular once upon a time?"

Damon shrugged and nodded, "They were," he agreed, "But it's not really the kind of thing that we do. Someone would need to find a fresh twist to make it worth our while and I'm not sure how fresh you can get with cooking games."

"Alien catering business," Lizzie said promptly. "Spaceship cook. Magical cooking school."

Damon laughed. "I expect most of those have been done. And I think the appeal of the cooking games is repetition of the familiar. Not too many people familiar with alien catering."

"They could be," Lizzie said, "That would be the fun part."

"You have a weird idea of fun."

"Cooking for aliens is a nice break from smiting and pilfering," Lizzie retorted. "That's what a lot of games boil down to."

Damon clapped a hand to his chest, pulling a wounded face though his eyes were smiling. "Tell me what you really think."

"I think," Zee said, putting his beer down, "that we should get on with this. Lizzie says you want info on Aubrey Carter and the Cestis in England."

"Yes," Damon agreed. "I'd like to know who I'm dealing with."

Zee's focus shifted to me. "Lizzie says she was less than chill toward you?"

"Not so much hostile as wary," I said, "Not sure she's a fan."

He nodded. "That would make sense."

"Why? I'm very likeable," I said, mock wounded.

Lizzie snorted at that and I balled up my napkin and tossed it at her.

"Well, you're outside the boundaries, really, aren't you?" Zee said, ignoring the flying napkin. "Didn't know you had magic, tangled with a demon, got plenty of magic, but still learning at your age. You're an example of the kind of thing that the Cestis in the UK works hard to prevent."

"Hey," Lizzie protested. "We work hard to prevent it as well."

Zee shrugged. "Yeah, but not in quite the same way they do. And they have a smaller population."

"My mom went out of her way to avoid the Cestis here. It's not their fault. She went off the grid and hid from them."

"Yeah, but she did that after she had magic," Zee said. "In England, a known witch vanishing off the radar would be followed up pretty quickly."

"They keep tabs on everyone?" I asked skeptically. "That seems impossible."

"It's different over there. They have well-established networks they've nurtured over centuries, they have staff, and they have, well, centuries worth of resources built up to help them do it," Zee said. "Children from known witch families are monitored carefully."

"My grandparents didn't have magic," I objected.

"No, but I'm guessing if you went back a couple of generations, somebody would have," Zee said. "And that's the difference over there. They have the records back generations, a lot of generations. They get, well, fewer surprises. The English seem to go along with it. They're an orderly lot at heart."

"Unlike us snooty colonial upstarts?" Damon suggested.

"Something like that," Zee said. "A lot more consideration to what's proper. Not so much so as there used to be, maybe, but there's still a healthy respect for the traditions."

"For the rules," Lizzie said. "And not breaking them."

I wasn't sure I liked the sound of that much control and

supervision. "All right, so they don't like me because I don't fit into a neat box," I said. "Why don't you tell us a bit more about what they think that box should be?"

Chapter Seven

Zee leaned back and swallowed more beer before he answered. "Everything's a lot more structured over there. They love rules and regs. Making them and following them. The Cestis own a building in the heart of London. They have formal hearings and times where people can bring complaints to them." He picked at the label on his bottle, shredding it one tiny strip of paper at a time. "They operate a lot more like a regular court here, I guess. Don't try to be quite so low profile. Most of the human population still don't seem to care much, unless they have a magical issue that impacts them. But they know where to go for help, if they do. And the witches, well, they definitely know who's watching."

"That doesn't sound so different," I said. Most people without magic ignored it and got on with their lives. Some tried to use it to their advantage, some of them resented the fact that others had it and they didn't. Humans were humans, after all.

"Yes," Damon agreed. "And you can't say our Cestis here go easy on anyone they catch doing the wrong thing."

"No," Zee said. "But they're less gung ho about trying to

put the fear of exactly what will happen if they do into everyone."

Damon looked at me, expression quizzical. I shrugged. "Don't ask me. I didn't grow up in a normal witch family. Sara avoided all forms of authority, not just the Cestis. She was more worried about telling me how not to get noticed by the cops than witches. And my grandparents, well, I doubt they ever got a parking ticket or a late fee. But they didn't talk to me about magic or the rules either."

Lizzie and Zee might not understand much more than me about how your average witch was raised to feel about the Cestis. Lizzie had run away from home when she was a teenager, trying to get away from her father who was a controlling, abusive asshole. She'd known she had magic, but she'd kept that secret. The Cestis had lost track of her, too, once she'd run, and Zee for that matter. Maybe Aubrey wouldn't approve of any of us.

Damon watched Zee picking at the beer label. "Okay. So they're more officious. And they talk to their counterparts across Europe regularly."

Zee's mouth twisted. "Yeah, and that causes its own problems. Even more bureaucracy and politics to get around."

"I don't think we have time for you to teach us about that tonight," Damon said. "And I have people whose whole job is navigating global bureaucracies. Let's focus on the personalities. Did you meet any of the Cestis while you were there?"

Zee flicked a fingernail against the beer bottle, once again considering his words.

"There are five of them, like here. Aubrey's the youngest. By at least twenty years," Lizzie said, when he didn't say anything. "The others are all in their fifties."

All four of them? That seemed weird. Lizzie wasn't quite that much younger than Radha, who had just turned thirty-nine, but then Cassandra was in her sixties. Antony had been a little younger than her. And Ian slotted in between, turning fifty soon. Lizzie had told me once that they tried always to keep a range of ages and perspectives in their ranks.

"Is that usual?" Damon asked, clearly thinking the same.

Lizzie shook her head, reaching for her wineglass. "In their case, it's bad luck more than anything. During the Second World War, most of them were serving in one way or another and they lost three members in a few months. The remaining two stepped down once the war was over, and they'd trained their replacements. Trauma, I guess. And given the casualties that Britain suffered in the war, it just happened that five people around the same age were chosen as replacements. Since then, well, they seem to recruit younger people around the same ages, train them, and then they replace them as they retire. So they've had a pretty consistent age range for quite some time. That was until Verity died. Verity Llewellyn. She had a heart attack. She's the one Aubrey replaced. She was the second oldest. I think their healer is the closest in age to Aubrey and she's fifty-two. But Verity died unexpectedly, which left them scrambling a bit. They always have their eye on possible replacements and apparently Aubrey was the strongest. They picked her to join despite the age gap."

"Okay, so she's the youngest," I said. "What else?"

"Well," Zee said, "Her grandma was on the Cestis as well. Her great-grandfather was, well, I don't remember exactly, but he had a title of some sort. Grandma was the oldest daughter, but the estate went to the son. But luckily, Granny had magic, and she married another witch, an academic. Aubrey's mom was their second or third daughter. She has magic, but not strong enough to be Cestis. But she also married a witch, and the kids are all magical." He looked at Lizzie. "I forget which Aubrey is."

"Third, I think," Lizzie said. "Three girls and a boy. All smart, all magical. But Aubrey is the most powerful, and the only one who had a chance at keeping up the family tradition as far as the Cestis is concerned. It seems her family pushed her in that direction once they realized how strong she was. She went to a better school than her siblings, and then to Cambridge—that's where her grandfather taught. She studied political science and international law, as well as whatever magical studies she did. That stuff is a bit more hush-hush, not in the public record."

"So, she was raised in the family tradition and dedicated to the cause?" I asked. I filed that away, trying to see how it meshed with what I'd seen of her. Focused. Proper. And a tad judgy. It fit.

Lizzie's earrings chimed faintly as she nodded. "And being the youngest member, she's got something to prove, I guess, to show that the faith that the others showed by choosing her is justified." She looked down at the table, mouth going flat.

Did she feel that way, too? That she had to prove herself. I'd never seen any of the other Cestis here treat Lizzie with anything but the utmost respect.

"And the others? The oldest is Leo Waite, is that right?" Damon asked.

"Yeah. He *is* a lord. An earl, I think," Lizzie agreed. "Old family."

"Does that mean he has a seat in the House of Lords as well?" I asked. "Isn't that how it works over there?"

"He does. But he's not allowed to vote because of his position. The Cestis have to stay out of normal human politics. His family goes even further back than Aubrey's. And the other three. Well, there's Ralph—pronounced *rayf*—Bright, who's another academic. Oxford, rather than Cambridge, I think, though he mostly guest lectures these days. He's the history keeper. In charge of the Archives. He's the one that Aubrey has to convince if they're going to digitize. Well, she'd have to convince all four of them but, if he was really opposed, I don't think the other three would be likely to go against him." Lizzie looked thoughtful.

"I had to go to the Archives there once, or at least the bit of it that they would let me see when I was looking at something for my case," Zee said. "I met Ralph. He plays the easygoing professor type. But I got the feeling you wouldn't want to cross him." His forehead wrinkled as he shifted uneasily on his seat.

"Why not?" I asked.

"He has that…I don't know…coldhearted feel to him. Maybe that's not the right word. Someone who won't hesitate to make the right decision, even if it's not necessarily the easy one. Even if it means…"

Taking someone out, if necessary. That was part of what the Cestis had to do. Unlike the human courts, they were judge and jury. If they deemed a witch to be too dangerous to let live, then they took care of it. Same with other magical threats like demonkind. It tended to be kill them first and deal with the fallout later. I was on board with that part. The executing witches was not something I liked. But, then, the thought of a serial killer with magical powers was terrifying. Keeping a witch like that in prison would be a challenge, and use resources that the magical community didn't necessarily have to spare.

"Like Cassandra," Zee continued. "She's ruthless at heart, when she needs to be."

She was. But in her, a big helping of compassion and caring tempered her steely sense of duty. But she could be ruthless. The Cestis had to be. After all, they'd subjected me to demon stone twice now, knowing that either time it could have killed me.

"The other two are Isolde Lark and Padma Barad. Isolde's a lawyer, by training. And Padma is their healer. Works as a surgeon now and then."

Unlike Radha—who was a psychologist, a counselor by training—surgeons, I'd learned from my experiences in the hospital with Gran, were another breed entirely.

"Well, they sound like a fun time," Damon said.

Zee shrugged. "I didn't deal with most of them. Just Ralph."

I blinked. "You never dealt with Aubrey? But you were working on something to do with the Fae, weren't you?"

He shrugged. "Well, I was undercover. So, no, not directly. Cassandra handled whatever admin was needed for me to be there, and it was too risky for me to actually meet any of them when I was supposed to be fitting in as someone on the wrong side of things."

That made sense, now I thought about it. Undercover wasn't undercover if you were caught hanging with the magical equivalent of the cops.

"But I heard about her," Zee added. "The people I was dealing with, well, obviously they were actively trying not to get noticed by the Cestis. It sounded like she was good at her job." He shrugged. "Which could be good or bad."

"What do you mean?" I asked.

"Being good at your job when you're dealing with the Fae all the time takes a certain kind of ruthless mindset of its own," Zee said.

"And not a little skill with politics and protocol, I'd imagine," Damon said. "Is that what you mean?"

"Yes," Lizzie agreed. "Aubrey must be a very good negotiator. Good at getting her own way. Or getting the way of the people she's representing. The Cestis wouldn't keep her in that role if she wasn't effective. To be effective with the Fae isn't easy. There's a reason why Cassandra usually deals with them for us. And Aubrey doesn't have Cassandra's years of experience behind her to lend some weight to her authority. I mean, she has the history of the Cestis over there, of course, and she's powerful. But, to the Fae, someone her age is still a baby. So, if they're willing to deal with her, then she clearly knows what she's doing. We have to assume she has some serious diplomatic skills to go along with her magic."

In other words, Aubrey wasn't someone to be taken lightly

or underestimated. Not that I planned on doing either, but knowing that Lizzie and Zee both viewed her a little warily just confirmed what I had already been thinking. I leaned back in the chair, wishing I could have another beer, but between the coffee and the alcohol, anything else was going to mean either not sleeping well or paying for it in the morning. So I said slowly, "What do you think our plan of attack should be? Is she someone we can trust?"

"Well, she is one of us," Lizzie said, "That's a good start."

"Not exactly one of us," I pointed out. No single Cestis operated the same as the others. So we couldn't assume their people thought like us.

"I know, but it's hard to be a black hat and make it into a Cestis." She hitched a shoulder. "I'm not saying it's never happened in history, but I can't think of the last time the Cestis had to deal with one of their own for a crime."

"Yeah, but being a good Cestis member doesn't necessarily mean she's our friend. The Brits will be playing their own angle, surely?" I asked.

"True," Lizzie agreed. "So, yeah, in that case, you should treat her as, well, not as someone who can't be trusted but someone on the right side, but with their own agenda." She turned her attention to Damon. "I guess if they decide to go ahead with digitizing their Archives, you'll get to learn more about that. You'll have to spend time with them. They'll probably try a hard bargain."

"Cassandra drove a hard bargain. Though in her case it was about whether to do it, not about how much it would cost." Damon said.

Mostly because Damon was funding the project here. But I doubted he'd do the same for other countries, unless they were willing to make some sort of alliance.

"But Cestis or no Cestis," he added, "I'm willing to back my team in terms of locking them down in a contract."

Lizzie laughed. "Yes, I saw the copy of the one that you made with Cassandra. It's thorough."

"Do you think it's a good idea? For them to digitize their Archives?" Damon asked. "Obviously there's a benefit to them, but the bigger picture would always be to work toward having shared resources. Do you think they'd be open to that?"

Had he already been thinking about this in the back of his mind?

"No idea," said Lizzie. "That's a whole other kettle of fish. It's part of the reason why we did it, but actually getting the Cestis to cooperate and opening lines of access in other countries, well, I can see that comes with its own set of problems," she said. "After all, in some countries, they've been squirreling away things in their Archives for a lot longer than we have. We help each other out with individual cases and resources where needed, but that's not the same as sharing everything. The tricky bit is really having the people who understand the context of the Archives. What the really dangerous books are, or how things are linked. You need a real person for that."

"Not necessarily, with the right metadata and a good AI," Damon said, but his expression had turned thoughtful the way it did when he'd just had an idea. Or had some information dumped in his lap about a project that he hadn't considered before. The digital version of the Archives he was building had a cataloging system and metadata, but I hadn't yet come across any sort of warning system. Possibly Damon and Cassandra had discussed it, and we just hadn't gotten to that part of the project yet.

"Good luck getting them to agree to try that," Zee said.

"Yeah, don't mention that part to Aubrey," Lizzie said. "Stick to the basics. It will be hard enough to get them to agree to share without making them think you want to make them redundant."

"Besides, no one wants an AI who can do magic," I said, joking.

Lizzie looked horrified.

"That was a joke," I added hastily.

"Not so much, when we don't know if it's possible. I mean, demons can invade virtual reality, as can Fae. Clearly magic can work there. So, that's definitely a *no*. Stick to sharing only."

Damon shrugged. "Well, we're used to dealing with trying to get lots of other individual countries to cooperate. I guess we can treat the Cestis in the same way."

Lizzie nodded. "Yes, that's not a bad approach. We're kind of like the Vatican is in Italy, each our own little bureaucracy and kingdom, and we all do things different ways." She tilted her head. "The problem you might run into is who you have in your team who can do the work for them that they would trust? They might want you in person."

Damon shrugged. "I guess we'll cross that bridge when we come to it.

Chapter Eight

Once upon a time, a three-way fight between a Fae, my boyfriend, and myself would have officially registered as weird. Lately, it had become just another night at the office.

Another *tiring* night.

Which wasn't what I needed. It had been around eleven when Lizzie and Zee left after dinner. I'd gone straight to bed, but Damon had woken early, and I'd tagged along with him to Riley and worked from there for the day. Mitch delivered his background briefing on the British Cestis but it matched up with what Lizzie and Zee had told us already, though Mitch had more detail. Callum arrived just after Damon and I had finished eating an early dinner in his office, and I was beginning to regret choosing a burger instead of salad as I sparred with them.

I panted as I backed away from the fight, trying to catch my breath. Callum and Damon didn't notice, both of them gleefully intent on defeating the other.

Technically, Callum came to the Riley campus to help Damon, who was still trying to figure out how Callum was able to escape from a game that had been deadlocked—one that had been hacked so that only someone outside the game could free the player from the VR.

So far, no matter what Damon did to the combination of programming and technology, Callum managed to free himself fairly easily.

Unfortunately, I hadn't been able to do it again without the impetus of sheer instinct and fear that I'd managed fighting the bruadhsiu. Callum kept trying to explain to me what he was doing. I understood some of it, but I couldn't replicate it. We hadn't yet worked out whether it was a lack of power on my part, or just a difference between Fae and witch magic.

So we kept trying. I wasn't sure if it was helping Damon—who needed a solution for humans, not Fae, to find a mechanism that would prevent people like Jack from turning a VR environment into a virtual prison—but Callum's patience with the process was growing shorter as the novelty wore off. Lately it had taken less and less time each session before he got bored and demanded to actually *do* something in the game rather than just trying to escape.

Something about the virtual reality environment seemed to fascinate him, and we had played through several games in Riley's back catalog already. It was probably just as well that human technology didn't work reliably in the Fae realm, or Callum might have been the first Fae to turn into a true game head.

Plenty of tanai were gamers and Cerridwen's theory was it appealed because it gave them some semblance of the powers the Fae had over their realm. But the true Fae had no need of that. They could change the realm—or the parts of it they had control over—to suit them and had access to magic beyond anything a game developer could dream up.

So whatever Callum's fascination was with Damon's games, it wasn't the magic. In fact, he seemed to prefer historical games rather than fantastical ones. But tonight we were playing something that combined both. *Coeur d'Acier* was set in a medieval-meets-steampunk version of a Europe ruled by France. With bonus dragons. It was an earlier Righteous game but still fun, with plenty of scenarios and locations to explore.

As usual, Callum had taken the first opportunity to turn our quest into a combat session. He called it training and claimed it was to benefit me, but I got the feeling the sessions were mostly a way for him and Damon to test their skills against each other.

They had become friends of a kind, despite the debt that lay between them, but that friendship involved a *very* healthy dose of male competitiveness. Which I usually found entertaining, when it didn't go on too long. It had the added bonus of me getting to watch them sparring in whatever ridiculous outfits the game world required. I'd developed a fondness for the ones where they went at it in breeches and floppy white shirts, wielding swords.

One day I might even get Damon to wear a costume like that in real life. So far none of his billionaire events had involved a costume ball, and he'd vetoed the idea for Halloween the previous year. Though he had ravished me in a thoroughly rakish fashion after we'd gotten home from the Riley Halloween party.

Tonight we were having a three-way duel on a spectacular rocky plateau somewhere in the dragon-infested, not-quite-Swiss Alps. Personally, I would have rather flown on the dragons, but at least fighting in VR was somewhat easier on my body than my real-world training sessions with Callum and Cerridwen. Still, even in virtual form, the guys were bigger than me and when they started focusing on each other, I often took the opportunity to back away and play spectator while saving my strength for sneaky attacks later on.

Damon ducked behind a large group of boulders, and I held back an impressed whistle when Callum, hot on his heels, ran up the side of the biggest one and vaulted over it, throwing in a showy sort of flip that was probably only feasible in virtual reality. Well, at least for a human, it would be. I wouldn't put it past the Fae to defy gravity in real life. On second thoughts, I decided not to ask if he could. He might expect Pinky and me to learn how to do it, and I really didn't want to add acrobatic training to my schedule.

I backed up a few more paces, wiped sweat off my forehead, tossed my sword to my left hand so I could wipe the right one against the heavy woolen trousers my avatar wore, and then tossed it back, waiting to see if the boys were going to head my way again.

The sound of clashing swords came from behind the rock, followed by a protesting "oof" that suggested someone had thrown a sneaky elbow or worse. Damon rounded the rock at a flat-out sprint, headed in my direction. Callum, predictably, appeared on the top of the rock. He leaped into the air, trying to pull off the flip again. His body twisted elegantly, but he landed with his right foot on a smaller rock, which promptly shifted underneath his weight and dumped him on his butt. A rare mishap for him. And one that the game mechanics apparently decided was bad enough that he was injured, because when he tried to climb to his feet, he flinched as he put his weight on his right ankle.

He started swearing—something low and guttural that didn't sound anything like the few Fae curse words he'd taught me.

"Language," I said playfully, and he shot me a glare, his irritation turning his gold-green eyes distinctly more wolfish.

"This game is ridiculous," he said. "I would not be so injured from a minor mishap in the real world."

"Yeah, well, sucks to be you," I said, not feeling sorry for him. He pushed me to my limits pretty regularly. Even with some healing assistance from Cerridwen and Lizzie, I still spent most of my time with bruises on at least one limb and muscle aches in places I didn't know you could ache. "You've got to remember that in here you're human." To keep things fair, we tended to play games where the characters were evenly matched. In this world, that meant human and only minimal magic. Nothing to give Callum an unfair advantage.

Callum took a step, wincing again. His face pulled into a scowl, which deepened as he tried another step before coming to a stop.

"Had enough?" Damon asked.

Callum's scowl deepened. "Your virtual body is faulty."

Damon twirled his sword, smirking. "Nothing wrong with my programming. You just got cocky."

Callum looked confused. "Cocky?"

By Fae standards he'd spent a lot of time in our world, but sometimes slang still tripped him up. Of course, he spoke at least four human languages that I knew of, and however many Fae ones on top of that, so in his place I probably wouldn't remember all the slang either.

"Overly confident," I said. "Gravity is a bitch." I pulled up his stats display, pointed to the medical data, where an amber symbol flashed a warning of the injury. "It's just a sprain, it'll heal in a few rounds of game play."

"I think your stats are wrong," Callum huffed.

"This is just how it feels when you get injured as a human," I pointed out. "It's why we invented painkillers."

"Humans are too fragile."

I couldn't argue with that. Despite advances in medical science, ultimately we were still pretty breakable. "Sometimes."

Callum sheathed his sword, huffing out another irritated breath. "If this will take time to heal, then I feel I must retire from the game for tonight."

"I thought the point of training was sometimes to push through the pain, so you know how to deal with it," I said.

Annoyed green-gold flashed at me again. "Quoting my own advice back to me isn't helpful."

I laughed. "Maybe not. But it feels good. Besides, you need to remember that how you feel now is how Pinky and I feel a lot of the time."

His expression turned offended. "I do not make you train when you have—what do you call this again?" he asked, scowling at his foot as he took another limping step forward.

"A sprained ankle," Damon said. "Damage to one of the ligaments in your foot."

Callum looked unenlightened.

Damon summoned another holoscreen, this one displaying the anatomy of Callum's injury. He peered at it. "No, wait, it's a minor fracture as well. Congratulations, you've just become dragon food unless you can find a healer. Or retire."

"Exactly," Callum said, "See, Maggie. I would not make you train with an injury like this. I would heal you. Or make you go see one of your human healers like Meredith."

"But you'd want me to keep fighting if we're in a real fight," I said.

He raised an eyebrow. "Well, I would expect that if we were in a real fight, you would want to keep fighting, too. If the choice is between a little temporary pain and death, choose temporary pain."

Couldn't argue with that logic. "Sure. But that's the difference between fighting and training, and you sometimes forget that what we are mostly doing is training."

I'd made this point to him before, the fact that when he was in the game, he got to experience things as humans did and that he should remember how it felt when he was teaching Pinky and me. Usually he agreed and promised to remember and then failed utterly to modify his approach. So I was just going to keep making the point and see whether it ever stuck.

I did feel some sympathy for him. Part of the fun for humans playing virtual reality is they got to do things that they couldn't do in the real world. Callum, so far, hadn't gotten to do much of that. Other than dragon riding. Though I was too scared to ask him if dragons existed in the realm. That was one of the things I could live with not knowing.

"We could switch to tourist mode," I suggested. "Visit one of the cities." He usually enjoyed that kind of thing. Though sometimes he looked a little wistful, making me wonder how he'd spent all those centuries stepping in and out of human lives.

Callum's expression didn't lighten. "No. I'm not in the mood. Perhaps we should just bring things to a close."

"Do you have somewhere to be?" Damon asked.

"Almost always," Callum replied. He smiled smugly, suddenly cheerful.

I didn't think I wanted to know exactly what that meant. Callum was a habitual flirt and not above sleeping with human women, though he assured me he was careful not to do anything that might leave them infatuated. Or impregnated. When he stayed in the city, he enjoyed himself. But I didn't need to hear about his conquests and if he was in the city on Fae business, well, ignorance was bliss.

Damon clicked his fingers, and we blinked back into the blank white space of the game's foyer, still wearing our avatars, though our outfits had morphed back to the default black and gray skinsuits that most avatars sported outside of a game. Damon had built Callum a custom avatar and even in just the skin, he was unfairly handsome. As was Damon in his. Damon had built my avatar, too, but, to my eyes, it looked mostly just like me. An average gal on the tall side with nice green eyes and these days, more muscle than I used to have.

Callum flexed his foot, looking relieved when it moved easily, but still not happy.

"Is something else wrong?" I asked. "You seem distracted tonight."

His strange eyes fixed on me. "Nothing to concern yourself with, just yet."

Just yet? Well, that was ominous. "Can you be a little less cryptic, please?"

"Just that there are things happening in the realm."

"Cassandra asked Cerridwen about meeting with Aubrey, didn't she?" I asked. I hadn't raised the topic earlier because Callum hadn't said anything, but from his disgruntled expression, something had to be happening.

"The request has been made, yes."

"And that is upsetting you? Or someone in the realm? Is there a problem with the English Cestis?" Damon asked.

Callum frowned, running a hand through his dark hair. "No. Not precisely. And it is not upsetting, precisely, merely disruptive. It gives those troublemakers amongst us cause to be difficult once more. Things were just settling down after the door and the walker."

"They were?" I asked. "Does that mean you've learned something about who let the bruadhsiu out?"

"No, sadly. But that incident and the impact here in your world allowed those of us who wish things to remain calm sufficient weight to press our point against those grumbling in the background about the door being difficult and that we should perhaps move it again. They had gone quiet for a time, but now between the afrit and wanting to meet with a strange human, things are bubbling up again."

Great. Hopefully the Fae politics wouldn't spill out into our world again. "The afrit was Cerridwen's fault, not mine," I pointed out.

"That may be true," Callum said, "but the fact that one has been discovered so soon is giving those who were not sure about the decision to reopen the door here some fuel. Where there are afrit, there are other demonkind."

"Yes, but nothing active or the Cestis would know about it. Afrits don't always come with their larger friends."

He waved a hand in an annoyed gesture. "I understand that. But it is also true that sometimes they do."

"Not this one, as far as we can tell," I said. "We killed it. We haven't found any others."

Cassandra, Lizzie, and Zee had gone over the building and the immediate surrounds and did whatever else the Cestis did to try to find traces of demon-related activity, but so far they'd been unsuccessful in locating any more live afrits. Which, from my point of view, was better than the alternative.

"Be that as it may," Callum said, "things are unsettled. Amongst our kind, unsettled does not always end well. The Lady is…displeased."

I shot him a sympathetic look. I wouldn't want to be around Cerridwen in a mood, so I couldn't blame Callum for not wanting to either. Luckily, I wouldn't have to see her for a few more days, because our next training session wasn't scheduled until next week when Pinky and I were meant to be going into the realm for a magic lesson. I stopped at that thought. "Is it safe for me and Pinky to continue with our usual schedule?"

Callum nodded. "The Lady hasn't told me to tell you otherwise," he said. "I'm sure she will keep you informed if she changes her mind."

Occasionally, Cerridwen came to the physical training sessions that we had with Callum. Once it was clear that the lessons were going to continue for some time, Damon had purchased a warehouse in Berkeley and converted it into a training arena far bigger than Sal's Gym, where we used to train. It seemed like overkill, but it meant that he could be happy with the security in place while I was there with Callum. It made life easier for the Cestis, too, because they could add their own layers of wards. Plus, it had better air-conditioning and didn't smell of twenty years of sweaty bodybuilder workouts like Sal's, so I wasn't complaining.

"Would Cerridwen prefer to have a session in Berkeley?" I suggested.

Callum looked at me. "I think, for the moment, it is probably better if she stays within the realm. If the factions are restive, then she needs to be close at hand in case she needs to…intervene."

Crap. I hadn't thought of that. Cerridwen had been locked out of the realm once already. It wouldn't be any good if it happened again, particularly not when Aubrey was here. Having other Cestis involved would only complicate the politics even more.

"Besides," Callum continued, "you cannot properly learn Fae magic outside the realm."

"Not learn it, no," I said, "But I can practice." The magic that Cerridwen taught me was always easier within the realm, which was so saturated with the energy that witches called magic, that it was almost like breathing it in. Or maybe standing in the eye of a hurricane, feeling the immense pressure all around me. The magic flowed easily, but felt overwhelming, as though it might swamp me entirely. I could adapt the techniques that Cerridwen had shown me when I was working magic here, but I couldn't do most of the things I could do in the realm outside of it.

Callum and Cerridwen herself said their magic was more limited in the human realm, but I hadn't seen any evidence of how that actually affected what they were able to do. Callum still changed form and used illusions and other tricks like he had used on Beanie Guy without thinking about it. None of which I would be able to do even with a hundred more years of training. Not that I would get a hundred years' more training unless there were some breakthroughs in life extension in the next few decades.

"Very well," I said, after a pause. "I guess we'll wait and see what she says next week. Does the fact that this is unsettling mean Aubrey's request will be refused?"

Callum shook his head. "I think that unlikely. Our far kin have ties with the English Cestis. It would be impolite to refuse to meet without good reason." He cocked his head at me as though asking if I knew of just such a reason.

I spread my hands, apologetic. "If you're asking for dirt on Aubrey, I don't have any, sorry." Mitch was digging around, but having to proceed carefully. And so far, what he'd told us about Aubrey and the other Brits had been all aboveboard.

"Very well. Until next week, then," Callum said.

"Wait," I said, before he could blink himself out of the game. "Aren't we having a session with Pinky on Sunday?"

He shrugged. "I think perhaps we can skip that one. An acknowledgment of the week you've had."

That seemed unlike him. Was the real reason for him putting us off that he thought it would be better if, like Cerridwen, he stayed close to home for a time? That made my stomach go cold. What exactly was happening if both of them were sticking close to home? Could one small afrit really cause so much chaos or indeed one not quite as small foreign Cestis member? I guessed I would have to wait and see.

Chapter Nine

I spent the next few days irritable and out of sorts. Cassandra hadn't called, and Lizzie merely shrugged when I'd asked her if she had heard anything. The waiting was frustrating, but I tried to focus on other things: confirming my next assignments with Riley Arts and reviewing requests from other potential clients to see what they were offering. Busywork, but it was also enough of a distraction to stop me wondering about what was going to happen with Aubrey's request.

Cassandra finally called around lunchtime on Sunday.

"Hey," I said, trying to sound like I hadn't been waiting for the call. "What's up?" I boosted myself onto the kitchen counter, chewing my bottom lip and telling myself there was no need to be nervous.

"Are you and Damon free?" Her voice was brisk, the sound slightly echoey. Like she was in a car, perhaps.

My stomach went cold. "Yes, I think so." I glanced toward Damon's study. He was in there working and I was supposed to be choosing something fun to do after lunch when he'd be done for the day.

"At the Archives?" I asked.

"No," Cassandra said. "We're meeting at Ian's. He and Aubrey are already there."

We. That meant the Cestis. Plus Aubrey. My stomach sank further. This had to be about Aubrey's request to meet with the Fae. If it was about the Archives project, there was no reason for us not to meet at Cassandra's. I tried to keep my tone light and said, "What's Aubrey doing with Ian?"

"He was taking her sightseeing. I believe they were spending a day going through the galleries."

Well, Aubrey had said she wanted to see San Francisco. It made sense that Ian would show her around. He had some sort of family money, I didn't really understand, had worked in something finance related, made another small fortune of his own, and retired early. He wasn't as rich as Damon, but he didn't need to work, and he loved art and the fine things, as his magpie's jewel box of an apartment demonstrated. He'd be in his element, showing Aubrey through all his favorite San Francisco art galleries, large and small.

"Hang on," I said, already heading to the study. "I just need to go ask Damon."

I found him sitting with his bare feet propped on his desk, reading something on his datapad while various graphs and dashboards flickered and shifted on the holoscreen hovering in the air on the other side of his desk.

He smiled distractedly, but then the smile turned to a frown when he noticed my datapad. "Something up?"

"Cassandra," I said, pointing at the datapad. "She wants us to meet her at Ian's. Aubrey will be there," I added. "Are you free?"

Damon nodded. "Yeah, I just need about fifteen minutes to finish this, so I guess we could be at Ian's by…" He glanced at the holoscreen, checking the time. "Let's say by one?"

"Great," Cassandra said. "I should be there about then."

Which meant she was already on her way.

"Fine. We'll see you there." I ended the call and left

Damon to do what he needed while I found my purse and shoes.

I wasn't as familiar with Ian's apartment as I was with Cassandra's house. I'd been to Ian's twice to be tested by demon stone and another few times when we were planning how to rescue my friend Nat from the demon. But I'd seen Ian mostly at Cassandra's since then. Damon and I had had dinner with him once, at a very exclusive Japanese restaurant near Damon's house, where the food had been almost too beautiful to eat, but, of all the Cestis, he was the one I'd spent the least time with.

Which was a pity, because he always had entertaining stories about his life, and his apartment was a treasure trove of intriguing and beautiful things. No doubt there were fascinating stories to go with each of them as well. But this visit would be yet another one where things would be all business. No time for long conversations about art.

Ethan, Ian's assistant, showed us into the living room with his usual unflappable poise. Ian was already there with Aubrey, Radha, Lizzie, and Zee. Their conversation broke off as we came in.

That didn't bode well. "Looks like the gang's all here," I said, trying for cheerful and landing on something more in the vicinity of awkward.

Lizzie smiled briefly, but she looked tense. Also not a good sign. Her default was bouncy cheerfulness. If she was subdued, something less than good was going on.

"Hi, Maggie," Zee said when no one else answered me. He sat with Lizzie on a small love seat next to the gold brocade armchair where Radha was sitting, her feet tucked up on the chair.

Ian and Aubrey occupied the matching armchairs opposite her. Aubrey was dressed far more casually than she had been in the Archives. Actual jeans, though they were paired with an expensive-looking, hip-length, dark blue blazer, over a dove-gray tee that I would bet was cashmere, and flat-soled tan boots. Another gold chair stood empty next to Ian and a second, slightly larger sofa done in peacock-shaded paisley, completed the circle of furniture. Ian had on black jeans and a weathered gray fisherman's rib sweater, a concession to the unseasonably chilly June day, which set off the burgeoning silver streaks in his dark hair.

"Hey, Zee," I said. "This is cozy."

Ian raised an eyebrow at me, and I realized I needed to try to play nice. "Aubrey," I said, pasting a smile on my face. "I hope you've had a good day. Cassandra said you've been sight-seeing with Ian. No better tour guide for art in the city."

Ian looked amused by my attempt at chitchat, but nodded, acknowledging the compliment.

I thought Aubrey was going to ignore me, but then she seemed to recall her manners and nodded. "Yes. I've had a lovely time. Ian is very knowledgeable. I could listen to him talk about art for hours."

Apparently I wasn't the only one capable of throwing around compliments. "Great."

Ian gestured at the peacock sofa. "Why don't you and Damon get comfortable? Cassandra will be here soon." I knew an order disguised as a suggestion when I heard one. I took the end closest to Lizzie and Damon slid up beside me rather than leaving the center spot empty between us.

Ethan bustled around, asking us if we wanted anything to drink and if anyone else wanted a refill. I didn't think anyone would appreciate it if I asked for a shot of scotch, so instead I requested sparkling water. That way Cassandra wouldn't be able to scold me for drinking too much caffeine. Damon asked for coffee and then the room fell silent again until Radha filled the conversational gap and asked Aubrey about Padma.

The rest of us let the two of them chat.

Ethan had only just returned with our drinks when the door chimed.

"That will be Cassandra," Ian said. Ethan nodded, passed out the drinks, and then retreated, returning promptly with Cassandra. She was uncharacteristically dressed in navy and dark green. She thanked Ethan but refused his offer of a drink. After the usual chorus of hellos was exchanged, we all fell silent, looking at her expectantly.

"Well, I won't keep you waiting," she said. "I've heard back from Cerridwen about Aubrey's request."

That didn't sound like she was pleased with the response, particularly not when she'd gathered all of us here to hear it.

Aubrey leaned forward eagerly. "What did she say?"

Cassandra straightened a little in her chair. "The Elder council agreed to meet with you, but they have some conditions."

"Of course. I wouldn't expect anything else."

"Those conditions are they want all of the Cestis to accompany you." Cassandra's mouth was flattened a little. Clearly, she didn't like the idea. "And Maggie."

"Maggie? Why do they want to see her?" Aubrey's expression turned puzzled.

"Well, other than myself and Lizzie, she and one of the tanai fol are the only people who've had regular contact with them since they returned," Cassandra said.

Aubrey's eyebrows shot upward. She shifted forward in her seat. "You didn't mention that. Why has Maggie met the Fae?"

Cassandra met Aubrey's gaze without flinching. "They were aware of the demon incursion that happened a few years ago. And they knew that Maggie was the one connected to the demon. They wanted to find out more about her. Lady Cerridwen's been teaching her some things to help her defend herself should her demon decide to try again."

Aubrey's head snapped around to me so fast I was surprised she didn't give herself whiplash. "You're learning Fae magic?"

Was that a trace of envy in the question? I glanced at Cassandra who nodded as if to say, *You might as well tell her.*

Cassandra might be happy for me to spill the beans, but I wasn't so eager to tell Aubrey everything, just yet. I decided to try to keep the details to a minimum. "Yes," I said, "Defensive magic as Cassandra said. They're very keen to make sure that I learn how to avoid a demon in the future. More combat than anything else." Aubrey couldn't object to me learning to fight by non-magical means, surely?

"I can imagine they would be," Aubrey said tightly. She looked back at Cassandra, blue eyes cold. "Is there a reason why you didn't tell me?"

Cassandra arched a brow. "It didn't seem particularly relevant to what you were coming to discuss."

"I would have thought it would be relevant for the Cestis to inform others that a human is being taught Fae magic," Aubrey gritted out.

"It's not prohibited," Cassandra said calmly.

"That might be because I don't recall a case of them ever offering before," Aubrey said.

This time it was my attention that snapped to her. Surely, I couldn't be the first human to learn Fae magic.

Cassandra made a dismissive little gesture. "Just because we haven't heard of it, doesn't mean they've never done this before. Many of the tanai fol learn aspects of Fae magic, and they're part human."

Aubrey frowned, "Because they're part Fae. Maggie's not tanai, is she?"

"Not as far as I know," I said flatly.

Her frown deepened. "Why would you not know?"

Maybe she hadn't ferreted out all my history. "My mother was…difficult. She never bothered telling me who my father was. Maybe she never knew. And he didn't stick around to find out that she was pregnant in the first place." I said, "But given that no Fae's ever crawled out of the woodwork to claim me as their own, I don't think whoever he was had any Fae blood. For one thing, it would have been *very* ballsy of my mother to do what she did with my demon if I had any Fae magic to consider. I don't think the Fae would react well to a tanai being bound to a demon, do you?"

"No," Aubrey agreed, "they wouldn't. Still, I'm surprised that they've let anyone who's had contact with a demon into the realm."

"I'm clear of any demon taint." I protested. "That's been proven several times. I think they're more interested in making sure that, if my demon tries again to get to me, that I am better prepared to defend myself."

"You killed your demon, though. So it's safely back in its own realm, isn't it?" Aubrey asked.

Cassandra snorted, "You know as well as I do, Aubrey, that demons are not always easily dissuaded. We cannot assume that this one is not going to try again."

I resisted the urge to clamp my hands over my ears and chant "I can't hear you." My demon coming after me again was a regular feature in my most unpleasant nightmares. I sipped water to ease my suddenly dry mouth. Damon inched closer, putting his hand on my thigh in reassurance.

"Is that why Jack was interested in you? Because of your connection to the demon?" Aubrey asked.

"Jack was interested in my technology," Damon interjected. "Not Maggie."

Aubrey's chin tilted up. "Are you sure about that?"

Damon opened his mouth to retort, but Ian cut him off with a quelling look.

"I think," he said slowly, "it would be prudent not to get into an argument about this when no one is in a position to understand Jack Miller's true motivation. While the man remains at large, any guesses as to what he was trying to achieve are merely that—guesses, and not a particularly useful pastime, I would think." His tone was vaguely chiding, and Aubrey had the grace to look, well, chided.

She settled back against the cushions and nodded her head, albeit a little reluctantly. "Very well, I agree. Let's not argue."

Damon was slower to ease back, but I put a hand on his arm, and he nodded and sighed out a breath.

Cassandra turned to Ian, "Anything else you have to add before I continue?" she asked, one side of her mouth lifting, as though she was perhaps grateful for someone else keeping the youngsters in line for once.

Ian settled back, "No, you have the floor."

Cassandra paused, expression stern, but clearly waiting to see if anyone had anything else to say. No one did. "So, we have the invitation from the Elder's council, but only if we all go. This is not a request they've made before, so we don't have a precedent, but my instinct is to refuse. I think it's too risky."

"Do you think there's any chance they would be willing to negotiate?" Lizzie asked. "Isn't there something in the contract?

"It's possible they will compromise, but no, it's not a scenario covered in the contract. Which is clever of them and less clever of our past members. I'm willing to ask." She turned her attention back to Aubrey. "But that will impact Ms. Carter. It is her request that may be turned down if they don't like our counteroffer."

Aubrey considered the matter, twisting her ring again. I expected her to push her point but, to my surprise, she shook her head. "No," she said. "I agree, it would be more prudent if you didn't all go. In fact, I would argue that it's vital that you not." She hesitated. "Of course, it's also possible that they're just testing you to see if you will push back. With them it's a fine line between being respectful enough that they won't throw a tantrum and not being a doormat."

"And if they say no?" Cassandra asked.

Aubrey squared her shoulders, her mouth set in a determined line. "Well, then they won't be able to say that I didn't try to pay my respects. But I don't think it would be wise to do as they asked. It's not a request that we would comply with, back home." She smiled tightly. "It's like the royal family. The current monarch and his heir don't travel on the same transportation. No point giving someone a chance to wipe you out in one shot."

"No," Damon agreed. "That would be reckless. We do the same thing at Riley with the board of directors. We don't all travel together."

"Exactly," Aubrey said. "I think you have to negotiate. You are already down in strength."

Cassandra's eyes narrowed a little at that, but she nodded. "I agree."

"And Maggie?" Aubrey asked.

"I'm perfectly happy to go," I said. Not exactly the truth, but if the Cestis couldn't take their full strength, then for once I would be an asset. I was familiar with the realm, or at least the small portions of it that I had seen, and could do some Fae magic. Witch magic worked a little in the realm, but against the Fae themselves, it wasn't terribly effective. I also knew how to work the door to get out of there if needs be. "But can you tell me what the Elder council is, first?"

Aubrey mouth went round before she collected herself. "The Fae are training you, but you don't know about the council?"

"Cerridwen is training me. She limits my contact with other Fae."

"The council represent the powerful Fae who have attached their territories to the door here," Cassandra said.

"Cerridwen is one of them. I'm still working on getting the information on who else might be there."

"That will be important," Aubrey agreed. "We can't walk in not knowing who we are facing." She turned back to me. "Are you sure you want to come? The realm is a difficult place."

I lifted my chin. "I have spent quite a bit of time there."

"Time with a Fae who likes you and is protecting you," Aubrey said. "That is different to facing those who may not be so welcoming."

I didn't like the idea, but I didn't want Aubrey to see that I was scared. "I grew up moving around a lot. I was always the new kid. I'm pretty used to having a lack of a welcoming committee."

"It's hardly the same thing."

"No," Cassandra interjected, "but it is Maggie's decision, and it will be useful not to have to fight them on two fronts. I doubt they'll agree on her staying behind when they are still so touchy about demons."

"What about Maia?" Damon asked. "I don't like the idea of Maggie going in unprotected."

Cassandra raised an eyebrow. "She'll be with some of the most powerful witches in the world. Maia is skilled, but she's not as strong as any of us."

He folded his arms. "Still, I'd rather Maggie was with someone who knows their primary responsibility is to protect her."

"So would I," Cassandra said. "But Maia would be hamstrung in the realm. She's not experienced with Fae, and she can hardly just open fire and shoot one without causing more trouble than any of us want. Her protective instincts may be likely to cause more harm than good. Don't worry. We will do everything possible to ensure that Maggie is safe."

"I could—," Damon started to say, but I cut him off.

"No," I said. "You're not setting foot in the realm."

Aubrey looked intrigued at my vehemence, and I clamped my jaw shut. She'd learned about my connection to the Fae, but she didn't need to know that Damon owed Callum an unspecified favor. Which was a reckless bargain on his part and, no doubt, one that Aubrey wouldn't view with any more approval than my training with Cerridwen. "You don't have magic, so you're at even more risk than I am. Besides, Mitch would probably have an aneurysm at the thought."

Damon scowled. "Mitch works for me."

"Mitch keeps you safe. Things work out better when you listen to him. And I'll bet you a thousand dollars that he would agree with me."

That earned me a disgruntled *humph*, but he didn't argue.

"Is everyone agreed, then?" Cassandra asked. "We will ask to renegotiate the terms of the visit, but we will decline if they insist on all four of us attending?"

"Unless they want to meet outside the realm," Lizzie said.

That seemed about as likely as her learning to shapeshift like Callum.

Radha lifted a finger. "Will this impact the contract? If we refuse?"

Cassandra shook her head. "No. They cannot compel us to do anything we don't want to do. Our predecessors were clear on that much."

"Very well, then. Yes, I agree," Radha said. "Two of us, that's all we can risk." Ian and Lizzie nodded.

"Very well," Cassandra said. "I will go back with a counteroffer." She looked at Ian, "Perhaps Ethan could bring some tea now? And something to eat."

"Of course."

I'd been ready for her to close the meeting. What was she up to now?

She turned to Aubrey. "I thought it would be useful if you could tell us more about how you would approach such a situation in England. We have our own ways of handling the realm, but we've had little need to do any of them for over a decade now. You deal with the Fae more regularly, so it would be useful to get your perspective, if you would care to share."

Aubrey considered the request. "I'll tell you what I can." She held up an apologetic hand. "But I'm not sure how helpful it will be in this situation. Particularly not if we don't yet know who we are meeting." She paused. "Did Cerridwen say how many members the council has here?"

Cassandra shook her head. "No. Just that it would be a meeting with them, not just with her."

"Then that's something else you should clarify, if they'll tell you," Aubrey said.

Cassandra nodded. "Very well. Go on."

Aubrey said, "Here's what I can share without talking to the others. I most often deal with Fae individually. There's a few that I'm in, well, if not regular contact, then we meet several times a year. Others less often. Some rarely face to face but there's correspondence. There's a door on Hampstead Heath. That's the one we most often use."

"You've been inside the realm?" I asked.

"Yes," Aubrey replied. "I have. Not regularly, but sometimes our work requires it." She tilted her head as though considering whether to say anything else, but then went on. "Because I'm dealing with individuals, Fae that I'm acquainted with, the protocols really just vary depending on whether I'm going into the realm or whether they are meeting with me outside."

"They meet with you in our world?" Radha asked interestedly. Other than Cerridwen, the Fae in San Francisco were currently keeping to themselves. Clearly their English counterparts weren't so circumspect.

Aubrey nodded. "Yes. The Fae in London are not so separate as they are here. They still disguise themselves, of course, but there's a healthy tanai population, and the Fae have their own interests in the city."

"And the rest of the country?" Ian asked.

"There are several more doors. Some of them have been there since before humans even reached the island, from what we can gather. There are some that have been established more recently. If, within the last thousand years or so is recent," Aubrey said with a wry smile. "I most often use the one in London, unless there is a reason to access the realm elsewhere. Regardless of the door, we don't often meet with groups of Fae. Sometimes a few members of one family, but rarely with one of their councils. I'm not even sure the last time there was a reconsideration of the contract between us and the Fae in England. It's been in place for so long. Ralph is the one to ask. He might be willing to share some records of the last meeting if that would be helpful."

"Yes," Cassandra agreed. "I've been dealing with Cerridwen and one or two others, but any precedents would be helpful."

"I'll send a message after this. I'm sure Ralph will be happy to help."

Zee and Lizzie and I exchanged a look at the mention of Ralph.

Aubrey must have noticed. "Zee, I believe you met Ralph, didn't you?"

Zee acknowledged this in a kind of liquid shrug. "Yes. Briefly while I was working there."

"And did you meet any of the Fae?"

"I dealt mostly with tanai," Zee said, waving the question away with a flick of his fingers. "We're talking about formal meetings, not the kind I had. I'm not sure anything I learned would be useful."

He'd survived whatever contact he'd had, that was good enough for me.

Aubrey shrugged. "Perhaps you can tell me more another time. So. This is how we manage it. There are protocols for arranging a meeting and more for approaching the door, for making sure no one who shouldn't will see anything happen. The doors are always well guarded. The illusions and wards are old. And complex. I imagine yours must be similarly protected."

She raised an eyebrow at Cassandra, who nodded. "After that, well, inside the realm, the usual rules apply. Don't agree to anything they ask of you. Be polite and respectful and try and phrase any questions in such a way that it would be difficult for them to prevaricate. They don't lie, and that is something we can use to our advantage. So choose your words carefully."

Cassandra nodded. "We always do."

"Other than that, no iron, no magic. If you want to take protective items in, it's better to tell them in advance." She shrugged and smiled a little. "Though usually I have one or two additional protections that I don't tell them about. It's better to be safe than sorry, and there are ways to make them, well, less detectable. I'm sure they know they're there, but by this point, we have a certain kind of trust in each other. As far as it's possible to trust the Fae."

Cassandra straightened. "There wasn't anything about protective magics in what they sent me."

"Interesting. That could be useful if they haven't put any restrictions on things. Don't bring it up, if they don't." She nodded at me. "What happens when you go into the realm?"

"Pinky and I just take food, water, backpacks. I have an old mechanical watch, so it doesn't get messed up like some technology does," I said. "Cerridwen provides the weapons that we train with, so I'm not sure exactly what they're made of, but nothing that would bother them."

"And they don't mind the chip?"

"Cerridwen's never made any objection, nor has—" I bit off the words. I'd been about to say Callum—"anyone else she's brought in to help me train. Pinky has a chip, too."

"Pinky's the tanai fol you've been dealing with?" Aubrey asked.

"Yes," I said, reluctant to tell her anything more about Pinky than I had to.

"And how did she get involved with you? My understanding was the tanai fol who remained here had essentially cut ties with their Fae families."

"That's a longer story," Cassandra said, in a tone that didn't invite argument. "And not really relevant. She is of Cerridwen's line, her mother is half-Fae, but they stayed behind when the door was closed."

"So, she's not particularly powerful?"

"No, but Cerridwen is fond of her, I think," I said, hoping that would warn Aubrey off trying to poke around in Pinky's business too much.

Cassandra's expression had eased slightly during the conversation. "None of this sounds like anything particularly different to how I would have approached it anyway. Which is useful to know, but yes, I'd appreciate it if you'd still ask Ralph for any information he can provide. I'll be looking at the Archives myself. Maggie, perhaps you can help me, seeing you will be coming with us. Then we can brief everyone else once we come to an agreement with the Fae."

Just what I needed—more homework.

Chapter Ten

"INTERESTING LOCATION," Aubrey said, as we stood at the top of the Berkeley Rose Garden two days later. The sun was beginning to set, the golden light making the sloping garden glow in a way that looked almost unnatural. Sunset wasn't a time I would have chosen to enter the realm. No time was truly safe to travel there, of course, but for some reason, night-time felt riskier. The garden was safe enough at night, the magic that kept the door hidden tended to scare away anyone with bad intentions. I assume Cerridwen—or the council, maybe—had chosen sunset because there was less chance of civilians being around to see us.

They shouldn't have been concerned. The garden was deserted. Usually there'd be a few lingering people walking themselves or their dogs, but we had it to ourselves. No sign of Lok and Kez, the gardeners who tended the roses, either. Which was unusual at this time of year, when the roses were at their peak. Even though it hadn't been a hot day, the fragrance of the blooms hung in the air, strong enough I almost expected to see rose oil shimmering in the twilight air above each bush.

"The Fae like roses, apparently," I said, stopping beside Aubrey.

"True," she agreed, still studying the garden, her expression intent, energy focused. She looked like a Cestis member ready to spring into action.

Hopefully she wouldn't have to.

"The wards will make sure that we're not interrupted." The arbor that hid the door was halfway down the hill. The climbing varieties that grew around it were the most abundant in the garden all year round. Their blooms nearly covered the structure completely, a riot of white and pink and red. Just as well the door had magic to move them out of the way. Fighting through plants that had thorns and weren't afraid to use them would be a painful experience.

I extended my magic, assessing whether the warding felt any different. Not that I could sense. But I wore a token from Cerridwen on my wrist, so I might be immune to the effects of any spells aimed at deterring humans from lingering.

Aubrey turned to Cassandra, "How long has the door been here?"

Cassandra made a little "that not entirely clear" gesture. "A long time from what I understand."

"It may be why the Rose Garden exists, rather than having been taken over by developers by now," Aubrey said. "The Elders are good at arranging things to protect their spaces."

She wasn't using the word 'Fae' so close to the door; that was interesting. She seemed unworried, but perhaps it was all an act.

Which I could relate to. "You think they're manipulating the city officials and the real estate market?"

"I think they do what needs to be done to protect themselves," Aubrey said, pursing her lips. "It is a slightly odd location for a flower garden, after all. They protect green spaces. Why do you think London still has so many huge parks and heaths? They link their doors to places of power. And then tend them carefully, because there's not much leeway to relocate them. That's how they survive for so long."

I'd never really thought about it, about whether it was just a coincidence that the Fae had built their door in the Rose Garden. Or whether, perhaps, they'd defended themselves by encouraging the Rose Garden to be placed around the door as San Francisco and Berkeley grew from small, sleepy human settlements to the large and busy cities they were now. There had been hippies around Berkeley for long enough that maintaining public parks and urban green spaces was something the city valued. But had the Fae also encouraged certain kinds of people to move here? It would be easier to explain the occasional weird occurrence if the humans were used to their neighbors dancing beneath the moon and doing other odd shit at all hours of the day or night. The Fae were supposed to stay out of human affairs, but where exactly did they draw the line?

I made a note to try to ask Callum about it. He was more likely to tell me the history of the door than Cerridwen. "We don't have something as big as Hampstead Heath," I said. "Well, not here in Berkeley. There are bigger parks around the headlands."

"But those might not be as optimal from a Fae perspective, if there's no nexus." Aubrey gestured down the hill. "And sometimes they seem to favor high spaces."

"Where are some of the other doors in England?" I asked.

Aubrey smiled, "You didn't learn that in the research you've been doing?"

"Cassandra had me researching Fae protocol, not doors," I said. I'd spent the last two evenings in the Archives, reading about Fae lore. Some of it was interesting, some of it was flat-out scary. Learning the truth about things that I'd never imagined might actually be real. I'd gained some insight into a few of the species and clans that we might encounter, but, of course, what the humans knew about any of them was only a fraction of the reality of the realm. The Fae had always been careful to only show the Cestis select parts of it. The Cestis had gathered more information from other people who'd had encounters—pleasant or otherwise—with the Fae and lived to tell the tale, but it still felt as though we were about to engage with an enemy who kept their true power shrouded in mist.

We were definitely David, not Goliath, at least when it came to the magical considerations. I had to keep reminding myself that David had beaten Goliath when it counted.

Aubrey shrugged and said, "Well, you can probably guess some of them. There's one not far from Glastonbury Tor, one in Cornwall. Those are two of the major ones. There are smaller doors scattered around, and I'm sure there are some they keep hidden from us. Convenient for the Fae to move around unseen, in such a crowded island. We don't have as much wilderness left for them to hide in."

"Kind of like one vast underground system." I still didn't exactly understand how the Fae moved around beneath the earth through their realm, but the doors were the anchor points to our realm.

"Yes," she said, "Something like that. It's not like they can use the actual underground. Too much iron for their tastes."

"But you said they move around London?"

"Yes, in cars or on foot. They can tolerate the amount of metal in a car. A train is a different proposition. It's bigger and then there are the tracks, and all the supporting infrastructure trapping them under the earth. I don't think it does them actual harm, but those of the full blood find it uncomfortable."

"Remind me never to suggest any of them take the BART, then," I said.

Aubrey looked at me strangely. "Is that likely?"

I squinted, trying to picture Callum's face if I suggested we take public transport rather than a car. Cerridwen, I wouldn't even bother asking in the first place, outside a dire emergency. "No," I admitted. I couldn't blame the Fae for not liking public transport. I wasn't exactly comfortable on the BART these days either. Being underground with the risk of earthquakes was not an attractive proposition to me anymore.

"Shall we?" Cassandra asked.

Was it too late to change my mind? Probably. I rolled my shoulders, trying to shake off my nerves. Just another trip to the realm. I would be fine. After all, I had three powerful witches and Pinky with me.

Lizzie nudged me gently as though she knew what I was thinking. I shot her a grateful smile.

She smiled back, and then turned her attention back to the arbor. Her hair was a relatively normal shade of red and, unusually, waving gently round her face, not a braid or pony-tail in sight. Between the hair and the subdued clothing, it would be easy to think she'd been swapped by the Fae, a changeling version of Lizzie. But her aura was reassuringly rosy pink.

"Ready when you are," she said to Cassandra.

Lizzie had asked Zee whether he wanted to come, but he'd been happy to stay out of the whole business. He had talked to me about some of the things he'd learned in the UK, and I'd asked Pinky if she had any advice. Other than "how about we don't go," she hadn't been able to tell me anything we hadn't already gleaned from the Archives. Her mom had also offered a tidbit about a charm to carry for clear sight in the realm, and we'd added that to the small protections we all had in our clothes and jewelry.

Aubrey had been intrigued by the bracelet Cerridwen had given me, the one that let me enter the realm. But she hadn't been able to make much more of the magic than Cassandra had, other than saying it felt familiar. I rolled my cuff back now to give me easier access. I'd asked Aubrey if she had a similar charm for the door she used. She admitted she had, but that she hadn't brought it with her because it was unlikely to work on the door here. Safer back in London where, if needed, one of the other Cestis could use it. And, if worse came to worst and Aubrey never returned, it was there waiting for the next person to take her place.

I must have looked alarmed because she'd smiled reassuringly. "Not that I'm expecting anything to happen," she said, "It's just a precaution. Like not all traveling together. Or not sending all the Cestis into the realm."

Cassandra had negotiated successfully for only two of the US Cestis to come to the meeting but, in return, Cerridwen had asked Pinky to escort us. Lucky her. And all of this because Aubrey had wanted to say hello. I wondered what trouble we were actually stepping into, and who we were about to meet. Cerridwen had said there would be four other representatives with her, this apparently covering off the major families who claimed territory with closest access to the door here. But she hadn't provided any details like names. We'd found a little in the Archives about how the geography of the territories had worked before the door had closed; there was no guarantee that they were the same now.

"No time like the present," Cassandra said.

Aubrey nodded. "We need to get to the door." Sunset— the time we'd been told to arrive—was in five minutes.

Cassandra moved off, the others following her. I hesitated, looking back at the big black Riley Security SUV we'd arrived in. Through the windshield, Maia's expression was flat and focused. She'd agreed to stay where she was unless I called for help, but she wasn't any happier about it than I was. I gave her a wave, trying to look confident, and hurried after Cassandra. My palms were damp as we walked toward the arbor.

I had friends inside the realm, I reminded myself; or, if not friends, then allies, at least. Cerridwen and Callum were on our side, and Cerridwen was on the council. But that left the other four members as unknown quantities.

Aubrey had explained more about how the realm was

divided, but I still wasn't sure I understood. Each territory was ruled by one Elder, one of the strongest Fae, but it might be populated by a family group of related Fae, or it could be something more like a kingdom with a mixture of Fae of varying kinds who were protected by their lord or lady. They were all connected and yet changeable, which made my brain hurt.

It was like trying to understand a map of feudal England where at any time the map might decide to magically reshuffle. But I didn't need to understand it all just yet. Today, I had to focus on meeting the four Elders accompanying Cerridwen. Not that the thought of meeting four vastly powerful Fae—who could probably turn any of us into a bug and squish us beneath their feet should they choose—was a fun prospect.

We were relying on our magic and the contract between the humans and the Fae to get through the encounter and, now that the moment had arrived, words on a piece of paper didn't seem like enough protection for what we were stepping into.

I was so busy worrying about it all I nearly crashed into Pinky, who'd stopped just inside the arbor. I caught myself just in time as the familiar sensation of the door's wards hit me.

"Two minutes to go," Aubrey said, glancing at her watch. "We should wait and open it exactly on time."

"Does it really matter?" I asked. Pinky and I always tried to be on time with Cerridwen, but she'd never chided us for entering the realm a few minutes early or late.

"For something like this, it's important. They said arrive at sunset. If we want to be respectful, then we should arrive at sunset."

"If you say so." She was the expert. Cassandra waved Pinky and me forward. We were the ones who could open the door, after all. As I got closer, I could feel the faint buzz of the wards reaching out to my bracelet. The sensation was one of something close to curiosity, as it always was. "It's just me," I muttered, half unspoken, and the sensation lessened slightly.

I gave Pinky a final questioning look. She just tipped her head at the door. "You do the honors."

"Gee, thanks." I stepped forward, taking a moment to fuss with my clothes.

On Aubrey's recommendation, we'd all dressed up. Not in the kind of gowns Cerridwen wore when we weren't doing physical training, or that I wore to events with Damon, but more upscale than my usual outfits. I wore the pair of diamond earrings Damon had given me, and outside the black silk of my top lay another diamond and gold and pearl necklace, also a gift.

Hidden beneath the silk was the amethyst and obsidian pendant that Cassandra had given me when we'd first met. It was designed for protection against demons, but it had become familiar, and I hadn't wanted to leave it behind. I'd added an amber bead next to the amethyst, and my skin was dabbed in various places with a tincture Cassandra had concocted with the rowan bark and other herbs that Pinky's mom had suggested.

Whether it would do any good was anyone's guess. I had my suspicions that these days it was the contract that kept the Fae in check, not the effect of a few gems and herbs that humans had decided worked against them. Not even iron worked like it did in the stories.

I studied the branches of the climbing roses, leaves ruffling gently in the evening breeze. No hint of a door yet. But the familiarity of the roses was soothing, and I breathed in the scent of flowers, reaching for calm. At least there were flowers right now to explain the scent. Even in the dead of winter, the arbor tended to smell of roses. Lok told me once that it was the scent soaked into the wood from the blooms over so many years and I'd nodded and smiled. He didn't need to know it was more likely that roses enchanted by the Fae had a perfume with staying power unlike other flowers.

Hopefully what waited for us inside the door would also be familiar.

Pinky and I had told the others about the parts of the realm we'd seen. But given that was only parts of Cerridwen's house, the forest glade where she usually trained us, and a few other random outdoor locations when she'd decided we needed different experiences, it wasn't very useful. Cassandra had described the chambers where she'd worked with Cerridwen and other Fae on the agreement. But beyond that, the realm was one big slab of magical unknown.

"Now," Aubrey said, from behind me.

I stretched my hand out toward the door. To my relief, it swung open smoothly, and we stepped inside the entrance chamber, which looked unchanged to me. The other three filed in behind us, and I closed the door. No one was waiting to greet us, which made me nervous. I'd expected Cerridwen to come herself, ensuring our safe passage. The door that led out of the entryway looked the same as always, and I couldn't feel any strangeness in the magics that guarded it.

"Do we wait here, or go on?" I asked Pinky.

She shrugged. Her hair was a subtler shade of pink than usual and her clothes sleek and black. More like her wife Ivy's taste than hers. "Was there anything in the instructions?"

Cassandra shook her head.

"Does everything feel normal to you?" Aubrey asked, eyeing me.

"Yes," I nodded. "Nothing out of the ordinary.'"

"Then I suggest we just get on with it," Cassandra said.

I approached the far door, beckoning Pinky to join me. She looked reluctant but didn't protest. "Feel anything weird?" I asked her, hovering my hand near the door.

Pinky mimicked my gesture. "No."

I released a slow breath and glanced back at the others. "Ready?"

The three women nodded. Together, they looked formidable, all of them straight backed and focused. Lizzie, like Pinky, wore all black. Weirdly, the lack of her usual riot of color made her look younger, not older. I'd tried not to think too hard about why Cassandra had chosen her over Radha or Ian. I suspected it was sheer unwavering pragmatism. That ruthless streak she needed to have to do her job. If anything happened to her in the realm, then Ian was the one who would likely take her place. And then Radha also had more experience than Lizzie, who'd only been with the Cestis five years. Lizzie was strong, as they all were, but losing her wouldn't be as big a blow to the Cestis as losing one of the others.

That might be the reason that Aubrey had been given the role of Fae liaison for her Cestis, too. Easier to lose the youngest member than someone like Ralph, whose years of experience and knowledge would be much harder to replace. Dealing with the Fae and surviving the process was a good way of proving you had earned your place.

I suppressed a shiver and turned back to the door. It swung outward at my touch, revealing a long corridor with walls and floor made of black-veined marble.

Definitely not Cerridwen's house. I took a few steps forward and glanced up. The ceiling had to be thirty feet high if it was an inch. More like a grand monumental building—a palace or a cathedral—than a house.

Not that the Fae had gods that they worshipped. At least not that we were aware of. I exchanged a look with Pinky. "Any ideas where we are?"

"No," she said, "but I guess we go forward. Someone will find us eventually."

"I hope so." We started walking, moving cautiously. The door swung shut once we were all through, leaving us with no real option. I looked for any clues as to what kind of building this was. There were windows set high in the walls, made of colored glass. Not depicting scenes like human-made stained glass might, but instead forming a shifting rainbow of iridescence, like mist over water refracting colors.

They certainly didn't reveal any hint of what the surroundings of the building might look like, other than it appeared to be day outside because there was plenty of light pouring through.

"So much for sunset," Pinky muttered.

I nodded tightly. "Time in here is weird," I replied, as much to remind myself as her. The Fae manipulated their realm to suit their whims. There was no point trying to keep track of time back in the human world based on whether it was still day or night in the realm.

We moved quietly, more intent on paying attention to our surroundings than talking. The realm's magic pressed around me, stronger than ever, making it hard to concentrate. We walked for a few minutes before we reached a junction where the corridor split off to the left and right. To my relief, on the right, just past the corner, Callum stood waiting. He was, for once, dressed as elegantly as I would expect a Fae to be, wearing an old-fashioned jacket, shirt and breeches made from velvet and silk and leather in shades of black and gray. Various black jewels danced in his ears and on his hands, and his hair was tamed back off his face.

I'd only ever seen him in training gear or human clothes and the change was startling. He was a good-looking man at the best of times, but seeing him dressed as a Fae drove it home that he was indeed Fae, too beautiful to be human.

Callum looked me over once, one eye arching fractionally before he turned his focus to Cassandra. He bowed slightly. "Lady Cestis," he said. Then he turned to Aubrey. "You must be Miss Carter."

"Yes," Aubrey said.

Callum's gaze turned briefly appreciative, and I couldn't blame him. Aubrey was wearing a long-sleeved silk wrap dress in a deep shade of berry red that did good things for her hair and skin.

"You are welcome here. I am sent to bring you to the meeting," he said. Then he turned back to me. "Maggie. Rosaline." I could almost feel the curiosity about who he was radiating off Aubrey. But Callum hadn't offered his name, and it would be rude of her to ask before they were introduced. So I stayed silent as he turned on his heel and led us down another section of the corridor.

Callum finally stopped in front of a pair of doors at least fifteen feet high and made of some silvery metal, etched with a design of stars and flowers. Two Fae men stood either side of them, also dressed in black. But their outfits matched and were simpler than Callum's, which made me think uniform and guards. Sure enough, when Callum pushed open the door and led us through, there were more men in the same uniforms guarding each corner of the room.

Room was too small a word. More a hall. The ceiling vaulted up to a dome made of the same iridescent glass as the windows. Centered beneath it stood a ring-shaped table carved from pale wood, ten chairs arrayed at equal distance around its circumference.

Behind the chairs on the far side of the circle were five Fae. The Elder council. Cerridwen was in the middle, her hair, pale browns and greens, braided elaborately, and silky robes in darker greens draped around her. To her left stood a man who looked as though he was more made of water than flesh, his skin and long hair shifting blues and grays. Past him was another Fae man. His face was perfect, more beautiful even than Cerridwen and Callum, but also more youthful. His eyes, disconcertingly, were totally black. No whites.

Disturbingly reminiscent of the demonkind I'd encountered. I hid my alarm. There was no chance that he was demonkind, but the eyes were a clear reminder that it would be wrong to take his beauty at face value.

To Cerridwen's right stood another woman, whose features blurred and shifted, her face changing from younger to older, though her hair and skin remained the same pale white shade with each new facade. Her eyes were piercingly blue, and they were the only constant thing about her, staying the same through each change. The final woman had golden skin and reddish hair, held back with a golden circlet that revealed sharply pointed ears. Her green eyes were slitted like a cat's and, when she smiled, I saw her teeth were pointed, too.

A few paces behind each of the Fae council, other than Cerridwen, stood another Fae dressed much like Callum, not as lavishly as the Elders themselves. Advisors, protectors, companions? Impossible to know.

Callum approached the table and bowed to the assembled Fae. "I have brought the humans," he announced, and beckoned us forward.

Cerridwen smiled as we walked, and I assumed it was meant to be reassuring. But even though the realm's magic wasn't so bad in this room, the power rolling off the Fae themselves was worse. Cerridwen, close up, was unnerving, but five of them at a time spoke to something deep in the instinctive part of my brain and told it that it would be best to run.

I set my teeth and waited, heart thumping too loud in my ears, while Cassandra moved ahead. She approached the table but stopped, inclining her head politely, when she was a few feet away from the middle chair. "My lady Cerridwen," she said, "thank you for agreeing to meet with us. My companions and I are pleased to have this time with your council."

"You are most welcome, Lady Cassandra," Cerridwen said. "It is too long, perhaps, since we have parlayed with the Cestis in a more formal manner."

Interesting. Cassandra had definitely been dealing with the Fae since the door had returned and I thought she had been dealing with matters of the contract and how it would continue to work. What was different about this meeting?

Cerridwen gestured at the other Elders. "I will introduce you. Lord Padran—"

The watery man nodded sharply.

"Usuriel, Lord of the Darker Hours." That was the black-eyed man.

"Lady Morgain, and Lady Orea."

Morgain was the woman with the shifting faces and Orea the one with the teeth. Cerridwen hadn't told us either of their titles. But Aubrey had said that the territory rulers chose their own, so perhaps they didn't use them.

Cassandra introduced us and then we all took our seats as Callum paced silently around the table to stand behind Cerridwen.

Cerridwen clasped her hands on the table in front of her and said, "Miss Carter, you wished to speak to us?"

Getting right down to business, it seemed.

Aubrey clasped her own hands in front of her, resting them on the table, a pose that I thought was designed to appear calm but, to my eye, she was clasping those hands just a little too tightly.

"My Lady Cerridwen," she said, "I came to convey greetings from the United Kingdoms of England, Wales, Scotland, and Ireland. The Cestis and witches there appreciate our long-standing relationship with the Elders. And I wanted to pay my respects to you here. We, too, appreciate our alliances."

Cerridwen began to reply when the blond-haired man to her left cleared his throat. Cerridwen cast him a sidelong glance, pausing to give him space to speak, but he merely kept those night-dark eyes fixed on Aubrey.

Who stared back at him for a long moment, the pulse on her neck beating fast. She swallowed once, as though she'd lost her train of thought.

"And what news of our far kin who live across the oceans?" Cerridwen asked when the silence began to stretch.

Was that a test? If what Aubrey had said was true and the realms were all connected, then surely the Fae had to keep an eye on how the various territories near each of the human lands fared?

"When I left, things were peaceable as usual," Aubrey said. "No matters of great importance were being dealt with."

"Is that why you have time to come halfway across the planet?" the watery man asked. His voice was deep and carried an echo to it, like the crash of a wave against the shore. "Because there is no trouble in your domain?"

"I came on Cestis business," Aubrey said, "but nothing that concerns the Fae."

His gaze turned to me, disconcertingly. His eyes were large in his face and the colors in them rippled through a hundred shades of blue, like water churning. "And does the Cestis of the Kingdoms United approve of the demon witch?"

Chapter Eleven

"Padran!" Cerridwen exclaimed at the same time as Cassandra said, "I beg your pardon, my lord?"

Lord Padran, for his part, kept his eyes on me. "It is a reasonable question," he said, his voice deep and cold as the icy blues shifting through his hair. "One I am eager for Miss Carter to answer."

Fuck. Was Aubrey about to throw me under the bus?

Aubrey lifted her chin. "We have no reason to be concerned with Maggie. I'm satisfied that the Cestis in the United States have handled her case correctly."

Padran's face twisted, his eyes turning a depthless stormy gray.

"As am I," Cerridwen said firmly. "I have known Maggie for months, and I have seen no sign that there is any remaining connection to the demon that bound her."

"A demon that bound her for many years. That must have left her marked in some way," Padran objected.

"She was bound against her will. Indeed, with no knowledge of the act on her part at all," Cassandra said, her voice as steely as Padran's eyes. "Maggie made no choice to cede her power. And the one who bartered her power away paid for their actions. And since Maggie learned of the bond, which was after it was already broken, she has done her utmost to learn to embrace her power and protect herself from any possibility of such a thing happening to her again. After all, she destroyed the demon and returned it to its realm."

"That only proves that she is powerful," Usuriel said unexpectedly.

His voice was like icy velvet. Compellingly beautiful, the sound of it almost like a caress. But, at the same time, it chilled something deep inside me that wanted to flinch away, something that scented danger beneath the beauty.

"Powerful," he continued, "doesn't always equal trustworthy. Or safe."

That was the pot calling the kettle black, coming from a Fae. I clenched my teeth against my instinctive desire to protest. Hypocritical or not, it was a useful reminder of exactly who we were dealing with. Me arguing with hostile Fae wasn't going to help.

"We have our own ways of testing for demons," Morgain said.

Reluctantly I turned my attention to her, shivers skittering up my spine as my brain protested that she couldn't be real. Looking at her was like trying to watch a vidscreen through blurry glasses. Her body moved and reshaped itself almost too fast to follow, her face shimmering from young to old and everything in between, like watching a time-lapse of a life looping on high speed. Her clothes, too, shifted with her face, from frills and lace to sleek silk to ragged. Her voice was low and clear, but it had a curious tone to it, almost like a chord rather than a single speaker.

"We do," Cerridwen agreed. "And I have already employed those methods. Do you think I would have invited her into the realm if I were not satisfied that she was safe?"

"Your motivations are above reproach, Lady Cerridwen," Lady Orea said firmly. She leaned forward so that she could glare at Padran fiercely, pointed teeth bared. "Lord Padran, you are being unreasonable. Lady Cerridwen's line has protected the realm through the ages. Do you really think she would be fooled by a human?" She sounded incredulous.

I chalked her name up as Team Cerridwen in my head. Morgain I was less sure of, but she was defending me for the moment.

"Humans have fooled Fae before," Padran growled.

"Perhaps," Morgain said, "but they've never fooled Cerridwen." Her voice sounded older, now, with a rasp to the sound that hadn't been there before, though it still had echoes or sub notes to it. Pinky was watching her, expression fascinated. Perhaps to her, Morgain's voice was a musical puzzle, not just plain weird.

"We have also tested Maggie," Cassandra added. "She has submitted to trial by demon stone, twice, and both times she has survived. All the members of my Cestis will swear on it. That is incontrovertible proof, Lord Padran. Unless you know a way to fool demon stone that no one else has discovered? "

Padran scowled, his hair lifting in a breeze I couldn't feel.

Cassandra folded her arms and stared back, no hint of fear in her golden-brown eyes.

Padran looked away first, back to Aubrey. "And you, Miss Carter? Have you witnessed these trials?"

Aubrey raised her chin. "No. Nor do I need to," she said, her accent even more crisp and polished. Polite but edging toward irritation, I thought.

Which took guts when dealing with a hostile Fae. But cowering wouldn't do any good either. I looked past Cerridwen to Callum who offered me a smile that flashed so briefly I wasn't sure I had actually seen it.

"Stay calm," his voice came in my head.

"Easy for you to say."

"No harm will come to you."

I wasn't so sure. I calculated the distances. Could Callum

reach Padran before Padran could reach me? Probably. Though I had no way to know how fast Padran could move or what magic he might have at his disposal.

"I trust Cassandra's word." Aubrey continued. "The Cestis share records of those who have passed a trial by demon stone. Falsifying those records would be a criminal offence. Our word is law, after all. There is no reason for Cassandra and her circle to lie about Maggie. And I see no benefit to subjecting her to another test. The outcome would not change. Maggie is untainted, and opposed to demonkind, just as we all are."

"Very opposed," I muttered.

Usuriel's mouth quirked, and Padran's gaze returned to me. "And what do you have to say for yourself?"

I stiffened. Took a moment to breathe to make sure my voice was calm. "I'm not sure what I can add, Lord Padran. As Cassandra has told you, I have no reason to be fond of demons. They stole my magic from me for years. They have tried to kill me." I raised my chin. "I have helped Lady Cerridwen in her work, and I have helped protect the human world. You can trust me, my lord."

"Well said," Cerridwen declared, putting her hands flat on the table with a soft thump. The rings she wore glittered and magic pulsed through the room. "This is not a matter for debate, Lord Padran," she said. "This session was not called for us to pass judgment on Maggie. The humans have come to us in good faith. Come to pay their respects, as is proper. Which, you will admit, is both right and brave of them. And even were there a vote, you would lose. Clearly, there are three of us who trust Maggie or are prepared to take the Cestis's word that she is untainted. Callum would also support this assessment. He has worked with her more closely than any of us."

Aubrey drew in a breath at that piece of information.

Dammit. Now she knew Callum trained me, too. But it

was too late to do anything about that, so I kept my focus on Cerridwen.

"Your dog will say what you want him to say,' Padran said.

Callum stiffened, his face going tight and angry. If he'd been in his other form, he would have been rumbling one of his low warning growls at the accusation. "Is that a question of my honor, Lord Padran?" he asked coldly.

So coldly, my hand slid down reflexively, reaching for the sword I wasn't carrying.

Padran turned in his chair, and the two men stared at each other for a long moment. Padran was clearly powerful, but Callum was apparently willing to press the point, and that would be just what we didn't need.

"There is no need for that," Cerridwen said sharply. "Lord Padran, you will accept the will of the council. We can take it to a vote if you think it necessary, but you are capable of counting as well as I."

Padran made a noise of displeasure like waves crashing, but then subsided. "Very well," he said. "Let us continue."

We stepped out of the realm into full dark and I set a fast pace back to the car and Maia, trying to hide that I was more than a little rattled.

In the moonlight, the rosebushes looked vaguely menacing. I didn't stop until I reached the car, climbing inside without waiting to see if the others were behind me. It took a concerted effort to leave the door open. I distracted myself by reaching for the datapad I'd stashed in the seat pocket, needing to see for myself how much time had passed. Only a few hours according to the clock. I hissed out a breath of relief as the others reached the car and climbed into their seats. I relaxed a little more when Cassandra closed the last of the doors and I heard the soft thunk of Maia activating the locks.

"Well, that was fun," I said. My voice was rough, and I cleared my throat.

Lizzie shot me a concerned look.

I looked away. "Ready when you are, Maia."

"Where to?" Maia asked.

"We'll take Cassandra home first," I said. "Thank you."

I clasped my hands in my lap, slowing my breathing with one of the exercises Cerridwen had taught me to calm myself as we pulled away from the garden.

"Did you get what you wanted?" I asked Aubrey when I trusted my voice to sound normal.

"Well, I paid my respects," she said. "Which means protocol was satisfied." She leaned back against the seat, one hand stroking her thigh, smoothing a nonexistent wrinkle in her skirt. Perhaps she was rattled, too. "But I wasn't expecting quite that amount of…controversy."

"You've done this before?"

"Paid respects to foreign Fae? Yes. In Europe a few times when we've had cases that crossed borders. It usually goes more smoothly." She wrinkled her nose, looking at Cassandra. "It is unusual for a council to show disunity in front of humans. Has there been trouble since the Fae brought the door back here?"

"Minor discord," Cassandra said. "From what I understand from Lady Cerridwen, not everyone was a hundred percent happy with them returning, but the realm needs the anchor of our nexus."

Aubrey digested that, expression tight. "It might have been nice to have a heads-up about that."

Cassandra shrugged. "I assumed you knew. Reestablishing a door is not just the decision of those intending to shift their territories. Besides, the Fae will make trouble for trouble's sake. Lord Padran may have another issue with Cerridwen. He might be choosing to be defiant just to be difficult."

I wanted to believe that, but somehow I didn't. "Assuming it wasn't that, any idea why he seems to be set against me?" I asked.

"He's lord of one of the water territories," Cassandra said. "They, in particular, from what I understand, have concerns about demons in the realm."

"Why?" I asked.

"Think about it," Lizzie said. "What are the main ways to kill demonkind?"

"Fire. Or electricity," I said slowly.

Lizzie nodded. "Exactly. Neither of those things mixes well with water. It may be that the water Fae feel more at risk."

"Can demons swim?" I asked. Imps could. The imp that had chased Damon and me through Dockside the night I'd discovered my magic had come out of the water.

"Yes," Aubrey said. "Even afrits. Don't ever make the mistake of thinking you can get away from them that way."

"My plan is to stick with 'fry first and ask questions later'," I said.

"Don't mention that to Lord Padran," she said drily. "I don't think it would improve his opinion of you."

"Do you think he might have been the one who let the bruadhsiu loose?" I asked.

"Wait," Aubrey said, "there was a dark walker here? When? I don't remember hearing of it."

"We took care of it," Cassandra said. "There was no threat to London or anywhere else for that matter."

Aubrey's mouth tightened. "How did you defeat a walker so quickly that no word spread?"

"The authorities agreed to report it just as a strange virus that vanished as fast as it arose. It was in the local newsfeeds but perhaps that wasn't picked up anywhere else," Cassandra said.

"That tells me how you contained the news, not how you defeated the walker."

"That's a longer conversation," I said. "It's complicated. Callum helped."

"Complicated seems to be a strength of yours," Aubrey said. "And Callum is another thing you all forgot to mention. Who is he exactly?"

"One of Cerridwen's warriors," Cassandra said. "A demon hunter."

"And he's training Maggie?" Aubrey asked.

I gestured at Pinky. "Both of us."

"Mostly Maggie," Pinky said. "I don't have a lot of power. But great grandma seems to be getting her kicks out of making me try. Probably because Mom and I stayed behind. She thinks it's bonding time or something."

"Great grandma is Cerridwen," I added.

"You call her *great grandma*?" Aubrey half-choked.

I felt a little sorry for her. Clearly she was used to things being more by the book. Maybe Cassandra could appease her with cookies.

Pinky shrugged. "Not so much to her face, but at home, yeah. Mom didn't like naming any of the Elders once they'd gone."

"I'd like to talk to your mother about that," Aubrey said. "About the impact on the tanai who stayed. The Fae in England would not take kindly to such a division."

"There's not much to tell," Pinky said. "We mostly got on with living our lives. Everyone's still trying to mostly get on with living their lives. Mom probably won't want to talk about it. So far, Cerridwen's the only one who has made overtures to her relatives. The rest are all waiting to see what happens. Most of them would rather be left alone. Mom definitely does."

"She doesn't like that you see Cerridwen, then?"

"She doesn't much like any Fae." Pinky shrugged again, looking regretful. "She doesn't really have anything to do with magic either."

"I see," Aubrey said.

"We're getting sidetracked," Lizzie said. "Maggie asked about the bruadhsiu."

Aubrey was frowning. "Lord Padran isn't the obvious one to have control of a walker. They're terrestrial creatures, not marine," she said. "That would be more Usuriel's realm."

"Cerridwen said he was Lord of the Darker Hours. Any idea what that means?" I asked. Usuriel hadn't been mentioned in any of the Archive's materials I'd studied. Which either meant he avoided interactions with humans or any humans he or his kind interacted with didn't manage to make it back to the human world to tell anyone about it.

And *that* was a thought I was glad I hadn't had in the realm.

"I'm not entirely sure," Aubrey said thoughtfully. "We'll have to see what we can find, now that we have names. But, judging by his eyes, he's one of the darker Fae."

I was aware that there were darker Fae. Though the Archives said that their name came more from their appearance than any truth that they were all ill-willed toward humans. "I always imagined the darker Fae would look more like creatures like Lady Orea," I said.

"In the realm, appearances are deceptive," Aubrey said. "I doubt Usuriel looks like that all the time. Who knows what his true form is? And Orea isn't dark Fae by any stretch. The families who have her kind of form are usually fairly reclusive. They have an affinity for nature. That's not a dark Fae trait."

"Well, if he can change his appearance, does that mean we can't necessarily go by his eyes?"

"He left them black for a reason. Perhaps he wants us to

see who he is. Or he assumed Cerridwen would tell us," Lizzie said.

Cassandra said, "I'll talk to Cerridwen, and you're right, we should consult the Archives. Aubrey, perhaps now we have a feel for how things might lie, you can ask Ralph if he has any more information about Usuriel or Padran? Or the others."

Aubrey nodded her head, "I will. The more we know, the more we can understand agendas at play. I haven't dealt with any of them before, but that doesn't mean my predecessors didn't."

"Do you have any idea where the San Francisco Fae went when their door was shut?" I asked Aubrey.

"There was some shuffling of territories, I believe. There was some concern from the Fae that we deal with regularly, but that was before my time, and it seemed to be solved peaceably enough. I couldn't tell you what door any of them were using. I assume probably somewhere in Europe. There definitely wasn't a big change in the tanai population in London, which suggests not many chose England."

"Too cold after California," Lizzie said, clearly trying to lighten the mood. "They'd probably prefer places like Italy."

I grimaced at her. "Helpful."

Lizzie patted my knee. "It's all right. It's not like they can do anything to you out here."

"Spoken like someone who doesn't have to spend regular time in the realm. I don't fancy being dragged to a watery grave. And there's always that handy trick of sending nightmare spider creatures to invade my dreams." I shuddered.

"He wouldn't have to drown you to kill you," Lizzie said cheerfully. I swatted at her arm gently. She just laughed.

"Lady Cerridwen will keep us safe," Pinky said firmly. "She gave her word on that."

I hoped her faith was justified. So far Cerridwen had

protected me, but Padran and Usuriel were Elders, too. Could they could get around her if they joined forces?

So, better not to think about it or I would freak the fuck out. I sucked in a breath, shoving my fear away. "I hope so," I said, folding my arms. "Are we sure we can't just get them to close the door again and go away?"

"Seconded," Pinky said. "There's plenty of tanai here who'd be happy with that."

"I think that horse has well and truly bolted," Cassandra said. "Barring another demon incursion—which I am assuming none of us want—I can't imagine they're going to close it again, not if they've decided it's necessary for the realm's stability."

"We're here," Maia piped up from the driver's seat before anyone could reply, and I jumped, startled. I hadn't been paying attention to the world outside, still trying to process what had happened. But when I peered out of the window, the familiar porch light at the front of Cassandra's house was glowing like a beacon.

"Are you coming in?" Cassandra asked.

"I'd rather just go home. Unless you need me for something tonight?"

"No, but if you have time tomorrow, perhaps you can come to the Archives. Now that we have some names we can target our research more."

I wasn't sure if I was curious to learn more or wanted to live in ignorance. The more I learned about the Fae, the weirder and scarier things got. But if it was me the Fae had an issue with, then I couldn't let the Cestis do all the work. "I'll see if I have time," I said.

"Very well," Cassandra said. "What will you tell Damon about tonight?"

"Well, not that there's a giant Fae made of the ocean who seems to not like me very much," I said. "I think I'll keep it simple, say that it went as well as can be expected."

Lizzie snorted. "Well, that's one way of describing it."

"Do you have a better idea?"

Cassandra shook her head. "No, I think keeping it simple is probably best."

I glanced at Maia in the front seat. She'd been listening to our conversation, and she would no doubt be filling in Mitch with at least some of the relevant details. I'd have to talk to her on the drive back to Damon's.

"Do you think this is likely to stir up any further trouble?" I asked Cassandra.

"Padran didn't put it to a vote, so hopefully not," she said. "If it does, Cerridwen will tell us."

***

"Such a spectacular view," Aubrey said the following evening as we drove across the bridge back into San Francisco. She gestured at the city, just starting to light up as the sun set. It glittered gold and black and silver, only the patches of darkness in places revealing it wasn't fully healed.

Neither was I. I'd woken early that morning from an uneasy sleep full of dreams of crashing waves and shifting landscapes and a woman whose face blurred as she said things I couldn't understand.

I'd done what any sensible woman with a hot man lying next to her would have and woken Damon with a kiss, letting him chase away the lingering weirdness of the night before with his touch. When we both lay panting in bed in the aftermath, he said, "What's the agenda for today?" I'd explained that I was working in the morning and then would be going to Cassandra's to the Archives again. He'd nodded and said, "Why don't you bring Aubrey back with you? I had something on tonight that got canceled, so we could do that dinner."

"Are you sure?"

He shrugged. "No reason not to, is there? The two of you

seem to be getting along better. You said she was useful last night in the realm."

He'd arched an eyebrow, inviting me to tell him more, but I didn't want to tell him more about the council than I already had. "She was. Alright, I'll ask. What time?"

"Say seven; we'll go to Perroni's. I'm sure they'll give us the private room."

I'd been sure they would, too. It was one of Damon's favorite restaurants and Anton Perroni, the owner, was an old friend who was always more than happy to help protect Damon's privacy. Anton made excellent cocktails, too.

Nothing I'd read in the Archives today had made me feel any better about Padran and Usuriel. Ralph hadn't yet responded to Aubrey. She'd asked me about Callum; while he was an easier topic, talking about the Fae training me to fight demons didn't exactly help me relax. I fully intended on dealing with my lingering unease in a mature fashion: with a lot of alcohol.

Aubrey was still gazing out the window, seemingly fascinated by the view.

"Cities on harbors are always pretty," I said. "Like London."

She turned back to me. "I guess. Bridges and water add a certain something, don't they?"

I winced.

Aubrey's eyes flared. "Oh, God, I'm sorry. That was thoughtless of me. I forgot about, what is it you call it? The *Big One*. The bridges were damaged, weren't they?"

"Yes," I said tightly. "The one we're driving over right now collapsed."

This time it was her turn to wince. "At least you've recovered from the damage."

I pressed my lips together, wanting to tell her that I would never recover from the loss of my grandparents. But there was no point being rude. She'd been trying to make polite conversation. She seemed to have thawed a fraction this afternoon as we'd pulled out references on Padran, Morgain, Orea, and Usuriel and their various Fae clans and families. There was more on the first two than the others, but Ralph was searching his Archives as well. We might know more in the morning.

"London has nice bridges, too," I said, attempting to steer us back to safer conversational waters.

Aubrey's smile was relieved. "Yes, although none of them are quite so spectacular as yours."

"I guess that is what we get for being a young upstart country."

She laughed. "Better engineering?"

"And settlers intent on making their mark, perhaps." Not just settlers. Damon had put a lot of time and effort into making sure San Francisco recovered after the Big One. He'd put his own stamp on the city.

I asked Aubrey more about London and we talked easily until we reached Perroni's.

The restaurant was busy for a Wednesday evening, but Stefan, the maître d', smiled at the sight of me and ushered us both through to the private room where Damon was waiting with Anton.

"Maggie, you look beautiful, as always." Anton greeted me with a smile and a kiss on each cheek and then exclaimed over Aubrey when I introduced her. "Best Italian you'll get outside Italy," he told her with a broad grin.

Aubrey laughed. "Well, I've been to Italy several times, so let's see."

Anton's grin widened. "Challenge accepted." He was about ten years older than Damon but, with deep brown eyes, olive skin, and cheekbones to die for, he was definitely not hard on the eyes. And knew how to wield some Grade-A charm. A necessary skill in a restauranteur.

He left us to it and almost immediately a waitress—Ana—came in, bearing champagne. She poured glasses, deposited the bottle into a silver ice bucket, and slipped out again. I sipped gratefully as Damon and Aubrey made polite small talk for a few minutes before Ana came back in and summoned the holographic menus.

The champagne was tart and strong and I started to feel relaxed as I read through the options. Relaxed, but in need of food if I was going to avoid getting way drunker than I wanted to. Fortunately, Ana returned promptly with a basket with enough bread for at least six people, along with dishes of olive oil and herbs and butter. I munched a slice rapidly while Damon and Aubrey ordered. Ana let me finish before she took my order and vanished again.

"Have you thought any more on the Archives? Will your colleagues go for it?" Damon asked, passing the breadbasket to Aubrey.

She took a slice, tore it into a few pieces before she answered. "Actually, I was talking to Ralph last night. He seemed intrigued, but I think he would possibly need to see more for himself. He has concerns, of course."

"Perhaps he should talk with Cassandra," Damon said. "She had concerns, too."

"I'm sure he will," Aubrey said. "Would it be possible for you to come to London and speak with the others in person?"

He nodded. "I'm there reasonably often. It shouldn't be an issue to work something out. How much longer will you be in San Francisco?"

"Another week or so," she said, "though most of it I guess can be sightseeing again, though I'd like some time with you to ask you some of the questions Ralph had."

"Of course," he said. "That should be easy enough to manage."

We were interrupted by the arrival of our appetizers. I tried to eat the shrimp I'd ordered more slowly, now that the bread had taken the edge off. Knowing Anton, there would be plenty more to come.

I was just pushing my plate away, having used more bread to mop up the delicious garlicky sauce when Damon's datapad began to chime.

"Excuse me." He pulled the datapad—one of the new tiny ones he carried at social occasions— from his jacket pocket. "I'll have to take it," he said after glancing at the screen. He stood and moved away toward the door, speaking softly into the handset for a few minutes. I reached for my champagne, trying to tell myself nothing was wrong. But when Damon came back, he was no longer smiling.

"What is it?" I asked.

He glanced at Aubrey and then seemed to decide that it didn't matter if she knew. "Another lead on Jack," he said. "He was seen somewhere in Slovenia."

I could hear the satisfaction in his voice. Almost see his eagerness to go. "Does that mean you're going after him?" I didn't really need to ask. Damon wouldn't pass up another shot at Jack.

Damon's eyes met mine. "Would you mind?"

I did. Because it would be dangerous. But Damon and I had already agreed that he was free to do what he had to do to catch Jack. So I hid my worries—like he did when I went into the realm—and let him get on with it. "Of course not. Everything's fine here." Which was true. There was no imminent threat. And if there was, Damon was better away from it. Besides, Jack needed to be dealt with. He'd left my life in flames, literally. He was too dangerous to be left free to plot God knew what. Nothing good, if his first foray against Damon was anything to go by.

Aubrey was watching the exchange with interest. "Slovenia will take some time; they don't have a suborbital station. You'd have to go to Frankfurt or Rome and then fly in. Are you sure the trail won't go cold again?"

"It's the risk we have to take. It's always a possibility. We have a team on their way, but he might get wind of them. I want to be there, regardless."

Aubrey looked puzzled. "If you want to get there faster, why don't you use the ways?"

Chapter Twelve

"What," Damon said, all his attention focused on Aubrey, "are 'the ways'?"

Aubrey's puzzled expression grew more confused. "You don't use the ways here?"

I was as bewildered as she looked and the tension that Anton's excellent food and booze had dissipated was returning with a vengeance. "Never heard of them."

"That can't be right. You're learning Fae magic," she objected.

"A fairly limited subset of it," I said.

"But Cassandra knows about them. She hasn't told you? Or you haven't come across anything in the Archives?"

"We're mainly focused on getting a good scan, rather than stopping to read," I said. Sure, there were times when I got a little distracted by reading one of the books, but I couldn't remember any of them mentioning anything called "the ways".

"So the Cestis here don't use the ways to travel through the realm?"

I spread my hands wide in a "I have no idea" gesture.

"The door here has been closed for over a decade, so not lately. Whether they did before, you'd have to ask them."

Cassandra had definitely never mentioned anything like that to me. She'd been more concerned about warning me not to go wandering around in there without Cerridwen or Callum.

Aubrey still looked confused, fingers drumming on the tablecloth. "I suppose I will." Her accent was clipped again.

"How about you explain it to us?" Damon's tone was closer to an order than a question. She'd definitely caught his interest. And I didn't like the idea of him traveling through the realm at all.

"If Cassandra hasn't told you, maybe I shouldn't," Aubrey said.

"Cassandra probably hasn't told me because it's never come up," I said. I wanted to know what they were. Now. Mostly so I could talk Damon out of using them. "She agreed to me going into the realm and learning from them. I doubt she would mind if you told us something that might come in useful."

"It's not something that's widely shared," she said. "You need to keep this to yourself." She frowned at Damon. "I'm not sure I should tell you at all."

Damon's eyes narrowed, meaning there was zero chance he'd drop the subject regardless of Aubrey's concerns. Not if it would help him get Jack.

"At this point, Cassandra thinks of him as an honorary witch," I said, hoping that would reassure Aubrey and avoid Damon going into master of the universe mode to try to convince her to tell him.

"Or, at least, a useful human ally," Damon added. "One who lives with a witch and is safer when I'm kept in the loop about what the hell is happening. Keeping humans safe is part of the Cestis's remit, isn't it?"

Aubrey smiled tightly. "I see why you're such a successful

CEO. You're good at getting to the heart of the matter, aren't you?"

"Comes with the territory," he agreed. "So how about you explain these 'ways' to us?

She sipped water, considering. Then seemed to come to a decision. She put her glass down, shifting back on her chair. "You understand that time can move differently in the realm?"

"Yes, that's one thing Cassandra made sure I knew." I tapped the watch on my wrist. "It's why I have this, remember, to keep track of the time outside. Plus I've read the stories, same as everyone." There are plenty of fairy tales about people who think they've spent a night in fairyland only to discover years or decades had passed when they returned. Maybe the Fae couldn't actually keep someone that long, but I knew better than to make assumptions about Fae magic. Or take unnecessary risks.

"Well, sometimes that aspect of the realm can work to our advantage rather than against us," Aubrey said. "Time doesn't have to go more quickly outside the realm than in. The reverse is also true."

I could feel my head starting to ache trying to understand. "Time can go faster inside the realm?" That had never come up in Cassandra's warnings. But I guess she was less concerned about me gaining time than losing it.

Aubrey nodded. "Yes."

"That would mean you can travel faster within the realm than you can out here," Damon said.

"Yes. And they call that using—or sometimes riding—the ways." She tapped her fingers again. "We don't know exactly how it works. They never explain when we ask."

Typical. "That's not exactly comforting."

"What is important is that they *can* do it," Damon interjected. "And I gather, they can move humans that way, too? Or you wouldn't have mentioned it."

"They can," Aubrey said. "And sometimes they agree to actually do so."

For what price? "Is it safe?"

"Hasn't Cerridwen ever moved you around inside the realm?"

"Yes," I said. "Are you saying she could zap me from here in San Francisco to a door that opens in Europe?"

Aubrey tilted her hand back and forth. "Not exactly. It's a little complicated. Cerridwen can move you in her territory by shifting it to suit her. To travel from here to London you'd have to cross multiple territories. But using the ways, you travel at a pace that seems normal, when really you are moving faster. Like a…well, the best explanation is the magic of the ways folds the realm closer together, so you move faster while seeming as though you're not."

"Like a wormhole?" Damon asked.

"I'm not exactly up on the latest in astrophysics, but the theory is similar, I believe. I'm not sure if it's exactly the same for Fae traveling alone, but when I did it, it felt like we traveled a good day in the realm but when we reached the door and came out again, only four hours had passed."

"So you've done this yourself?" Damon asked.

"Only that one time," Aubrey admitted, "when we were tracking someone from England into Lithuania. There was a tanai in danger, there was a ticking clock, and the Fae offered to help. Of course, it's not as far from London to Vilnius as it is from London to San Francisco."

"No. And you're not crossing an ocean either," Damon said. "Is that even possible?"

"Honestly, I have no idea. If the Cestis here don't use the ways, then maybe there's a reason. Maybe we should ask Cassandra."

"Better to go straight to the horse's mouth," Damon said.

I blinked at him, startled. "You want to ask Cerridwen?"

"No," he said, pulling out his datapad. "I think we'd have more luck with Callum."

Callum? "Do you think that's a good idea?" I squeaked.

"If he won't tell us, he'll just say so. He has no trouble saying no."

"Or he might try to work it to his advantage," I pointed out.

Aubrey straightened at that.

Dammit. We hadn't told her about the favor yet. I wanted to keep it that way.

"He and I have an understanding. It shouldn't be a big deal to explain something to us that clearly the Fae shared with some humans in the past," Damon said, brushing off my concern.

Aubrey eyed him, her expression calculating. "The Fae take obligations seriously, though."

Damon nodded. "I'm aware. But if this would get me and some of my team over there faster, then that might make the difference between catching Jack or not."

"You really think it's worth the risk of going through the realm?" I asked him, heart sinking. If he really made his mind up to do this, it would be hard to dissuade him.

Damon said, "We want to stop Jack. That's my first priority."

"Well, my first priority is your safety," I said. "And I'd imagine if we asked Mitch, he would agree with me."

Damon's eyes narrowed. "We're not going to ask Mitch."

I gaped at him, and then snapped my mouth shut. "And how well do you think that will go over?" Mitch was uncompromising about Damon's safety.

Damon shrugged off my protest. "No point worrying him until Callum tells us if it's even possible. Then I'll discuss it with Mitch, but we don't have much time. The suborbital can be ready in two hours. If we can't sort this out before then, I'll just take that." He hit a button on the datapad.

Callum must have answered because Damon said, "Hey, it's me. Can you talk?"

I couldn't really hear the response despite my best efforts.

"Where are you?" Damon asked, then, "Good. We're at Perroni's. Any chance you could drop by for a quick discussion? I just need a couple of minutes of your time, but I'm working against the clock."

He listened for a few more seconds, then ended the call and pocketed the datapad, smiling with satisfaction. "He's on his way."

Crap and double crap. "Where is he?" I asked.

"Well, as luck would have it, he was already dining in the city."

Interesting. Callum should be sticking close to home in the realm after what had happened yesterday. Had Cerridwen sent him out to look for more afrits? Or, being Callum, had he gotten bored and left? Unlike Cerridwen, he seemed to relish time outside the realm.

While we were waiting, Anton came back into the room. He must have sensed the change in mood, because his smile dissolved into something more concerned. "Is everything all right? Nothing wrong with the food?"

Damon waved him away with an apologetic gesture. "Everything was fantastic. It always is. I've just had an urgent matter come up."

Anton rolled his eyes, looking exasperated. "You work too hard, Riley. You have two beautiful women dining with you and you're going to do business?"

"Someone has to keep all the balls in the air," Damon quipped. "You work just as long hours as me."

"I don't have thousands of employees to help me," Anton countered.

Damon snorted. "The thousands of employees just increase the workload. A colleague of mine, Callum Dune, should be here any minute. If he asks for me, please show him in. Jake knows what he looks like."

Jake was guarding our private room from the outside, sitting at a table near the door, no doubt ignoring Anton's attempts to feed him.

"Very well," Anton said. "Should I send Ana back to take your dessert orders?"

"I'm sorry," Damon said, "but I think we'll probably have to leave. Perhaps coffee? I promise you we'll come back soon and make it up to you. I was looking forward to that *Delizia al limone* you were telling me about."

Damn. No dessert. Anton's food was all delicious, but his desserts were my favorite part. Damon had a fondness for lemon, but I loved the tiramisu. Because Perroni's made it with real coffee. Which meant it was more expensive than any tiramisu had any right to be, but it was worth every penny.

"Just as well you're a good customer," Anton said, his mouth quirking. "Otherwise I'd be offended. But fine, I'll send coffees in." He turned to Aubrey. "Ms. Carter, how do you like yours?" She told him and he left, shooting one last troubled look at Damon.

A few seconds later, the door opened again, and Callum came in, followed by a male waiter carrying an extra chair. He slid it into position at the table and departed before Callum had crossed the room.

I studied Callum as he took his seat, trying to judge his mood. He didn't look annoyed. Which hopefully meant he'd been at a business dinner, rather than on a date. The night we'd met he'd told me his family had interests in art and Pinky had confirmed that his family did indeed, have human-run businesses. Or tanai-run, more likely.

His clothes didn't offer any clues. A very sharp, dark-blue blazer over dark jeans and a white shirt. Which would work for a date or a casual business dinner. He looked, as he often did when he was outside the realm, as though he'd just stepped off the pages of a male fashion magazine. Aubrey, who'd looked impressed with him in the realm, blinked as he removed the blazer, hanging it over the chair before he sat, a faint blush staining her cheeks. Hopefully, she knew better than to get entangled with a Fae, but that wasn't my main concern right now.

"Good evening," Callum said, nodding a greeting.

"Hey," I said. "I hope we haven't interrupted your evening."

He waved dismissively and started to say, "No, it is no prob—" He broke off when the door opened again and Ana carried over a tray of coffees, including, I noted, tea for Callum. She must have caught him as he came in.

None of us spoke as she dealt with the drinks.

"Thank you," I said with a smile when she stepped back with her now-empty tray.

"Anything else?" she asked.

Damon smiled in thanks. "No, this is perfect."

She looked more dazzled by his smile than mine, but left us alone. Anton's staff were all flawless at their jobs. Friendly, efficient, and able to read a room.

Callum reached for his tea. "And what have you summoned me for?"

Damon leaned in. "I just had a message from Mitch that one of our teams in Europe has a line on Jack. In Slovenia."

Callum frowned. "That's a long way away. Even with your modern transport. Are you going after him?"

Even by suborbital, California to London was six hours at least. Frankfurt or Rome would be much the same, though I wasn't sure of the exact figure. Plus whatever it would take for the second part of the journey.

Damon shrugged, but the movement came off more tense than casual. "I'd like to, but as you said, time is of the essence."

"And you need to tell me this, why?" Callum asked, his frown deepening.

"Cerridwen has expressed interest in finding Jack in the past," I reminded him.

Callum's expression turned vaguely wary. "Yes. Which is only to be expected given what you learned of him the last time he was here."

"Aubrey thought you might help us use the ways," Damon said.

Callum's eyes sparked more gold as he turned his attention to Aubrey. "You know about the ways?"

"Yes," she said, "from your far kin."

He arched a brow. "It is not something we tell many humans about."

She arched an eyebrow to match his. "I'm a witch, not a human, and I'm one of the Cestis. Sometimes the Elders who use the English doors have assisted us to move quickly when there has been need."

That had him looking startled again. "You've *traveled* by the ways?"

"Once," she said, "when we were dealing with someone who'd kidnapped a tanai fol. I was surprised to hear that Maggie hadn't heard about them."

Callum shrugged. "From what I understand, they are not often used here. There are not so many doors and the lesser ones are in locations not very useful for picking up a trail."

Meaning doors in the middle of nowhere. The other doors in the States were mostly in places like national parks.

Aubrey stirred sugar into her coffee. "But theoretically, though, could you go from here to London, or—Damon, you said Slovenia, yes?"

Damon nodded.

"Then Ljubljana presumably," Aubrey continued. "I assume there's a door there somewhere."

Callum's expression turned distant a moment as though he

was trying to remember. "I believe so, yes. And theoretically, it's possible, but it's not as simple as that. For such a distance, you would have to move through multiple territories."

"Is that a problem?" I asked.

That earned me a fluid Fae shrug. "Crossing over into a territory that doesn't belong to family, or allies, is not always simple."

"I thought you could change the realm to your will," Damon said.

Callum shrugged. "When we move our own territories, yes. It is considered impolite, at best, to do it in someone else's without permission. Not to mention it takes a lot more power to countermand the magic of whoever rules the territory. That can slow down the travel somewhat."

"You mean it would take as long as out here?" I looked at Damon, "You might as well just get on the suborbital, if that's the case."

Callum's head shook slowly. "No, not so long as that. We could still make it faster, maybe get there in five or six hours of your time, but it wouldn't necessarily be without risk. You'd be safe enough in Cerridwen's territory, and she has other allies along the way, but we can't get to the door we need without crossing some territories that are neutral at best and others that might be actively against us."

"I'm not sure I understand," I said. "If Cerridwen can manipulate her territory, can't she just move it to be closer to the London door, and we could stay in her territory the entire time?"

"I am afraid it doesn't work that way. Or life in the realm would be infinitely simpler. Territories are important to the Fae. They guard them closely. The door that your territory is closest to is the one that you have most influence over. Cerridwen came back here because she believes so strongly in the need for the door here to be anchored and for there to be guardians here against the demons. If she were to pull her territory away from this door, then—"

"She loses her influence here?" I said.

He nodded.

Well, damn. "Then people like Lord Padran might get to have their way and make life difficult," I continued. "You think they'd take the door away again?" Cerridwen was determined to keep the Berkeley door open. She wouldn't risk that.

"Perhaps not, but it's not something the Lady would be willing to chance. After all, it took ten or more of your years for there to be an agreement to put the door back. Even though that may not be a long time for us, she's not going to let all that work fail just to move you a little more swiftly." He looked at Damon and hitched his shoulders apologetically, "I'm sorry, but she would not see it as a justifiable risk in this case."

Part of me was relieved to hear that it was not actually a viable option, but Damon, instead of dropping the idea, was still looking thoughtful.

"And if we were willing to take the risk?" he asked.

Callum looked at him, "Are you asking for another favor?"

Aubrey made a startled noise.

Damn. She didn't miss much. And she'd just learned Damon owed Callum something.

"Well, I assume I would need someone to escort me and whoever came with me," Damon said before Aubrey had a chance to interrupt, "I'm not foolish enough to think I can do it on my own."

"No," Callum said, "that would be a near certain way to get lost in the depths of the realm. You need a Fae just to travel safely, let alone access the ways."

"Someone who knows his way around multiple territories," Damon said. "Which sounds like the kind of knowledge someone who hunts those of the dark must have."

Callum acknowledged this with a displeased twist of his mouth.

"So you could do it?" Damon pressed.

"Could and will are two different things," Callum said. "Neither the Lady Cestis nor your Maggie would thank me for putting you in danger."

Damon sat back, considering. Callum sipped tea, watching Damon, his expression carefully neutral.

"Thank you," I said to him mentally. *"Try to make him see it's a bad idea."*

Callum ignored me, focused on Damon.

"How does it even work?" I asked. "If the realm can move around, how do you even determine what territories you'd need to go through?"

Callum focused back on me. "Well, for one thing, the territories themselves don't move that often. It does happen, of course, and there are a few clans that are more…nomadic, you might call it…but the more powerful ones tend to eventually settle near a door that they favor. But in answer to your question, there are boundary stones that link the points between different territories. They…make parts of the realm touch temporarily, so that you can move from one to another. So, using the boundary stones it's not so complicated. *If* the right protocols are followed."

Or perhaps if you had the knowledge of how to get around those protocols? I couldn't see Callum stopping to ask for permission when he was chasing a target.

"Our maps show boundary stones, not necessarily the landscape," Callum continued. "Though we know roughly what to expect in the more stable territories." He grimaced. "However there are those who like to keep their domains more private. Like Lord Usuriel. He and his Nichtkin don't welcome outsiders often."

Nichtkin. Right. One of the bits of information that we'd

found on Usuriel was that he was also known as Lord of the Nichtkin. Reading between the lines of the spidery handwritten note from a century ago, it seemed to confirm him as one of the darker Fae, though exactly what his Nichtkin were like wasn't something whoever had written the notes had cared to divulge. Nor had I had a chance to ask Callum what he knew. That could wait until we returned.

"It sounds like that would make life interesting," Damon said.

"It is not always so. Usually we have time to familiarize ourselves with the safest ways. And long lives to learn many of them."

"So, you could get me to Slovenia faster than the suborbital? My team in Europe is already on the way," Damon said.

Callum leaned back in his chair. "Why not let them just do this? Presumably, you have sent people with the correct skills to apprehend a man with possible connections to demonkind."

Aubrey made a thoughtful hum, as though she hadn't thought about that aspect of going after Jack.

"We have suitable resources, yes," Damon said.

"Then it would seem more sensible for you to stick to your human transport and meet them there," Callum said, his voice suggesting that he was being polite in not saying "don't be an idiot."

Damon's answer was a scowl. He leaned forward, stabbing a finger at Callum. "Jack kidnapped me. Who knows what he was planning to do to me. He burned Maggie's house down. I want to catch him myself. That way I'll—"

He cut himself off, but I realized what he'd been about to say. That way he'd be certain Jack was no longer a threat. Fuck. If he'd decided the only way to keep me and the other people he loved safe was seeing to Jack's capture himself, then there would be no convincing him to let his team handle it.

Callum looked from Damon to me slowly. "A matter of honor, then?"

Damon nodded, his face set.

"Honor worth risking your life for?"

"If Jack Miller goes free long enough, God knows what he'll do," Damon growled. "I'd imagine quite a few lives might be lost in the process. I'm not willing to let that happen. You understand promises. My promise to Maggie and my family and my employees is that they will be safe. I will keep them safe. Which includes stopping Jack fucking Miller. So, will you do it? Will you take me through the ways?"

"Say no,*"* I said to Callum mentally, heart pounding at the thought of Damon actually traveling through the realm.

"This is not your decision," Callum replied, his gaze not shifting from Damon. *"He must make his own choices."*

I controlled my urge to scowl at him, not wanting to give any hints we were talking. But if Callum wouldn't help, I'd have to convince Damon myself. "He just said it's dangerous," I said flatly. "I agree. You should let your team take care of this. You can still meet them, once Jack is in custody, if you need to see for yourself."

"It's my decision," Damon said, his voice as flat as mine.

Fuck. He'd really made up his mind. Master of the universe. Willing to risk his own stupid life.

"Your decisions affect me," I said, trying not to panic. "You need to think this through. Call Mitch. Ask him what he thinks. You said you would, once you talked with Callum."

Damon looked like he was going to ignore that suggestion.

"Call him, or I will," I said, giving Damon my best "I'm not joking" face. "I'm sure Mitch could lock you up in whatever he has that works as a cell if I tell him this is a very bad idea."

"It's not that bad—" Callum started.

I turned my glare on him.

"No more talking until Damon speaks to Mitch."

Callum held up his hands in surrender. "Very well."

"Well?" I asked Damon.

He didn't look happy, but he pulled out his datapad again and walked to the far end of the room. I tried to look casual, like I wasn't trying to hear the conversation.

Callum leaned closer. "I could make it so that you can hear."

"Not the best idea," I replied, ignoring the sneaky part of me that really wanted to take him up on the offer.

I watched Damon instead, trying to judge how the conversation was going, hoping Mitch would shut the idea down. They were clearly arguing, though Damon had mastered the art of keeping his voice low on a call. Either that or he had some new tech to muffle the sound. But just when I was starting to relax, his expression turned from unhappy to fierce. "Good," he said, sharply. I didn't need to be any sort of lip-reader to understand that. "Then we're going with Plan B."

He ended the call and came back to the table.

"What did he say?" I asked.

"He doesn't love the idea," Damon said.

"So then don't do it."

"He doesn't love it, but apparently there's an issue at the sub-port. Everything's delayed. Seems we wouldn't be able to leave until early tomorrow."

By which time his team would have already caught Jack or Jack would, once more, be in the wind.

"So let the team take care of it," I said, in one last attempt to make him see sense.

But I could see he wasn't going to.

"No. I need to go."

I wasn't going to change his mind. I bit my lip, wanting desperately to tell him "No" but knowing I couldn't. Our agreement was that he let me do witch things he considered stupidly dangerous, so I had to let him take the risks he judged necessary as well.

Damon looked at Callum. "Will you take me?"

"Take us," I said tightly. I looked at Aubrey. "He shouldn't go alone, right?"

"No, that would be foolhardy, at best," she said.

"And you've been there before. So you'd come with us?" I asked "You said Damon should ask the Cestis for help. Your Cestis, I mean."

Damon nodded. "You did. So, Miss Carter, if I request your assistance to catch a wanted criminal, one who has magic and consorts with demonkind, will you help?"

She hardly had a choice when he put it like that and the way her knuckles whitened as she clasped her hands on the table told me she knew it. "Cassandra is not going to like it if you go," she said, looking at me.

"Unfortunately, Damon's not a witch, and I'm not Cestis," I said, "so I'm not entirely sure she could stop me."

"She could keep you in the Archives till you saw some sense," Aubrey said.

"Cassandra is just as keen for Jack to be stopped as I am," Damon said.

"Still," I said slowly, "Aubrey is right. We do need to tell Cassandra what we're planning. We can't just disappear into the ether."

I didn't like the idea of telling her, but I liked the idea of not telling her even less. After all, the Cestis had done a lot for me, and even though, yes, they would agree that catching Jack was important, I wasn't sure they would think this particular method was worth the risk.

Damon looked back at Callum. "But will you do it?" he asked.

Callum said, "I believe the Lady would want me to, so, yes, I will assist you."

"For a price?," Damon asked, eyes steely.

I opened my mouth to say "over my dead body" but Callum had apparently learned his lesson because he shook his head.

"You already owe me a favor," he said. "This I will do for free."

Chapter Thirteen

I WAS right about Cassandra's reaction.

"Have you completely lost your mind?" She wasn't quite yelling, but it was as close as I'd ever heard her come.

I winced and held the datapad farther from my ear, leaning back into the leather seat of Damon's limo. We'd made a quick detour to his house to change clothes. Fortunately, Aubrey was about my size, so I loaned her a spare jacket, jeans, and boots. Damon provided the nanoarmor to go under it all. Apparently he kept multiples. I wasn't sure whether it was sweet that he kept backups for me or horrifying that my life required multiple sets of body armor.

I was trying not to think about the armor, or the fact that my sword was in the trunk of the limo, as Cassandra continued to chew me out.

"Callum thinks he can get us there safely," I said when she finished. "There's an issue at the sub-port. We can't get there fast enough any other way."

"If something goes wrong in the realm, you might not get there at all," Cassandra snapped.

"Nothing's going to go wrong," I said, sounding far more confident than I felt. "I trust Callum. He wouldn't deliberately put us in danger." Well, no more danger than any trip into the realm entailed.

"Perhaps," Cassandra said. "But we haven't used the ways from this door in a very long time. Not in the entire time I've been in the Cestis."

My stomach twisted. "Any particular reason why not?"

"Because it was deemed too dangerous. Things have gone wrong in the past. And there's never been anything urgent enough that it was worth the risk. I'm not sure this qualifies as urgent enough, either."

"Maybe not," I said. "But that's Damon's call to make, not yours. He's the one going after Jack."

"And you're going with him," she said. "Putting both of you at risk. There will be other chances at Jack. Chances that won't be so dangerous. What if something happens to you?"

I understood her concern. I even shared it. But while I could handle the idea of something happening to me, losing Damon could break me. I couldn't just sit back and let him try this alone. And I knew I couldn't stop him going.

"If I don't go and Damon is hurt, I'll never forgive myself," I said. "I can use some Fae magic. I can help if I go." And I'd be no use to anyone if I stayed behind. "I'll lose my mind if I just sit here and wait."

"You can't tell me you haven't already lost it, if you think this is a good idea," Cassandra said. "But I guess I can't stop you. When you get back, I think we need to have a serious discussion about risk versus reward."

"Jack burned down my house," I said, repeating what Damon had said earlier. If I was going to do this, then I might as well climb all the way on board. "He cheerfully would have killed me and Lizzie and Zee and possibly Damon. I get that there's risk in going after him, but there's a lot more if we don't stop him."

The limo was silent as we neared the rose garden thirty minutes later. Damon had spent much of the trip talking to Mitch, and I wasn't sure his conversation had gone much better than mine with Cassandra. However, in the end, he'd said, "I'm doing this. I'll make contact as soon as we're through. Don't worry," and hung up.

No one had said much after that.

But now that we'd arrived, we had to snap out of it and work as a team.

Damon waved his datapad at Callum as Jake parked. "Is there any point in me bringing this?"

"You can try. It may malfunction once we're inside," Callum said.

"He means it may get fried. Not just that it might not work," I clarified. Pinky and I had both lost a couple of datapads before we'd stopped taking them into the realm. Which Damon understood. The fact he was double-checking told me he was nervous, even though he was clearly determined not to show it now that he'd made his decision.

"Worth a shot," Damon said. He spun the datapad idly, as he waited for Jake to give the okay for us to leave the car.

"It might be safer to write down some of the numbers. Mitch and whoever you need from the team in Slovenia," I suggested. "Paper will survive." Barring an unfortunate encounter with an angry water Fae like, say, Lord Padran. But no point borrowing trouble when we already had plenty.

"That would be helpful, if I had some," Damon said.

I'd also grabbed my training backpack. There was a notebook and pen in it, and I handed them to him. "Didn't you once tell me you were a Scout? What happened to being prepared?"

He smiled lopsidedly, acknowledging the point. "Strangely there was no badge for prepping to go into the Fae realm. What else have you got in there?"

"Water bottle, protein bars, nothing terribly exciting." A

clean T-shirt. Some mints. A basic first aid kit, to take care of the bumps and bruises that sometimes Cerridwen didn't think were worth healing after the sessions that Pinky and I had with her. She always healed any serious injuries but the minor ones she seemed to consider just part of the process. Hopefully we wouldn't encounter anything in the realm that required so much as a Band-Aid.

Damon scribbled some numbers from his datapad, before tearing the page free, folding it, and tucking it into the back pocket of his pants. He wore the same tactical gear his security team wore when they were dealing with a serious threat. No doubt made of the same sort of indestructible nanofibers as my jacket. He passed me back the notebook. "I guess we should all do the same."

Callum shifted impatiently. "If you want to do this, we should get moving," he suggested. "We've already wasted an hour or so."

We had, but it was still faster than waiting for a suborbital that worked.

"I already have my contacts," Aubrey said. She'd left her purse at my house but had slid her ID and a few things into various pockets of the clothes and backpack she'd borrowed.

"I know Lizzie and Cassandra's numbers," I said. "I'm not sure who else I'd want to call."

"I'll give you Mitch's and the teams' as well," Damon said as he powered his tiny datapad off and slid it into one of his jacket's inner pockets. "Then we should get going." He pressed the button to lower the privacy screen between us and Jake.

Jake's expression was tense. Mitch had clearly filled him in on the plan at some point in the journey. "You sure this is a good idea, boss?"

"I'm sure," Damon said. "I hope Mitch isn't in too bad a mood when you get back."

Jake looked torn. "You sure you don't want me to wait

here in case something goes wrong, and you have to come back through this end?" At least he hadn't asked to come with us. If Maia had been on duty, she might have tried, but with no experience in the realm, despite her own magic, she'd be a liability.

"If we have to come back through this door, then we'll call Cassandra. No point in you sitting here all night," Damon replied.

Jake shrugged reluctantly. "All right, you're the boss."

We climbed out of the car and trudged through the garden. As we got to the arbor, I almost shrieked when Zee stepped out of the shadow of one of the pillars.

"Sorry," he said, conjuring a faint glow of light in his hand so I could see his face—and his apologetic grin more clearly. "Didn't mean to scare you."

I put a hand over my racing heart. "Well, you did," I managed. "What are you doing here?"

He glanced toward the roses that concealed the door. "Cassandra thought you might need some more backup."

"You're coming with us?" I asked. "Are you sure?" Aubrey was doing her duty. I was trying to keep Damon safe, given he'd decided to throw caution to the wind. But Zee didn't have to risk his neck for any of us.

"It's Cestis business," he said.

"You're not Cestis."

"I'm on the team." He sounded as though that was all the argument he needed. Loyalty was definitely one of his strengths.

"They have other resources."

"Not with experience with the Fae, they don't. At least, not close by. Unless you'd prefer Pinky?"

Oh no. I wasn't letting her get dragged into this. Zee had much stronger magic than her.

"I'd prefer neither of you," I said. "Aubrey is Cestis. And she has more experience than you with the Fae."

Aubrey stayed silent. I didn't know if she was reluctant to countermand Cassandra or whether she just thought another witch on our side was a good idea. Either way, not helpful.

"Maggie has a point," Damon said to Zee. "Trueno need you, too."

As did Lizzie.

"Not your choice. Either of you. Cassandra asked me. I said yes. And if I said no, then Lizzie would insist on coming with you." His tone had gone flat.

Yeah, he wasn't going to let that happen. It was my fate to be surrounded by stubborn protective men, it seemed.

Well, there were worse things to deal with.

"Besides, Mitch agrees with Cassandra," Zee said. "I can fight. With weapons that will work in the realm, unlike any of your team." That last part was directed at Damon. "So I'm coming with you."

"I—" I started.

Zee cut me off. "We're wasting time arguing. I know the Fae a little, I know some of the British tanai." He tipped his chin at Aubrey, "And when we get to the other side, well, I know how to get things done in ways that she might not."

That was a good point. We were chasing a criminal. Which might mean deploying some outside-the-box thinking of our own. Still, I didn't want him risking his life. "Are you really sure?"

"I'm a big boy, Maggie, I can make my own decisions." He leaned down and picked up a backpack, unzipping it and pulling out a cloth pouch before passing it to Aubrey. "Here," he said. "Cassandra thought these things might be useful."

Aubrey untied the pouch and had a quick look. She nodded, re-tied it, and shoved it into her backpack.

"What's in there?" I asked.

"A few magical supplies." He reached into his pack again. "Cassandra also sent these." He handed out charms like the ones we'd worn into the realm for the meeting. Callum looked at them with a raised eyebrow, but didn't say anything.

"Anything else?" I asked.

He dug into the backpack again and handed me a very small notebook.

"What's this?"

"Key terms of the contract with the Fae," Zee said. "Just in case."

Just in case we needed to argue our way out of a sticky situation. I swallowed and shoved the notebook inside my jacket.

Zee looked at Callum. "I assume you can provide weapons inside?"

Callum nodded. "Better than you'll find out here."

"Good," Zee said. "And no point bringing a gun?"

"No," Aubrey said. "Trying to carry a human gun through the realm would be one sure way to pit everyone we encounter against us."

"Yeah," Zee said, "that's what I figured." He patted his hip, and I noticed a dark sheath strapped to his leg. A knife of some kind. So he hadn't come completely unarmed.

"Alright," he said to Callum. "I guess we get going."

I looked at Damon one last time, "You're sure you want to do this?"

He didn't hesitate. "Yes."

We stepped through the entryway's second door into yet another unfamiliar place, a cobbled yard of some sort, the gray stones gleaming ever so faintly in the moonlight. Still night. That meant nothing, but it was somehow reassuring. Across the yard from the door was a small building made from some kind of light stone. The windows were barred. There were no signs of a visible lock on the door, but I could sense the strength of the warding from where I stood.

"Where are we?" I asked Callum.

"First stop, weapons," he said, nodding at the building. His outfit had changed to his usual hunting gear as soon as we'd stepped through the door. He blended with the shadows as he led us across the yard. The door's wards yielded to his touch, and we stepped into what could only be described as an armory. The kind of thing I'd only ever seen in VR. Rows of swords and knives and various sorts of leather and metal armor hung on the wall in neat rows. They were beautiful, as most Fae things were, but the blades caught in the light Callum raised with a wave of his hand in a way that told me they were also deadly. The sword I carried was a Fae blade Cerridwen had given me when we'd started more serious training exercises. It looked like some of the swords on the wall. So this was Cerridwen's armory, presumably.

Maybe we were at the house she'd taken Pinky and me to before?

Risky, if we were trying to avoid attention, but I could understand why Callum might choose speed over stealth when we were in a hurry. Clearly he was allowed to be in the armory if he could disable the wards so easily.

"Maggie, you need a knife. Look there." Callum pointed at a rack of knives on the left-hand wall, before he turned his attention to the others.

I moved across the room and studied the knives without touching them, trying to see if any of them resembled the daggers Cerridwen trained me with—those stayed in the realm, unlike my sword. I carefully didn't touch while I considered the options. Who knew what wards they might have?

I only half-registered the sound of the door opening again until a female voice said, "Well, isn't this interesting?"

I whirled, reaching for my sword. In the doorway stood a

woman a few inches shorter than me, but unmistakably Fae, her face sharply beautiful. She wore clothes similar to Callum's. Leather pants and vest, dark shirt, knives strapped to her thighs, and a sword in a scabbard strapped to her back. Her dark hair was braided back from her face and black metal rings decorated her ears. The only color other than the golden tone of her skin was the startling green-gold of her eyes. Just like Callum's. Callum, who didn't look pleased with the intrusion.

"Go away, Gráinne,'" he said tersely. "I'm busy.'"

Gráinne. I filed the name away, more worried our mission had just been thwarted before it began, than with who she was.

"Busy in the dead of night arming humans from our armory?" she said, unperturbed by the snap in his tone.

"The armory is *my* business," Callum retorted.

"I help pay for it," Gráinne snapped back. "Which makes it my business, too. Even before we consider the other factors."

Other factors? I looked at Aubrey, wondering if she had any idea who the woman was, but she was watching the two Fae, her mouth twisted.

Gráinne put her hands on her hips. "What trouble are you causing, Callum?"

"No trouble, merely helping some friends of the Lady."

She rolled her eyes, clearly unconvinced. Something in the angle of her head reminded me of Callum in his other form. "Helping them do what, exactly?"

Callum's expression turned annoyed. 'You are not my keeper, Gráinne."

She frowned, equally unimpressed. "No, but I am one of the keepers of this armory. And I don't wish to have to explain to the others that I let you sneak off into the night with a group of humans when you inevitably get into trouble doing whatever this is." She snapped her hand at the four of us, irritation clear in the gesture.

"There will be no trouble. I am taking them to the door in Ljubljana."

Her eyes widened. "You're using the ways? On your own?"

I swallowed, trying to ignore the increasing swell of nerves in my stomach. Were we insane to attempt this, when her first thought was we were going to get into trouble?

"We will move fast; it will be fine," Callum said blithely.

"That's what you think." Gráinne's green-gold eyes swept over us. "Three of them are witches, I see, which might make it easier, but that one is human." She nodded at Damon. "One of you to protect four of them is unwise, particularly given the state of things."

"What state?" I asked.

Her gaze shifted to me, eyes narrowing. It was an uncomfortable sensation. I was beginning to get some idea who she was. Or what she was, perhaps.

"You're the one he's been training," she said slowly.

I nodded. "I am."

She tossed her head, braids swishing in the air. "Well, I guess that makes you slightly better than completely useless, but the ways are not always straightforward, and the path you take crosses at least one territory that isn't particularly friendly to our Lady." She looked at Callum. "You said she had requested this?"

"I said they were friends of the Lady," he corrected.

Her lip curled back, the expression once again reminding me of Callum. "So you haven't told her. Did you perhaps hit your head on something while you were beyond the realm?"

"No. I know what I'm doing, and I am not under your command, so perhaps you could do me a favor and mind your own business for once."

Zee's mouth quirked at that. I might have been more

amused at the clash of wills between them if Gráinne hadn't made it clear she thought we were unlikely to succeed.

Gráinne made an exasperated noise and crossed to the armory wall, yanking down a few weapons without looking. "Why don't you let me help you? That way your chances of pulling this off will be vastly improved."

Callum looked appalled, and I almost laughed.

"Aren't you going to introduce us to your friend?" I asked. "Is she one of the s'ealg oiche?"

Her attention snapped back to me. "As it happens, I am," she said, with a familiar rumble underscoring her tone. "Do you need a demonstration?"

"No," I held up my hands to show I had no quarrel with her. "I've seen how it works."

She smiled, baring her teeth, then aimed her ire at Callum. "Why don't you answer their question, Callum? Tell them who I am."

He dragged a hand through his hair, clearly exasperated, and sighed, "You're going to insist, aren't you?"

She nodded, "You bet."

That sharpened my attention. It was a distinctly un-Fae term, which suggested that she, like Callum, was someone who spent some time outside the realm.

Callum sighed again.

"Perhaps it would be wise if you made the introductions," Damon said, his voice carefully polite. "So we can continue." He shifted his weight, eager to be underway.

"This is Gráinne," Callum said, "As you've already determined, she is one of the blades who hunts with me for the Lady Cerridwen."

I looked at the two of them. Now that they were standing closer, there was a definite similarity. Curiosity got the better of me. "Do all the s'ealg oiche look alike, or just you two?"

Gráinne shot me a smile, "Not all of us," she said. "There

are a number of different families who make up the blades who serve the Lady."

Good to know. But they had to be from the same one, surely? "Then are you two related?"

"Gráinne is my sister," Callum gritted out.

Gráinne's smile widened, "His twin, to be precise."

I couldn't help smiling back as I watched Callum's brow crease. "You have a sister? And you're a twin?" Pity their poor mother. Or not. Some of the Fae weren't terribly fertile. Twins would be cause for celebration.

"He has several sisters," Gráinne said when Callum didn't answer. "And some brothers, too. But only one me." She smirked at her brother and his scowl deepened.

"Huh." I'd always thought of Callum as the mysterious, lone-wolf type. Perhaps it was closer to think of him as having a pack, which made sense, I suppose. I knew that Cerridwen had more than one person who worked for her hunting demons and the dark side of the Fae.

"Who's the older?" Damon asked, clearly trying to hide a grin.

"I am," Callum said firmly. "Which means she has to do as I say."

"You wish," Gráinne said. She came over to me and studied the sword I was carrying, looking at the hilt. "Ah, so that's where that one went. Has he taught you how to use it properly?"

"Of course," Callum said.

Gráinne looked me up and down, lips pursed. "Let's hope so." She moved to Zee and hit him with a dazzling Fae smile. "Now you, you need something nice and big."

"Don't flirt," Callum growled.

"I wasn't flirting, I was stating a fact," Gráinne said pertly. "Besides, he has that taken air about him."

Zee looked startled at this, and I snorted, filing that one away to tease him about once we were all safely home.

"What about this one?" she asked Callum, looking at Damon.

"His name is Damon. He belongs to her," Callum said, jerking his head in my direction. "So behave yourself." Gráinne looked between us, then nodded. "So I see," she said. She prowled back to Aubrey, an appreciative light in her eyes. "Then perhaps I'll stick with this one." Aubrey shot her a glance, blushing slightly.

Callum rolled his eyes. "If you are going to stay, perhaps you can help me outfit them, and then we can be on our way," he said.

"I'll do a better job than you can," Gráinne said. "It won't take long."

Callum waved her back to Zee. "Help Zachariah."

He looked a little wary as she approached, but obeyed when she said, "Hold out your arm." She studied him briefly, then walked to one of the racks of swords, pulled one out, and passed it to him. "I hope you know how to use this."

"I'm familiar. And the name is Zee, not Zachariah," he said drily, gripping the sword. He stepped back away from everyone and took an experimental swing. His form looked good to me, which made sense given he trained with Trueno on all sorts of weapons. "Nice balance," he said to Gráinne.

She smiled at him, looking pleased.

He looked at the sword, then back at her. "You made it?"

"I did," she said. "I made all of these."

"Gráinne has some skill with metal," Callum said grudgingly. "Not as large as her talent for being annoying."

"You're just jealous, big brother," she said. "You wish you had my charm."

"I have charm enough," he said, "and I need to be on my way."

She studied him a moment and then dismissed him with a flick of her hand, crossing the wall and selecting two more swords. One she handed to Damon and the other to Aubrey.

It only took her a few more minutes to find them matching daggers and sword belts and sheathes for everything, helping them fasten the weapons securely. Callum also passed out small metal pins, that he said would work the way my bracelet did and make the others easy to find if we got separated.

I didn't want to think too hard about that possibility, so I watched Gráinne as she finished getting us all outfitted.

"We can stop by the kitchen for some supplies," she said when she was satisfied everyone had as many weapons as they could handle.

We? "We have food," I said quickly, hitching my backpack so she could see it.

"Good," she said, "But more will be useful."

Aubrey opened her mouth to say something, but Gráinne smiled reassuringly. "You needn't worry. Callum and I aren't going to give you anything that would trap you in the realm." She nodded at me. "The Lady Cerridwen likes her and I'm guessing that the two of you must have some connection to the Cestis at least to venture in here so calmly. She'd have our heads if any of you came to harm, wouldn't she, brother?"

Callum shrugged, "Nothing's going to happen to them. But if everyone's ready, I agree; we should get going."

"Do they need armor?" Gráinne asked.

I tapped the chest plate under my shirt. "We have human body armor.

"Does it work against enchanted weapons?"

"No idea," I said, "I'm hoping there will be no need to find out."

"Good plan," Callum said, "which is why we need to get going. I'd rather use the dark to keep us out of sight while we can."

"No need for so much caution for the first part," Gráinne said. "What route are you planning on taking?"

"I thought we'd go via Morgain's and then cross the tip of the Mists. After that we can cut through Nine Hills to

Rannoch's lands. They're closest to the door we want at the moment."

She frowned, "Well, the Mists and Rannoch aren't a problem; Nine Hills, we'll have to be more careful about. The Lord of the Lochs is a friend of Lord Padran's."

Right, so she knew about Padran at least.

"I'm not an idiot," he said. "It's why I want to get going and move fast. Nine Hills is quieter at night."

Gráinne didn't argue with that. "What is so important that they need to use the ways anyway?"

"We're hunting a witch who deals with demonkind," Callum said.

Gráinne's gaze sharpened, her attention locking in on him. I recognized the expression from him. It was the one that meant he was in hunting mode. "You should have said that in the first place. Very well. I'm definitely coming with you."

Chapter Fourteen

"No. You're not," Callum said, stepping into his sister's path as though he had half a mind to physically remove her from the situation. Or maybe just spirit her elsewhere in the realm? Could he do that? And if he did, could she just spirit herself right back? Was there some sort of hierarchy of Fae powers? Other than the obvious ones with the lords and ladies.

I watched them warily, reminded again how little I knew about the realm and what we were about to face.

Gráinne put her hands on her hips, meeting Callum stare for stare. "Don't be an idiot, brother. If you wish to do this safely, then you need help."

"We're trying to go unnoticed. The more people we have, the harder that is." He shook his head vigorously enough to make his hair lash around his head. Almost as though it was trying to lift like his hackles would in dog form.

His sister remained unmoved. "Are you honestly trying to tell me you think I can't go unnoticed if needed? If we had more time, I'd make you eat those words. Don't be a caoirgh-brained dolt. Another set of eyes and ears, someone else who can work the ways, if needed, can only be a benefit to them."

She waved a hand in our direction, distracting me from wondering what the hell a *caoirgh* was.

"What will you do if something happens to you? The four of them will be stranded, only able to move at their own pace. How do you rate your chances, their chances, then?" Gráinne continued.

"Nothing's going to happen to me," Callum rumbled.

"No. Because I'm coming with you."

Callum scowled, eyes glinting very gold.

"It's either you let me come with you, or as soon as you leave, I will go to Cerridwen and she will send someone, if not several someones, after you. And I'll be one of them," Gráinne said.

"The Lady—" he started.

Gráinne held up a hand to cut him off. "Yes. I understand the situation. It was not that difficult to deduce that our Lady may not be entirely happy with this venture." She shrugged. "But it is our way, is it not? To help those that fight against the dark. If what you have told me about Maggie is true, then she is an important ally to the Fae. That is before I consider that you said that the man you seek communes with the dark. It is our duty to defeat such a one. Mine as much as yours. You can't deny that." Her expression turned smug, as though she knew he wouldn't think of a counterargument.

Callum looked like he was about to lose it. "It is your duty," he said tightly, "to defend the Lady."

Gráinne blew out an exasperated breath, waving an arm back toward the main house. "She has plenty of people guarding her. Hundreds, in fact. Stop being so stubborn, you're wasting time."

He stared at her. "You're really not going to let us go in peace, are you?"

"No."

He sighed, his expression turning contemplative. Was he still trying to find a reason for her to stay behind? I, for one, thought having more protection sounded great. Though I wasn't sure saying so would defuse the situation.

"And don't even think about trying to send me to the kitchens for supplies and sneaking away while I'm gone. You know I'll just catch up to you," Gráinne said.

Aubrey stepped forward. "It does sound like a sensible idea to have some additional help," she said diffidently. "It will make things easier for you, Callum."

Callum didn't look like he agreed, but Gráinne clearly wasn't giving in.

"I think so, too," Damon said. "If Gráinne won't hold us back, then it seems like the smart thing to do."

Gráinne's gaze shifted to him, her eyes narrowing in irritation. "I won't hold you back, human. No more than old stubborn head here would."

Callum growled. But he nodded. "All right. You go to the kitchens, get what we need. We will wait here."

She cocked her head. "Why don't you meet me in the stables?"

"Stables?" I squeaked.

"I assume we will be riding, or you four will at least," Gráinne said, looking puzzled. "It will let us set a faster pace."

"Riding?" I squeaked again, my brain going blank.

I had *seen* horses, of course. Difficult to spend half your childhood in various small towns in rural areas of the country without encountering livestock. But Sara had never been in the position—or had the inclination—to pay for so much as a pony ride at a fair. It hadn't taken me long to figure out that there was no point in me trying to make friends with any kids at any of my schools who seemed to have money. That would just help Sara narrow in on their parents as potential marks. And farm kids were out, too, because she never wanted to ferry me around.

Once I'd returned to Berkeley with my grandparents, well, horses weren't something I was into. Riding for pleasure was the domain of the wealthy. Outside of the odd police horse, horses just weren't part of my world. Certainly I'd never ridden one.

Gráinne was frowning. "You've never ridden?"

I swallowed hard, shaking my head.

"Not even in a game?" Callum asked.

"Once," I said. That had been enough. Westerns were not my favorite genre and definitely not Nat's. When I'd played anything in the kind of fantasy setting that might involve horses, there were usually other options for transport that I could choose. "It didn't go well." I'd fallen off several times and then decided that the saying about "having to climb right back on" could bite me.

Damon was struggling not to smile. "Not a fan?"

"No."

"What about the rest of you?" Gráinne asked.

Aubrey raised her hand. "I can ride."

Of course she could. It sounded like a very fancy English thing to do. They no longer had fox hunting, but if she'd grown up with the kind of wealth-and-privilege background Lizzie and Zee had talked about, it didn't surprise me that she'd ridden.

Gráinne looked pleased at that, shooting Aubrey a smile that made her blink.

I couldn't blame her. Callum was distractingly pretty enough on his own. Having two Duinnes in the same room, was…a lot. I stepped closer to Damon, hooking my arm through his and taking a breath in. Inhaling him to remind me of what was real. It didn't matter how uncannily attractive Callum or his sister were, Damon was mine. We had each other. And each other's back. Which was the only reason I wasn't making a strategic retreat back to the door, Jack or no Jack.

"I've ridden occasionally, and I've done it plenty in games," Damon offered.

"And you, big one?" Gráinne asked, looking at Zee.

He rubbed a hand over his hair. "In games, not in real life."

Well, at least I wasn't completely alone in never having ridden. But knowing Zee, "in games" was code for "thoroughly across everything to do with horses"…virtually at least. Professional gamers had to master many skills.

"And that is why I hadn't suggested riding," Callum said.

Gráinne looked at him as though he may have grown a second head. "It will make things faster, and you know our horses will not let them fall."

Fae horses. Yikes. The only Fae horses I'd read much about were the Kelpies. And those were supposed to be bad news. Once they convinced you to climb onto their backs, they carried you off and tried to drown you in the nearest river. Water beasts like Lord Padran. Which meant they had no more reason to like me than he had.

Something of my concern must have shown on my face, because Gráinne said to me, "Don't worry, they are horses, not waterfolk. They won't do you any harm." She lifted her chin slightly. "In fact, the Lady's horses are famed throughout the realm for their beauty and abilities."

Clearly that was a point of pride. Which made it harder to say no. "I'm sure they're very pretty, but won't it slow us down if half of us don't know what we're doing?"

She dismissed my concern with an airy wave. "You won't need to do much more than hang on. We can charm you, so you won't fall. And the horses know what they're doing, so you don't need to. They will follow Callum and me."

"The two of you won't be riding?" I asked, lifting an eyebrow. Callum was big and fast in his other form but keeping up with Fae horses seemed like a stretch.

"No," she said. "We can travel mostly in our other form. We're just as fast as the horses that way, and perhaps better placed to take care of threats," She looked back at Callum.

"Or we can take turns. Split our time between riding and running."

"That might be wise," Callum agreed.

"Very well," Gráinne said. "I'll go to the kitchens and then meet you at the stables." She turned on her heel and slipped out through the door before Callum could mount another argument.

He just huffed an irritated breath as she left and then double-checked our weapons. "Let's go. It will take a little time to get the horses ready."

My stomach twisted. Magic horses. This was really going to happen. And, unlike in a game, I couldn't just hit the kill switch and opt out.

I was tempted to follow Gráinne, but I'd probably just get caught and ruin everything. Reluctantly, I trailed after the others as Callum led us through the darkness to a building at least ten times the size of the armory. Two large doors were lit by two lanterns on either side, but they gave enough light for me to see that it was far grander than I would have expected a stable to be. The windows were arched, the walls had columns and carved inlays, and what I thought might be gargoyles perched near the edge of the roof. It did, however, smell strongly of horses, though not exactly the same as the few human horses I'd ever been close to enough to smell. There was a difference to the scent, something wilder and sharper, a tang almost like ozone.

Callum put his palm on the door, and a smaller door opened within it. I'd seen that kind of thing in barns. A smaller door made less work to open and close as people went in and out. Apparently the Fae also viewed it as more efficient, even though I suspected they could probably just make the larger doors open and close with a thought.

We slipped inside the building, and lanterns hanging above each stall door winked into life, illuminating a lengthy corridor of stalls. The not-exactly-horse smell was stronger inside, mingling with notes of wood and straw and leather that made it more familiar.

Callum studied the stalls, looking from us to the horses who were starting to put their heads over the doors, looking sleepy and confused as to who was interrupting them at this hour.

A muffled thump came from above, followed by a male voice demanding, "Who's there?"

"Just me. Callum," Callum answered without looking up. Whoever was asking, clearly Callum wasn't surprised that he was there.

"What are you doing here so late?" the voice came back, rumbling with irritation.

"The Lady has a mission for me. I'll be taking Tor and four others. They'll be back in a day or so."

The voice snorted. "They had better be. But very well. Don't do anything foolhardy, wolf. You know where everything is?"

"Yes," Callum replied, "go back to bed." He waited a moment, but no further comments came, so I assumed whoever was sleeping above had taken his advice.

We headed down the row of stalls, Callum walking near silently on the paved floor which made our footsteps seem extra loud. I tried not to gape. The inside of the stables was more luxurious than most apartments I'd lived in, with gleaming wood, polished brass, white stone, and touches of the pale greens and browns that Cerridwen favored used in tiles and paint. Even the cobbled floor was spotless.

As we walked, the horses stretched their heads farther over the stall doors, shaking their heads and whickering at Callum. They seemed bigger than an average human horse—not that I was an expert—and more finely built, like an Arabian drawn by someone who wanted them to be both more delicate and more imposing at the same time.

There was intelligence in the eyes that watched us pass,

eyes that weren't just brown or blue, but shades of red and gray and yellow, too. Their coats under the lamplight were unusual, too. White and black and gray and brown tinged with other colors, like Cerridwen's hair, shades of green and brown and silver, almost shimmering, so I couldn't tell whether it was an effect of the lanterns or the horses themselves. But it was clear they weren't normal horses. I kept to the center of the aisle between the stalls, not wanting to stray too close, despite Callum and Gráinne's reassurances that these creatures were safe.

It might have been easier if they were real horses. The coat colors and the just-different-enough scent had my brain convinced they couldn't be real. That it was a game. Horses like these weren't real and so none of it could be real. I'd experienced flashes of a similar feeling in the realm before, but this was worse. Maybe because I was already on edge. Or maybe seeing creatures other than human-seeming Fae was pushing my ability to process the difference to its limits.

I shoved a hand into my jacket pocket, clenching my fist, trying to focus on sensations. The fabric against my skin, the stones under my feet, the air moving through my lungs. Things to anchor myself in this reality. Because it wasn't a game. There was no easy way out. If we got hurt—or worse— here, it was real. No do-overs. I had to stay sharp.

Callum led us to a small room filled with horse gear of various kinds. Most of which I couldn't have named if you paid me. Saddles were the things you sat on, reins were for steering, those were attached to bridles, and that was the limit of my knowledge.

The saddles and bridles here were as beautiful as the horses, the leather tooled, the metal parts gleaming silvery gold. There were fancier versions still with bells and gems hanging from some of the racks, but Callum ignored those and directed us toward the plainer ones, directing each of us to a specific saddle and bridle.

The scent of leather partially blocked out the strange horse scent as we carried everything back out to the main aisle between the stalls. Callum gestured again and five of the stall doors swung open without any further intervention.

The first horse to emerge was large and mostly black, though it was a black that reflected more colors than a black horse should. The beast stamped a foot, drawing a spark of light from the cobbles, and then whickered imperiously at Callum.

"None of that nonsense," Callum said. "Come here." The horse tossed his head and stamped again, but then did as he was told. Callum rubbed his ears and the horse nudged at his pockets searching for treats like a dog.

Once the black had settled, four more horses walked out of their stalls and stood waiting, their odd eyes fixed on Callum.

He just patted the black's neck and then waved us closer. "Watch me do this and then I'll help you one at a time so you can get acquainted with your horse before we set off."

It didn't take Callum long to saddle the stallion—I assumed the big black creature was a stallion—and loop the reins loosely over its neck, telling it to wait.

That earned him an impatient hoof stamp, but the black stayed put. More obedient than his master in canine form, that was for sure.

Callum paired us with the other horses, helping us put the saddles and bridles on. The horse he gave me was, to my relief, quite a bit smaller than the stallion, and a pale, dappled gray sheened with rainbow shades of pale pink, purple, blue, and yellow.

"Her name is Daima. That means dragonfly, or close enough to it," Callum said. "You can pet her, she won't bite."

I put my hand on her neck, part of me still struggling to accept that she was real. I'd seen similar horses in games, fanciful creatures like unicorns or pegasi, but this was a living, breathing animal. Her skin was warm under my palm, and she made little pleased-sounding huffs as I scratched her neck tentatively.

Aubrey looked delighted with her horse, a deeper gray with a mane closer to true silver. Zee's horse was a dark rich brown with a golden streak down its nose and Damon's was a deep blood red. Not a color any human-bred horse had ever been. Particularly not with bright green eyes.

Callum instructed me on how to hold the reins to lead Daima. The others didn't need instructions. We walked out through the far door of the stables into a yard beyond. Daima was perfectly behaved, moving when I moved and stopping when I stopped. Reassuring, but my heart still thumped with panic at the thought of actually having to ride her.

I was tall, but these animals were a lot bigger than me. And magical.

Gráinne was waiting for us in the yard, a pile of leather sacks at her feet.

Callum nodded to her. "Get what you needed?"

"Of course." Gráinne bent and sorted the sacks into two distinct piles, one that looked like waterskins and the others holding food most likely.

"Fasten those on to Tor, and we'll get going," Callum said.

She rolled her eyes. I'd never had a sibling, but recognized an annoyed sister when I saw one. "I know what I'm doing."

Callum ignored the eye roll. "You didn't have any trouble in the kitchen?"

"No, no one saw me. We're fine." She jerked her head back to the stable, "What about Ruagh? Did he hear?"

"He woke up, but he didn't come to see what I was doing or who was with me," Callum said.

"Well then," Gráinne said, "we'd best get started. Do you want to ride or run?"

In the end, Callum rode while Gráinne ran ahead. Aubrey's slightly alarmed face, when Gráinne had first shimmered into her wolf-dog form, was enough to make me feel better about my nerves. She might have ridden, but I, at least, had some experience with the s'ealg oiche.

But my temporary smugness only lasted until Callum boosted me into the saddle, and we started to move.

At first, we wound our way carefully through the dark. The horses seemed to have no trouble seeing. Gráinne, who was big and black like her brother in her wolfish form, trotted some distance ahead, melding into the shadows with ease. We followed a paved road until we reached a gate in a fence made of pale metal twisted into a thousand shapes of trees and flowers and strange creatures, stretching in either direction as far as the eye could see. I could only tell where the gate began and ended because two tall pillars topped with a flame icon marked its boundaries.

I was too focused on staying in the saddle to appreciate the artistry. The rocking, swaying motion of the horse beneath me, even though Daima's gait seemed smooth, was unfamiliar, and my hands on the reins were already sweaty. Not that I was willing to let go to wipe them off. I didn't yet trust that I wouldn't plummet off Daima like a greased stone.

"Everything okay?" Damon asked. He was riding beside me, looking perfectly at home in the saddle. Annoying.

"Well, I'm riding a magical horse through a mystical realm in the middle of the night," I said. "So, you tell me."

He smiled reassuringly. "Hopefully, we won't be here long."

I hoped so too. I was fit these days, but as Cassandra was fond of telling me, learning new things used new muscles, and I could already tell that riding was going to put a strain on my thighs, not to mention wreak havoc on my butt.

Callum halted once we were all through the gate, and it

swung shut behind us. "All right. Are we ready to move a little faster?"

I bit off the "no" that rose instinctively in my throat and tried to look relaxed. Terrified or not, clueless or not, I'd keep up if humanly possible.

Callum caught my eye and smiled encouragingly. "You won't fall, Maggie. Trust me. The ways are safe."

That was the crux of it, wasn't it? I was trusting my safety entirely to Callum's goodwill at this point, not to mention the safety of the man I loved, and my good friend. And I had reasons not to trust Callum totally. But we'd made the choice to come here, and now I had to go with it.

"All right," I said, forcing myself to smile back.

Callum moved his stallion back into the lead, focused on the path ahead rather than on us. Clearly he had no concerns that the other horses wouldn't follow.

A soft howl came from the darkness in front of him, and I caught a glimpse of Gráinne springing into a run just before Callum's stallion took off after her. Daima went from still to running in one easy motion, keeping her spot not far behind Callum with ease. I spent a few panicked minutes convinced I was about to fall as the world to either side blurred as we ran. I wasn't sure if it was just the speed of the horses or whether it was an effect of the ways—or if we'd even entered the ways— but it was disconcerting, either way.

I started to relax a little when I realized I wasn't jolting in the saddle with each stride Daima took. I still didn't feel exactly comfortable, but I got the feeling it would take an effort of will to actually fall. The path ahead glowed faintly enough that I could see a little of where we were going, even though what loomed on either side of the road, which seemed to be open grasslands of some sort, was mostly cloaked in the darkness.

Above us, the sky glittered with stars, the moon hanging large and full, seemingly closer than it was in the human world. I wasn't sure how long we ran for. The horses seemed to enjoy it, occasionally blowing out a breath or nickering, but none of them ever faltered or even seemed to be breathing hard. They just ran through the blurred landscape, hooves drumming softly on the path, following Callum and Tor. Eventually, Callum slowed, and our mounts followed suit.

We walked on a little farther, and then Callum directed his stallion off the road, heading for a line of trees. We passed through the trees and stepped into a familiar-looking glade. I couldn't have sworn it was exactly the same one as where we trained with Cerridwen, but it was remarkably similar, other than the fact that the leaves of the trees were glimmering in the darkness, giving off a soft silvery-green glow.

"We'll take a break here," Callum said. "Drink some water, stretch your legs. I don't want you all unable to walk on the other side."

"No, that would be unfortunate," Gráinne said, stepping out of the trees in her human form. Unlike the horses, she was breathing a little heavily. But other than that, she showed no signs of just having run God only knew how far. She came up to each of us, moving around the horses, patting noses, and offering them something from the flat of her hand.

The horses weren't even sweating and, once we'd all dismounted, drifted around the edges of the glade, snatching at the grass. I took a couple of steps, realized that I was definitely already starting to stiffen up, and took the opportunity to begin a cycle of Cerridwen's stretches.

Gráinne came over to me. "Anything too sore? I can ease it if you have need. I am better at healing than my brother."

"I appreciate the offer, but no, thank you," I said. "At the moment, I'm fine."

She nodded. "Very well. But when we break again, it would probably be best if you let one of us help you a little. Riding works muscles that you aren't used to."

"Yeah, I've noticed that. So I'll probably take you up on

that offer." I looked around. "How much farther until we reach the boundary?"

"Another hour, I would imagine, or a little more. And from there, crossing Morgain's territory should be about the same. After that, we will see."

Right. Because beyond Morgain's lands were the territories that weren't so friendly.

I swallowed, and must have looked nervous because Gráinne reached out to pat my arm. "Do not worry. All will be well."

Easy for her to say.

Chapter Fifteen

I FINISHED STRETCHING, trying, with limited success, to ignore the spikes in my pulse every time the trees rustled behind me. Being in the realm at night just increased the level of weirdness. Maybe the blurry too-fast-to-see-riding thing wasn't so bad after all. Better than the knowledge that almost anything I could imagine might be lurking in the dark, just waiting for a chance to attack.

But Callum hadn't set any wards that I could sense, so I had to trust that he knew what he was doing. We were still in Cerridwen's territory, after all.

I turned my back on the tree line. It probably wouldn't make any difference if I saw something. I had to assume most Fae could move faster than me. My watch told me thirty minutes had elapsed since we'd entered the realm. Hopefully it was right. Gráinne had said we'd traveled for an hour. But that was the point of taking the ways.

Callum stood with Aubrey and Zee in the middle of the clearing. Gráinne stood off to their right, near Tor, stroking his nose. And Damon was on the far side of the clearing, also stretching. And, from his focused expression, taking mental notes about everything he was seeing. Probably squirreling away details to use in future games. Or, like me, worrying about what was out there in the dark.

I didn't want to distract him, so I joined Gráinne. "Do the horses need anything? Food? Or water?" That was the one thing I remembered from games involving horses. They required lots of attention.

Tor's head turned toward me, his dark eyes alert, ears pricking forward. Did he understand what I said? He was, after all, a Fae horse. In a game, he'd probably join us and spout some pearl of wisdom about the quest we were about to undertake. But, if he could talk, he wasn't choosing to talk to me.

"They're well for now," Gráinne said. She nodded toward the far side of the glade where the path stretched into the darkness. "There's a stream over there, so we'll let them drink once they've cooled more. But they can run for many hours with no ill effects. Much longer than one of your horses. They like it, in fact, don't you?" she said to Tor, reaching up to scratch his ear. He snorted and bobbed his head, as though in agreement, and she laughed. "They won't say no to a treat, though. Come with me."

She led me over to the pile of leather pouches she'd removed when she'd changed back from wolf dog form, grabbing one from the top of the pile. She unfastened the flap, extracted some lumps of something sticky-looking and held them out to me.

"Honey," she said, "from the Lady's bees. It will sustain them. You could try one yourself." I stared at the yellow-brown lump. It smelled like honey, richly sweet. Probably delicious. But I wasn't quite ready to sample Fae food, even if it looked harmless. "Thanks," I said. "I'll give one to Daima."

She seemed satisfied with that and tipped a couple of the lumps into my hand. "Are you enjoying the ride?"

"It's a frantic gallop through fai—er, a magical realm—

heading toward territories where there are Fae who might hate me. I'm not sure enjoyment is the correct term."

She shot me a feral grin that reminded me of Callum at his most annoying. "It's an adventure."

"I think your idea of fun and adventure might be different from mine."

"Quite possibly, given you are human, and I am not." She fed Tor one of the honey lumps. "But my brother speaks highly of you, so perhaps you will find your adventurous spirit in here." She nodded at the horses. "We will slow down a little as we approach the border, so you will see more of the Lady's territory. It's a pity Callum is choosing to travel in darkness, it hides too much of the land and its treasures."

I nodded, not wanting to tell her that I was perfectly happy not to encounter the treasures—or terrors—of the realm up close and personal anytime soon. The sense of magic still pressed around me, stronger again now that we weren't moving so fast. It was taking all of my training not to let it distract me. If I let my attention stray and let it sneak under my defenses, I'd end up half-drunk with power. And be useless if anything happened. I strengthened my grips on my shields.

"You feel it, don't you?" she asked, gesturing at the air. "The realm. The power."

"I can feel the magic, yes."

Her eyes lit with curiosity. "What does it feel like?"

"Like I'm trying to swim through an ocean that wants to pull me under," I admitted.

"I can see how that might be." She patted my arm in what was probably intended to be a comforting gesture. "But it appears that so far, you can swim without drowning. So just keep doing that."

She looked back at Aubrey and Zee, talking to Callum. Zee's posture was alert, but neither of them looked particularly concerned. "And they are swimming, too. You should check on your Damon, perhaps. Humans feel it differently."

Crap. I hadn't thought of that. Things had moved fast back at the armory, and I'd been too intent on keeping up, to think about preparing Damon for what he was about to experience.

I strolled over to Daima and gave her one of the lumps, which she gobbled gratefully before returning to the grass, clearly not that interested in my presence. And then I took the other over to Damon who had finished his stretches and was standing by his horse.

"What's this?" he asked when I offered it to him.

"A treat for your noble steed," I said, smiling.

The dark red horse looked at me and ambled over with his neck outstretched as though he already smelled the honey. He snuffled the lump out of my palm, his soft lips tickling my skin. I patted his nose tentatively.

"Not so bad, are they?" Damon said, smiling at me.

"They're beautiful," I said. "I'm not sure whether good or bad comes into it." I loosened my shields a fraction to check his aura. It was a steady bright blue though it seemed to shift and stretch more than usual. I chalked that up to the realm. "How are you feeling?"

"A bit sore," he admitted. He swept his arm at the trees. "But this is amazing, so it's hard to worry about the state of my quads."

I looked around the darkened glade. It was beautiful. Even more so under moonlight than it was during the day. And probably more so to someone who hadn't spent time in the realm before.

"Is it like this when you train here?" Damon asked.

"Well, usually it's daytime," I said. "Cerridwen trains us in the forest quite often, but it doesn't look like this," I said, pointing at the nearest branch of glowing leaves. "In daylight, you can't see all of that."

We'd had a few training sessions where she had changed the appearance of the glade to night, but during those I'd been too busy fighting to notice much about what was happening around me. Damon, on the other hand, kept glancing around, looking slightly dazzled.

I stepped closer. "You'll tell me if you feel strange?"

"Strange how?" he asked.

"Intoxicated, I guess. Or, you know, if you get a sudden urge to throw off your clothes and dance under the moonlight." I put my hand on his chest. I couldn't feel the pendants he wore under his body armor. And I didn't know if its protection would be enough. So I needed to be the one who kept him safe. "In here, it's safer to think first and act second."

He put his hand over mine, blue eyes serious, as he gazed at me. "I'm aware. It's alright. I don't feel any need to run off into the woods and find a sexy nymph."

"Good," I said, "Because she'd have to fight me for you." He laughed at that, the sound loud in the relative quiet. The others turned their heads toward us.

"Come here, nymph," he said, and bent to kiss me.

When we turned back, Callum was shaking his head. "Humans," he muttered. Gráinne, however, looked approving.

Zee came over to join us, carrying an insulated flask and a couple of small plastic cups. "Tea?" he asked, offering a cup.

"Let me guess," I said, "Cassandra?"

Zee nodded and shrugged. "She said it would be helpful."

In that case, for once, I wouldn't complain about drinking tea. In the realm, I was willing to take any advantage I could get.

He opened the flask and poured the tea when I held out my cup. I sniffed tentatively, smelling a familiar grassy undertone. "Well, here goes nothing," I said, and chugged mine back. As Cassandra's teas went, it wasn't too terrible, and I swallowed and handed the small cup back to Zee. He refilled it for Damon.

"How are you feeling?" I asked Zee.

He shrugged. "So far, so good." He glanced at the trees. "I'd forgotten the feel of the place. It's stronger out here."

"Yes," I agreed. "I think when we're with Cerridwen, she suppresses it a little to make it easier for us." But Callum and Gráinne clearly weren't doing whatever she did. Or maybe they couldn't, because it was her territory, not theirs.

"That might be it," Zee agreed, eyeing Damon. "But we should be on the lookout, keep an eye on each other."

"I already told Maggie I'm not feeling any desire to run into the woods," Damon said.

"Good," Zee said. "That would be jagged up."

"We're in Cerridwen's territory. This part should be safe, shouldn't it?" Damon asked.

"Even in Cerridwen's territory, I imagine there are things that might not be so friendly," I said.

"Better to ignore the pretty and act like you're hacking your way through the Amazon with snakes and spiders and other critters lurking that could take you down with one bite," Zee added.

Damon's mouth turned down briefly. "You two take all the fun out of things."

"Just trying to keep you alive, buddy," I said, and he laughed.

From the tree line above us, as though to prove my point, came a chirping sort of trill. I looked up, saw a pair of glowing golden eyes, and stumbled back in alarm, dragging Damon away. "Watch out!"

Gráinne bounded over in a few quick strides. "What's the matter?"

I pointed at the tree, heart hammering. The eyes were still visible about three feet above my head.

"Oh, that's nothing to worry about," Gráinne said reassuringly. "Watch." She made a clicking sound with her tongue, and before I could protest, a smoky-black, feline-like creature sprang from the tree, landing with a thump on the saddle of Damon's horse. Where it stayed, regarding us curiously. It wasn't quite a cat; it was too big, for a start, its muzzle was slightly more foxlike, and there were not one but two luxuriantly fluffy tails twining around its legs. "What is that?" I asked, warily.

"A *nixling*. A night cat," She moved closer to the horse and extended her hand. The cat regarded her warily for a few long seconds, then deigned to sniff it. Perhaps it was more catlike than foxlike, after all.

"Hello, little hunter. Seen anything of interest?" The nixling tilted its head and chirped a series of sounds that were clearly in response to her question.

"Good. That's what we like to hear," Gráinne replied gravely.

The creature looked around the glade and then chirped again, the sound clearly curious.

"Something for the Lady," Gráinne said. "But nothing that should trouble you or your kind."

Another trilling chirrup.

"No, you will just have to leave with that curiosity of yours unsatisfied."

The cat creature bared its teeth at her, ears flattening briefly.

"Don't be impolite," Callum said to it as he came to join use. He also extended his fingers toward the cat, "Speaking of nothing troubling, we must be on our way."

The nixling butted its head against his fingers, trilling again.

"Good hunting," Callum said. It leaped and scrabbled up the bark, blending back into the darkness of the leaves as though it hadn't been there, leaving me wondering all over again what else might be watching us from the shadows.

I lost track of time again as we rode on. I had more confidence that I wouldn't fall, as Daima skimmed over the road at an uncanny pace, but I still wasn't willing to let go of the reins to check my watch. The darkened fields of Cerridwen's territory blurred past as we raced through the night. Unlike our first ride, where I'd been too concerned with falling to care much about my surroundings, now that I'd met the nixling, uneasiness prickled at the nape of my neck. The blur was no longer comforting, instead it just seemed like something that was hiding anything lurking in the night—so it could sneak up on us.

I needed to ask Callum or Gráinne to explain more about how the ways worked and whether they offered us any additional protection. I couldn't quite shake the sense of threat, no matter how I tried. The last time I'd felt this sort of creeping dread had been in the game with the demon.

After a while, my butt began to ache with each repetitive pound of Daima's hooves on the road. My thighs were also starting to feel like they were on fire. I'd definitely have to take Gráinne up on her offer of healing when we stopped.

Eventually, we began to slow. I straightened in the saddle, glancing round and trying to see what terrain we were dealing with. We'd passed through a few more bands of forests in our flight, but now we were back in a long rolling open plain, the moonlight above us illuminated fields stretching out to rolling hills.

Damon moved his horse into place beside mine as Gráinne began to slow her horse and the others followed the stallion's example.

"Are we stopping again?" Damon asked, half shouting.

"Your guess is as good as mine." Despite my screaming muscles, I was all too aware of time ticking away.

But the decision wasn't mine to make. Ahead, Gráinne pulled the stallion to a halt and then swung down.

Callum, who had been pacing ahead in his animal form,

trotted back, and then changed forms, looking unbothered by the fact he'd been running for an hour or more. He beckoned us all to bring our horses closer, and we dismounted with various degrees of ease.

"We're approaching the border," he said. "When we get to the stone, we'll take you across in two groups. It's easier that way."

"Whose territory are we crossing to?" Aubrey asked.

Callum glanced back at the road. "Lady Morgain's. It shouldn't be any trouble. Once we're there, it should be a short ride across to the next boundary." He sounded confident.

I tried to tell myself I had no need to be nervous when he wasn't. Still, I stretched surreptitiously and checked all my weapons as I waited beside Daima. We took a few minutes to drink, Gráinne came and blasted each of us with a shot of icy power that was only a little less unpleasant than Cerridwen's brand of healing, and then we remounted. This time, Gráinne led us at a walk for fifteen minutes or so until the path began to blur in a different way, the air around us turning to an impenetrable mist, so only the path and some sort of clearing ahead were visible.

We dismounted once more and began to lead the horses. As we got closer, I saw the mist surrounded the clearing, blocking any view of what lay beyond. The small round space was empty except for a marble column, about waist high and a foot wide, that seemed to sprout from the ground in its center. The top was angled, as though someone had taken a neat slice through the marble, and inlaid with a golden metal plaque.

"That's the boundary stone," Callum said.

I'd figured out that much. I was close enough to make out symbols etched into the metal in graceful characters of some kind. Fae, I assumed. But while I spoke a few words, I couldn't read it.

Callum barely glanced at the symbols before he turned back to us. "Maggie, I'll take you and Damon through first, and Gráinne can follow with Aubrey and Zee."

I took a deep breath and nodded. Moving through Cerridwen's territory was disconcerting but leaving it for a territory controlled by a Fae whose motivations I knew nothing about was flat-out terrifying. But we needed to keep moving.

"Stay close," Callum said. Damon and I shuffled closer, our horses crowded behind us until we were only an arm's length from the pillar. Callum reached out and touched the plaque, and suddenly the mist swirled around us, sparkling with a thousand colors before opening in front of us.

Callum lifted his hand. "Follow me."

We stepped somewhat disconcertingly from night to dawn in the space of a few strides.

Damon bit back a sound of surprise, but Callum didn't react, just kept walking until we and the horses were clear of the mist.

I started to slow, but Callum urged us on. "A bit farther. We have to leave space for the others to cross." He moved on another twenty feet or so from the mist, which on this side, had lost the colors and looked as it had before, pale gray and opaque and obscuring what we'd left behind. I waited nervously, straining to catch sight of the others.

It didn't take long for them to emerge. Aubrey and Zee looked as startled as Damon had at the change to morning, but they recovered quickly and followed Gráinne to join us. The mist closed up, leaving no glimpse of the clearing.

So that was it. We'd left Cerridwen's territory. Now I really had to pay attention. I scanned the surrounding area, waiting for Callum to tell us what our next move was.

Morgain's territory seemed to be more woodland than plains. Mid-sized trees with widespread branches dotted swathes of vibrant green grass, their leaves startling shades of green and blue and yellow. In the distance they grew closer and taller, forming a massive forest that rolled on for miles toward a range of towering mountains. The snow on the peaks was tinted pink and purple from the rising sun.

As a panorama, it was glorious, more spectacular than anything I'd seen in real life. I doubted even Damon's most talented designers could come up with a vista so beautiful.

Not a game, I reminded myself for the thousandth time. Damon was squinting toward the mountains, one hand shading his eyes, once again seemingly cataloging everything he was seeing.

I nudged him with my free hand. "Not a game," I muttered. "Pay attention."

He smiled sheepishly. "It's glorious."

"It's potentially deadly. Don't get distracted." He could take mental notes for game design after we were safely back in our world.

Callum, who'd been conferring quietly with Gráinne, looked up at that, eyes narrowed. "So far, so good."

Gráinne nodded. "Yes. So we should move on. Do you want to take point or shall I?"

His hand strayed to the sword at his hip. "You ride and we'll switch at the next border."

He passed her the reins of the stallion, but before she could mount, the air about ten feet away from us shimmered and a door carved from silver-veined marble appeared. It swung open, and a tall woman dressed in dark green leathers, similar to the black ones Gráinne and Callum wore, walked through. She strode across the grass, stopping about five feet away from where we all stood. She had long blonde hair pinned back from her face and eyes almost as dark a green as her clothing, huge and round in her pearl-pale skin. But she stood like the warrior she so clearly was, her expression confident if not downright arrogant.

Callum muttered something under his breath that didn't sound polite or happy.

The blonde's eyebrow lifted. "My mistress sends greetings," she said in a lilting voice. It sounded friendly, but she had one hand on her right hip. Helpfully close to the silver hilt of the sword that rested there.

Callum grimaced, but then bowed politely. "And greetings I return on behalf of my Lady and ourselves. We will not be long in her land. We are merely moving across to the next border stone."

The blonde looked amused. "My mistress will speak to you first."

Chapter Sixteen

WHAT THE HELL? My stomach dropped like a stone. We couldn't afford any delays. Morgain's was supposed to be the easy territory.

Callum squared his shoulders, his focus not shifting from the woman in green. "My apologies to Lady Morgain, but we need to make haste. We will not be in her lands long."

Her expression cooled a little. "That is as may be, but she wishes to speak to you. And the ways here will not open for you until she permits. Nor will the border stones."

Fuck. So much for an easy territory. What was going on? And how were we going to get across the other territories if they could all just block us?

Gráinne and Callum exchanged a wary look. "The matter we are pursuing is running to a tight timeline." Callum said.

That earned him a shrug from the blonde. "Then let us not tarry, and my mistress will not keep you long."

"Very well," Callum said. "We will pay our respects and be on our way."

"Wait," Damon said, stepping forward. "We need to keep moving."

"We can't cross the territory without the permission of

Lady Morgain," Callum said. "Not now that she's expressly denied us."

Damon scowled. "Can't we just go back and find another way?"

Callum's eyes flashed annoyance, though he kept his face calm. "Unlikely. Morgain may have closed that way as well. Besides, the next closest territory is more dangerous and will take us longer to cross."

"Longer than whatever this is?" Damon asked, nodding at the blonde. His voice was tight. "We can't afford to waste time."

"I can take care of that once we're back in the ways, but the fastest way will just be to see what the lady wants. She is an ally, so we should not be delayed too long," Callum responded, keeping his gaze more on the waiting woman than Damon. Not entirely sure where we stood, it seemed. Or if she was friend or foe.

"Your lady grows fonder of humans it seems," she said, flicking one of her braids back over her shoulder. She said it as a human might say "oh, you're starting to like dogs, now.".

"She seeks allies who can help us on our mission and keep the realm safe," Callum corrected. "As she always has. And your Lady has supported her in this, has she not?"

The woman in green shrugged. "Yes, but the Lady also listens to the realm and to what the fates tell her."

Gráinne's expression, I thought, shifted a few degrees more wary at that pronouncement, but she moved to stand beside her brother. "Very well, we will pay our respects. But we need a guarantee of safe passage. These humans are under Lady Cerridwen's protection and cannot be harmed."

That was perhaps overstating things, given Cerridwen didn't know we were here. Hopefully the blonde didn't know that.

She bowed her head. "Lady Morgain is aware. Come

along." She turned and began to walk back to the door, obviously expecting to be followed.

"That wasn't exactly a promise not to harm us," I said silently to Callum.

"No, but I doubt she will. Morgain and our Lady have long worked together." Callum replied. *"Besides, we need the border stone to work, so we have no choice."*

Perfect. The very first step we had taken out of safe territory and things had already gone wrong. I wanted to grab Damon and flee back to Cerridwen's territory and then back home. But I didn't think I'd convince him to leave. Not yet. I swallowed against the fear, trying not to let it show on my face.

Callum nodded, mouth turned down, and Gráinne began to walk. Tor moved with her, his bridle jingling faintly in the morning air.

The blonde turned back at the sound. "You can leave your steeds here. They will be unharmed. There is food aplenty." She waved a hand, and an enclosure seemingly made from golden vines sprang up about ten feet to the right of where we stood, a gap just wide enough to walk a horse through in one end.

"I thought Fae horses stayed where you told them to," I said.

Gráinne shot me a warning look. "The enclosure will be warded to protect them. They can defend themselves to a certain extent, but it is a gesture of good faith to provide additional defenses."

Wouldn't it be a gesture of good faith just to let us go? I bit back the words. If Callum and Gráinne both thought it pointless to argue, it was pointless. We were going to have to do things Morgain's way.

I suppressed a shiver, remembering her shifting, blurring face. Even though Lords Padran and Usuriel had been more openly hostile, I had found her more unsettling than them, if only because she had looked as though she could see straight through me into my soul.

Of the four Fae Elders we'd met, she was the one we'd found most about in the Archives. The one who'd made it into human myths and legends. Some of the material had linked her to Morgan le Fay of the Arthurian tales, a wielder of powerful magic who couldn't be trusted. Others to the Morrigan, avatar of war and fate, predictor of doom or victory. Ralph had unearthed more references to her as a mystic or seer. Whichever was true, I wasn't exactly enthusiastic about meeting her again.

Callum and Gráinne walked the horses into the enclosure and removed their saddles and bridles, arranging those on the fence of vines. When they emerged, the blonde gestured and the gap closed.

"There, they will be perfectly safe," she said. "Let us make haste." She began to walk and this time Callum and Gráinne followed. The sky had lightened but, as I glanced back, the mist still seemed solid behind us. No way back. Only forward. I sighed and jogged to catch up.

Callum glanced at me when I reached them. "Best not to get separated here." His tone was…cautious.

The blonde shot him a glance back over a shoulder with a half-smile. "So wary, wolf."

"My kind have learned to be wary. It serves us in good stead."

"Perhaps. But you have asked for my Lady's good faith, so you must offer it in return."

If a supposed ally of Cerridwen's ordering us into a meeting when we had no time to spare was good faith, then what was bad? I slid my hand to my sword.

Callum didn't say anything else, but his jaw was tight as he stalked after our escort. At least in the sunlight we should see anything approaching. Unless, of course, something effectively stepped out of thin air as she had.

In less time than it should have taken, we reached the edge of the forest. I slowed instinctively, not wanting to set foot in an unknown fairy wood. But instead of breaching the tree line, the blonde stopped and then held out her hands, making a series of graceful gestures. The same silver-veined marble door appeared in front of her, shimmering prettily in the dawn light and buzzing with magic that felt similar, but not exactly the same, as the door to the realm in Cerridwen's territory.

"This way," she said and swung the door inward.

Damon slipped his hand through mine. We stepped from the outdoors into a hall, nearly as imposing as the one where the council had met, though on a slightly smaller scale. It was decorated in shifting pearl shades that echoed the dawn outside, if the dawn was veiled in the faintest of mists. Beautiful but also unsettling, because my eyes felt like I couldn't quite focus on any particular detail.

"Wait here a moment," the blonde woman said. "I will go through and tell my Lady that you are here."

Callum waved her on a little impatiently, as though eager to have this thing done with.

I understood how he felt. I sidled over to Aubrey, half dragging Damon with me.

"Any idea what's going on?" I asked in a low tone.

Her mouth twisted. "Some sort of Fae power play, perhaps. Flexing her strength to prove a point to Cerridwen. Or else the Lady Morgain wants something from us."

I swore in my head. Dammit. I should have tried harder to convince Damon to let his team do their thing and wait for the suborbital.

Our escort came back through the door. Her clothes had shifted from hunting leathers to a far more formal gown made of deep green velvet and embroidered in shimmering silks in a pattern of vines and leaves that twined around her arms and across her chest and shoulders to disappear behind her back. "Lady Morgain will see you now," she announced.

Lucky us. But I followed the others through. I thought we would be going somewhere like Cerridwen's study, but instead we filed into another hall where two long tables ran nearly the entire length of either side of the room. The chairs were filled with Fae who were busily eating breakfast or whatever they called their morning meal. Green-clad servants moved around the tables carrying crystal pitchers filled with variously colored liquids, and silver platters of food.

Enticing smells wafted from every direction, and my stomach gurgled in response. But I was determined not to eat anything prepared by Morgain or her…clan…or whatever the correct term for them was. Not until I had some reassurances about her intentions.

A third table sat across the head of the room. Morgain had the middle seat with Fae on each side of her. Two women, three men. All of them were cut from the same blonde-haired, green-clad mold as our escort.

Our blonde led us up the aisle between the two tables, and the sounds of all the voices lowered to murmurs as we passed, made me wish I'd learned more Fae. None of it made any sense to me and if Zee or Aubrey understood, they gave no sign of it. Probably wise. Damon had defaulted to his impassive CEO face, no hint of his feelings allowed to show. Heads turned to follow our progress toward Morgain, the room gradually falling silent as we reached her.

Our blonde friend bowed briefly and moved to stand behind Morgain in the same position Callum had taken behind Cerridwen at the council.

So. She was some sort of trusted advisor and one who I had to assume was well able to protect Morgain should she be called on to do so.

Damon moved closer to me as Callum stepped forward.

"Lady Morgain," he said with an elegant bow. "Health and peace on you and your lands."

"Lord Duinne," Morgain said.

I only just stopped my mouth from gaping. Callum was a Lord? Of what, exactly? Ugh. When we got back, I was going to start spending even more time in the Archives. Sleep was for the weak. But Callum's title wasn't exactly the most pressing issue right now, so I dragged my attention back to the conversation.

"Does your mistress know why you are here?" Morgain asked, her face blurring to the old woman. "She sent no word of you crossing my territory."

"We who hunt the dark do not always provide notice in advance, Lady," Callum said, his tone polite but tense.

Morgain nodded. "But you do not appear to be hunting the dark; you are escorting humans." She looked at me. "Unless you were wrong at the council, wolf, and these humans are connected to the dark?"

I sucked in a breath. The last thing we needed was for Morgain to decide Lord Padran was right about me. Damon moved fractionally closer, clearly ready to intercede.

"No, Lady. Quite the opposite. We are escorting them to help them reach a human who is assisting the dark, so they can stop him. They are on our side. We need to move swiftly, or he may avoid capture. Walking the ways is our chance to get ahead of him in the human realm," Callum said.

"I see," she said, sounding skeptical. "Still, now that you are here, you should break your fast, and then continue on your way refreshed."

Callum and Gráinne glanced at each other.

"What's going on?" I asked Callum. He flicked a hand at me in one of the signs we used in our training, the one that meant "be quiet".

Did he mean "don't distract me" or "don't talk because others might hear?"

Gah. I hated not knowing. My muscles tensed, ready to spring into action if needed. What game was Morgain playing?

"We have not long eaten," Callum said. "We started on our journey just recently."

"The ways burn through your power, though," Morgain said. "You should take some refreshment." She looked past him to me, her face young again if you ignored the depth of her gaze that made the hairs on my neck stand up. "Your humans need not be concerned that I am trying to trap them here with tricks." She wrinkled her nose as though the very concept was insulting. "Their tales of such things are misleading."

From what I'd read in the Archives, that wasn't strictly true. There were cases of people who had gone missing in the realm and never reappeared. Or who had been found years later, insisting that they'd merely spent a night or two. It wasn't common, particularly not since the agreement with the Fae, but the lore was similar in enough countries to suggest that it definitely happened. And I, for one, was not prepared to waste my life away in the realm.

But annoying Morgain might just make her stretch the encounter out even longer.

Callum was clearly thinking along the same lines. "Tea would be welcome. Riding can be thirsty work, even in the ways." It was his charming voice. Whether it worked on Fae like Morgain was anyone's guess.

Morgain nodded. "Very well. But a word, if you don't mind, Lord Duinne."

She didn't sound particularly charmed. And it wasn't as though he could refuse. Not without starting some sort of fight that we were unlikely to win. We were surrounded by her people.

Morgain rose from her chair, beckoning at Callum. As she turned, one of the servants—a young woman—who had been approaching with a crystal pitcher of some clear liquid, had to jump back quickly to avoid a collision. The liquid in her jug sloshed but didn't spill.

"My apologies, Lady," she said, bowing her head.

Her accent, I realized with a start, was British. Aubrey stiffened. So she'd noticed, too.

The young woman had dark-blonde hair, braided back from her face. Her head lifted again from the bow as Morgain walked past her. She was pretty, but didn't have the unearthly beauty of a full Fae. The sunlight streaming through the windows played over her hair, revealing a pearly sheen to the color that was nothing human. Tanai, then. Her eyes were a more human shade of pale blue, but perhaps slightly larger than would be usual for a human. Pinky looked no different to any other human, but the tanai could take more after one parent than the other. Perhaps the woman favored her Fae side. She smiled apologetically, and I felt a moment of déjà vu, as though I knew her.

I searched my memory. But no. I didn't remember her. And she was striking enough to leave an impression.

Callum turned to us and said, "Enjoy the tea. I'll be back shortly." He stared meaningfully at Gráinne, though if they were talking the way he and I did, I couldn't hear. Gráinne nodded and his expression eased.

No doubt he'd given her instructions not to leave us alone to do dumb human things in a strange Fae territory.

Gráinne nodded again and Callum stalked off in Morgain's wake. The blonde who'd escorted us followed Callum.

Before there was any chance for me to ask Gráinne what the hell was going on, another servant approached and ushered us to the very end of the table on the right-hand side of the room, where there were now empty seats. Since they'd all been full when we walked in, I assumed some Fae had hastily vacated. Certainly, the ones remaining gave us curious looks as we sat. Two more servants produced delicate white China cups decorated in graceful vine patterns and poured steaming tea before backing away silently.

The other Fae resumed eating and talking, ignoring us.

Aubrey leaned toward Gráinne. "That girl with the jug, she's English," she said softly.

Gráinne shrugged. "Perhaps."

"Is she tanai?" I asked, leaning in, too. None of the Fae around us reacted.

"Hard to tell. I would hope so, given she's here in the realm." Aubrey looked unhappy. She hadn't touched her tea either.

"Is that normal? For a tanai to be a servant?" Zee asked, equally low voiced.

"It is an honor to serve one of the high families," Gráinne said with a shrug. "It would entirely depend on who her Fae parent is, and what status they hold."

Aubrey's face, while still calm, suggested that she wasn't entirely satisfied with this explanation. She twisted her ring and glanced in the young woman's direction.

I nudged her with my elbow. "Don't do anything rash."

Aubrey frowned. "I'd like to make sure she's here willingly. If she's English, she's in my jurisdiction, after all."

"Your concern is the witches, not tanai."

Tanai, if they hadn't split from their Fae family, weren't technically part of the Cestis's remit. Not unless they used their Fae magic against humans or witches.

"And if I was sure she was tanai, then I could rest easy." Aubrey nodded toward her. "But I can't tell by looking, can you?"

I shook my head. Her hair was an unusual shade, but that could just be the effect of sunlight here in Morgain's territory. Not proof she was tanai. She was too far away for me to sense if she was using magic and in the realm it would be hard for me to tell.

"If she's human, she's definitely my concern," Aubrey continued. "I need to know that she's here voluntarily. I'd like to talk to her."

Gráinne's eyes flared wide, and she shook her head once. "Drink your tea. We can't afford trouble."

Aubrey ignored her. I hid a grimace. On one hand, Aubrey was correct about her responsibilities. But, on the other hand, causing a scene would be dumb given where we currently were. But I doubted I'd be able to dissuade Aubrey from doing anything she considered her duty.

"Callum said to stay put," I said, to add weight to Gráinne's order. We didn't need trouble, we needed to get back to the ways.

"I can stay put and try to speak to her," Aubrey said, her mouth set.

She nodded toward the head table where the girl was pouring water for one of the Fae still seated there. Maybe she'd stay there. I didn't think Aubrey was ballsy enough to just waltz up and interrupt.

Unfortunately, the girl finished, looked at her pitcher, which even I could see was nearly empty and began walking back down the room toward us.

Aubrey pushed her chair back a little. "I just need to speak to her."

"Don't make a scene," Gráinne said. "It'll just draw attention you don't want."

"I'll just ask her where the bathroom is or something. I assume this place has a bathroom?"

"A refreshment chamber," Gráinne corrected. "It would be wiser to stay put. Once Callum returns, we need to be ready to make a quick exit."

"I can hardly ask her if she's here of her own free will around all these Fae," Aubrey said in an even lower voice. "If she's not, then they're likely the ones holding her here."

None of the Fae reacted to this. Callum's hearing was

exceptional, surely theirs was, too. The hairs on the back of my neck spiked with alarm. The whole situation could go bad fast. But Aubrey was right: this wasn't the place to ask a servant whether she was being held captive.

"If you're going to do it, you need to be fast." I nodded at the table where the girl was only a few feet away from us now.

One of the Fae had stopped her, and she was pouring water again. But when she stepped back, her jug was definitely empty. Hopefully that meant she'd have to leave the room to refill it. Unless, of course, it would just magically replenish itself as it would in half the fantasy games I'd ever played.

"I know what I'm doing," Aubrey retorted.

The girl moved toward us, and it seemed to me like she was studiously not looking at the group of humans, unlike some of the others who were casting carefully curious glances when they passed.

"Excuse me," Aubrey said, rising. "I would like to wash my hands. Is there a room where I might refresh myself?" She used her most clipped English accent, making it unmistakable where she was from.

The servant's pale blue eyes widened for a second, her mouth opening in surprise. But she merely bobbed her head and said, "Of course, my lady, I can escort you. This way."

Chapter Seventeen

"Crap," I muttered as they left the room. I surreptitiously checked my watch. Another half hour had passed. Not good. But I noted the time so I could track how long Aubrey was gone.

Zee tipped his chin at the door. "Want me to follow?"

"No, that will only draw attention," Gráinne said immediately.

"Aubrey knows what she's doing, doesn't she?" Damon asked. "She must deal with this kind of situation regularly."

I chewed my lip. Dealing with the Fae on Hampstead Heath was one thing. How often had Aubrey actually confronted the Fae alone in an unfamiliar, if not hostile, part of the realm? Not that Morgain was necessarily hostile, but she was being difficult. And Aubrey interfering with one of her servants was unlikely to improve her mood.

"I hope so. But I don't like this. Can't you follow them?" I asked Gráinne.

Gráinne shrugged. "I don't like it either, but no. It would be odd for me to wander around Morgain's house unescorted. I'm sworn to Cerridwen. It could be taken as an insult. That's the last thing we need."

I upgraded "crap" to "fuck" in my head, shifting in my chair, fighting my instinct to go after Aubrey. "All right. So we stay put and wait. She shouldn't be long." Hopefully, Callum would return soon. That would solve both problems, because we could find Aubrey and leave. Needing a distraction, I stared down at my tea, wondering if I should drink it to avoid drawing attention.

Gráinne was sipping hers, and she nodded at me over her silver-rimmed China cup. "It's safe, as far as I can tell."

Safe for her wasn't necessarily safe for us. Cassandra had taught me some basic ways to check for obvious drugs or poisons, but there were probably hundreds of things the Fae could access that she'd have no idea about. And checking required me to use magic, which, one, might draw attention and, two, I wasn't certain was wise when I was still doing my best to keep the effects of the realm's magic at bay. Since we'd stepped into Morgain's territory, it felt different, sinuous and slippery, sliding around me rather than just surrounding me. Perhaps that was a reflection of Morgain herself with her blurry, shifting face. It made sense—using the logic of the realm—that the magic might feel different in her territory.

I turned the cup on its delicate saucer, trying to decide what to do.

Damon and Zee were watching the Fae around us and hadn't touched their tea either.

"At least pretend, if you don't believe me," Gráinne said, her voice even quieter. "It's polite."

That brought the attention of both men back to her. Damon lifted his cup and put it to his lips, appearing to swallow. He might have been just faking it, which was probably the safer option, but I couldn't tell from where I sat. I lifted my own cup and did the same.

Cerridwen's silver bracelet on my wrist caught the sunlight, and I blinked, reminded that I had another resource at my disposal if this situation got out of hand.

I could use the charm embedded in my bracelet to summon Cerridwen, or at least alert her to trouble. But I wasn't sure that we were in trouble yet. Though it was tempting to just call for her and let her sort out Morgain. But that ran the risk of her pulling the plug on our using the ways.

Plus, there could be consequences if she just arrived in Morgain's territory without an invitation. They were allies, but that didn't necessarily mean they were friendly enough that they could move freely on each other's lands. I had no doubt Cerridwen was powerful enough to move across a boundary if she chose, but without a strong justification, the breach of protocol would just cause more problems if Morgain took offense.

I shook the bracelet back on my wrist, tucking it under my sleeve so I wouldn't be tempted, and then put my cup down, peeking at my watch again. Five minutes had passed. Aubrey still hadn't returned. "Should it be taking this long?" I asked Gráinne.

"Do you mean Callum or your friend?"

"Either," I said.

Her mouth quirked. "It's hard to rush Morgain. She can be difficult if she is seeing something that disturbs her. But Callum's dealt with her before, so he will talk his way clear soon enough." She didn't look concerned.

I *was* concerned. And I didn't like the sound of Morgain "seeing" anything to do with any of us. I looked back at the door. One of the green-clad servants standing near it was a young-looking blond man. He met my gaze and his eyes, which were brown perhaps, suddenly seemed solid black.

Like Usuriel's. I blinked and looked away. No one from Usuriel's territory would be serving Morgain, would they? I was just letting nerves get the better of me. Jumping at shadows that clearly didn't exist in this very sunny room.

Still, I couldn't shake my unease. I leaned closer to

Gráinne. "What can you tell me about Lord Usuriel's territory?"

She blinked. "Usuriel? We should not be passing through his lands. Why do you ask?"

"Just curious," I lied. "We don't have much information about him."

"No, he would see to that, I would imagine," Gráinne said. "He guards his lands and his Nichtkin. It serves him to stay in the shadows."

That didn't sound ominous at all. "Any reason a Nichtkin would be here?"

"There's no love lost between Morgain and Usuriel, so I doubt it," Gráinne said. Her forehead creased briefly. "Why do you ask?"

"There was a servant by the door. He looked like he had… eyes like Usuriel's."

"You've met Usuriel?"

"At the council meeting. Didn't Callum tell you about it?"

"I haven't seen him since then. I was on a mission, and he has been in your realm. Our Lady didn't tell us to be on the lookout for any threat from the Nichtkin."

Hopefully that meant Cerridwen wasn't concerned.

"Are you sure of what you saw?"

I twisted to look at the door, Gráinne doing the same. But the servant had vanished. Unease crept down my spine. I pushed back my chair. "I think I'll go look for Aubrey."

Zee, whose attention had drifted back to the group of Fae sitting closest to us, snapped his gaze back to me. "What's wrong?"

"I'm not sure exactly, but I saw someone who looked like, well, our blond friend from the council." I tried to avoid using Usuriel's name again. Names had power in the realm.

Zee's brows creased. "That seems unlikely."

"I agree. That's why I think I need to go check on Aubrey."

Gráinne was frowning again. "He is not an adversary to take lightly. And it would be difficult for him to place someone in Morgain's court without her knowledge."

Difficult wasn't the same as impossible. "Are you sure about that?"

She put down her tea, frowning. "I think you should remain here. Lady Morgain has this place well-guarded and well-warded. Aubrey will be fine."

I wanted to believe her, but my gut was telling me something was wrong. I twisted back to check the door again, "I think I should check. This doesn't feel right."

"This is an uneasy court, due to Lady Morgain's powers. You may just be catching a sense of how the fates converge here," Gráinne said, shaking her head.

What the hell did that mean? Nothing good. "Maybe, but I'd still like to make sure everything is okay," I said, lifting my chin. There was another servant standing near us, an even younger girl whose hair was both green and made of slender vines with actual leaves sprouting from them. No mistaking her for human. I beckoned to her, "Can you show me where I might refresh myself, please?"

"Of course, my lady," the girl said, bobbing a curtsy. "This way."

"Be careful," Gráinne hissed, and I nodded and followed the girl out of the hall. We turned to the left, and ahead, I thought I saw the blond youth at the far end of the long corridor, just turning around a corner, heading right.

"This way, my lady," the girl said, leading me in the same direction. I chafed at her slow gliding pace, itching to try to catch up. Finally I faked a noise of discomfort and said, "Do you mind if we move, er, faster? It is a matter of, er, urgency."

Her eyebrows lifted, and she flushed. Maybe the Fae didn't get caught short in matters of the bathroom, but I hoped she had gotten the message. Her pace picked up and I hid my sigh of relief. But by the time we took the same right turn, there was no sign of the blond man. No sign of the possibly-British tanai or Aubrey either. The girl gestured at a door on the right-hand side of the corridor about fifteen feet farther on.

"That is the refreshment chamber."

"Thank you," I said, hoping I looked pleased and relieved rather than worried.

"You are welcome, my lady. I will wait here to escort you back to the hall."

That was a relief. I didn't rate my chances of not getting lost in a Fae building if someone decided to play games and lead me astray. "I won't be long."

I walked to the door and pushed it open part way. I didn't want to interrupt Aubrey if she was talking to the tanai girl, but I couldn't linger, or *my* escort might get suspicious. I couldn't hear any voices inside, which seemed strange. Was it possible Aubrey had been shown to a different refreshment chamber? That seemed unlikely. The girl who'd brought me hadn't hesitated about where she should take me.

I slipped through the door and found myself in a room more like a small living room than a bathroom. Several low chairs covered in embroidered green silk were arranged around a small fireplace in the right-hand wall. Greenery and flowers were garlanded over the marble mantle, scenting the air with a sweetness that seemed to urge me to sit and rest.

Not an option. There was another door opposite the one I'd just come through. Beyond it was a larger room that was more like a bathroom. Four objects I recognized as very ornate basins were set into green-veined marble along the left-hand side of the room. Less familiar was the fact that they didn't have faucets. Instead, about a foot above them, the wall stepped, providing a channel for what looked to me like an entirely natural stream, complete with rocks and plants. Above each basin a rivulet like a tiny waterfall, sprayed down, providing a stream of constant water.

I stopped, impressed, then pulled myself together. Find

Aubrey first, admire Fae plumbing later. She definitely wasn't in this room, nor was the servant girl. The far end of the room ended in a green velvet curtain hanging from a golden vine. Green, it seemed, was Morgain's favorite color. I hesitated before touching it. "Aubrey? Are you in there?"

No answer.

That wasn't good. My apprehension back in the dining hall was rapidly turning to outright fear. "I'm coming in." I said, warningly. I yanked back the velvet curtain. No sign of Aubrey but the tanai girl lay unconscious on the floor.

"*Fuck.*" I dropped to my knees beside her, feeling frantically for a pulse. She was breathing, I realized, as I touched her neck, her chest rising and falling slowly. She was very pale, but not necessarily paler than she'd been in the hall. I patted her down quickly but found no weapons or anything resembling a human ID. She wore a bracelet woven of silver wire and dark green and black stones around one wrist but that told me nothing.

She didn't move a muscle as I searched her, nothing but the soft sound and movement of her breathing proving she was alive. This was a problem I didn't know how to solve. And I didn't have time to waste with Aubrey missing.

I stood and hurried back out, stopping only once to call Aubrey's name again in the room with the basins. No response. The woman who'd escorted me looked around, eyes startled, as I flung the outer door open.

"My lady?" she said.

"Fetch help," I hissed. "Someone's hurt."

She looked alarmed, but nodded. I didn't wait to see if she left but went back inside to watch the girl. I couldn't see any bruises or wounds. No blood. She just seemed to be fast asleep and unresponsive. It reminded me of Beanie Dude. And if she had been charmed asleep, then I didn't know how to wake her. So I just stayed watching, one hand on my dagger.

Aubrey wasn't here. The most likely explanation was

someone—or something—had taken her. And it could come back. I'd never thought I'd feel fond of Dockside, but waiting there alone, knowing I was relatively defenseless in the realm, was far scarier. I could take care of most things that might attack me back home. Here, I was…well, prey not predator.

My heart pounded, my palm slippery against the hilt of my dagger. I tried to stay calm, but my mind raced. Where the hell was Aubrey? She definitely wouldn't wander off on her own. And I definitely couldn't see her knocking someone out without provocation. And if there had been provocation, the tanai girl should show some sign of a scuffle, surely?

Which left me with only my first theory. She'd been taken. That thought made my pulse race faster, until I was almost light-headed.

It didn't take long before I heard the sound of footsteps and then Callum calling. "Maggie?"

"In here," I yelled, keeping my eyes on the girl. More foot-steps. Enough to let me know he wasn't alone. Callum barreled through the door, followed by the blonde who'd first escorted us to Morgain. She rushed past Callum when she saw the girl.

"What did you do to her?" she demanded, glaring fiercely.

I held up my hands. "I didn't do anything. I found her like this. Aubrey asked her to show her the refreshment chamber, that's all I know."

Callum was scanning the room. "Where is Aubrey?"

"Your guess is as good as mine. She wasn't here when I got here," I said.

The blonde's head snapped up, her green eyes flaring wide. "Your companion is missing?"

"Yes," I said. "She wanted to talk to this girl. She's English, right?"

The blonde paused, brow wrinkling. "I think so. I do not know the personal history of all our servants. She is tanai fol.

It is possible she is from anywhere in your realm." Her tone was semi-dismissive, which made my back bristle.

"Well, that means she's a human citizen," I pointed out.

"Hush," Callum said in my head. *"Arguing isn't helpful."*

"None of this is helpful," I snapped back, but outwardly I bit my lip.

"She's asleep. Like Fae asleep, I think. Can you check?," I asked Callum. He dropped to a crouch beside the girl and touched her forehead. His mouth went flat.

"She is bespelled," he said over his shoulder to the blonde. "This is not good."

"Who would do such a thing?" she asked. "There's no reason to attack one of our own."

I cleared my throat and both of them turned to me. "I thought I saw someone who looked like Lord Usuriel. Back in the hall."

An actual low growl escaped Callum's throat. "What? When? Describe him," he demanded.

"He was blond. And younger. He wore what all the servants are wearing. But his eyes were black. He looked right at me. I think he left the hall not long after Aubrey did.

Callum stiffened. "One of the Nichtkin?" he asked. He looked over his shoulder at the blonde. "What is one of the nicht doing here?"

"No Nichtkin serve in this territory. The Lady would not allow it." The blonde's eyes flared brighter green as she glared at me. "You must have been mistaken."

"His eyes were black," I insisted. "I saw Lord Usuriel at the council. His eyes were like that."

She slanted me a look that told me she doubted I was telling the truth. But unlike Callum, she hadn't accompanied Lady Morgain to the council.

"I know what I saw," I insisted.

"There are other Fae with dark eyes here," she protested.

Callum looked at her. "That is true, Yssola, but not dark enough to seem black."

Her—Yssola's—own eyes were deep green, but they had whites. Not like the entirely black voids of Usuriel's.

"Totally black," I added. "No whites."

Callum nodded at Yssola. "Yes. That would be a rarity here, would it not? It shouldn't take you long to find out if there are any such amongst your staff. You can gather them and find out where they all were with little effort."

Yssola's lip curled. "I need more than *he was blond*." She gestured at her own hair. "Most of us are."

"He was young. In human years, I would think nineteen or twenty. Tall. Skinny. His hair was short." I hovered my hand at my ear lobe to demonstrate the length. Most of the Fae in the hall had had longer hair.

She looked blank. "I'm not sure that's enough. But I'll arrange for the servants to be summoned."

"And what about Aubrey?" I asked. "Who's looking for her?"

"We don't know that she is missing yet." Yssola folded her arms. "Perhaps she snuck off on her own recognizance. Spying in the Lady's hall."

"She didn't even know we were coming here," I objected. "Nor does she know this place. What could she possibly be looking for?"

"Anything," Yssola said. "Humans do foolish things."

"This particular human is of the Cestis. And she knows something of our ways. So it seems improbable she would do something likely to offend your Lady," Callum said gently. "Perhaps you can search the house for her as well." He looked at the sleeping servant. "And perhaps you should fetch your Lady and see if she can wake this one."

"You can't do it?" I asked.

He touched her forehead again, then shook his head. "It's not exactly the same as my magic. I may do more harm than good. Lady Morgain's power is stronger than mine. And she is skilled in the ways of the mind. If anyone can bring this girl out of sleep easily, it will be her." He frowned slightly. "Though if it was one of the Nichtkin, it's possible she was dosed with something, rather than just a spell."

Yssola grimaced, "Perhaps. But she looks normal enough. A potion fashioned by one of the nicht would most likely leave a trace. They don't always care about covering their tracks."

The more I learned about Usuriel's people, the less I wanted to meet any of them. Any human criminal not concerned with covering their tracks most likely didn't intend that victim to survive to identify them. Or perhaps, to never be found.

"True," Callum agreed. "But arrogance is sometimes their downfall." He bent and sniffed near the woman's face. "I can't smell anything out of place," he admitted. "But still. We should bring her to Lady Morgain."

Yssola nodded, "Very well." She turned on her heel and marched back out to the door and started issuing orders.

"Who is she?" I asked, as Callum continued to study the unconscious tanai.

"Yssola? Captain of Morgain's guard."

"Huh." In that case why hadn't she been with Morgain at the council?

"Also, her youngest daughter," Callum added.

"Huh," I repeated, still trying to process this. Then I lowered my voice. "She doesn't look like her mother..." I shimmied my hand back and forth to indicate Morgain's ever-shifting appearance.

"No," he agreed. "She has not her mother's affinity for the fates, which is probably just as well for her. It is not an easy task to read the magic and the fates the way the Lady Morgain does."

I could imagine it wasn't. I had more questions about Morgain and children and how that worked with a body that changed endlessly, but they could wait. "So you knew who she was all along?"

Callum shrugged. "Yes, I've met her before."

"You could have told us.

"There wasn't a convenient time," Callum pointed out. "She found us at the boundary, and she brought us straight to the hall. Do you think I should have stopped and asked her for introductions?"

"A heads-up that she was Morgain's daughter might have been nice." I snapped. Then I stopped. Took a breath. I wasn't angry with him, but with everything else.

Before I could even ask any more questions, Yssola returned with four men dressed in green leather as she had been earlier. Probably the guard uniform, given her rank. "Take her to the Amber Chamber," she ordered, and the four men bent to lift the girl, after Callum and I moved out of the way.

"What's her name?" I asked Yssola as they carried her out of the room.

Yssola frowned. "Gwen, I believe. Come along, we will see what the Lady has to say."

Lady, not mother. Interesting. Another quirk of Fae protocol, perhaps. If she was serving as Captain of the Guard, then she couldn't treat her mother merely as her mother.

Yssola clicked her tongue as though to hurry Callum and me along. "They are searching the grounds and the building for your friend. I'm sure she'll be found soon enough."

I wasn't so sure.

Chapter Eighteen

WE FOLLOWED Yssola and the guards carrying Gwen to a sunny room with a row of empty beds along one wall and shelves lined with various bottles and jars of herbs and tinctures along the other. The air smelled of something sharp and citrusy. The Fae equivalent of a hospital, I guessed. Or a healer's workroom.

The guards laid Gwen on the bed nearest the door. and stepped back. "Anything else, Captain?" one of them asked.

"No." Yssola nodded at the tallest guard. "Thomas, you remain and watch the door until Lady Morgain comes. The rest of you go join the search. I want that servant found. And the human, of course," she added, glancing sideways at me.

"Yes, Captain," They bowed their heads respectfully and filed out, moving silently.

Gwen was still fast asleep or unconscious or whatever it actually was. The change in location hadn't roused her at all.

I watched her, trying to judge if anything had changed. A scattering of freckles dotted her cheeks, standing out against the pale skin. With her blonde hair and blue eyes, she was the stereotypically pretty white girl who could be from anywhere in Britain. Or even somewhere else like America or Australia if you ignored the accent. More important than where she was from was whether or not she was in the realm voluntarily. And even if she was, my first instinct was to try to convince her to leave.

But as we waited for Morgain, I started having second thoughts. Something had brought her to the realm. Wherever her human home was, what was her life like if serving a Fae was a more appealing option? No point dragging her back to something awful.

But that was Aubrey's—or the Cestis from wherever the girl was from—job to sort out.

Of course, that required Aubrey to be found, or we'd most likely have to leave her here. Neither Zee nor I had the authority of a Cestis.

I didn't have too long to stew on it before the door opened again and Morgain walked through, Damon, Gráinne and Zee trailing behind her. They were followed by yet another man in the guard's leathers, though a slightly fancier version, with silver embossing on the shoulders and across his chest. He was tall with true silver hair that marked him clearly as Fae. The same man who'd guarded Morgain at the council, I realized when he skirted to take his position behind her.

Lady Morgain walked over to the bed and studied Gwen where she lay.

"She was found in the refreshment chamber," Yssola said. "By the human." She looked at me somewhat sourly.

"It's Maggie," I said, not looking away. She clearly wasn't going to like me no matter what I did, and I was equally determined not to let her think she could intimidate me.

Lady Morgain arched an eyebrow. "I have not forgotten your name, Maggie Lachlan." She stretched out a hand, her face blurring to what I was coming to think of as her middle face—the woman who looked to be around forty—and touched Gwen's brow. "She is sleeping, something is keeping her that way. A moment."

She closed her eyes, and I felt a pulse of magic. Not as cold and sharp as Cerridwen's, more subtle. But unmistakably strong.

"There. She should wake shortly. There was something else in her veins besides magic." Morgain cocked her head at Yssola. "Was there anything in the room where she was found?"

"Other than the human, you mean?" Yssola said, slanting another glance in my direction.

"I don't think the human has the power to overcome a tanai fol and send her to sleep in this manner," Morgain said.

Yssola flushed pink, frowning. Nope. Not going to be joining my fan club any time soon.

"That is," Morgain continued, "Unless Cerridwen has been less than forthcoming with me about what she has been teaching you."

I shook my head. "She hasn't taught me how to magically whammy someone. I didn't even know it was possible to make someone fall asleep until I saw Callum do it a few nights ago." Witches with healing talents could soothe someone to sleep but they couldn't keep someone that way for long without drugs to assist the process. Or, I didn't think they could. And, judging by Cassandra's reaction to my few attempts at making her teas, she didn't think my healing abilities were anything to get excited about.

Morgain arched her brows again, her face still unchanged. It was probably the longest she'd stayed in one form since I had met her, which told me that perhaps it was something of a choice as to how she appeared, and that shifting, blurring thing she did was intended, at least partially, to intimidate. "A magic whammy? What is that?" she asked.

"A whammy is a… well, a drug, I guess," Damon offered. "Something used to knock you out or make you unconscious."

"I see…" Morgain studied him a moment and her attention shifted back to Callum. "This man is her…?"

"They are together, though not wed as the humans count it," he replied.

Her smile turned approving, as though she thought Damon was worthy in some way, or maybe, like most females, she just thought he was hot.

"You said there was something else besides magic, Lady?" I asked. "Captain Yssola said something about the Nichtkin using potions."

Morgain's face shifted then, moving to the older version, grim-faced and stern. "There are no Nichtkin in my territory."

"The human thought she saw one, Lady," Yssola said. "She said there was a servant at the rear of the hall, whose eyes turned black. But she may have been confused."

"It's possible," I agreed, "but he reminded me of Lord Usuriel." I held out my hands and shrugged. "I admit, my knowledge of the Fae is slight, but he looked out of place somehow, and he left the hall between the time I noticed him and when I went to look for Aubrey. He was some way ahead of me, but I saw him go toward the refreshment chamber. The servant who was escorting me probably saw him, too."

"And how long did it take until you reached the refreshment chamber?" Yssola asked.

"Two minutes at most," I said.

Lady Morgain considered this. "In that case, he would have had to work fast to have taken your companion somewhere."

"Couldn't he have just opened a door like Yssola did when she came to greet us by the boundary?" I asked.

"Only if he was more powerful than any servant should be," Morgain said. Her frown was deepening with every word. "And it would take a great deal of power to open a door to escape my territory without my sensing it."

"It could be done, though," Callum argued. "It is not acceptable behavior, but it is possible. And not something that

I would put past the Nichtkin. Their lord did not seem kindly disposed toward Maggie at the council, even though he let Lord Padran make all the noise."

"That is true, but I do not see what he would stand to benefit from taking a human, or how he would even have learned that she was here." Morgain shook her hair back. "I need to think about this."

"If he took her, where would he have gone?" I asked.

Callum's mouth went flat. "Well, if he was nicht, presumably he returned to Lord Usuriel's territory. I can't think of any other likely destination. Lady, could you tell if a door was opened in the refreshment chamber?"

Morgain nodded. "I should be able to feel a trace, but I can't tell where a door will lead if it is not mine," she said. "It's not like a boundary stone where the wards are designed to make a record of who crosses over and where they are headed."

"So you have no way of knowing where Aubrey might be?" Damon asked, face grim.

"If she's still in this territory, I should be able to find her. But if she was taken beyond my borders, then no."

I checked my watch again. Only about twenty minutes since Aubrey had first left, hardly any time at all. My gaze fell on the bracelet that rested next to my watch. "What about Cerridwen?" I asked Callum. "Couldn't she tell where Aubrey was?" I pointed to the pin on Damon's collar. "You gave her one of those. One of Cerridwen's tokens, right?"

Callum's face cleared. "Yes." But then his frown returned. "We would have to summon the Lady here."

Morgain's face shivered into the old woman, not pleased, I gathered, at that particular suggestion.

Callum added, "We would only do so with your permission, of course, Lady Morgain."

We should call for Cerridwen. Regardless of Morgain's permission," I objected silently.

"I'm trying not to make this worse than it is," Callum replied, not looking at me.

Quite frankly, if Aubrey wasn't found in the next few minutes, Morgain could suck it. Explaining to the British Cestis that we'd lost one of them in the realm wasn't a conversation I had any desire to have.

"We will let the guards complete their search first," Morgain said, "then I will consider what the appropriate actions may be."

Damon was chewing his lip. No doubt thinking of Jack and the time slipping away. So was I. Every minute gone, regardless of what Callum said he could do and the ways to make up the time, felt like another opportunity for Jack to elude us yet again. I closed my eyes, wishing we could go back and just wait for the damned suborbital. We still might not have caught up to Jack, but Aubrey would be safe.

"I think she's waking up," Damon said, suddenly.

My eyes flew open. Sure enough, Gwen's eyelids were fluttering.

Morgain touched her head once more, and the magic pulsed again. "Wake, child."

Gwen's eyes snapped open. Confusion flooded the pale blue, then she registered who was standing beside her. "My Lady," she gasped, struggling to sit.

Morgain pressed her back down. "Rest, child. You're not in trouble."

"What happened?" Gwen asked, still looking bewildered.

"We're rather hoping you can tell us the answer to that question," Yssola said, her tone less gentle than her mother's.

Gwen's eyes flared wide, her skin turning even paler, but she shook her head as though she had no idea what we were talking about.

"You were taking Aubrey to the refreshment chamber," I prompted, "do you remember?"

Gwen gulped and cleared her throat. "Yes."

"And when you got there, what happened?" I pressed.

Gwen looked away.

"Speak the truth, child," Morgain said. "No harm will come to you if you are honest."

Gwen was twisting her hands, and my eye was caught again by the strands of silver wire around her wrist.

"I showed the lady the refreshment chamber. Waited for her," she said. "She was washing her hands and talking to me."

"What did she speak of?" Morgain asked, frowning.

"She was asking me about my accent, my lady. She's English, like me."

A look passed between Morgain and Yssola that I couldn't quite decipher. "You are half-English," Morgain corrected.

"Yes," Gwen agreed. "She was asking whereabouts in England I'm from."

Morgain hummed encouragingly. "And what did you tell her?"

"I was starting to tell her that I was born in Surrey when we were interrupted."

"Interrupted by who?" Morgain asked.

Gwen looked puzzled. "One of the male servants, I'm not sure of his name. I was surprised he came into the room. He approached the lady, and he…he. I'm sorry, I'm not sure," she said, eyes widening in what was a very good imitation of distress if it wasn't real.

"He must have put her to sleep," Yssola said, shaking her head impatiently. "She can't tell us anything useful."

"No," Gwen said. "I mean, yes, he touched me, but he opened a door first." She looked startled. "I didn't think that was possible inside the hall."

"No," Morgain agreed, "because it shouldn't be."

But it seemed it was. "Well, that seems clear enough. If he opened the door, he must have taken Aubrey through it."

"Yes," Callum agreed, "and the fact that he left the girl behind suggests they wanted us to know they have her."

"Does that mean we're waiting for some sort of ransom request?" Damon asked. "If they've taken her to gain some advantage, shouldn't they be asking for something?"

Morgain looked undecided. "I do not know. I need to consult the fates." She glanced at Callum. "But if this one is telling the truth, I think that, yes, perhaps you should summon your Lady and see if she can work out where Miss Carter was taken."

Yssola cleared her throat. "We are not prepared for a visit from the Lady Cerridwen."

"She is not an invading army, my dear," Morgain retorted. "You can manage her and a few of her companions if she arrives with any. After all, her blade and his sister are already here. That is enough for her to come to visit this court at least. Unlike other courts, she knows she is safe here." She waved her hand at me. "As are the rest of you. You have my word on that."

That would have been more reassuring if Aubrey hadn't been snatched out from under her nose, but I tried to look grateful.

"Very well," Callum agreed. He touched one of the leather cuffs around his wrist, and something like a chime rang in my ears, though no one else reacted. Perhaps it was something in my bracelet reacting to his. He went still after that, head tilted as though listening, talking to Cerridwen perhaps.

After a moment, he nodded. "She will be here shortly. If you allow her to open a door, Lady."

Morgain inclined her head. "Of course. Tell her to aim for the usual spot in the garden, and we will meet her there."

Yssola escorted us out of the hall, hurrying us back through the house and into the garden. Damon questioned me about exactly what had happened while we walked.

He gritted his teeth when I stuck to my story. "Based on what I saw, I think Lord Usuriel took her."

"And he is one of the Fae you met at the council you went to, with Aubrey? The one who gave you trouble?"

"No, that was Lord Padran," I said. "But I don't think Usuriel's necessarily on Cerridwen's side regarding whatever's been going on here in the realm. He's Nichtkin."

"You never really explained what that means."

"Ever played a game that had dark elves? Or an unseelie court…like monsters?"

"Yes."

"Well, his line is one of those. Not so nice by our standards."

"What did he look like?"

"Pretty. Like a young hot blond guy," I said. "But his eyes are solid black."

Damon was frowning. "So, if he's a bad guy, is he the one who let the walker out?"

Damn. I'd been hoping he wouldn't make that connection. "It's possible." According to the Archives, there were lesser Fae—creatures or monsters or such as we'd call them—of all varieties in most of the territories. Even the horses we'd ridden here could be classified as lesser Fae, given they seemed to have some sort of magic. But like called to like, maybe. There were definitely creatures who we would consider nightmare fuel. There was a reason why Callum and his kind found things to hunt inside the realm as well as out of it.

"And what do we do if he has her?" Damon asked.

"That's why we need Cerridwen."

"How long is this going to take?" Frustration shaded his voice.

I'd been expecting that question. "I'm not sure." I understood his concern. This was hardly the short interlude Callum had promised us. "It'll be fine," I said, hoping I sounded certain. "We'll figure this all out."

"I'm sorry." His arm tightened around my shoulder.

"What for?" I asked.

"This is a mess. We should have just waited for a plane."

"Maybe," I said. "But you would have missed Jack."

"Perhaps," he agreed, "but it's not looking good now, either, and we've lost someone in—"

"The realm," I interjected, before he could say something dumb like fairyland in front of Yssola and Morgain. Callum didn't mind it, but all the Cestis's records were clear that it wasn't a term most Fae appreciated.

"At least Aubrey got to meet Gwen, see whether anything is going on with her that shouldn't be."

His frown deepened. "I don't think Gwen told us everything that she knows."

I glanced warily at Morgain who was talking with Yssola as they walked. "No," I agreed. "I'm not sure she did either, but, given the circumstances, I think I'd be wary, too. She doesn't know us, after all. And depending on her situation, she might not want to talk in front of either us or the Fae. It's possible she told Aubrey something. When we find her, hopefully she'll know if Gwen needs help."

"And what happens if she does?"

"That part we leave to the Cestis and the Fae to sort out."

Damon didn't look particularly inclined to help anyone just then. "Well, let's hope Cerridwen can find Aubrey fast."

"I'm sure she will," I said reassuringly. "Cerridwen will want to help us get to Jack if she can. Callum wouldn't have agreed to help us if he didn't know Jack is a priority for her."

"All right," Damon agreed, still sounding unhappy.

I leaned against him. "I don't like this any more than you."

"I doubt that," he muttered.

"We will wait here," Yssola announced, halting our little procession.

I hadn't been paying much attention to where we were going, but I did now that we'd come to a stop. The garden beds around us were formal, but full of flowers and plants I didn't recognize. Beyond them were stretches of lawn and more beds and then an area that looked like a field of wildflowers spilling in a thousand shades across bluish grass before ending at the edge of another forest. Or the same one we'd seen at the boundary. Impossible to tell from here. There were mountains in the distance, a trio of peaks towering over rolling foothills, but there was no way to work out how far they might be. Or if they were real at all.

That thought made my brain hurt, so I concentrated on the flowers, letting myself just be taken in by the beauty for a minute or two, hoping to clear my head.

But there wasn't much time to do anything before a familiar wooden door appeared, and Cerridwen came through it. She was wearing the leathers she wore to train in. Which meant she was ready to fight. Not a good sign. No one came out after her and the door vanished as she nodded briefly at Morgain.

Morgain's face was blurring again, shifting between her three forms in rapid succession.

"Lady Morgain, greetings," Cerridwen said politely before her gaze shifted to us. "And what trouble have the five of you managed to get yourselves into?" Her tone was far less polite. "Though Callum tells me there should be six of you." She narrowed her eyes at Callum, something close to anger flickering over her face, making me want to step back. I managed to stay where I was.

"Don't be angry with him," I said. "We asked him to bring us, to find Jack."

"So he was explaining to me," Cerridwen said, turning her displeasure on me. "It didn't occur to you to ask for help?"

"We thought you were dealing with more important things, Lady," Callum said, for once sounding apologetic. "We were not expecting…trouble."

Cerridwen made a, well, not a snort. I didn't think the Fae actually snorted, but it was close enough to it. "Have you learned nothing then, my blade? Our kind thrive on trouble, and this is hardly a time of unbridled unity in the realm. Perhaps next time you'll consider asking for my help at the beginning, instead of when things have gone too far and quite wrong."

"I perhaps underestimated the situation," Callum admitted. "But you task me to hunt the dark. Jack Miller sides with the dark."

"I cannot argue with that," Cerridwen said. "But you do not help our cause by being reckless, my blade." Her gaze switched to Gráinne. "Neither do you."

Gráinne bowed her head. "I thought I should help."

"Your loyalty to your brother is always admirable," Cerridwen said. "But sometimes ill-considered."

"We made a mistake," I said. "But can we do apologies later, Lady? We could be running out of time. Callum told you what happened when he called for you. Do you think you can find where Aubrey is?"

"If she still carries my token, I will be able to sense it, unless steps have been taken to cloak it."

"What reason would Lord Usuriel have to take her?" I asked.

"As to that, I am not entirely sure," Cerridwen said. "It is a bold move to take one of the Cestis, especially right out from under Morgain's nose. But Usuriel, if it was him, plays deep games." She shook her head. "I agree, Maggie. Time is important. Better not to speculate when we can act."

She slanted a glance at Callum. "Do not take that to heart, my blade. You could well do with some more speculation, or contemplation."

Callum tipped his head in acknowledgment.

"Action has my vote," Damon said. "We are working to a timetable here."

She turned her silvery eyes on him. "As to that, I think the wisest thing to do would be for you and Zee to continue on to the door to your destination. Gráinne can take you, and perhaps Morgain would spare a guard or two."

"No," Damon said flatly, with one sharp shake of his head. "I'm not leaving Maggie behind."

It hadn't occurred to me that we could split up, but as Cerridwen set out her plan, I couldn't help agreeing with her. Firstly, because I wanted Damon out of the realm as quickly as possible and safely back with his security team. And, secondly, because, well, frankly, he would only slow us down. He didn't have magic. That was a liability. If the Fae could take someone like Aubrey so easily, then Damon was truly defenseless. I needed to get him out of the realm.

I turned to face him, taking his hands. "You should go," I urged. "Find Jack. It's important."

"I'm not leaving you behind," he said gruffly.

"I'll be fine," I reassured him. "I have Cerridwen and Callum."

His head gave another quick shake of rejection, fingers tightening on mine. "You're not Fae, though."

"Neither are you. But we dragged Aubrey into this, and I'm not leaving her behind. There's no reason for all of us to stay when you can still reach the door and find Jack. That's important, too, right?"

"Right," he agreed, but he was frowning at me.

"Then go," I said. "I'm sure we won't be far behind you."

I looked into his blue eyes, willing him to believe me, even though it could be a lie. But I'd told him the truth about Aubrey. I couldn't leave her behind.

"Zee could go after Aubrey," Damon said.

I rejected that option with a shake of my head. "Zee will

be more use to you in Europe. He has contacts there. With people your team might not. You don't know what might make the difference. Go. I'll be fine."

Damon looked as though he wanted to argue, but I could tell he was torn.

"Go, you're wasting time," I repeated. "Catch Jack for me. That's your job. This is mine."

I knew how much he wanted to stop Jack. Hopefully enough that it would outweigh his need to stay with me. "And I need you to do your job," I said. "That way we'll be safe again. We'll catch up with you before you know it. Right, Callum?"

"Say yes," I added in my head. *"I want him out of here."*

"Right," Callum said. "With the Lady helping us, it should be a few hours at most."

Chapter Nineteen

"THAT'S NOT SO LONG," Damon said. "I could wait."

Dammit. What could I say to convince him? "Why risk it? You know you want to be there."

His fingers were almost too tight on mine now. Like he didn't want to let go. "The team can get him."

"I want you to catch him for me."

He flinched, blue eyes burning into mine. "I don't want to leave you alone."

And I don't want you to stay in the realm. But that wouldn't convince him. That would only show him I was afraid. He wouldn't leave if he thought I was scared. "I'm not alone, and you're not alone either." I freed my hands, gave him a little shove. "Go. The quicker you're out of here, the quicker we will be, too."

"She's right," Cerridwen said bluntly. "We will be faster if we divide. You cannot do what we can do in here. And in your realm, you can do what needs to be done."

Damon looked torn, eyes still fixed on me. "Are you sure?"

"Yes." I waved him away. "*Go.*"

His face twisted, but he nodded reluctantly, his hand flexing. "Very well, I'll go," he said to Cerridwen. "You're right, it will be faster this way. But keep Maggie safe."

"I value her, too," Cerridwen said, her expression softening. It may not have been the warmest sentiment in the world, but it was nice to hear.

I looked at Gráinne. "Keep him safe. All of you be safe," I said, fighting to keep my voice calm. God. If anything happened—

No. I cut off the thought. I couldn't function if I was panicking. Damon would be fine. Far safer out of the realm. But Aubrey was Cestis. I had to help her. The Cestis had helped me every time I needed it, without question. One of them had died for me. If Cassandra or Lizzie were here, there was no way in hell they'd leave without Aubrey. I couldn't either. I owed them too much to not try to help.

Gráinne nodded. "I will." She nodded at her brother. "Don't do anything stupid."

He flashed her a cocky grin. "I won't if you don't."

Morgain looked at both of them with something like exasperation and then stepped forward and raised her hand. On it appeared a golden pin. She passed it to Gráinne. "Here, this is my token. It will get you through Padran's territory if you need to cross it. And bearing this, most of the other boundary stones should open to you."

That gave me pause. How powerful was Morgain if her token was a free pass?

But there was no time for questions. Morgain lifted her hand and a familiar marble door appeared. She shooed the others toward it. "Hurry. You need to get back to the border and through Nine Hills as fast as possible. If the Lord of the Lochs decides to be troublesome, he could alert Padran. Or Usuriel."

I watched as they went through the door, keeping my eyes on Damon until the door shimmered back into nothing and he was gone. Beyond my help for the time being.

I wanted to beg Morgain to open the door again so I could go after them. I swallowed hard. *No.* My priority had to be Aubrey. Damon had protection; she was all alone.

In a court of beings that, to humans, were monsters out of our darkest whispered stories.

I made myself turn away from where the door had been. "All right. What's the plan?"

"First, we find Aubrey," Cerridwen said. She closed her eyes, and I held my breath as seconds stretched slowly. Just when I really did feel as though my last nerve was going to snap, her eyes opened, burning bright silver. "She is in Usuriel's territory."

"Can you tell where?" Callum asked.

"Yes," she said. "Though I am not sure what we will find there. Usuriel, well, his territory tends to be more changeable than most. It could be he's holding her at his court. Or she could be elsewhere."

Teleporting into the center of a court full of hostile Fae didn't sound like fun. Or safe. But it was too late to back out. "So how do we get her?"

Callum's eyes were glowing with anticipation. Apparently he did think it was going to be fun. "The usual way. We sneak in. We work out where she is. Then we steal her back."

"You make that sound easy," I said, highly skeptical.

"Hopefully it will be," he said. "The fact that the Lady can locate her tells me he hasn't realized she has a token, and he has no need to suppose we know where she is yet. If we move fast, we should still have the element of surprise."

"Good," I said. "And if it all goes horribly wrong, then we call for backup and fight our way out?"

"Yes," Callum agreed. Then he grinned. "But I'm not sure Usuriel will want to argue with the Lady."

If we made it out of here alive, I'd make Callum focus less on swordsmanship and more on Fae diplomacy. If I stuck to my guns and kept working with Cerridwen, this wouldn't be the last time I'd have to deal with contrary Fae.

"That remains to be seen," Cerridwen said. But she looked as though she might be looking forward to finding out. "He has been mercurial of late. I'm not sure whether Padran has been in his ear, or if he has genuine concerns about something, but who knows what he is plotting."

"Could he have been the one who released the walker?" I asked.

"Maybe. There are walkers in his territory, though we found no evidence to link that particular one back to him." She arched a brow at me. "Possibly it would have been more useful if we could have questioned the creature."

Sure, but I'd been busy trying to stay alive. "Next time I'll try to remember that you need to talk to the thing that can steal into people's nightmares and kill them, before I kill it."

Morgain looked slightly startled at this, her face shifting to its youngest version. Callum just grinned approvingly at me.

"You did well," Cerridwen said. "In your place, I possibly would have done the same. But, still, it leaves us without proof of any crimes to lay at Usuriel's feet."

"Other than the fact he's stolen Aubrey," I pointed out. "Which I'm sure breaks half a dozen clauses in the contracts between you and the Cestis."

"Yes." Morgain said. "I don't understand what he thinks he can gain by taking her."

"No," Cerridwen agreed. "If he wants to threaten us somehow with her, then perhaps we would have expected some sort of communication by now. What else could he want her for?"

"Perhaps there's something he wants from the Cestis?" I suggested.

"It seems a strange way to gain their goodwill. Usuriel, though, can be charming when he wants. It's one of the reasons he is dangerous. He's very good at convincing people that his way is the right way. He hides his real motives and his true self. His court is known as the court of mirrors for good reason. He is never quite as he seems."

I wondered exactly what that meant. That he wasn't the beautiful golden youth that he had appeared? More something far darker that went with those black eyes? Or that he was maneuvering on more than one level at all times? All questions for after we had Aubrey back. For now, I just had to trust Cerridwen and Callum and do what they told me to do. "How do we do this?"

Morgain waved a hand toward what I was calling east based on the position of the sun. "Usuriel's border is that way, and there's a boundary stone. But if you cross there, then he will sense it."

Callum shrugged. "I know some additional ways in. Ones that shouldn't trigger the boundary stone."

"Let us try some more straightforward methods first. Save that for the actual crossing into Usuriel's land." Cerridwen said. She twisted to Morgain. "What kind of temper is Feagon in lately? Do you think he would mind if I crossed via a door rather than the boundary stones?"

"He is his usual contrary self," Morgain said. "But I can talk him around. He is currently in my debt."

"Good," Cerridwen said. "Usuriel won't anticipate us using a door. Or perhaps even recognize that it is my door if Feagon lets us through. We need all the advantages we can get." She grimaced at Morgain. "We will work out a way to balance things after."

Morgain nodded. "As you say. Let us get to work."

I shouldn't have complained about how it felt riding the horses along the ways, because being dragged through various doors and boundaries and ways at the merciless pace set by

Cerridwen left me feeling as though I'd been caught in a riptide, spun, tumbled, and half drowned.

Dizziness made me gag, as I half stumbled through what I devoutly hoped was the final door for a while. I had to bend over and breathe deep for a minute to avoid throwing up.

When I'd regained control and risked standing upright again, I faced the now-familiar sight of a border mist. This one looked different. A darker shade, faintly purple like the beginnings of twilight, moving in wisps and streaks that seemed to suggest screaming faces. Or perhaps that was just my screaming head making my imagination run wild. The effect did nothing to settle my still complaining stomach. I closed my eyes, breathing deep.

"Are you feeling unwell?" Cerridwen asked.

I held up a shaky hand to wave her off, keeping my eyes closed. "I'll be fine, just give me a minute."

"Don't be foolish. I can help you with that. The ways are not always easy on humans. The horses are the more sensible way to go. It helps your brain adjust to the travel because you feel like you're moving more than you do when we do it this way."

"Awesome," I said. "I'll remember that for next time."

Callum said, "You've done fairly well for a human. The last time I had to move someone so fast through the realm, they came out puking their guts up."

I sent him a shaky smile. "I'm not entirely sure that's not going to happen."

Cerridwen came over and put a hand on my back. "Just keep breathing."

A shock of magic ran through me, like being plunged into ice water. It stole my breath, and I gasped and flinched, and then realized as I did so that the nausea had vanished. Once I managed to get my breath back, I managed a slightly steadier smile and said, "That is better. Thank you." It might have been somewhat masochistic to thank her for dumping the magical equivalent of a bucket of ice over me, but it had worked, even if it had been unpleasant. And it was no worse than drinking one of Cassandra's more unpleasant teas.

"Good," Cerridwen said. "We need you ready to fight."

I couldn't see a boundary stone, but Callum had said he could sneak us in a different way.

Cerridwen looked at him, "Very well, my blade, why don't you show us how this works?"

He lifted an eyebrow at her, and I couldn't quite interpret the expression.

Did he think perhaps that she should know? How long had it been since Cerridwen had actually hunted at the side of the s'ealg oiche, rather than sending them to do the killing for her?

She arched a brow back and Callum nodded, sketching a shallow bow. He straightened, frowned, and walked closer to the mist, extending his hand until it hovered a few inches away from the surface of the swirling fog. As he closed his eyes, I braced my shields and let my sight slide into the magic, intrigued.

As usual, the magic was nearly dazzling. Callum's smoky blue-gray aura even brighter than usual. I ignored the magic tugging at me, watching Callum. I didn't feel anything, but slowly the color of his energy field morphed, until it was a near match to the mist, the shape of it swirling as the mist did.

I flinched, the change disturbing me for reasons I couldn't have explained. Cloaked in the twilight shadow, Callum extended his other hand, then slowly brought them both together. Two long breaths and he carefully drew them apart again. As he did so, a narrow corridor opened in the mists. He opened his eyes, a satisfied smirk playing on his lips.

"That's a useful trick," Cerridwen said.

"Yes," Callum agreed.

"Where did you learn it?" she asked.

"From one of the Nichtkin, many moons ago."

"Interesting. They don't usually give up their secrets so easily."

Apparently neither did Callum, if Cerridwen hadn't known he could do this.

"Well," Callum said, "I did have a sword to their throat at the time. They chose cooperation over death."

Cerridwen's brow shot up. "Alright, perhaps you can tell me that tale another time. And explain why you haven't told me it before. For now, we should cross."

Callum's smirk faded, and he bowed again, apologetic. "Mostly because it is useful, but it's not the easiest thing in the world. Gráinne can manage it sometimes, but none of our other pack kin can do it. I didn't think that you would have much call for it, so I kept it secret. Better to have a few tricks up my sleeve."

Cerridwen looked at him, considering. "Perhaps. But now is not the time to argue the point."

Callum stepped back. "You go first, Lady. Maggie and I will follow. The mist will close once I am through."

Cerridwen nodded and walked toward the mist, moving in the same stealthy, silent stride that Callum used. I did my best to copy her, moving cautiously, not wanting to make contact with the shifting mists.

Even though Callum's aura looked different, to my magic, his energy still felt the same. Whereas if I tried to feel the mist, what I felt was absence. As though it was draining energy from the places it covered. And it felt…hungry. As though it might just drain me, too. I let go of the magic and focused on my shields once more, shoring them into place with everything Cassandra and Cerridwen had taught me.

To my relief, nothing reached from the mist to drag me into the dark depths in the few paces it took to cross. By now I was learning to be less surprised by what I might find on the other side of a boundary. We'd crossed three, no, four territories to reach this point, and the time of day and the landscape had altered with each one. Now we were in darkness again, but not quite full dark. The sky above had a deep blue tinge, like the death of dusk. There were stars, but fewer than I'd seen in other territories, and their light had a particular coldness to it.

"Now, what?" I asked as Callum joined us, the mist closing behind him.

"Now, we continue." Cerridwen said. She pursed her lips, looking us over. "But first, I think, disguises."

I looked down at what I was wearing. "How?"

"Illusions," she said. "There are some who live in this territory who appear as the Fae you have met so far, but there are more who do not. And you, in particular, look very human."

Great. "Well. You can tell me what I should look like, and I can try an illusion." I rubbed my wrist, twisting the bracelet and gliding my thumb over the faint scars on either side of my chip. In a game, of course, it would be easy. I could conjure an avatar to make me look like anything, but this, as I was continuing to remind myself, was not a game. This might be Aubrey's life or, indeed, mine.

"I will take care of the illusion," Cerridwen said. "It will take more power for you to hold it than is sensible. You may need your magic for other things." She looked at me meaningfully. "Just remember, many of the nicht are not overly fond of light or fire."

I digested that. My strongest magic had always been fire. That had been the first thing I'd done with it, acting instinctively to protect Damon and me from an imp. Of course, I'd also burned myself in the process, but now I could control it far better. I'd even killed a demon with lightning, though here in the realm. I had no way of knowing if I'd be able to do so again.

I'd never actually attempted to replicate that feat in the

human world. But fire I could manage, if needed. "I'll remember."

Cerridwen nodded, and then I felt a cool sheen of her magic, far less icy than before, settling around me.

I turned to Callum and nearly took a step back. He wore a twisted version of his usual impressive wolfish form. One that stood upright on two legs and had far too many jagged yellow teeth and long black claws jutting from leathery hands. His eyes had lost the hint of green and shone an angrier shade of gold.

Like every nightmare version of a werewolf, in fact. I swallowed, reminding myself it wasn't real. Or, if it was actually one of his forms, it wasn't one he chose to use. "Okay," I managed. "What do I look like?"

"Not like him," Cerridwen said. "You're a rancaigh. More like Lady Orea. If she was more ferret than fox. It works with your green eyes and brown hair."

Great. Callum got to be a scary werewolf. I was some sort of weasel girl.

"Well, you'll have to point one out if we encounter one.

"Hopefully, we won't," Callum said. "They're vicious little things. Bloodthirsty when they want to be."

I lifted an eyebrow at Cerridwen, "Are you trying to tell me I need to channel my bloodthirsty side?"

"Just be on alert. I'm hoping no blood will need to be shed in this venture." She waved a hand over herself and became a figure more like Morgain, a woman who looked like she was woven from mists, semi-transparent. Though in Cerridwen's case, the mists were near black, making her look even more ominous than Morgain.

"And what is she?" I asked Callum, who was eyeing Cerridwen nervously.

"A banshee," he said. "Or what your human tales of banshee are based on. Best not to say their real name here."

An omen of death. Just what we needed. Hopefully, Cerridwen wasn't planning on having to evoke the real thing.

Cerridwen put a finger to her lips. "Quiet. I need a moment to find Aubrey."

I nodded and patted my hip. The familiar weight of the sword was still there. Maybe I was spoiling the illusion, but the weapon comforted me too much to worry that anyone who was watching us from the darkness might wonder what I was doing. Hopefully, Callum and Cerridwen were shielding us from sight.

Eventually, Cerridwen's pale eyes snapped open. "I think I have her. Are we ready?"

"Ready as I'll ever be," I quipped and stepped back to give her space as she opened yet another door.

Chapter Twenty

We didn't use the door immediately. Cerridwen held us back with a gesture, and then poked her head through before nodding with satisfaction. "The grounds on the outskirts of Lord Usuriel's court."

Grounds? "I thought we were going straight to Aubrey?" Surely that would be easier. Grounds suggested we'd have to navigate our way into the actual buildings. That sounded... not fun.

"This is safer. I can study his wards a moment before we take the final step. Stay quiet," Cerridwen instructed and beckoned us forward.

We emerged in a garden, or what passed for a garden in a land that I suspected was eternally shrouded in night. But night or not, there were plants in the beds. Plants whose blooms seemed to reflect the cold starlight glowing faintly in a thousand shades of gray and silver and pale purples and blues, their leaves and branches deeper blacks and charcoals. They twined and writhed, jockeying for position, reaching. The paths between them were narrow, which, given the wicked thorns I could see on some of the plants, seemed like a choice made to make navigating the garden dangerous, if not deadly.

If the Nichtkin liked poisons, then that might well include their choice of vegetation. I made a mental note not to touch anything.

Beyond the garden was a sizeable house. It stood out in the darkness, made of white marble that gleamed like the flowers, night mist colors shifting across the walls in drifts. Which, in a way, was as unsettling as the garden.

So was the fact that there were no people anywhere. Tall metal lampposts holding lanterns shining cool white light were set at intervals along the paths and light also came from the windows, which had no shutters or blinds. But there was nobody visible in any of them. So where was everyone? Nichtkin meant 'people of the night' and even if this was the true night of a sunless land, surely some of them should be around? It all felt just that bit too convenient.

Cerridwen stared silently at the house, her expression intent, all her attention focused on it. If she'd been a s'ealg oiche in canine form, her ears would have been pricked. Her tail twitching. Ready for the hunt. Once she was sure she had the scent of her quarry.

"Should it be this quiet?" I whispered to Callum.

Even through the illusion I could tell that he was on edge. "It may be just a quiet hour," he said. "But, no, I would expect the grounds to be patrolled, at least."

"That's not good."

"No." His golden eyes scanned the garden restlessly, even as Cerridwen made an impatient gesture, warning us to be quiet. I moved closer to Callum, leaving enough room to draw my sword, if I needed, and joined him in his silent surveillance.

"How long do you think she needs?"

"She's checking the wards and other defenses. Not something to do hastily. Just watch and be ready."

I did as he suggested, heartbeat spiking with every rustle of leaf and branch in the icy breeze.

"This way," Cerridwen said, eventually. She stalked forward, not looking back to see if we were following. I'd only taken a few steps before a hissing growl pierced the silence and shapes began to coalesce like mist around us.

"What the h—" I started to say, but Callum was already drawing his sword, and so was Cerridwen, so I shut up and pulled mine. The mist began to shape itself into dogs, not as large as Callum in his other form, but sleek and night-black, their fur reflecting subtle glints of the starlight. The only color came from fiery red eyes glaring at us, and white teeth long enough to also catch the starlight.

"What do we do now?" I hissed at Callum.

"Take care of them, and then we'll use the door," he said matter-of-factly.

"Doesn't the fact that they're here suggest that whoever's inside also knows we're here?" I hissed back.

"Focus, Maggie," Callum snapped as the snarling growls grew louder, more of them appearing behind the first group. He reached out and put a hand on the hilt of my sword, muttering something I didn't understand.

"What was that?"

"Night wraiths need more than simple steel to kill them," he said. "The spell will help. Aim for the neck."

Night wraiths. Yeah, that definitely sounded like something that would be easy to kill. Why couldn't I ever get attacked by sentient marshmallows or something? Though those would probably win because I'd be too distracted by their cuteness to fight. Just as I was being distracted now, I realized, as the growls stopped simultaneously. All the hairs on the back of my neck rose in response.

Fuck. It was all I had time to think before the nearest wraith thing leaped toward me. I countered intuitively with a slashing blow. To my dismay, just before my blade struck, the wraith turned misty, so my sword passed through it rather than making any contact. As I ducked and the beast flew over my shoulder, I saw it had some sort of collar around its neck. Close enough to the color of the beast itself that it was hard to see.

I straightened and turned, trying to spot the next attack. Callum and Cerridwen fought side by side, their blades flickering almost too fast for me to see, night wraiths vanishing as their blades swept through them.

"Aim for their collars," Callum yelled. "They need that to stay solid."

That piece of information barely registered before a growl came from behind. I spun on my heel and saw yet another wraith. Or maybe the same one that had attacked me initially. I managed to get my sword up to swing as it sprang, jaws snapping. My arm hit its leg, enough to knock it off course slightly so that its teeth caught the edges of my jacket at my shoulder rather than connecting with my throat.

I heard a yelp from my left and saw one of the beasts collapse at Callum's feet. He bounded past me to strike at another one that I hadn't even registered was coming. "Look sharp, to your right," he shouted. I turned again and saw another beast gathering to spring. This time I had a second to center myself, take a breath and let my focus narrow to the movement of my hand and the sword. When I struck, the sword connected with the collar, sending a shock up my arm. The beast crumpled and vanished, leaving only the severed collar lying on the dark grass, glimmering faintly.

Callum dispatched another one and, as I turned to face the next one, I realized there were no more night wraiths.

Cerridwen was already sheathing her sword. She wiped her forearm over her brow and crooked her fingers at me. "Hurry."

Callum crouched to wipe his sword through the damp grass as Cerridwen's hand curved a line through the air to open a door. Then he straightened and grabbed my hand, half dragging me toward the door at a run. He pushed me through, and I stumbled, almost falling, only to have Cerridwen catch the hem of my jacket and pull me upright.

I panted as I found my balance. We were in a small, dimly lit room, decorated in navy and gold and black, satin and silk, and polished black wood. Candles in black brackets on the walls offered the only light. Aubrey stood at the far end of the room, staring at us in astonishment. Possibly because of the illusions we wore. But even as I had that thought, I saw Callum return to his usual human form. Apparently our disguises were no longer required.

Aubrey looked unhurt. I heaved a relieved breath. "Are you okay?" I asked, and she shook her head, mouthing something I couldn't make out. I started to move forward, but Cerridwen's hand clamped over my arm, pulling me back as the air beside Aubrey flickered into golden sparks, and Lord Usuriel appeared. He wore black, stark against his golden skin and hair. His nails were long and black, too, which they hadn't been at the council. Here in his court, he might feel free to let more of his true self show.

He gave Aubrey a stern look and then turned his attention to us. "I'm sorry. Did you think that you could just walk in here and I wouldn't notice?"

Cerridwen raised her chin. "Well, you seem to think you could just walk into Morgain's territory and steal one of our allies. You cannot expect us to follow the rules when you disregard them yourself."

Usuriel inclined his head as though acknowledging the point. "I saw an opportunity," he said. "I took it. I wish to understand more of certain matters." He looked at Aubrey, and I saw her eyes flick to me and back. Had he been pumping her for information about me? I wasn't sure how much more she could tell him that I hadn't already told the council. So, what did he really want?

"Regardless of opportunity and your misplaced curiosity, we will be taking Miss Carter and leaving. You cannot simply abduct a Cestis witch and expect there to be no repercussions. We cannot afford to have the humans turn against us, Usuriel. You should know that better than most. After all, your people are the ones they've turned into tales of fear and horror. The ones they would behold and see proof that all those fears were real. You know humans. You know what would happen next if the Cestis were not there to intervene," Cerridwen said.

It was hard to read an expression in those black eyes, but I thought I saw his face flicker and shift to something less pleasant before it solidified back in place.

"As to that," he said, "I'm able to defend my own."

"You are delusional if you think you can defend your people if the humans decide to try to destroy us," Cerridwen countered. "There are billions of them. They have weapons now that you cannot imagine. We cannot win against that."

I hadn't considered that. But if the Fae feared a demon getting into their realm, then what might happen if one of our countries learned about the Fae, decided they were a threat, and acted as humans have been wont to do throughout history and tried to destroy them. How many nukes would it take to blast the Fae realm away from the human one? And what would it do to us and them? I shivered. Surely, Lord Usuriel wasn't willing to start a war to prove a point.

"Come now," Cerridwen said. "We reached a concordance about the door in San Francisco. It is necessary for the stability of the realm. That means we take what comes in San Francisco."

"And you are happy for demon witches to be one of those things?"

Not this again. Suddenly my fear died away, replaced by anger. I sucked in an outraged breath. What the fuck would it take to convince him? "I am *not* a demon witch and Aubrey couldn't have told you anything different. Because it's the truth."

"Humans lie."

"We do," I agreed. "But why would I lie about this? If I was actually working with a demon, well, I've had access to the realm for months now. I could have brought it through at any time. Do you think a demon would wait to attack once it found a way in?"

"She is right, Usuriel," Cerridwen said. "Any of the Greater Dark would have already struck at us."

"So you say," he sneered.

"Yes. I do. With hard-won certainty. My family has bled to keep our realm safe. To keep all of us safe. I have bled for it. We may not be friends, and we may not always agree, but I am a bad enemy, Usuriel." Cerridwen's voice was matter of fact and the two Fae stared at each other.

My anger sparked again. I didn't have time for Fae politics. I wanted to take Aubrey and get to the door. Get to Damon. The fact that Usuriel hadn't just appeared with a squad of whatever he used for guards and tried to kill us, and hadn't attacked Cerridwen just now, suggested that he wasn't willing to really piss her off. Yet.

Time to play dumb human and change the subject and get us back to rescuing Aubrey.

"How did you find Aubrey, anyway?" I asked. "You shouldn't have known where we were."

"You'll come to learn that the Fae are not such a trusting people," he said. "We tend to keep an eye on things."

"Knowing we are in the realm is one thing," I said, "Knowing exactly where to find Aubrey is another. How did you do that?"

Aubrey's eyes flared wide at that question. I couldn't tell if she was scared or worried. And I didn't have time to figure out why she might be worried.

"As to that. It is easier when you have assistance," Usuriel said.

"You have a spy in Morgain's house?" Cerridwen asked, sounding shocked.

"As though you don't send your agents into other realms," Usuriel scoffed.

"I send my hunters to hunt creatures that have broken our laws," she replied icily. Something in the way she said it made me think she was suggesting to Usuriel that he didn't want to be one of those creatures.

Cerridwen didn't move her gaze from Usuriel. "Hunt them because it is my role. Tasked to me and mine by the broader council for these ages past."

"Those of us who have other roles to play need resources too, Lady," he said. "San Francisco is dangerous. Two demons in too short a time. We all need to defend ourselves."

We were getting back into posturing territory. "So, was it the blond kid?" I asked.

Usuriel turned those eerie black eyes on me. "Who?"

"I saw a young man, blond hair, black eyes kind of like yours. Was that him? Or—" I cocked my head at him—"was that you?"

Usuriel smirked, clearly not going to answer.

Cerridwen shook her head reluctantly. "It would be difficult for Usuriel to walk Morgain's halls without her knowing. She would feel the change in the fates if nothing else."

Usuriel's smile turned a little smug at that, but he didn't contradict her. Which didn't equal a denial. It made sense. In his place, if I had a way of moving undetected that I didn't want the others to learn of, I wouldn't be offering it up to Cerridwen either.

"It was Gwen," Aubrey said. "At least she did something that opened a door. She shoved me through. I don't know who knocked her out. Maybe that was the boy you saw."

Usuriel scowled at her.

"The tanai?" I asked, ignoring him.

"Yes. Is she all right?" Aubrey asked.

"She was last time I saw her," I said. "Someone knocked

her out, but Lady Morgain woke her. Enough for us to know that you had been taken."

Usuriel didn't look particularly surprised or upset at this news. "I was wondering how you found me so fast. I underestimated Morgain, it seems. I believe there were more in your party. Where are the others?"

Oh no, I wasn't giving out any information about where Damon and the others were.

"Gone from the realm," I said flatly. "Lady Morgain sent them home. They will be well into the human world by now." That was a lie, if I was any judge of time here, but I didn't want Usuriel trying to interfere, and hopefully he wasn't good at knowing when a human was lying.

Usuriel's black eyes were unblinking. "I wonder if that is true." He took a step toward me. "It would be easy enough for me to find out."

"If you fear me because you think I'm a demon witch," I said, dropping my hand to my sword. "Then I would suggest that it is better that you do not upset me. If you interfere with my friends, I will be upset."

He did blink at that. "Is that a threat, little human?"

"It's a statement of fact," I retorted.

"Maggie," Cerridwen said sharply. She turned to Usuriel, "Forgive her forwardness, Lord Usuriel. The humans tend toward impulsiveness. It is, I think, a reflection of their short lives."

It was a reflection of my desire to ensure that no one hurt Damon. I fought to not draw my sword.

"How did you even get to Gwen?" Callum asked. "If she is in Morgain's service?"

"I have my ways and means of seeking out the dissatisfied. Something in their nature calls to me." Was that how he enticed people over into his night court? The ones who weren't Nichtkin to begin with? Which surely Gwen wasn't, if Morgain had allowed her to serve in her territory.

"Dissatisfied how?" I asked.

Usuriel shrugged. "The tanai had changed her mind. She wishes to return to the human realm." He glanced off to his side and stretched out a hand. "Isn't that right, my dear?" He made a tugging gesture, and Gwen appeared out of nowhere, stumbling toward Usuriel, eyes wide with terror. Her hands shook as she held them up to ward him off.

Well, fuck. Not good. He'd lifted her out from under Morgain's nose, too.

Gwen went to her knees at Lord Usuriel's feet. "Yes, my Lord," she said in a soft, shaky voice. "I wish to return home." She looked up at him. "I did as you asked."

Usuriel stared at her for a long moment. "Not exactly. I asked for that one," he nodded at me.

"You said a human woman traveling with the s'ealg oiche," Gwen said. "The blonde one felt more powerful to me. I assumed she was who you wanted."

Aubrey and I didn't exactly look alike, so I wondered if Usuriel hadn't bothered to give Gwen a proper description.

"I did as you asked, my Lord," Gwen repeated, pleading.

"You delivered the wrong human, tanai," he said. "So our bargain is not yet complete. We will have to find another way for you to satisfy me before I let you go."

"If she's human, and she wants to leave the realm," I said, "then that's her right under the contract."

I looked at Aubrey for confirmation.

"Well, that is not exactly true," Lord Usuriel said. "They can leave the realm if their parent allows them to do so."

"This one, however..." He reached down and cupped Gwen's cheek with his hand, and she flinched away, cringing as his nails pressed into her skin. "This one has no knowledge of her Fae parentage. She followed some other tanai into Morgain's court, and the lady took her on as a servant. She made that agreement; now she's made another one with me.

Until she fulfills those agreements, she is ours to do with as we please."

"No. She is not." Aubrey said. She moved sideways, putting space between them. "You are mistaken, my Lord."

Usuriel didn't let go of Gwen, but his head turned to Aubrey. "What are you talking about?"

"Under the contract your people hold with mine, if one of the tanai tells the Cestis that they wish to return home, we are allowed to help them negotiate that return." Aubrey said. "I'm sure Lady Morgain will see reason. Her agreement is the original one. Obtained without coercion."

"I did not coerce her."

"You didn't give her all the information she needed to complete your task. A lie of omission is still a lie. And that is forbidden under our agreement," Aubrey said. Her voice was steady, her accent growing more precise with each word. "Maggie, do you have that copy of the contract?"

I nodded and dug into my jacket pocket. I felt it and pulled it out, offering it to Aubrey. She took it, making a show of flipping through the pages.

"I can find the chapter and verse for you, my Lord, but if Gwen has asked to return home, then I am honor bound to take that request to the Cestis. As Lady Cerridwen said, you need to honor our agreement, or the consequences can be difficult for everyone."

Particularly difficult for Gwen, who seemed to be facing a life of enslavement in the Fae realm if this didn't work. Which meant we had to try to convince him to let her leave with us.

And the Fae, according to nearly everything I'd learned about them, didn't often do things without wanting something in return. There were exceptions, of course. Like Cerridwen and Callum, who didn't make every interaction into a trade. But I doubted Usuriel was inclined to altruism. So, what could we offer him for Gwen? The answer came to me almost immediately, souring my mouth with fear.

I swallowed, forcing myself to speak. "You said you wanted me, not Aubrey," I managed, the words coming slowly as though part of me didn't want to say them. "Why is that?"

Cerridwen made a warning sound, and I waved her off. "No, if Lord Usuriel wanted me so badly, he can tell me why."

"Perhaps I merely wish to satisfy myself that you are indeed no danger to us."

"And how are you intending to do that?"

"I do not need demon stone to recognize demon taint," he said. "My people are closer to the dark than some of our kind. We know the power they can wield. I would sense it in you, should it linger."

"Are you asking if you can read me in some fashion?" I asked. "Will that put an end to your nonsense once and for all?" I didn't like the idea, but I would do it if it meant that we could all get out of here.

Cerridwen made another warning noise. "You do not wish to do this, Maggie," she said quietly.

"I want to go home. And I don't want to have to spend the next fifty years wondering if Lord Usuriel is going to move against me. If we can relieve him of his fears, it is better for all of us." I spread my hands. "What do you want to know, my lord?"

"That you're not going to destroy us all by walking in the realm," he said bluntly.

"And how do I convince you of that? You've already heard that I've been tested. You know that my binding was involuntary and that I killed the demon that was trying to recover me."

"And how exactly did you do that?" he asked, disbelieving.

"I called lightning. As I told the council."

"A human should not be so powerful."

Aubrey shook her head. "I must correct you again, my Lord," she said. "There have been humans through time who can do extraordinary things. Maggie is powerful, yes, but her magic is her own."

"Perhaps she is not entirely human," he said.

"I am certainly not tanai," I retorted.

"Yet Cerridwen is teaching you Fae magic."

"I teach her such magics as will be useful for her in fighting the dark. It is because she is late to her human training that she can understand a little of it, unlike most witches whose minds become closed," Cerridwen said, voice tight with irritation.

Aubrey looked intrigued at that. It wasn't exactly true, though. Cerridwen was teaching me because I could learn and because she was using me as a loophole to aid the Cestis. The Cestis would not take such a large favor from an Elder. Could not risk the debt. But Cerridwen could teach me, and I could share my knowledge once I had learned. Better that Usuriel not know that, of course.

"Still," Usuriel said, "I would satisfy myself." He took another step toward me.

Callum moved between us, standing sideways, one arm stretching to Usuriel to block him. "He's dangerous. You should not let him inside your mind."

"I can shield myself."

"You may not be able to keep him out. He's an Elder. And skilled at manipulation," Callum said.

I gritted my teeth against the shiver of fear that slid through my gut. When I was sure I had control, I let myself answer. "I've kept a demon from overwhelming me. Not even the walker could keep its grip on me."

Usuriel hissed at that. "You killed the walker?"

I smiled, teeth bared. "Still want to touch me?"

His eyes narrowed. "You are bold, human."

"I will protect what is mine. And I do what is right. The Cestis believe in protecting those who need protection. Like tanai who wish to come home. So. A trade, my Lord. I will let you touch me, touch only; and in return, you will let Gwen leave with us, and you will let us return from your territory and the realm unharmed.

"All that for a touch?" he asked.

I nodded. "Whatever it is you're afraid of, you want to stop it badly enough that you are willing to kidnap a witch and risk endangering the realm. You can determine that I am not what you fear with your touch. Isn't that worth letting her go?"

Chapter Twenty-One

Usuriel just stared at me, unblinking.

"Do we have an agreement?" I asked.

He nodded. "Yes, I—"

"Wait," Cerridwen said. "Lord Usuriel, if you wish to accept this offer, we will negotiate the terms."

"Yes. We should do this properly," Aubrey agreed.

Usuriel's brow lowered, and he drummed his long black nails on the side of his thigh. I stood my ground, chin lifted. No showing fear. Not with Gwen still kneeling, tears rolling down her face. In my place, Cassandra or Lizzie would be doing exactly what I was doing. I wouldn't let them down.

Eventually Usuriel came to a decision. "Very well. We will negotiate the terms of the contact, and at the end, if I am satisfied, you can take the tanai."

"We will take the tanai regardless of your satisfaction," Cerridwen said but she moved to stand by Usuriel, gesturing for Aubrey to join them. Gwen remained kneeling, whether through obedience or fear. I wanted to tell her to stand, but didn't want to make things worse just when the tide might be turning in our direction.

Callum moved back to stand at my side, whether trying to

guard me or support me, I wasn't quite sure. But I was grateful.

"This was a foolish idea, Maggie," he said.

"We can't leave her here. And he's just going to keep coming after me if he thinks I'm a threat. This takes care of both those things."

"At what cost?"

"I'll be fine. Between Cerridwen and Cassandra, my shields are strong." At least I hoped they were. I'd never faced an Elder Fae intent on winning his way before.

"You're brave. I'll grant you that. Cerridwen was right to cloak you in the illusion of a rancaigh. They are also brave. And prone to reckless-ness," he added with a mental chuckle.

"Not helpful. You're making me nervous."

"I could change form. You could pet me."

"Are you offering to be my emotional support shapeshifter?" The thought made me smile. *"No, I think you're better off staying human for now. If Usuriel decides to summon reinforcements, then you need to be ready to fight."*

"If he's agreed to a negotiation and is setting the terms, he will not break them."

"No, but you Fae are sneaky. So he's going to try something."

"Undoubtedly. But that is a problem you will deal with after the more pressing one, which is surviving his touch unscathed. He is powerful. Do not falter or he will find a way to make you let him inside your head."

"I'll be fine. I've survived demon stone. That was pretty unpleasant."

"And he is lord of the Nichtkin. He rules the creatures who walk human nightmares."

I bared my teeth in a strained smile. *"I've lived with night-mares since I was thirteen. He can't be scarier than a demon."*

"For your sake, I hope not."

Before I could respond, Cerridwen said, "Very well, my Lord. Do we have an agreement?"

My focus snapped back to Usuriel. I couldn't read anything in those black eyes. I just had to make sure he wouldn't be able to read anything in me.

"Yes," he said.

"And you will hold to the terms?" Cerridwen asked.

I held my breath.

"Yes," Usuriel said.

Cerridwen glanced back at me. "Very well, Lord Usuriel needs to touch you, Maggie. And then he will let Gwen come with us."

"I will let you take her," Lord Usuriel agreed. He beckoned, black fingernails glinting in the light.

Too long. Too sharp. My stomach turned and I looked at Cerridwen, suddenly frozen.

"This is your choice to do this. I cannot stop you." Her tone suggested she would like to at least advise me not to do it, but then we would be at an impasse. And I wouldn't leave Gwen behind, trapped by a monster. Sara had done that to me, even if I hadn't been aware of the demon. Usuriel might not be a demon, but I doubted he was merciful, and I couldn't let Gwen be punished for not delivering me.

"But I will not force you if you have changed your mind," Cerridwen continued.

Despite Callum's boast earlier, I wasn't entirely sure three of us—or four counting Aubrey—could fight our way out of the realm alone. Certainly, I wasn't sure how we would take Gwen. So regardless of how scared I was, I had to do this.

"Let's get this over and done with," I said.

Usuriel's smile turned sharp. "Come here," he said, his voice silky and somehow enticing. I took a half step forward before I realized what I was doing.

"Guard your shields," Callum snapped.

I yanked every mental barrier that Cerridwen had ever taught me in place, piling protection upon protection.

Usuriel crooked his finger. "Come here," he repeated.

I resisted just long enough to let him see that I could, and then I moved. He extended a hand, and I reached for it. His hand touched mine, his skin strangely cold. And before I realized what he was doing, he yanked me forward and pressed his lips to mine.

I don't know how long the kiss lasted. He didn't try to deepen the contact. But the feel of him was like a nightmare pressing against my skin. Darkness crawled around me, and I focused on not drowning in it, on holding my shields firm. My magic wanted to flare, the urge to burn the threat away growing strong. But before I lost control, he let me go.

I stumbled back, wiping my mouth with the back of my hand, the crawling sensation fading slightly. My skin felt chilled, as though I'd been kissed by a creature of ice.

"That was unnecessary, my lord" Cerridwen said, the words tight with anger.

Usuriel was still smiling. "Perhaps," he said, "but I enjoyed it."

I stared at him, fighting the urge to draw my sword and bury it deep in his guts. Perhaps he had truly meant no harm, but his touch had been horrifying—closer to the sensation of the demon than anything else I'd felt.

"And are you satisfied?" I managed to ask.

The corner of his mouth lifted, his half-smile nearly a smirk I wanted to slap from his face. "Yes. I agree, you are free of the demon's taint." His expression turned more curious. "And how you have achieved this interests me."

I shook my head. "Oh no, our agreement is done. If you want information, you can deal with the Cestis."

"Or me," Cerridwen said, stepping between us and reaching for my hand to draw me to her side. "Maggie is under my protection. And you got what you asked for, Mirror Lord."

Usuriel's face tightened.

I straightened my shoulders, still fighting to maintain a semblance of control. Pretending would have to do until it became actual control. "Now, give us Gwen and we will leave."

Usuriel lifted a brow and walked back to Gwen, placing a hand on the top of her head. She shuddered under his touch and my jaw clenched. "I didn't say I would give her to you," he said, smiling in a smug way I didn't like at all. "I said that you could take her."

Aubrey swore softly and I realized that he had managed to sneak that wording in.

"What does that mean?" I demanded.

"On your feet, girl," he said to Gwen.

She rose to her feet, trembling. Her face was drained of any hint of the color she had regained back in Morgain's, looking as pale as it had when she'd been unconscious. He shoved her, and she stumbled forward a step or two. Before any of us could move to help her, he waved a hand, and the mists sprang up around her.

"What the—?" I stumbled backward as streaks of the mist extended slightly, reaching toward us. Aubrey flinched back, too. And even Cerridwen and Callum fell back a step. The mist acted like it did at the border, extending to the roof in a perfect circular column perhaps six feet wide. Not much room inside for Gwen if she wanted to avoid touching the mists. Which, if she had any sense, she would.

"If you want her," Usuriel said to me, "then you can take her. Otherwise, she stays within the mists." He smiled, not bothering to hide his satisfaction.

I looked at Callum.

"Oh no," Usuriel said. "I said you could take her. *You*, Maggie Lachlan."

Fuck you.

I didn't say it, but my hand curled round the hilt of my sword. I really, really wanted to stab him. To control my temper, I made myself watch the mists, letting my senses slide to magic while still holding my shields fast.

"I don't suppose you can give me a ten-second crash course in how you do that trick of yours?" I asked Callum.

"I can try. But it is complicated."

"Just tell me." I stared at the shifting mists as I waited for him to reply, trying to recall the feel of it and the changes in Callum's aura along with the feel of all the doors that I'd been dragged through recently. There was something…similar about all of them.

"Is it something to do with matching the energy of the mist?" I asked.

"Not exactly. The boundaries are formed by the realm. You have to convince the realm that you are one with the mist. The mists are raised by those who control the territories. That means having a little of their essence."

"How exactly?"

"The Nichtkin who taught me, gave me a memory of its, well, you humans would call it a soul. If I use that I can convince the mists to part. Well, the mists here around Lord Usuriel's lands, at least."

I didn't have a convenient memory of a soul, I realized, but I had just been kissed by the Lord of the territory. I knew him now, more than I wanted to. Knew the touch of his power, and the fear he wielded as a weapon. He shouldn't have been so quick to try to overwhelm me. His arrogance may have led him into a misstep. I moved closer to the mist, considering, tracing the flow of magic in my head as it shifted and swirled.

"If it touches you, it can drag you inside with her. You could be trapped," Cerridwen said warningly.

"No one's managed to trap me yet," I said. "Now, let me concentrate." I stared at the mist and did something that I rarely did in the realm, reaching for its magic rather than my own.

Here in Usuriel's realm, there was an icy feel to the power. Something cold and dark and deep that made me want to shiver. But the touch of it also resonated with the mist. It had the same twilight darkness to its energy that I'd seen at the border. And the same darkness that I'd felt flowing over me when Usuriel's mouth had been on mine.

"Feel the energy, change the energy," I muttered under my breath. Though in this case it was become the energy, perhaps. I pictured my aura. How would I change that? I drew a blank at first, still shaken by the memory of Usuriel's touch. But then it struck me that he might be the answer. I had to try, had to let the darkness in for once, instead of trying to keep it out. There was darkness, after all, buried somewhere in my mind. The sensation of being bonded to a demon. The knowledge that my mother had only ever seen me as a means to an end. The moment Nat had died. The moment I'd let rage and fury and grief fuel my magic and called lightning to slay the demon. If that wasn't darkness, what was? Usuriel had said he was closer to the darkness than most.

So was I, if I let myself be.

I let the memories resonate through me, trying to push that feeling outward. Something shivered through me, and the mist shivered in response. I stretched my hands out in the gesture that Callum had made, drawing them together as I reached for the darkness. The realm pressed around me, the magic threatening to swamp me. I wouldn't be able to hold it for long. I pulled my hands apart, pushing my magic forward.

A corridor opened in the mist. It wasn't nearly as deep as it had been at the border. Gwen was huddled on the ground inside, sobbing.

I moved closer. "Get up." I extended one hand while keeping the other one outstretched. The mist shimmered a little, and I could feel my magic beginning to strain, my heart beating faster. The realm was pushing at me, fighting my control, and I didn't know how long I could hold it back.

"Get up," I shouted. Gwen lifted her head. "Get up if you want to go home." That got her moving. She scrambled to her feet and took a lurching step forward.

"Don't let the mist touch you," I warned, beckoning.

"Why are you helping me?" she asked, the words cracking.

"Because I understand what it's like to want to find a home. Take my hand, walk through."

She reached out and took my hand, pale blue eyes full of fear. I yanked her out through the gap in the mist, practically running backward.

Without a second to spare. As soon as Gwen passed the edge of the mist, my magic began to collapse. I tugged at Gwen, pulling her farther back, in case the mist moved as I lost control. The whole column shivered, trembling in place, before Usuriel raised his hand, and it vanished. He was staring at me, his face blank in a way that told me he was hiding his reaction. Cerridwen looked impressed, and Aubrey was, quite frankly, gaping. Then she seemed to recover herself and moved to stand on Gwen's other side.

"Well, that was unexpected," Callum said drily.

I bit back a sob of laughter, trying to remember how to speak, as I banished the memories and the darkness, trying to picture myself shielded in light. Gwen hadn't let go of my hand, and the tightness of her grip grounded me in a fashion.

Cerridwen faced Usuriel, "Very well, Usuriel, I believe that satisfies the terms of your agreement. You will let us depart."

Usuriel didn't look happy, but he nodded. "You are free to go." He nodded at me. "I believe we have more to discuss, Maggie Lachlan."

I set my teeth. "I believe I've had enough of talking with you for now, my lord. I am no danger to you and your kind, unless you force me to be."

He blinked once, slowly. Then nodded. "Very well. Do not fear that I will send anything to stop you. After all, my forces are occupied elsewhere."

Cerridwen's head whipped around.

"What the hell does that mean?" I demanded.

Usuriel just smiled. "I suggest you leave. Run. Run to the borders of the realm. Time is moving swiftly, after all."

I really, really, really wanted to stab him. Or burn his whole damned night court to the ground. "We need to go," I said urgently to Cerridwen.

"Agreed. Lord Usuriel, until next time," she said in an icy voice that suggested he wasn't going to enjoy their next encounter.

We gathered around her as she opened a door. As we moved through, I felt a surge of power swamping me, like nothing I'd yet felt inside the realm. The magic crushed around me, feeling like it was both compressing me and stretching me through an infinite distance. Light flared wildly around us until suddenly we tumbled onto grass. In the distance, I could hear what sounded like a fight.

Cerridwen looked at Callum. "*Go*, my blade," she ordered. "Help them."

Callum shimmered into his other form, racing away almost as soon as the change was done.

"What's happening?" I asked, looking around wildly. "Where are we?"

"Near the door."

"I didn't think you could take us that way."

"Normally not. But Usuriel broke the rules, which allows me some freedom even though I am sure I will have to do some fast talking to explain myself."

She pointed at Aubrey, jerked her head in the direction Callum had taken. "The door is half a mile ahead. If I'm not mistaken, Usuriel has sent some of his people to stop your friends from crossing. We may have to fight."

"I can fight," Aubrey said.

Cerridwen looked at Gwen. "And you? Can we trust you?"

Gwen blinked, pale eyes confused, looking as though she had no idea who or where she was. "Are you taking me home?"

"Yes," Cerridwen said. "But we need to reach the door to get you there."

"I can fight," Gwen said, "if someone gives me a knife." She was tanai, and that didn't mean she couldn't necessarily lie, but she didn't seem like much of a fighter. Nor was I sure that I trusted her.

Cerridwen, however, pulled a knife from a sheath in her boot and passed it to the girl. "Maggie, you and I will take the lead. Aubrey, you stay with Gwen. Don't engage unless you have to. We'll distract them. You focus on getting to the door."

Aubrey looked torn.

"Please," Gwen said to her, voice catching. "I know I called Lord Usuriel, but it felt like my only chance to go home."

Aubrey's lips were pressed together. "We can talk about that once we're through."

"Get to the door," Cerridwen repeated. "Don't get distracted.

The four of us ran, heading toward the sound of clashing metal. When we got there, Gráinne and Callum were fighting in their four-legged forms. Biting and snarling, warding off creatures straight out of the big book of "oh god I didn't need to find out these existed". Damon and Zee had their swords drawn, backing toward a door about fifty feet behind them.

"Is that the right door?" I asked Cerridwen.

"Yes," she said. "It should open for you because you carry my token. If you can get them through—if you get the chance —take it. Don't worry about us."

"Alright," I said as one of monsters, something that looked like a tiger crossed with a giant porcupine, sprang toward me.

I swerved and thrust at it. It squealed and dodged, moving too fast for something its size. As I tried to track the movement, something sliced across my thigh. Fiery pain bloomed and I bit back a shriek.

The creature came at me again and I gave up on the

sword and summoned a flame, throwing it at the creature. To my surprise, it worked, and the thing caught alight as though it had been doused in gasoline.

Around me, the sounds of battle went quiet, the night wraiths flinching away from the blaze. Right. They didn't like light or fire.

I could give them that.

I summoned another flame then backed it with the illusion of more, ignoring the pain in my leg as I burned a path through the monsters, trying not to breathe in the acrid smoke rising from the dead Nichtkin.

"Damon!" I yelled, and he looked in my direction, his gaze locking onto mine. Something like fury crossed his face and he began to fight like a man possessed until the monster he was currently battling lay dead at his feet.

"Maggie!" he shouted, and I ran for him, my hand outstretched, needing to touch him more than I needed to breathe.

"Maggie," he said, his hand catching mine and pulling me close.

"No time," I panted. I smacked a quick kiss on his cheek. "The door's behind you. Let's get you through." Aubrey was making her way around behind the circling Nichtkin, pulling Gwen in her wake.

Damon looked confused. "It's closed."

I shook my wrist with the bracelet. Zee was still watching Callum and Gráinne and Cerridwen fighting the Nichtkin who seemed to be recovering from their fear of my fire. "I can open it. Zee, come on!" I yelled.

"I can't leave those three to fight these things off," he protested.

"It's Cerridwen. If she and two of her blades can't deal with this lot, then we're all in trouble. We need to get Damon and Aubrey and Gwen."

Zee looked startled. "Gwen? What's she doing here?"

"Long story," I said, lunging to stab another of the smaller Nichtkin as it sprang at me, testing my illusion. I sliced at it, and it fell back, yipping. Aubrey and Gwen were catching up to us, making use of the fact that most of the creatures had turned their attention to Cerridwen and the two snarling wolves.

"Let's go," I said to Damon, moving toward the mist, summoning the charms in my head to conjure the door. For a moment, the magic resisted me, but then a door appeared. Solid wood, like the one in the Rose Garden. I hoped like hell I hadn't summoned the wrong one and ran toward it, reaching for the handle..

"Aubrey, Gwen, run!" Aubrey was half dragging Gwen, but the two of them bolted past me and through the door.

"Damon," I said, "*go.*"

"Not without you."

I blew an exasperated breath at him. "I'm right behind you. Move."

Zee was already falling back toward the door. "I'll guard the other side," he said.

Crap, I hadn't even thought about what might happen if one of Usuriel's creatures got through the door.

"We can't hold it open much longer. They could get through. Go!" I yelled at Damon, shoving. "Go *now.*"

Chapter Twenty-Two

I stumbled after Damon, dragging the door shut behind me, hoping we hadn't just abandoned Cerridwen, Callum, and Gráinne to be killed by the Nichtkin.

Hands dragged me forward, and I jerked back instinctively, still in fight mode.

"Easy," Aubrey said. I blinked, dizzy, her face blurring in front of me.

"You're bleeding." She sounded concerned.

And now that she'd mentioned it, the pain in my leg roared back to life. The dizziness intensified.

"Yes," I managed as my knees started to buckle.

Damon caught me and lowered me to the ground. "Help her," he snarled.

Good plan. My leg was on fire. I clenched my teeth, trying not to give in to the pain, struggling to breathe through it. Sweat trickled down my face. Not good. Poison. Hadn't someone said something about the Nichtkin and poison?

Damon went to his knees beside me, dumping the contents of his backpack out. "I've got a first aid kit in here somewhere."

I nodded, unable to speak as the pain arrowed up and down my leg.

"Hang on," Damon muttered. He produced a pocketknife and widened the cut in my pants, before dumping the contents of a small dark bottle onto my leg.

The burn intensified. "Fuck." I groaned, digging my fingers into the grass. "What the hell was that?"

"Antiseptic," he said. "I'll find some painkillers."

Aubrey touched his shoulder. "Hold that thought. If Cerridwen comes through, she'll be able to help Maggie better without human drugs in her system."

"And if she doesn't?" Damon snarled. "Maggie's in pain."

"Zee and I will see what we can do. Until help arrives."

Help. Like Damon's security team. "Are we in Ljubljana?" I managed.

He looked around. "We're in a park. It's early. Other than that, I don't know."

"Try your datapad," I managed.

"Right. Hold this," he ordered Aubrey, and I realized he was pressing a gauze pad to my leg.

She put her hand on my leg, waving him away. "I'm certified in first aid. Leave me to do this."

"Right." He pulled out his datapad, tried to power it on. "Fuck. It's dead." He looked around again. "This is a park. We can't be too far from civilization."

"I can go find someone, find a phone." Zee offered. "Someone will have a public data point."

Was I the only one thinking straight? I tapped Damon's thigh where he was kneeling beside me. "Panic button," I gritted out as my leg throbbed harder.

Relief washed across his face. "Right."

He could trigger an alert from his chip if there was a network nearby. I still carried a physical button in case I was ever out of range. "Inside pocket. My button."

Damon reached into my jacket, found the pocket, and pressed the button.

"They'll be here any minute," he said. "Just hold on."

I nodded gratefully and passed out.

I opened my eyes, blinking, when an icy jolt of magic swept through me. Cerridwen was kneeling beside me, her hand on my leg.

"Welcome back," she said as I pushed up on my elbows, to work out where I was. Still in the park.

"Thanks, I think." I winced as my leg throbbed. But it was a different, healing sort of throb. And not nearly as bad as it had been.

Cerridwen sat back on her heels, removing her hand. "That is healed, but you need to be careful with it for a few days. It will take some time to truly mend." A streak of black blood marred her perfect face, stretching across her cheek and hair. "You're lucky it was only a gairogh claw, not a poison blade. Nichtkin do not fight fair."

If that pain hadn't been from a poison, then I definitely never wanted to experience a Fae poison. "Hopefully it won't be an issue I have to deal with again.

Cerridwen nodded. "Let us hope so."

I looked past her. Callum and Zee and Aubrey stood a few feet away. Aubrey saw me and headed in our direction "Where's Gráinne?" I asked Cerridwen.

"She's fine. I sent her home. I just came through to make sure you were all well here." She looked around. "Is this where Damon needed to be?"

Where was Damon? I pushed myself into a sitting posi-tion, wincing, until I spotted him about ten feet away, talking with four men in familiar-looking dark clothes. "Well, that looks like one of his teams. So I hope so."

Aubrey nodded. "Yes, they arrived a few minutes before you, Lady. This is Slovenia."

"And your quarry?" Cerridwen asked. "Was he caught?"

I studied Damon's back, and something in the line of his shoulders told me perhaps not. "I'm not sure."

"Very well. Callum will stay with you. He can call for me if I'm needed. But for now, I should return. There will be some, well, how is it you humans say it? Feathers to unruffle. And then, of course, I need to talk to the others about Usuriel."

"Do you think he'll keep causing trouble?"

"Well, he did not get his way this time," Cerridwen said. "But hopefully, you have proved to him that you are not the threat that he suspected you were. Though, by manipulating his mists, you may not have really eased his mind."

I hadn't thought about that. What I'd revealed about my magic. My strength. "I had to get Gwen out."

She nodded approvingly. "I know. And this was always a possibility when I agreed to teach you." She rose to her feet, brushing grass from her leather trousers. "Don't worry, I have been doing this for a long time. I can manage the likes of Usuriel. "

"Thank you for the help."

"We are allies, you and I, Maggie Lachlan," she said, bending to touch my cheek briefly. "And our hunt continues."

She walked away. The door appeared before her, and as I watched, she stepped through it without looking back.

"Well," Aubrey said, "that was something." She turned away. "I should see to Gwen."

Gwen. I hadn't even asked how she was. She was sitting on the grass beneath a tall oak tree about twenty feet away, her arms around her knees, and a silver recovery blanket wrapped around her shoulders.

"Is she alright?" I asked.

"We'll see," Aubrey said. "She's been through some things,

clearly, but we have ways of helping the tanai who have lived in the realm adjust to life out here again. The hardest part might be getting her back to London. She doesn't have any sort of identification, much less a passport."

"Will that be a problem?"

Aubrey shrugged. "I should be able to navigate the local authorities."

The benefits of being Cestis. Friends in high places. I snorted softly, still feeling weirdly disoriented." And you?" I asked, "Did Usuriel hurt you?"

She blinked, then shook her head. "He didn't kiss me. If that's what you're asking."

I shivered suddenly. I'd forgotten about the kiss. "No. But you were with him for a while. What did he want?"

"He was asking about you," she said.

"I don't see why I'm such a concern."

"No," she agreed. "There might be something more going on, driving him, but if there is, he didn't tell me." She shuddered then. "He's not… He was trying to be pleasant, but I don't think I would like to spend much time alone with him."

Definitely not. I nodded and then stretched out my hand. "Here, help me up."

"You sure your leg will take it?"

I shrugged. "Cerridwen healed it. Can't ask for much better than that." It was sore, but Cerridwen wouldn't have left me unable to stand or walk. Aubrey took my hand and pulled me up.

The leg throbbed harder as it took my weight. "Ow. Did we figure out what time it is?"

"Just past seven," Aubrey said.

I tried to work out the time difference, decided it didn't matter, and took a wary step. The ache intensified, but the leg felt strong enough. I limped over to Damon. "Hey," I said. "What's going on?"

He whirled. "Maggie!" He yanked me into his arms and

kissed me soundly. I let him, ignoring the leg and everything else, while the familiar touch of his lips reassured me that he was real and safe.

We broke it off when someone whistled low and slow. Callum, most likely.

Damon ignored it and kept his arm around my shoulders, turning us back to his team as he made the introductions. Stanislav, the team leader, nodded politely when Damon had finished. "Ms. Lachlan. We were just debriefing Mr. Riley." His English had only the faintest trace of an accent.

"Do we know where Jack is?" I asked.

He grimaced, "No. Our contact went dark two hours ago. We checked the last place they reported seeing Jack, but there was no sign. We're scanning footage from all the local feeds and cameras."

Fuck and double *fuck.* "He got away?"

I looked at Damon. His face was grim. I squeezed his hands, knowing how disappointed and frustrated he must be. If Morgain hadn't interfered, could we have been early enough? But then we wouldn't have been able to save Gwen.

"Yes," Damon said. "Callum said there's no way we could have arrived two hours earlier. And Jack might have been gone before then."

That made me feel a little better. But not much. And Damon, I imagined, was furious. Maybe even at me. If Morgain hadn't stopped us...maybe we would have made it. "I'm sorry. I slowed you down."

He shook his head. "It's not your fault. We got here as fast as we could. So did the team." His eyes turned steely. "We'll get him next time."

I hoped so. My jaw clenched. *No.* Not "hoped". We would get him. I needed the hunt for Jack to be done. Needed him to be safely locked away for the rest of his miserable life. So did Damon.

"So, what happens now?" I asked.

His hands tightened on mine. "Right now? The team will see if they can pick up the trail again. We can't do much more until then." He looked away for a moment, expression bleak, bleak before he turned back to me and pulled me closer. "I don't know about you, but I want to go home."

"That sounds good," I said, before I glanced back to where Aubrey was sitting with Gwen. Aubrey was talking, but Gwen didn't seem to be responding much. "How about we go via London?"

The benefits of having a billionaire as a boyfriend were many. His ability to conjure up a private, luxurious charter jet to wing us to London in the time it had taken his team to pile us into two dark 4x4s and drive us to the airport at Ljubljana was definitely one of the more useful ones. Better yet, the jet had a bathroom and a bedroom. After seeing everyone was seated and being well taken care of by the very professional flight attendants, he dragged me toward the other end of the plane.

"What are you doing?" I hissed.

"I thought I'd lost you," he muttered. He pulled me into the bedroom, slammed the door, and pushed me up against the wall. "I thought I'd *lost* you," he repeated.

"I thought I'd lost you, too," I admitted, staring at him and remembering the pit of fear opening in my stomach when Usuriel had announced his forces were busy elsewhere.

"Can you ward the room?" he asked.

I nodded and pressed a hand to the wall to do just that. "You mean the billionaire doesn't have soundproof bedrooms on his jet? You're not conforming to stereotype, Riley," I teased, my tone mock disappointed.

He grinned, his eyes very blue. "Not my jet. But we'll just have to make do."

His lips descended on mine. Just as well the wall was there, because the taste of him went straight to my head, turning my blood to fire. He was here. He was safe. We had survived. And I wanted his hands all over my body until I forgot that any of that was ever in doubt.

I made a hungry noise against his mouth and his hands went to my thighs as though he was going to lift me, but then he stopped, pulling his mouth away from mine.

"What?" I protested.

"Your leg." Worry filled his eyes.

"My leg is fine." There were other parts of me with far more pressing needs. I started to tug his head back down, but he resisted.

"It won't be fine if I do you up against the wall."

"Isn't that my decision to make?"

"Nope." His hands went to my waist, tugging me into him. Then he spun us and started backing me toward the bed. When the backs of my knees touched the mattress he paused and started kissing me again, his hands busy unbuttoning and unzipping.

I tried to help, but really, it was unfair the things he could do to me with just his mouth on mine, and I lost myself in the sensation.

Before I really knew what was happening, I was naked on the bed and so was he. Damon pushed my legs apart gently before he buried his head between them, and I stopped thinking altogether. I came fast and hard, bucking against him, groaning his name.

"Come here," I managed when the pulse of my inner muscles started to subside. I couldn't yet lift my head, but I could lift a hand and I tugged at his hair.

"Bossy," he murmured.

"You bet," I said. "Come here and fuck me."

"Are you sure those wards are working?" He chuckled, the sound low and rough and making my stomach curl.

"Too late to worry about that," I said, unable to bring

myself to care that much. "If they're not, everyone already knows what we're doing."

He laughed again. "You were quite loud."

I raised my head at that, narrowing my eyes. "You like that I'm loud."

"Sure do," he agreed and proceeded to push himself up and then lower himself over me. He slid against me, his cock hard against my clit and I dropped my head back, seeing stars.

He seemed to take that as encouragement, because he thrust again, this time sliding into me, the sensation so good, I made all the noises he liked so much and wrapped my legs around his waist. Bad leg be damned. The only thing I could feel just then was him.

And I wanted to feel more. I opened my eyes, saw the wild dark blue of his.

I didn't have to ask. Damon started to move, fast and hard, his gaze never leaving mine, as though he also needed to prove this was real. I brought my head up to kiss him, curling myself around him, arching and writhing to meet his thrusts. It was fast and hard and sweaty and so perfectly what I needed that I came again, almost before I was ready. Damon didn't stop, he just hitched my right leg higher on his hip and changed the angle slightly and I started to climb again, plea-sure sweeping through me like a wave that I could no more resist than I could resist the ocean. So I let it catch me, let him take me where we both needed to go, until he was the one testing the limits of the wards, calling my name as he came, too.

It was almost two hours before we emerged. I'd taken advantage of the shower once Damon and I were done and then changed into the new clothes his team had provided for me. They were basic black and a little large, but didn't include a gaping rip across my thigh where the gairogh had caught me, so that was an improvement.

My leg was still a little sore, but I wasn't limping when I wandered back out to the main cabin. Callum was awake, watching something on a datapad. Gwen was sleeping in one of the seats closest to the cockpit and Aubrey was also curled up, eyes shut, in the seat opposite hers.

I took a seat next to Callum. "Do you think she'll be all right?" I asked him.

"Aubrey or Gwen?" he asked.

"Aubrey. Do you think Usuriel did anything to her before we got there?" Aubrey had kept her head throughout everything that had happened, but the fact remained she'd been kidnapped by a Fae. That had to be terrifying, even if she was putting on a brave face.

Damon dropped down in the seat next to mine. He looked good in basic black, his hair still damp, some of the tension gone from his shoulders. Not all of it, but some. That was probably as good as I could hope for, for now. He made a "go on" gesture at Callum.

"I can't sense any trace of magic on her, if you're worried about whether he's glamoured her," Callum said.

"Not necessarily," I said. "That man doesn't have to spell you to hurt you."

Damon frowned. "What do you mean?"

I swallowed. There hadn't really been time to talk about Usuriel yet. But I'd promised myself I would tell him. No lying. No secrets. So I explained what had happened.

When I got to the end, Damon wasn't looking relaxed anymore. In fact, he kind of looked like he wanted to punch a wall. Just as well we were several thousand feet in the air where he had no way to even start looking for a way to get back into the realm. Otherwise I suspected he would be charging in there to do something foolish.

"I'm fine," I said, nudging his knee with mine. "It was

nothing I couldn't handle." Not that I'd care to repeat the experience, but it was true. I was fine.

"He put his hands on you."

"To be fair, I gave him my hand willingly enough. I had to save Gwen."

"He kissed you," he growled, eyes flashing blue.

"I didn't kiss him back," I promised. "Don't worry, Cerridwen will be keeping a close eye on him. Usuriel is not our problem."

"No," he agreed. "Or not the main one." He huffed a breath.

Right. Jack.

"Any updates about what happened?" I asked.

He nodded. "I got a message while you were in the shower. They found the contact they were using dead in some back alley."

"He *killed* someone?" I asked. That was new. Jack had evaded Damon's security before, but I didn't think he'd left dead bodies in his wake in the past. Or maybe he had, and he'd been better at hiding them. He'd certainly seemed willing to let us all die when he set my house on fire.

"Him or whoever he's working with, perhaps," Damon said.

"How was he killed?" Callum asked.

"A gunshot."

He nodded, looking relieved. Had he been worried that Jack was working with a Fae?

"So, what happen next?" I asked.

Damon leaned his head back against the rest, looking exhausted. But the look in his eye was resolute. "We're not going to stop until we find him."

When we landed in London, lack of ID wasn't an issue. An immigration official came onto the plane, spoke briefly with Aubrey, and then scanned Gwen's fingerprints and issued her with some sort of temporary ID card with instructions on how to get something more permanent once she had a datapad. They cleared all of us for entry at the same time. Apparently the combination of Cestis and billionaire was enough to get strings pulled where necessary.

Another of Damon's teams was waiting for us on the tarmac with more cars. Callum left us, declaring he'd find his own way home. Whether he meant to the realm or back to San Francisco was unclear.

Damon and I went in the first car with Aubrey and Gwen. Zee went in the second with the security team. I got the impression he wasn't exactly thrilled to be meeting the Cestis again. Aubrey gave the driver an address, and we settled in for the long drive into London from Heathrow.

I half dozed against Damon's shoulder; he worked on his datapad and took calls. Aubrey and Gwen were mostly silent.

We pulled up outside a normal-looking concrete-and-glass office building. Not exactly how I'd imagined the headquarters of the British Cestis to look. Only the fact that you couldn't even get through the front door without a body scan and other checks and that all the windows on the ground floor were mirrored, blocking the interior view, suggested there might be something important within.

Once we'd passed the scans and been issued visitor tags by a very efficient man in the kind of dark gray suit I associated with Damon's security team, we were shown through a second set of doors into a marble and dark wood foyer that was more like what I'd been imagining. It couldn't be that old, but it *felt* old.

Waiting for us was a woman perhaps a few years younger than Cassandra. But where Cassandra was curvy and short and kind of made you think of Mrs. Claus, this woman was tall and thin, her posture and clothes screaming elegance. Pearl earrings and neatly French-rolled, dark-blonde hair and a pale blue silk shirt over navy pants that probably cost more than the rent on my first apartment. Diamonds and various stones winked from the rings on her fingers.

"Isolde," Aubrey said. She sounded happy to see her, so possibly my first impression was unfair. Isolde was the lawyer, I reminded myself. Not going to be a pushover.

"Hello, come inside," Isolde invited. She looked past Aubrey at Gwen. Damon's team had found clothes for her as well, so she was wearing jeans, sneakers, and a hoodie. Without the dark green servants' gown, she looked more solidly human, though she was still an unusually pretty girl. She kept tugging at the cuffs and sleeves as though she wasn't used to the sensation of human clothes anymore. She did so now as she nodded at Isolde, a little wild-eyed, as though she wasn't sure what was happening.

"Don't be alarmed," Isolde said. "You're safe now. We'll get you back to your mother." She tilted her head. "It is your mother, who lives here, yes?"

In other words, it was her mother who was human. Which was the more usual scenario with tanai fol. Fae women didn't seem to seduce human men as often. Or, at least, were better at not letting their affairs result in children.

"No," Gwen answered. "My father."

Isolde's brows lifted briefly, and she glanced at Aubrey. "I'll take Gwen to the infirmary. You take your other guests to the council room. Leo and the others are waiting for you."

Having been questioned by the Cestis back home before I'd known any of them well, I wasn't looking forward to having to go through a similar grilling. But better to get it over and done with and then at least I'd know where I stood. I took Damon's hand as Aubrey led us through the building.

In the end, it wasn't too bad. Ralph turned out to be tall and wiry with pale ginger hair and bright blue eyes and freckles, dressed in a beautiful but somewhat wrinkled navy pinstripe suit. He stayed mostly silent, leaving Leo Waite, who was a short but imposing guy with steel-gray hair and dark-blue eyes, and Padma Barad, whose beautiful dark eyes studied the three of us carefully, to do the questioning. Most of them were directed at me, but Damon and Zee also came in for their fair share of the polite interrogation. With Aubrey supporting our story, the other Cestis seemed, if not pleased about the situation, at least inclined to believe us.

"Very well," Leo said at the end. "I concede you needed to help the girl once she asked. The rest, well, we will have to see how it plays out in the realm." He had the same sort of plummy upper-class accent, if not even more so, than Aubrey. He peered at me over thick, black-rimmed glasses. "Hopefully that will be Cassandra's issue to deal with. And now we are aware of your interest in Jack Miller, Mr. Riley, perhaps you will remember that we may be able to assist you if he surfaces again in Europe."

"But you'll help Gwen?" I asked before Damon could answer that somewhat brusque instruction.

Leo nodded. "Of course. Padma will examine her once we are done here. She wanted to make sure the three of you were well, too."

Padma nodded, sending the ends of her chic black bob swinging around the gold and ruby hoops in her ears. "Is your leg paining you?"

"It's a little sore, but fading," I said. "I'll be fine for the flight home."

"I'll make sure you have some painkillers to take with you."

"Thank you." I didn't mention that Damon's team traveled with medical kits as well stocked as most drugstores.

"And once we're happy that Gwen is healthy, we will begin the process of locating her father," Aubrey said to me. "She'll be reunited if that's what she still wants."

"She doesn't know who her Fae parent is?" Ralph asked. His voice was lovely, low, and velvety. If he'd been born a century earlier he would have made a killing as a radio announcer.

"No. That's what Usuriel said. She couldn't ask for permission to leave because she didn't know who to ask."

He grunted. "Perhaps her father will talk to us if he hasn't told Gwen before now. He may have his reasons, but it is better if we understand the situation. If only to help her connect with the relevant tanai families." He nodded at Aubrey. "But until then, she needs to stay away from the realm. Do you think she will?"

Why would she not? I thought of Gwen, kneeling in terror for Usuriel. Surely she'd learned her lesson?

"Hard to say," Aubrey said. "We've seen it before where tanai get addicted to the magic."

"I think she's pretty scared of Usuriel," I offered. "Which is understandable."

Damon shot me a sharp glance at that.

"We will just have to wait and see," Leo said. He rapped his knuckles on the desk. "Thank you for your time, both of you. And Ms. Lachlan?"

"Yes?"

"Thank you for going after Aubrey. That was brave."

"Of course," I said. "I couldn't leave her there." That earned me a first look of something close to approval.

Ralph stood. "If you don't mind, perhaps you could come to the Archives with me, and we can record some more details about what happened." He peered at me. "After breakfast, perhaps. You all looked tired."

"I'd take some coffee, but we ate on the plane," I said. I was past the point of needing to sleep. But I had to admit I was curious to see the London Archives. So I climbed to my feet when really a big part of me just wanted to stay put and have nothing happen for at least six months.

"Perhaps in return," I suggested, "you can let Damon tell you about what he's doing for the Archives back home."

Ralph raised his eyebrows. "Very well," he said. "I have to admit, from what Aubrey has told me, I'm curious, though I have reservations."

"Of course," Damon said. "I understand why."

We said goodbye to Leo. Padma said she'd walk with us part of the way as we were heading in the same direction as the infirmary. It took a few minutes before we parted ways and then a few more before we reached the first security check for the Archives. The building was either deceptively deep or there was some sort of illusion cast on the exterior. Or both. I wanted to ask Zee what he thought, but it seemed rude in front of Aubrey and Ralph, so I decided to wait until we were back on the plane.

The security controls were even more complicated than Cassandra's and we passed through several more layers of checks. The weight of wards and protections started to buzz against my skin as we progressed through each. And I could feel them weighing on me heavily. So I wasn't entirely surprised when we stepped through the final doors to reveal a space that had to be ten times as big as the Archives back home.

It looked like every picture I'd ever seen in a movie or TV show of a British museum. Wood paneling and rows of bookshelves and carefully shaded lamps. Staircases with beautiful carved bannisters led to the upper floors, the same carved wood forming the railings that ran along the edges of each floor where it met the central square atrium. The air felt the same as at home. Slightly odd because it was humidity and temperature and contaminant controlled to protect the contents.

Wards shimmered around the shelves, making it difficult to see exactly what they held. But there was a familiar row of tables in an open space off to one side. Unlike the more utilitarian tables at Cassandra's, these looked like antiques, dark, gleaming wood polished to perfection and lit by rows of green bankers lamps. Ralph led us to the closest table and we began to talk.

He hadn't said much in the other meeting, but apparently Ralph had a mind like a steel trap; he hadn't missed or forgotten anything we'd said. He pulled out a datapad and began to type notes as he asked us to go over the experience again, pressing for tiny details about the realm and the Fae we'd encountered that the others hadn't. It went on for about an hour before I felt myself begin to flag and wish I'd asked for food after all. Aubrey must have noticed because she said, "That's enough for now, Ralph. You can talk to them more over vidlink if you need more. You can't squeeze every detail out of them in one sitting."

Ralph, to his credit, went a little red. He pushed the datapad away. "Apologies. I get a little single-minded when I'm in information-gathering mode. Damon, why don't you tell me about your project and then we can let you get back to the airport. Unless you're staying in London?"

"Not this time," Damon said. "But I think we'll be back soon."

It would have been nice to stay a few days—I'd never been to London before—but at the same time, I just wanted to go home. So I rested my chin on one hand and tried to stay awake while Damon began to explain to Ralph how the Archives could go digital.

Epilogue

Seven hours or so later, I woke on a plane once more. Damon's arm lay heavy and comforting over my waist, the sound of his breathing reassuring in the dark.

I closed my eyes, hoping to fall back to sleep, but my mind started whirring wildly. Ralph had been interested in what Damon had told him about digitization, but hadn't made any promises yet. Damon would probably win him over. Before we'd left to return to the airport, Ralph had promised he'd look for any information they had about Jack, as well as passing along anything more he found out about any of the Fae we'd encountered.

Then he'd reluctantly let us go. We hugged Aubrey and promised to make sure the luggage she'd abandoned in San Francisco was sent back to her as soon as possible. She seemed a little sad that her trip had been cut short, but said she wanted to stay with Gwen and get her settled, rather than return with us.

One of Damon's own jets was waiting to take us home. This one apparently had a soundproof bedroom, but I'd been too tired to do anything but crawl into the bed and fall asleep as soon as the captain had cleared us to leave our seats after takeoff. I wasn't sure exactly how much time had elapsed, but I could tell falling asleep again was off the table. And my stomach was growling. So I slipped out of bed, leaving Damon to sleep, pulled my clothes back on, and left the bedroom, realizing as I did so that my leg was no longer hurting. Cerridwen did good work.

I'd barely sat down before the attendant—Jon—appeared and asked me if I needed anything.

"Coffee, please. And food."

"Anything in particular?"

I was fairly certain that he could produce just about anything I wanted. But my brain couldn't cope with thinking of anything complicated. It just knew it was hungry. "Toast or a sandwich? I'm easy," I said. "How much longer do we have?"

"We'll be landing in a few more hours," he said brightly.

No point figuring out what time it was in San Francisco. My backpack was still stowed in the compartment above the seat I'd used for takeoff, so I retrieved it and found the new datapad Damon's team had given me. I'd messaged Lizzie and Cassandra with updates, telling them we were on the way back home, on the drive back from London to the airport, but wanted to check and see if they'd replied.

They hadn't. I couldn't help feeling relieved.

There would be much to discuss at home but, for now, I could ignore it all. I wanted to watch a mindless movie and drink coffee and crawl back into bed with Damon.

Jon came back with the coffee as though my thought had conjured him, sliding it into place, and the scent of it made me want to cry. The Cestis in London had tea and syncaf, not real coffee. I sipped gratefully, the caffeine clearing my head almost immediately.

"I'll be back with food," he promised. As he disappeared into the small galley space, I heard the bedroom door open, and Damon came out, wearing jeans and a T-shirt, padding barefoot down the aisle. He looked deliciously rumpled, and I regretted my decision to leave him in bed.

"Hey," he said, around a yawn. "What time is it?"

"I'm not entirely sure," I waved the datapad in the air. "This says midnight, but I haven't checked what time zone it's on. Jon says we have a few more hours." That was all that mattered. It would be easy enough to ask the local time, but there didn't seem to be much point when we'd be home soon.

He yawned again, stretched his arms, arching his back with a sleepy groan, and then sat down beside me. "Couldn't sleep?"

"I was hungry," I admitted. "I only woke up a few minutes ago."

"Food sounds good." He blinked sleepily, clearly not yet quite awake. Which told me a lot about how exhausted he was.

"Well, Jon should be back soon."

Damon nodded at my datapad. "You're not working, are you?"

"No," I said, "I was thinking of watching a movie." I went to swipe the screen off. But just before my fingers hit the glass, a message popped up on my screen. "Ralph," I said as Damon peered across.

"What's Ralph emailing you about at this hour?"

"I don't know. But he cc'd you." Curious, I opened the message. "Huh. He works fast."

"What?" Damon asked, his voice sharpening.

"He sent out word to the other Cestis, seeing if anyone could find images of Jack anywhere in their records. He's attached some photos from various places. Not in the UK, but there's some from other places." I looked at the locations Ralph had listed: Russia, Ireland, Switzerland, just to name a few.

I pulled up the photos one by one. Seeing Jack's face again was weird and so was seeing him get younger, then older again as I flicked through each image. Jack had apparently been spending time in various parts of Europe for a few decades. The very last file simply said Caribbean.

Different. But I doubted it would tell us much more than any of the others. Jack got around and he was a good-looking guy at any age. I clicked on the file as delicious smells of toast and bacon started to emanate from the galley. My stomach growled, distracting me until the image popped open, filling the screen. I froze. The Jack in this picture was much younger, his hair gleaming dark, but it wasn't him that made my appetite vanish. No, that was the young, beautiful woman standing beside him. Damp red hair curling around her shoulders and down her back. Her skin, for once, golden tan against a deep-green bikini that was almost as pretty as the color of her eyes.

Damon must have noticed something in my face. He leaned closer to the screen. "What is it?"

Numbly, I tilted the datapad toward him so he could see better. "He's young there," Damon said, and I nodded. He tilted his head again. "Maybe in his thirties?"

"Yes," I said. My lips felt funny. As though I was speaking a language I didn't understand. The picture didn't make sense. I caught my lip between my teeth, trying to tell myself it had to be a coincidence.

"What's wrong?" Damon asked, sounding concerned.

I tapped the screen, touching the face of the redhead. "Her," I said. "That's my mother."

THE END

Join my VIP readers to get an EXCLUSIVE TechWitch short story

Maggie and Damon's adventures continue in
Wicked Deeds - ORDER NOW

A note from M.J.

I hope you loved reading WICKED WAYS. I always love writing Maggie and Damon's books and the next one will be WICKED DEEDS.

As an indie author, it really helps me when readers get the word out about my books, so if you enjoyed the book, please consider leaving a review at the store where you purchased it and tell your friends!

If you want to stay up to date with all my news, find out about new releases and sales, then please sign up to my newsletter at www.mjscott.net or using the QR code below.

About the Author

M.J. Scott is an unrepentant bookworm who grew up in a family that fed her a properly varied diet of books. This cemented her story addiction and love of fantasy and romance. So it's not surprising she grew up to write books with both. When not wrestling with the magical worlds in her head, she can generally be found reading, doing something crafty, binge watching, and avoiding housework. She lives in Melbourne, Australia in a small house packed with books, cats, and craft supplies. She also writes romance as Melanie Scott. Her website is www.mjscott.net.

Also by M.J. Scott

Urban fantasy

The TechWitch series

Wicked Games

Wicked Words

Wicked Nights

Wicked Dreams

Wicked Ways

Wicked Deeds

Wicked Lies

The Wild Side series

The Wolf Within

The Dark Side

Bring On The Night

Romantic fantasy

The Four Arts series

The Shattered Court

The Forbidden Heir

The Unbound Queen

Courting The Witch (Prequel novella)

The Daughter of Ravens series

The Exile's Curse

The Traitor's Game

The Rebel's Prize

The Half-Light City series

Shadow Kin

Blood Kin

Iron Kin

Fire Kin

Romance (writing as Melanie Scott)

The Cloud Bay series

Don't Blame Me

Right Where You Left Me

You Belong With Me

The New York Saints series

The Devil in Denim

Angel in Armani

Lawless in Leather

Playing Hard

Playing Fast